LIVE BAIT

A TOM KNIGHT MYSTERY

Charlie Hodges

This edition published in 2021 by Farrago,
an imprint of Duckworth Books Ltd
13 Carrington Road, Richmond, TW10 5AA, United Kingdom

www.farragobooks.com

Print ISBN: 9781788422659
Ebook ISBN: 9781788422642

Cover design by David Wardle

For Gervase Bradford, 1931- 2017.

Chapter One

Blanketed in snow, the identical bungalows went on in an unvarying pattern for half a mile in every direction. It was as if the grey monotony of the estate had been magicked away and supplanted by something otherworldly, courtesy of Pixar.

An old man was moving slowly from door to door, supporting himself with a stick as he crossed the treacherous patches where the snow had been trodden flat. His army greatcoat clashed oddly with the wellington boots and red bobble hat, the only speck of colour in a sea of white. He carried a satchel on his shoulder.

Try as he might to cast himself in the role of Arctic explorer, Knight could not shake off a profound sense of underachievement. Far from bearing rations for a polar trek, the satchel contained leaflets inviting the citizens of Eastbourne to buy conservatories, double glazing and Indian takeaways. At the creeping pace of which he was capable he was earning at most four pounds an hour. He had been tempted to dump half the load but the agency made spot checks along the route.

It pained him to have reached the age of seventy-three only to find himself in a state of penury. A new knee was a fine thing, but for six months while he recovered he had been unable to work. The pain of turning cases away was followed by an even deeper gloom as the offers dried up. Credit cards, loans and unpaid bills joined together in a grim battalion against which his modest state and army pensions were outgunned. Short of a miracle, he would soon no longer be able to live at his beloved flat. And he didn't believe in miracles.

These were not the only woes to afflict him as he trudged through the snow. For some time now, a question had taken to posing itself when his mind wandered from the drudgery of survival. Given his age, it might have seemed to the world at large an impertinent or even inappropriate question, which was why he kept it to himself.

Yet to him it was, if not a matter of life and death, certainly something that stirred up a degree of existential angst he could do without. The question was whether he would ever have sex again. His wife had died in a car crash some three years ago. Six months ago there had been a woman, Fran, with whom he had fallen briefly in love, perhaps obsessively so. She had been much younger, a mere sprite of fifty-three. Their short, unconsummated affair had roused him from sexual slumber only to dash his hopes. It had also been responsible for the damage to his knee.

Understandably, and indeed sensibly, there was a part of him ready to raise the white flag over the whole matter of romance. But there was another part that saw things otherwise. Surrender was cowardly, treacherous even, and to accept that his sex life was over was to take a knowing step towards the grave.

The fact that he had no libido was used by both warring sides to advance their arguments. The surrender faction took it as cast-iron evidence that they were in the right, while the diehards insisted it was the direct result of a poor attitude.

At this particular moment, the diehards had him playing a game he had learned on Sunday afternoon walks at boarding school. You picked a number, say three, and the third female that passed by would turn out to be your next lover, or indeed your first for those foolish enough to admit their lack of experience. In the original version, much of the entertainment arose from the rule that it could be a female of any species, though for present purposes Knight was restricting himself to the human race.

He regretted having chosen the number five. The streets were deserted and the pickings slim. His third sighting had been ages ago, a meals on wheels driver who had hooted at him for jaywalking; the fourth was a nonagenarian in the process of being stretchered from her bungalow to an ambulance. It had been callous, he now reflected, to congratulate himself on dodging a bullet.

He was approaching the edge of the estate. At the far end of the road was a small car park next to a remote stretch of beach, a few miles from the town centre. A girl's body had been washed up here two weeks ago.

She had been wearing a wetsuit and flippers, leading to suggestions that she belonged to a diving club, but no one had claimed her. Further speculation had it that she was a refugee who had drowned while trying to cross from France, though there was no upturned boat to support the theory.

He was close enough now to see a motor scooter and a helmeted figure perched beside it on an iron railing. Whether it would prove to be number five was hard to tell, but there was less doubt as to the sex of the person now entering from the beach. As she stopped at a battered Nissan and fished in her handbag for the keys, the scooter owner darted forward and pushed her to the ground. She screamed as the bag was snatched from her hands.

It may have been that her possible status as his next lover let loose in Knight an instinct to protect, or that his various resentments coalesced into a wrath he chose not to contain. Either way, he was filled with a righteous fury that felt surprisingly pleasurable.

While she struggled to her feet the thief was on the scooter, speeding down the road in Knight's direction. As it approached he stepped out and swung the heavy satchel. The blow glanced off the scooter's windscreen, and would have done no damage had the rider not attempted to swerve. Losing traction on the compacted snow the scooter skidded, spilling its owner before careering into a lamp post.

Only now did it occur to Knight that his action may have been unwise. If he had caused serious injury he could find himself enmeshed with the law, while if his victim was fit enough to seek revenge he was ill-equipped to run away. Already the thief was struggling to his knees, unleashing a torrent of obscenities. The voice was male and every bit as angry as the fierce red acne visible through the visor.

The knife that slid from the top of the boy's boot confirmed Knight's worst fears about his earlier decision, but it also made the next decision simpler; attack was the only form of defence.

Pausing to steady himself, he slid his walking stick through his fingers until he was holding it by the tip. The crook was made of solid steel, painted to look like wood and intended to inflict severe injury. It was technically only an offensive weapon if used to deliver offence, but the presence of the knife, in his view, gave him carte blanche to wreak as he saw fit.

The boy was meanwhile on his feet, approaching gingerly over a patch of ice. He too was having second thoughts. He had never actually stabbed anyone, so far at least. The only blade wound he had ever inflicted had been upon himself in a drunken duel involving carving knives at the catering college from which he had recently been expelled. He pointed the weapon at the old man's face, the only part of his body exposed to view.

'What the fuck you do that for?' he protested shrilly.

Knight swung the metal crook at his assailant's wrist. The boy bellowed, or rather whinnied, and clutched his hand to his chest as the knife fell.

'The same reason I did that. Now get on your bike and fuck off before I do it again.'

There was a grandeur in the old man's voice that the frustrated predator had only ever heard on television or in court. It had a menacing poshness that made him want to flee all the faster. Somehow he heaved the scooter up with one arm and wobbled away, chastened though not necessarily wiser for the experience.

Knight hooked the handbag with his stick, letting it hang for a moment like a trophy fish plucked from the sea. For a moment all thoughts of debt or failure left him and the world lay at his feet. Number five meanwhile was shuffling through the snow.

'That was rather brave. Thank you.'

It was said in a matter-of-fact way, almost as if she were entitled to receive the service he had just performed. Inside the hood of her shapeless coat he could see a narrow, somewhat gaunt face with a thin nose and a receding chin. A few wisps of grey hair hung down over her forehead; several more had taken up residence above her upper lip. Play was abandoned for the day.

'You're more than welcome – with any luck he'll think twice about trying that again.'

He held out the handbag. She hesitated for a moment before taking it, as if expecting him to remove it from the stick and present it to her.

'Are you hurt?' He knew from bitter experience the price one could pay for a fall.

'No, not at all. The snow, you see.' She said it as if he had obliged her to point out the obvious. Now she was burrowing in the bag.

'I really ought to give you something.'

Knight was irritated that his gallantry should be reduced to a matter of hard cash, however much he needed it.

'No, please! I wouldn't dream of it.'

'Nonsense. You can't be making much delivering those.'

The leaflets lay scattered across the road, clear evidence of his fall from grace.

'Well, you see...' he cast around for a more flattering account of his activities. 'I was actually doing this for a friend who couldn't get out today.'

'Yes, but all the same,' she said dismissively, as if it didn't matter whether she believed him or not. She was opening a frayed leather wallet.

'Would three pounds be enough?'

Knight was struck dumb. She had an air that made her seem at once distant from the world yet confident it would do her bidding. He held up a hand in polite refusal, even though this was now the only money he would earn today.

'The truth is,' he replied, 'I'm a private investigator. I'm observing these streets for a client and the leaflets are my cover. Tom Knight, how do you do?'

He held out his hand and, after a moment's hesitation, she took it as she might a substandard offering from the fish counter.

'Clementine Lever. The artist.' As if he ought to know.

He offered her his arm and they walked back to the Nissan. Knight did not warm to her. The behaviour with the money was bizarre, and the lecture that now followed on the seashore-themed art movement she claimed to have founded grew swiftly tedious. Her self-importance hung about her like a force field.

When they reached the car she didn't offer him a lift, not that Knight wanted one. Instead, she looked him up and down as if assessing him and produced her wallet again. Knight decided he would take the money this time, but rather than the three pounds she produced a card.

'I may have some work for you,' she said, as if conferring a rare privilege. 'Perhaps you'd like to give me a call?'

Chapter Two

Merv was worried about Knight. The new knee was clearly a result, but the Mad Major was pushing himself too hard. Sooner or later there would be another disaster, such as the incident at the library. Knight had mistaken his painkillers for sleeping pills and fallen asleep for several hours with his phone on mute while Merv searched the town for him. At least the library was warm, which he suspected was why Knight had gone there in the first place.

He knew that Knight was broke. The problem was, he wouldn't talk about it. Every time Merv mentioned the empty fridge he got a lecture on the nation's wasteful eating habits. When he drew attention to the freezing temperature in the flat he was told that central heating had made society soft, which he knew Knight didn't believe; computer games had done that. But now, if the old man would let him, he had thought of a way to help.

On the workbench in his allotment shed was a lobster pot. True, it was technically a plastic crate and a few feet of chicken wire, but it worked and he was proud of it. For the past month it and several others had brought him a modest but tax-free living, all because his mate Charlie Fleece was in prison for benefit fraud. Charlie's downfall had come when one of his greyhounds escaped at the dog track. Something of a fitness fanatic, he had recovered it with an ease that would have put a younger man to shame. Sadly, the inspector investigating his claim for mobility allowance had videoed the incident.

Merv didn't approve of benefit fraud, which to his mind was completely different from tax evasion. Benefit fraud put you down among the scroungers and the layabouts, while hanging on to your own money stopped the government from doing stupid things with it. Charlie had gone down in Merv's estimation, but he did have a sixteen-foot cabin boat that he kept in Sovereign Harbour, and to his credit had said Merv could use it while he was away. His plan was to offer Knight the job of helmsman. It was not strictly necessary, and in truth he preferred to work by himself, but he could say that he needed someone to stop the boat from drifting while he lifted the cages in and out of the water. The problem was, the old bugger was proud and there was no point in having him along if he wouldn't take the money.

*

Knight squeezed the teabag with a spoon until the water turned a faint yellow. He had kept a fresh one for Merv, hoping to avoid further questioning about his welfare. Merv, he felt, had a tendency to cluck, and in any case he had a horror of being a burden to anyone. He was in a pit of his own making and would not be inviting his friend to share it with him.

The pit itself had nearly doubled in size overnight. A letter had come from the managing agents requesting a cheque for twenty thousand pounds towards a new roof and the redecoration of the exterior. Altogether he now owed just under fifty thousand. Even in his past life, in the world of commercial espionage, it would have been a significant sum, but manageable through further borrowing. That option no longer existed; he was maxed out on all fronts and his creditors were growing restless. Yet fifty thousand was also a trifling sum, it seemed to him, a paltry bonus for a junior City trader. He felt all the more humiliated that it should be so far beyond his reach.

Against these forces his new employment was no more than a token gesture. However, it enabled him to cling to the notion that something might turn up, which in turn stopped him thinking about the flat. Things did turn up – they always had in the past so why shouldn't they again? As if to prove his point the doorbell rang, reminding him that Merv had invited himself over with some more weed.

Merv was relieved to see that Knight had not begun to let himself go. A few items of misplaced clothing and used crockery lay scattered about the flat, more than enough to fail a barracks inspection, but by male standards the place was tidy. The heating, however, remained off, so that it felt almost as cold inside as out, where the temperature hovered around three degrees.

'Bit parky in here; you thinking of opening a morgue?'

Knight grunted noncommittally as they faced each other over the coffee table, Merv on the ancient Chesterfield opposite the worn leather armchair. In his rucksack were some tins of stew and soup which he would put in the cupboard when Knight was not looking.

'So how's the leafleting?'

'Oh that. I decided to pack it in for a bit. Wait for the weather to clear.'

Merv crumbled the buds. He had grown the plants in the shed, hidden in a dustbin under a light powered by a solar panel on the roof. Disappointingly, it was the last there would be for some time, an unknown thief having stolen the panel. He asked himself sometimes if he was doing Knight a favour by sharing the weed with him, whether perhaps it clouded his judgement, but what other pleasures did he have? He was not sorry that Knight had given up the leafleting, though it meant he'd have even less money.

'Good idea mate, you don't want to be out in this lot. Get this going while I put the kettle on.'

Knight didn't want him to see inside the fridge but Merv was already on his feet, and now, with the lit joint in his fingers, the effort of getting up did not seem worth it. He felt the familiar tang in his throat and wondered whether to tell Merv about the job.

Merv smuggled the tins into the cupboard where they joined a forlorn collection of beans and lentils.

When he opened the fridge for the milk, he was greeted by an ailing lump of cheddar and a bag of carrots, along with a few rashers of bacon wrapped in cling-film. It was hardcore self-denial, but then Knight never did things by halves.

'Bit Mother Hubbard in here,' he said casually.

The weed was already making Knight feel hungry. He pictured the fridge in its glory days, packed with salmon, prosciutto, olives, the stuff of distant memory.

'I know. Haven't had time to get to the shops.'

'You sure you're getting enough to eat?'

Merv wished the words back in his mouth before he'd finished the sentence. He sounded like a social worker, and in his experience they weren't much better than the police. He saw Knight's face cloud.

'I'm absolutely fine, thank you. Do you want some of this or not?'

Merv returned from the kitchen and took the joint.

'Got a proposition for you. Could be a nice little earner now that you're off the leaflets.'

Knight heard him out. He was not averse to a sea voyage but spotted immediately that the position on offer was essentially redundant. It wasn't just that he disliked accepting charity. Given that Merv would obviously be in charge, there was something about the reversal of roles that made him uncomfortable. He was glad, therefore, to have a golden bridge over which to retreat.

'Well, it's very kind,' he ventured diplomatically, 'though I don't honestly see what use I'd be. And anyway, I've just taken on a new job.'

Merv rejoiced. It had happened, Knight had turned a corner. He also felt relieved that he wouldn't have to look after him on the boat.

'That's brilliant, mate! I knew they'd start coming back. What you got, an obbo?'

'Not exactly, just something I'm doing for a woman I met the other day.'

Merv grinned.

'Oh yeah, you going into the gigolo business then?'

'We didn't discuss that; I'm not sure she could afford my rates. She's an artist as it happens.'

Merv waited.

'Well, go on then, what you doing for her?'

Having been in two minds whether to tell Merv, he had painted himself into a corner where there was no alternative.

'She's asked me to model for her.'

There was a short silence.

'Model? You mean like getting your kit off?'

'Yes.'

The news united with the weed to create a rare moment of perfection in Merv's life.

'You are fucking joking, mate! You are going to get bollock-naked in front of some bird and she's going to pay you for it? Why?'

'Presumably because she sees in me a thing of beauty that you couldn't possibly appreciate.'

Merv exulted in the outrageousness of it. He didn't care that it wasn't an investigation, what mattered was that Knight had turned a corner, one that might herald the return of the old days. He was less pleased by what Knight said next, which caused him to question again the wisdom of giving him marijuana.

'You know, going back to your earlier suggestion, I quite fancy the idea of being a helmsman, not for money, of course. When were you thinking of going?'

Chapter Three

Adrenaline Rush was a small, slow motorboat in the shape of a bath toy, with a wheelhouse no larger than a sentry box and a cramped aft deck exposed to the elements. She took her name from Charlie Fleece's much mourned favourite greyhound, whose dope-fuelled winnings had paid for her.

Although lacking her namesake's speed and agility, she lumbered efficiently enough through the gentle swell. Encased in a lifejacket strapped rather too tightly over his coat, Knight sat outside on the built-in bench, enjoying the steady roll over shallow peaks and troughs. They were a mile or so offshore.

He had mixed feelings about his imminent appointment with Clementine Lever. It was not that he was body shy, he had the army to thank for that, and compared to leafleting it was a far more efficient way to scrape together a few pounds. But the fact of being naked in the presence of a woman other than a doctor led him back to the war of the white flag. The diehards proclaimed the appointment a step in the right direction, though they were unclear as to the destination. For this they were ridiculed by the surrender faction. If to be naked with a woman was a benchmark of progress, what did it say that the woman was Clementine Lever, towards whom he felt not the least attraction? There was a brittle coldness to her, an assumption of superiority he found offensive.

She was also mean. Five pounds an hour was more than an insult; it spoke of some odd pathology he didn't want to know about. But beggars couldn't be choosers, and it would at least be warm.

Merv came out of the wheelhouse.

'Right, you're on.'

They were approaching a trio of plastic jerry cans some twenty feet apart, anchored to the seabed by buckets that Merv had filled with concrete. Between them, not far beneath the surface, ran the rope from which the traps hung. Taking Merv's outstretched hand, Knight swayed to his feet and groped his way cautiously to the wheel. Save for a fishing boat a few hundred yards to starboard, he was lord of all he surveyed.

It was a simple matter of adjusting the throttle and the wheel to keep the boat in place while Merv hoisted the rope with the boat hook and hauled up the cages. On the dry run by the harbour buoy he had passed with flying colours.

Now that they were on the high sea the task was more demanding. Merv hooked the rope without difficulty, but against the oncoming swell Knight overdid the throttle and the boat lurched forward. Merv cursed as the rope slipped away.

Knight reversed the engine and backed up. Was it his imagination, or had the swell become stronger?

'What the fuck's he playing at?' Merv shouted.

Knight thought Merv's anger was aimed at him until he turned and saw the fishing boat bearing down on them, pushing a strong bow wave in front of it. It was about three times the size of *Adrenaline Rush*, with a bristling array of masts and winches. A stout man in bloodstained overalls was standing on the foredeck, clutching the rail.

'You're on my water!' he barked. The boat was less than fifty yards away and closing fast. *Adrenaline Rush* pitched violently, causing Knight to swing the wheel further as he clung to it for support. Merv was yelling at him to cut the throttle.

With vastly more aplomb than Knight had demonstrated, the fishing boat hove to at their side, towering over them. A young man sneered down at them from the wheelhouse, casually giving Merv the finger, while a second man joined their skipper at the rail. The latter was berating Merv in colourful language for trespassing on his patch and stealing his lobsters. Merv was giving as good as he got, insisting correctly that he had a right to take three lobsters a day wherever he liked, not mentioning that, on occasions, he had caught as many as ten.

'You think you've got rights out here?' the skipper bellowed. He looked to be in his sixties, his face an unhealthy puce. He shouted something to the man in the wheelhouse.

The fishing boat's prow bumped the side of its puny adversary, enough to send Merv to his knees on the deck. Knight clung to the wheel, the small boat pitching erratically as it was prodded away from the buoys. Somehow he managed to open the throttle again and turn *Adrenaline Rush* away from her tormentor. The skipper leered at them with grim satisfaction, the fish blood on his overalls combining with the colour of his face into something unpleasantly demonic.

'Next time I see you two idiots out here, I'll sink you.'

He hadn't finished yet. As *Adrenaline Rush* retreated to a safe distance he produced a boat hook and hoisted up Merv's line. When the cage surfaced, he hauled it aboard. Incensed by the blatant act of piracy, Merv grabbed the wheel and tried to turn back towards the fishing boat, where his second cage was about to be taken. Guessing his intention, Knight wrenched the wheel.

'No! We can't take on three of them!'

'You want to bet? Watch me!'

They both clung to the wheel in an absurd tug of war. It was evenly matched at first, Knight possessing remarkable upper body strength for a man of his age, but he knew he would be the first to tire.

'For God's sake, Merv, who do you think's going to sink if you ram them?'

'It's my boat, let go of the wheel!'

Knight lost patience.

'Merv, will you use your bloody brain!'

He delivered the last four words with a roar that left him out of breath. Nevertheless, it pierced the part of Merv's psyche that still twitched at the sound of an officer at parade ground volume. He let go of the wheel.

'All right,' he said petulantly. 'What do you suggest?'

'I don't know.'

Their nemesis was now cutting the ropes to which the buoys were tethered. The ropes sank into the sea and the jerry cans floated away to join the travelling family of flotsam drifting through the Channel.

Merv watched sullenly as the fishing boat moved off, heading further out to sea.

'I'm sorry I shouted,' Knight said quietly. 'I just didn't fancy a swim today.'

Merv said nothing. Knight had never shouted at him like that before. He was right, of course, he could see that now, but it had touched a raw nerve, a fear and distrust of authority that ran deep, the one that had regularly prevented him from rising above the rank of corporal.

Sensing the resentment hanging in the air like a damp fog, Knight cast around for something reassuring to say.

'We could go to the police,' was the best he could manage.

'Yeah great, their word against ours, that'll work. We didn't even see what their sodding boat was called.'

Knight picked up the binoculars and peered through the wheelhouse window. The words *King of Sussex* were visible on the fishing boat's stern, but then a flash of orange bobbed in the sea further ahead, and then another. Beyond the vessel lay a line of marker buoys several hundred yards long.

'I think he's got his pots out there.'

He passed the binoculars to Merv. The *King of Sussex* was approaching the far end of the line of buoys and appeared to be slowing down. Still gripped by rage, Merv knew immediately what he had to do.

'I'm going to have them.'

It was reckless but not suicidal, and Knight sensed he had pushed Merv far enough. He also resented the humiliation inflicted on them by the fishermen; it felt cowardly to back off.

'Don't see why not. We'd have to be quick, though.'

Merv steered towards the opposite end of the line from the *King of Sussex*. Busy winching their pots aboard, the crew paid little attention at first. This time, Knight's performance at the wheel was exemplary. He held the little boat steady while Merv landed the first pot and hoisted a second. Only now did the fishermen understand what was afoot. They had seen the course Merv had taken, but it never occurred to them that he would be foolish enough to take their catch. By the time they had shut down the winch, the thief was running at full throttle to Sovereign Harbour.

The *King of Sussex* was no more built for speed than its quarry. It was still a hundred yards away when they were in plain view of the harbour tower and the dog walkers on the beach. At the wheel, Knight relaxed; a public ramming seemed unlikely.

Behind him Merv transferred the occupants of the pots into a crate and threw the pots overboard. If third parties became involved there would be no evidence, just the word of two against three. Knight doubted it would come to that. From what he had seen, their persecutor was a man who preferred to settle things personally. He was not surprised when the fishing boat chose to turn away rather than follow them into the harbour, though he had a strong premonition of more to come.

Chapter Four

Built on a vast bank of shingle that had once accommodated seabirds and rare wildflowers, Sovereign Harbour lay to the east of the town centre. It consisted of four interconnected mooring basins surrounded by houses and apartment blocks. With its chain restaurants and proximity to the retail park, it lacked perhaps the glamour of Saint-Tropez or Monte Carlo, but to its population of retirees, renters and second-home owners it afforded a taste of the sea without most of the discomfort. The high proportion of part-time residents also offered a degree of anonymity, which to some of them was highly convenient.

The mooring basins were separated from the outer harbour by a lock operated from the control tower that stood directly above it. The lock opened on the hour and half hour. Having missed its chance to enter, *Adrenaline Rush* waited in the shelter of the outer harbour wall.

Knight's own surge of adrenaline had long since abated. It was still only mid-morning, but he had been up since six and the unwanted skirmish had left him drained. He was also ravenous.

He watched while Merv slid a thick rubber band onto a captive's claw. The liberated pots had yielded no less than eight lobsters, which flapped and scrabbled in their crate, ignorant of their destiny. The jaws of the banding tool opened wide as he squeezed the handles together, stretching the band to let it pass over the claw. He snapped it neatly into place and withdrew the tool in one smooth motion.

Beside the crate lay the last of Merv's home-made traps. It was a simple affair, with a tapering tunnel of chicken wire that offered a one-way journey to the bait beyond. Having passed through and taken its fill, the unfortunate diner was unable to make its way out again and so took a step up the food chain instead. Knight was not untouched by their plight, but would happily have consumed one there and then had there been anything to cook it in.

'You fancy a go at this?'

Knight took the banding tool and selected a lobster. He wasn't wearing gloves, so it was unfortunate that he picked one whose fighting spirit was still surprisingly intact. At three pounds it suffered a severe weight disadvantage but it jabbed and writhed vigorously, making it difficult for Knight to aim the tool.

'Cheeky bastard that one – want me to do it?'

'No thank you, I can manage.' Knight sounded sure of himself so Merv sat back and watched.

He set down the lobster and grabbed clumsily at its right claw, only to receive a sharp nip on his fingertip. He grabbed again, irked that his reflexes had been outclassed. But the lobster, evidently a southpaw, caught him with a sucker punch from the left and hung on tight. Merv reached over but Knight waved him away.

'I said I'm fine!'

'You're not fine, it's going to have your sodding finger off!'

Had it been much bigger it might have done so. Even then, the pain was intense, the claw's serrated edges clamping him like a pair of blunt scissors.

'Use the tool!'

Knight slid the jaws of the banding tool between the pincers and squeezed the handles to prise them apart. His finger was bleeding. Without thinking he banged the animal against the side of the boat. Momentarily stunned, it dropped its guard long enough for Knight to snap the bands in place.

'Well done, got there in the end. Let's see the damage.'

'It's just a scratch, there's nothing to see.'

'Fancy doing another one then?'

The joke fell on deaf ears. While Merv dealt with the remaining catch, Knight inspected his finger. The skin was broken, exposing a glimpse of raw flesh from which a few drops of blood were oozing. In the matter of body armour, the lobster had also won hands down. Yet the outcome had never been in doubt. Baffled by the geometry of the trap, then flailing wildly in the alien brightness of the world above the sea, the creature had stood no chance. Quietly saluting his opponent, Knight found he had lost his appetite.

The lock gates creaked open, allowing *Adrenaline Rush* to enter the inner harbour. Ahead of them and to either side were three further basins, each accessed by a short canal that passed under a drawbridge. Their destination was the basin to the right, which involved a trip past half a dozen or so piers lined with moored boats.

The yachts and motor cruisers gleamed white in the wintry sun. Most of them dwarfed the tiny vessel, conjuring up in Knight's mind a world of complacent affluence in troubling contrast to his own. Nevertheless, his belief that the ordeal was nearly over raised his spirits, if only for a minute.

'Where did they come from?!'

Waiting for them on the drawbridge over the canal between the two basins were the angry skipper and his sons. Knight recalled that a small colony of fishing boats occupied part of the beach about halfway back into town. In the time that *Adrenaline Rush* had been waiting for the lock they could easily have landed and driven here.

Merv stopped at the end of the middle pier. Like Knight, he wanted this morning to be over. One of the trio lifted his hand in an ironic wave.

'There's not much they can do to us; the place is full of cameras.'

Merv felt only slightly better as Knight pointed them out. Dotting the buildings that lined the quays were enough CCTV cameras to monitor every corner of the marina.

'Yeah, but they're going to do something aren't they? They haven't come to say sorry we nicked your lobsters and please keep ours; they're here to give us shit.'

Knight put himself in their shoes. While he and Merv could claim to have earned a creditable draw in the contest, to the fishermen the taking of their catch was an intolerable affront.

'They want the lobsters. It's not going to be much of a fight against two of us, and even if there is they'll just say they're taking back their property. Their word against ours again.'

'So what, we just hand them over?'

The thought soured in Knight's mind. The lowlife on the bridge could not be indulged.

'Maybe not. If you back down this pier I think I can get off without them seeing me.'

There were two rows of boats, one on either side of the pier. Merv reversed down the side furthest from the men, whose view was blocked by the forest of masts. Halfway down was a small sloop that sat only a few inches higher in the water than *Adrenaline Rush*.

Knight stood on the bench behind the wheelhouse. Held in place by the slowly turning engine, the stern nuzzled against the sloop's open foredeck. Merv darted across and stood ready to catch him. All he had to do was step from one gently bobbing platform to the other, catching the opposing deck just as it began to descend. He was too slow and took the full force of it coming up, so that Merv had to grab him and haul him over. In a similar vein they reached dry land, where Merv handed him the tray of lobsters and returned to the wheelhouse.

Screened by the rows of boats, Knight's intention was to reach the end of the pier and wait until the men followed Merv to his mooring. A brisk walk around the side of the basin would then take him safely to the car park. Reaching the corner, he craned round the hull of a yacht. They were just visible through the lattice of masts and superstructure, watching as *Adrenaline Rush* approached the raised drawbridge.

Knight moved across the open gap to the next pier and waited by a vast motor yacht. It had caught his eye on the way out, a thirty-metre Sunseeker with three decks and extravagantly sculpted contours. It was called *Mamma Mia*, which struck him as appropriately vulgar. *Adrenaline Rush* was passing under the bridge and the men were following; he had a clear run now to the car park.

It was awkward carrying the tray while holding his stick under his arm, but the quayside had been swept clear of snow and he marched briskly, not for the first time blessing the surgeons for their work. At the next junction he stopped again to check. He was glad that he did. One of the younger men had returned and was walking back from the bridge. Knight's absence had been noticed.

He turned and fled. Any second now the man would reach the corner at the end of the pier and see him. Ahead of him, level with the quayside, was an open platform that formed part of the stern of *Mamma Mia*, Without looking back, he walked straight on board.

A staircase led from the platform to the main deck. He took the steps one at a time, concentrating on the tray as if he were delivering breakfast to a lover's bed. Only at the top did he dare to look over his shoulder. His pursuer was staring up and down the quayside, and only needed to raise his eyes to see him. The door to the salon was open, an offer that could not be refused.

A cream calfskin sofa snaked around one side of the room, opposite a lavishly stocked bar. Beyond lay a black marble dining table and a dozen white chairs. The darkened glass walls reduced the sunshine to no more than a glimmer, allowing the lighting system to cast a soft, seductive glow. For a moment Knight forgot about his pursuer. It was as if he had stepped into a page of *Hello!* magazine; he half expected to find a grinning celebrity toasting him from behind the bar.

'Can I help you?'

The indignant voice came from the far side of the dining table. A tall, slim man in his fifties wearing an obtrusively branded polo shirt was staring at him. Knight clearly wasn't welcome but there was no way he could leave yet.

'Are you the gentleman who ordered the lobsters?' he asked graciously. He walked boldly forward and set the tray down on the dining table, then removed the cloth with a flourish. It was an impressive sight, the perfect prop to complete the picture of plutocratic bounty. The man relaxed.

'It must be a mistake. Sorry old chap, who did you say they were for?'

'Hopkins,' sighed Knight, 'I take it that's not you?'

'No, sorry about that. Afraid I can't help you.'

Despite the faint tone of regret, it was a signal for Knight to leave. He picked up the tray and walked as slowly as he could back to the saloon door, intent on staging a dizzy fit when he reached the sofa.

'Wait!'

The man came forward, clearly no longer considering Knight with suspicion.

'Let's take another look at those.'

With the air of one accustomed to getting what he wanted, he swept back the cloth and beheld the gleaming array again.

'How much for the lot?'

Knight guessed they weighed about fifteen pounds altogether; he could not remember when he had last paid for one.

'I think it was a hundred and twenty, but I should really get them to Mr Hopkins.'

'Tell you what, I'll give you a hundred and fifty. What do you say?'

24

Scarcely believing that fortune had chosen at last to smile on him, Knight waited while the man went to find the cash, willing him to take his time. When he finally walked out, the quay was empty. As he passed over the bridge he saw Merv walking towards him from the far basin. The fishermen were walking behind him, shouting a stream of threats and insults that he was wisely ignoring. Feeling an unaccustomed benevolence towards the idle rich, Knight continued unhindered to the car park.

Chapter Five

The rolling fields had become the dunes of a ghostly white desert. Snow was still falling, a straggling shower behind a blizzard that had passed in the night. Knight proceeded at a snail's pace on the ungritted B road, glad to have it to himself.

A day's rest and a simple celebration with Merv had done wonders for his outlook. Merv had insisted that he take half the money, so he was a princely seventy-five pounds in pocket, although fifty of that had already gone on petrol. His army pension would arrive tomorrow, covering the credit card interest. To straws such as these he clung as he searched for the turning to Hillside Grange.

Clementine Lever lived on a lane that descended from the road into an empty hillside. No vehicles had passed and the snow lay several inches deep; he would have to walk. His leg was still stiff from the operation, so that it took a full five minutes to change into his wellingtons. Yet this too was a blessing; a few weeks ago he could not have done it on his own. Imbued with a spirit of renewal, he left the Skoda at the end of the lane and set off.

Hillside Grange, when it appeared fifty yards later, was not what he expected. Her manner had suggested something pompously Gothic rather than the hovel that stood before him. It was a rare thing in southern England; a humble farm labourer's cottage that had been overlooked by property money. Even at this distance he could see that the window frames were rotten and the brickwork crumbling. Perhaps on a summer's day it had a quaint rustic charm, but exposed on the snowy hillside it was profoundly bleak.

Somewhat reluctantly, he rapped the tarnished brass fish that served as a door knocker. When no one came he was tempted to leave, but persevered to the other side of the building where he found a second door and a window through which he could see a kitchen. It was cramped and shabby with 1970s fittings.

'Ah, you're here – I was wondering where you'd got to.'

Knight spun around. The artist was looking irritably at her watch, though he was only five minutes late. She was wearing the same thick coat but now the hood was down, revealing a long grey plait that hung over her shoulder. Knight thought they were going inside, but instead she led him around the back of the cottage to a corrugated iron shed attached to the rear wall.

'The studio is separate from the main house,' she explained crisply. 'You can leave your clothes behind the screen and I'll call you when I'm ready.' There was no word of welcome, let alone an offer of tea.

He followed her through a jumble of paint-spattered tables, shelves and boxes amongst which was a tattered Chinese screen. Undressing behind it, he reminded himself of the diehards' most recent salvo. His body had been chosen as raw material for a work of art. That made it a special body, therefore, in some way, a beautiful one too. It followed that there must still be women on the face of the earth who would desire it, and they wouldn't all be as unappealing as Clementine Lever. The surrender faction had, as yet, nothing to say.

Ready to be admired, he poked his head around the screen.

'Mrs Lever?'

'It's Miss Lever. Are you ready yet?'

Busy fixing paper to an easel, she didn't look up.

'Not quite. I was going to ask if there was any heating. You may not have noticed, but it's rather cold in here.'

She looked disappointed.

'Well, if you must. It does cost a lot.'

With bad grace, she went to a battered gas heater that lay hidden in the clutter and prodded the controls until it lit, though only at the minimum setting.

'Are you ready *now*?'

Sitting on the chair, Knight hooked his underpants off his toes with his stick and raised himself to his feet. Showtime. Keeping the stick more for moral than physical support, he advanced from behind the screen.

'Over there,' she pointed.

A grubby white sheet hung from wires attached to the ceiling. In front of it was a cheap leatherette sofa in a state of advanced ruin. The upholstery was tattered, hanging in flaps that showed signs of mould. At one end, a spring poked through. Even by the standards of what he had seen thus far, it hit a dismayingly new low.

'Do you want me to get on that?!' he spluttered. She looked disappointed again.

'I got it specially,' she said brusquely. 'Can you sit against the armrest with your head to my left and your outside leg on the floor? I don't need the stick.'

At least she didn't expect him to sit on the exposed spring. He put the stick down beside the sofa and eased himself into position, flinching at the cold kiss of the leatherette on his bare skin.

She was staring at him disapprovingly.

'You're still wearing your socks.'

'They take rather a long time to take off and the floor is damp. I didn't think it would matter.'

'Of course it matters. Can you really not get them off?'

'Yes, but it'll take a few minutes, and you seemed in a hurry.' He was happy for her to hear the edge in his voice.

With an impatient sigh, she came to him. He was bending over to remove the first sock but she brushed his hands away and did it herself, making a point it seemed of avoiding eye contact. Her plait hung down and grazed against his calf, like a snake judging its way onto a branch. The ends had been left to grow out in spidery strands. As she turned her attention to the second sock, she did not so much as cast a glance at the rest of him. Admiration seemed in short supply thus far.

'There.'

To his surprise she smiled, or tried to; a momentary twitch of her thin lips that didn't carry to her eyes. Under the cold exterior he detected a nervousness that he hadn't noticed before. The diehards slyly suggested that this might be the effect of seeing him naked, in which case her admiration could be of the suppressed variety. She returned to the stool and peered at him critically over the top of her pencil.

'Can you crook your inside leg and turn your head sideways on the armrest so that you're looking up at the skylight.'

It was an awkward pose. Uncomfortably splayed, his frozen genitalia at vanishing point, he watched the snowflakes falling and summoned what powers of endurance were left to him.

'So you're a private detective?'

Knight wasn't in the mood for small talk, but it was the first time she had expressed any interest in him.

'Yes, before that I worked in commercial intelligence and before that I was in the army.'

She nodded, but didn't seem that impressed.

'Aren't you rather old to be a detective?'

That stung. He wasn't about to tell her that he couldn't afford to retire, that he had lived for many years from hand to mouth. He wondered if she believed his story about the leaflets.

'I like to keep my hand in. I'm still perfectly good at it and I enjoy the work. Perhaps the way you enjoy your painting.' He hoped that would shut her up.

'But do you really follow people around without them knowing you're there?' She made it sound ridiculous. 'Isn't that just something you see on television?'

'Well, yes, of course I do. It's part of the job.' He didn't exactly snap but didn't disguise his irritation either.

From the corner of his eye he saw her smile again, the same nervous twitch.

'So how *do* you follow people? It must be such an interesting thing to do.' She sounded almost contrite now.

Losing himself in the snowflakes, Knight reeled off random items of tradecraft. Now that she appeared to have thawed a little, his irritation lifted. He felt a small pang of sympathy for her.

'It must be extraordinary to be somewhere and know that the person you're watching can't see you. It must be like being invisible.'

Feeling more generous, Knight reeled off further scraps of information. Disguise, cover, escape routes; normally he wouldn't have revealed his hard-learnt skills to a stranger, but she was a harmless eccentric and lonely; it would not hurt to offer this small entertainment.

She worked on for another thirty minutes, occasionally asking him about cases, once or twice adjusting his limbs with the same clinical efficiency, though she did manage to look him in the eye and perform the twitchy smile. At last, she said he could get dressed.

The picture embodied the worst predictions of the white-flaggers. The execution was by no means bad, owing something possibly to Bacon or Freud. What repelled him was how his body seemed to have caved in and spread over the sofa like an excrescence, as if it had grown there with the mould. Most damning of all, she had drawn him with his eyes closed.

'It's part of a series of works about decay and death,' she explained. 'I chose you to represent the mid-to-late stage of the spectrum. That's why you're juxtaposed with the mould, some of it's alive but most of it's dead already.'

Taped to various shelves and cupboards were sketches of rotting leaves, a dung ball and the decaying corpse of a badger. Even though he was now fully dressed, Knight felt chilled to the bone. The painstakingly assembled notion of pride in his body fled the field, leaving the white flag to fly unchallenged.

'I think I've caught you rather well,' she said, almost cheerfully. 'I suppose you'd like some tea?'

The furniture in the tiny sitting room was threadbare, albeit a vast improvement on the shed. While she made tea he looked at the pictures lining the walls. These included several male nudes whose treatment was markedly more flattering than his own. They all bore her signature, prominently displayed. Interspersed between them were certificates boasting diplomas and prizes, charting the flat arc of her career from St Martin's to obscure artist. It seemed to him a shrine, a prop to the illusion of importance that kept her going.

Beside the chimney breast was a picture that was different from the rest, a print of a Chinese painting depicting an old man at an easel. He was looking across a valley at a wood. Above the trees a flock of birds, possibly ducks, was flying away into the distance. It was a quiet, graceful scene that he preferred infinitely to everything else on show. In the bottom corner were some Chinese characters which he took to be a kind of commentary, or perhaps the picture's title. He was still absorbed in it when she returned with the tea.

'Why are you looking at that?' He thought she must be displeased because he was not looking at one of hers.

'I've been admiring all of them,' he reassured her. 'They're really very good. This one is obviously not by you, of course,' he petered off lamely. He wanted to go, but his comment unleashed a further lecture about the significance of her work. It became clear that he was going to have to ask for the money. Eventually, she paused to draw breath and he dived in.

'Actually I do have a few more things I need to get done today. Would you mind very much if we settled up and I got going?'

A flicker of distaste crossed her face. Her handbag seemed hard to find. He wondered if this was a ploy not to pay him but, eventually, the ragged wallet was opened.

'Ten pounds then.'

She made it sound like a fortune, which it possibly was. Empty of notes, the wallet contained a handful of coins which she began to count out. Knight could not bear to watch.

'Look,' he said, 'if it's too much, just... please don't worry if you can't afford it.'

'Of course I can afford it!' she snapped.

'Are you sure?' He tried to speak kindly. 'It's just that it doesn't look quite like that to me.'

He had struck a raw nerve. Her mouth dropped open as if he had made a lewd proposition.

'I am not a poor person, Mr Knight!' she shouted. 'What you see here is not who I am! Someone stole from me, do you understand?! It was never meant to be like this!'

The vehemence of the outburst took him aback, and her too it seemed. They sat in silence for a moment.

'I'm sorry,' she said, while he was still wondering whether to apologise, 'it's none of your concern.'

She went on counting out the money. He looked away and caught the eye of one of the nudes. It leered back with a familiarity that taunted him.

'I expect you earn a lot more as an investigator,' she said offhandedly, as if her outburst hadn't happened. 'How much do you charge as a matter of interest?'

Knight quoted a figure. It seemed to shock her.

'Well, I hope you get some work soon.'

So did he. She showed him to the kitchen door and he stepped out gratefully into the snow, relishing the prospect of the plod back up the track. But she was not quite finished with him.

'Could you do another session for me?'

He thought he had misheard her, but now she was proposing a date and a time. When he made an excuse a truly plaintive expression overtook her, one he hadn't seen before. For an instant her guard dropped, revealing a small, fearful child about to be crushed by disappointment. Infuriatingly, his heart softened.

Knight regretted his charitable lapse as soon as he turned away. He tried telling himself that ten pounds was ten pounds, but it rang hollow.

Chapter Six

The car park at the discount supermarket was full. A break in the snow had brought out a crowd of shoppers, anxious to stock up before the next heavy fall. Knight edged the Skoda through the slush in a depressing melee of cars looking for a space. A pair of elderly pensioners were picking up food that had fallen from a ruptured bag, a morbidly obese woman was shouting at her son because he'd left his gloves in the café. He mourned the days of Waitrose.

It had been a stressful forty-eight hours. A final demand for the service charge excess had sent him into a panic, forcing him to engage with the situation and look for other places to live. This had panicked him still further. After clearing expenses and debts and leaving a modest cash cushion, the best he could hope for was a one-bedroom flat above a shop, or a small bungalow far from the sea.

In the end, he did what he had done many times when his back was to the wall; he made an appointment to see his accountant in London. Reuben Gerwitz had been a staunch ally for more than twenty years, keeping the taxman at bay and devising ingenious stratagems to revive his cash flow at minimum cost; perhaps he would conjure another rabbit out of the hat. But when he went to the station the trains were not running, courtesy of a body on the tracks just outside the town. Reuben was going on holiday the next day and would not be back for a fortnight, leading Knight to curse the deceased for a lack of consideration. Now, en route to his second appointment with Clementine Lever, he had stopped off to complete another mission, one that promised to transform his meagre larder.

A few days earlier, he had noticed out-of-date stock being removed from a shelf, and had watched while it was taken to a storage area at the side of the building. Here it was dumped in an open container before being sent to fester wastefully in a landfill, not even by way of a food bank. When challenged for his presence in the area, he had pretended to be lost and confused, and was guided back to the store by a security guard. But what he had seen excited him, for the container stood directly beside the access road from the car park. He could be in and out in thirty seconds; even if he was stopped it would not be in the supermarket's interest to prosecute a frail pensioner for taking condemned food. Nor did he feel any shame. It was simply a question of living off the land, something he felt perfectly capable of and saw no reason not to try.

At last, he found a space. It was on the far side of the car park from the access road but it would have to do. He set off with his stick and a wheeled shopping bag he had bought in a charity shop for a pound.

The access road was deserted. He trundled the shopping bag to the side entrance of the warehouse and peered through a thick plastic curtain. The container was immediately to his right. Opposite him a woman was unloading cartons into a wheeled cage, ready to be taken to the shelves. As soon as she disappeared into the store, he made his move.

The container came up to his chest and was only a third full, so that the intended booty was out of reach. Most of it was processed food in uninspiring permutations of fat and sugar, but he could also see a chicken and some sausages. These were prized calories; if cooked tonight they offered several days of healthy feasting. The only way to reach them was to tip the container towards him on its wheels and scoop them out.

The bin tipped easily enough. He lowered it with both hands then held it steady at waist level while he reached in with his stick, hooking the chicken and some of the sausages before scooping them out. Imagining some kind of casserole, he seized a bag of frozen roast potatoes. There were no other vegetables. He hunted instead for something to use as a sauce, but by now the bin was weighing heavily on him. Abandoning the idea, he scraped several boxes out indiscriminately and was about to call it a day when a pot of mushroom soup in the far corner caught his eye. It would make an excellent sauce.

He lowered the bin almost to his knees and bent over to reach in. The soup remained tantalisingly out of reach. He strained until the stick reached the carton, only to lose his grip on the bin. It wasn't a loud crash, but enough to alert the security guard behind the stacks of pallets. He switched screens from the porn on his phone to the monitor showing the old man who'd wandered in the other day. He was shovelling food into a trolley bag. The guard felt deeply offended. The bin was his preserve, shared only with a cashier he fancied, who didn't mind an out-of-date pizza. Knight was halfway down the access road before he caught up.

'Oi, you! Bring that back!'

Knight was annoyed with himself for compromising the mission; the soup was not worth the price of a rearguard action. He opened the bag and took out a pack of frozen onion rings.

'Everything you see here is about to be thrown away, as I'm sure you are well aware. I'm not doing anyone any harm, so I'd be grateful if you would let me go on my way.'

Perhaps he should have played it scared and pitiful, but the idea that anyone should object annoyed him as much as the sight of the onion rings offended the guard. Knight tried to walk on, but the guard clamped a hand on the trolley bag.

'You can't have it, mate, health and safety. I'm taking it back!'

Knight told him not to be ridiculous, but found himself losing the tug-of-war that ensued. The guard was not a big man, in his thirties perhaps, but with Merv's wiry build and strength. A non-violent escalation of tactics was required.

Without loosening his grip on the bag, he unleashed a violent coughing fit followed by a medley of strangulated gasps with his mouth open wide like a suffocating fish. It was a well-rehearsed ploy that seldom failed, its performance a source of professional pride. He clutched his chest and patted his pockets frantically.

'My heart pills! They must have fallen out in the warehouse!'

The guard was horrified. He didn't want to lose his job over a dead pensioner, not with the gambling debts that hung round his neck.

'Please, go and get them for me,' Knight wheezed. Gabbling into his radio the guard dashed back.

Knight was out of breath from the coughing fit. Trailing the heavy bag and using his stick as a hiking pole, he hurried towards the first row of cars as if late for a flight. It was too fast. His breathing became more laboured and he began to feel dizzy, but he was damned if he would stop. Next he was leaning on the bonnet of a car, doing his best not to fall.

As he steadied himself he became aware of something very big approaching. It was the woman who had been shouting at her child.

'You all right, love?'

She picked up the fallen stick and helped him off the car, plucking him effortlessly yet gently in her massive arms. Borne aloft as if on wings, Knight glimpsed the zip tattooed around her wrist, and the words 'open here'. At first, the sheer size of her provoked a feeling of absolute abhorrence. But either the humbling effect of the painting was still at work, or the dizziness alarmed him, for when her chest enveloped his head like the softest of beanbags he felt pleasantly soothed.

'Where's your car then?'

'It's at the end of the last row. Don't worry, I'm sure I can make it.'

'Don't be daft!' She turned to the boy, who, by now, had thankfully been reunited with his gloves.

'Don't just stand and gawp, Carl. Take the gentleman's bag for him!'

Knight's repeated assertions that he could manage fell on deaf ears. She clasped him round his shoulder and made him put his arm around her waist as far as it would reach, which was barely past her spine. Like a pair of front-row forwards they proceeded down the row of cars with the boy behind them.

'You're like my grandad,' she said. 'He always says he can do it on his own and the next thing he's arse over tit on the floor.'

He disliked the comparison, but they were making far better speed than he could have achieved alone.

'This is really very kind if you,' he said, remembering his manners. 'I'm extremely grateful.'

She cackled. 'You're a bit posh for here, aren't you? I thought your lot went to Waitrose.'

Clutching her belt, Knight settled comfortably into the ride. He had been in tanks on exercises and felt a similar thrill of invincibility, confident that any obstacle in his way would be obliterated. For some reason, this did not seem to apply to the guard, who was now blocking their way. Having found no trace of the pills, it had belatedly occurred to him that he had been hoodwinked. The sight of the old man hurrying away with a known troublemaker was ample proof.

'Right you two, that's far enough! Just give me the bag and leave before I have you nicked.'

Knight sensed his new friend was no great stickler for etiquette, yet she plainly didn't tolerate impoliteness from people in uniforms.

'What's your problem? Get out the sodding way!'

The guard pointed to the trolley bag.

'That is stolen goods. You either give it back or I call the law.'

She let go of Knight as if he were contaminated.

'You what!?'

She glared at him with a sudden menace. Sensing the need for speedy rehabilitation Knight rounded on the guard as if he were a delinquent private on a charge.

'You,' he said, taking a step forward and thrusting his face towards him, 'are an appalling little shit! I've already told you, the food in that bag is going to be thrown away, yet you persist in harassing me and insulting this good lady here.'

The astonished guard was cowed long enough for the woman to take a pizza from the bag and inspect the sell-by date. To Knight's relief, her fury refocused on its original target.

'He's telling the truth! Let him keep it you tosser!'

The guard made a grab for the bag but she snatched it away. When he tried again, he made the mistake of trying to wrench her fingers from the handle.

'Don't touch me!' she bawled.

She shoved him in the ribs, sending him staggering onto the boot of a car. In two strides, she was pinioning him with the full weight of her body.

'Think you're hard? Wanna try that again and see what happens? You hard enough for that?'

The guard squirmed, his legs flailing uselessly. A second guard appeared. He tried to pull her away but a sideways blow from her tremendous forearm caught him in the solar plexus. The boy remained unperturbed, having seen much worse.

'What the hell's going on?' croaked the second guard. 'Where's the old man with the heart attack?'

They looked around.

'He's gone,' said the boy.

Knight picked a gap in the traffic and shot across the carriageway, narrowly missing the arriving ambulance. On the floor beside him, the trolley bag brimmed with the spoils of war. He blessed his Samaritan and felt remorse for the abhorrence that had seized him earlier.

Fifteen minutes later, he reached the B road. This time it was gritted; the weather warnings were coming thick and fast on the radio. They were probably overdone, he thought, the usual nannying exaggerations that kept people in a state of unnecessary anxiety. Despite his resolve not to let Clementine Lever under his skin, he felt a growing unease about the fact that he was going to be late. He tried to resign himself to the encounter as if it were a visit to the dentist; however unpleasant, there would eventually be an end to it.

Knight froze. A police car was parked in the track leading down to Hillside Grange. He tried to remember if he'd seen a camera at the supermarket. But even if they had his number, how could they possibly have tracked him here? He was about to drive on, but already his presence had been noted. Sitting in the car was Detective Constable Bullock, an inept yet troublesome nemesis who would take delight in whatever breach of the law he may have committed. Realising he would only heap more suspicion on himself if he fled, he stopped the Skoda and crossed the road. Bullock wound down his window.

'Good afternoon, detective constable, how very good to see you,' he exclaimed jovially. 'What brings you to this far-flung corner of the world?'

Bullock frowned, equally displeased to see Knight and not bothering to hide it. The fact that Knight had saved his life barely six months ago did not change the fact that he was an interfering old git who had an annoying habit of making his life less pleasurable than it should be.

'That's funny, it's what I was going to ask you.'

There was a suspicion in the detective's tone Knight didn't like, but it still didn't make sense that anyone could have been expecting him.

'I have an appointment with Miss Lever at Hillside Grange. Is everything all right?'

Bullock stared at him curiously.

'An appointment eh? You're a bit late then.'

Somehow, Knight didn't feel relieved that Bullock hadn't mentioned the supermarket.

'She went under a train yesterday morning. She's brown bread.'

Chapter Seven

The day had started badly for Bullock. His boss had reprimanded him for failing to check the dead woman's home for a full twenty-four hours after she was identified by her driving licence. Anyone with half a brain could see it was a suicide. Now another idiot had arrived to torment him.

'She a friend of yours then?'

Knight had been struck dumb for a moment, stunned by the sheer horror of it, though not above feeling a twinge of relief that he would no longer have to see her.

'Well, I … I knew her slightly; we weren't close friends.'

'When did you last see her?'

He counted back the days uncertainly, wondering if this was some elaborate hoax.

'On Monday, I think.'

'The day before she topped herself. What were you doing with her?'

'She'd hired me to do some work, something unimportant, not an investigation.' He needed to change the subject. 'How do you know it was a suicide?'

Bullock's pudgy lips twisted into a sneer.

'Well, maybe she just fancied lying down on the track to see if the current was on. In which case, it was a tragic accident. So what *was* the nature of your business with her, Mr Knight?'

Not feeling up to concocting a story, Knight reluctantly confessed the truth. The price of his honesty was the delight Bullock took in goading him about his new career. But the opportunity to humiliate him put Bullock in a better mood.

'Well, you take good care you wrap up warm, Mr Knight, I think I'd keep my clothes on in future – could have been the sight of you that pushed her over the edge.'

He knew he should interview Knight but he couldn't be bothered. Besides, when his shift ended in an hour he was due to sample the delights of the magnificent Katya, and he didn't want to be late. Knight was best forgotten.

Knight himself was in a layby half a mile down the road, trying to come to a decision. The thought of Clementine Lever was even less appealing in death than in life. He wanted to have nothing to do with it and tried to convince himself that Bullock was right. But the vehemence of her outburst about the thief rang in his mind. He recalled how she had asked him how much he charged. It had occurred to him at the time there might be something else she wanted him for, but he had shrunk from the very thought of it. Perhaps if he hadn't, she would not have died. His conscience prickling, he resisted the temptation to drive home and forget he had ever met her. He should at least see for himself the place where she had met her end. It would be a small but salving act of respect for the dead.

The snow was thickening by the time he reached the bridge on the north west of the town. He had seen something of it on the news, little dreaming that the body might belong to his new employer. There was a barbed-wire fence that denied access to the steep embankment, but that was not where she had gone onto the line. The car had been found further on, where the land flattened out and the track disappeared behind a line of trees. The police tape was still there. One end had come away and was flapping in the wind.

As he trudged through the ankle-deep snow, it struck him, someone would need to know the area well to be aware that the track could be accessed here. Could she have been a rambler? Or did she have friends nearby? He tried to imagine who her friends would be. Ahead of him another strand of tape marked a broken section of fence where she had gone onto the line.

He made his way cautiously along the side of the track, heading back towards the bridge. True to form, the trains had admitted defeat early on and were not running, though perhaps with reason. The wind was now whipping the snow into his face and eyes, so that it might have been wiser to turn back at this point. But his mind had slipped into morbid speculation. If she had lain down across the track as Bullock claimed, her body would have touched the third rail and received a shock of 750 volts. It didn't always kill first time, but if you lay there long enough it would finish the job without difficulty. It was a hideous way to die. And the walk was a good three hundred yards – he tried to imagine doing it in the knowledge that such a grisly end awaited him. Was she capable of that? Was anyone?

The bridge itself supported no more than a narrow country road so there was no tunnel to speak of beneath it, merely a short stretch of cover where you could only be seen from the track, and only in daylight; the train had hit her shortly before dawn. Knight was loath to enter but he needed to escape the snow.

There was nothing to see. The police and medics had done a thorough job of removing any trace of human remains before the line was reopened. He cast his mind back again over their conversation. She had asked him questions about how he worked, which he had taken as a belated attempt to be civil. Without thinking anything of it, he had given her a beginner's lesson in investigation techniques. Had she tricked him into revealing his tradecraft so that she might pursue some investigation on her own? Given her extreme reluctance to part with money, it seemed plausible.

He tried to remember what he had told her: how to track a target, how to conduct a stakeout and stay hidden from your enemies, how to leave a trail of coloured gravel for your friends if you needed them to find you. There was no gravel under the bridge, but it didn't mean there wasn't any buried beneath the snow outside.

He made his way back down the track, no easier with his conscience. If she had tricked him, it was an absolution of sorts, but it didn't change the fact that he had sensed her vulnerability and turned away from it. A more pressing issue was the snow. By the time he reached the road, the car was covered from front to back. Weary from the long walk, he brushed the windscreen with his sleeve and slumped into the seat. It was dark now. He crept at a snail's pace into the whiteout, the headlights reflecting off the dancing flakes. Merv was coming round in half an hour; he should text him.

*

Merv knew about the second modelling appointment. He was also aware of the weather, having spent the afternoon nursing a leaking shed. It was worrying to learn that Knight was out in the blizzard. He texted straight back, demanding to know where he was.

Knight felt a familiar twinge of irritation as he replied. Merv had pointed out twice that he should return before the snow arrived and would cluck all the more on discovering why he had failed to do so. Any distinction meanwhile between road and roadside had ceased to exist. Far from being persuaded to stop, he grew all the more determined that the elements would not defeat him. At a slow walking pace, he missed a corner and slithered down a shallow bank into a hedgerow.

Clinging to the bonnet, he slid down the short slope to inspect the damage. The bumper was hard against the roots of the hedge, the wheels firmly embedded in the twin furrows they had ploughed. He looked around in vain for a flat stone or a fallen branch, realising how pitifully equipped he was to deal with the situation. Years of mild winters had whittled away the discipline of snow tyres and chains, leaving him with nothing but a collapsible shovel that was completely useless.

His AA membership had long been cancelled, which meant that a tow truck would cost a small fortune. The police would give him a hard time for ignoring the weather warnings and, if it got back to Bullock, he would have yet more to mock him with. Or he could call Merv, which would oblige him to admit that he had acted stupidly. Then he remembered a pub, The Lamb, about a mile down the road. There might be someone who could help him, and it was a more inviting prospect than remaining in the car. With the wind in his back, it should take no more than twenty minutes.

Knowing his friend's sensitivities, Merv waited for half an hour before texting again. When there was no reply he tried calling. After the library incident he had thought of asking Knight to install a location-finding app on his phone, but it was obvious what he would say. Now he regretted not having pushed it. He made a solemn vow to himself: if he ever saw the old fool alive again, he would install the location app without telling him. He weighed up the options: he could wait and see what happened, or he could go and find him.

Like an apparition from a ghost story, Knight shuffled on. There was no sign of the pub; he seemed to have misjudged the distance. He was wearing an ancient rugby jersey and a thick sweater under his coat, not enough to insulate him from the icy blast in his back. Having foregone the warmth and comfort of his car, he felt his resolve to conquer the elements begin to slip. It didn't help that his bladder was full to bursting. He fumbled with his trousers and stood defiantly with his legs astride, watching the sparkling liquid shoot into the snowflakes. It took him a moment to realise the reason for the sparkle was the headlamps of an approaching car, to which he was technically exposing himself. His bladder still unemptied, he abandoned the project and fumbled again with his trousers.

'Are you all right?'

There was something distinctly accusing about the question. A woman's head was leaning out of a Range Rover. As Knight approached he made out an expression of severe disapproval.

'I'm so sorry to trouble you,' he apologised, with all the charm he could muster, 'but I'm trying to find The Lamb. I thought it was along here somewhere.'

The lordly tone did little to reassure her.

'It's about half a mile down there.' She pointed in the direction from which Knight had come. 'Are you sure you should be out in this weather?' She hadn't accused him of anything; it seemed he was in the clear.

'I'm afraid my car broke down. You couldn't possibly give me a lift could you? If you're going that way, of course.'

She pursed her lips, sizing him up. She was in her forties, wearing a Barbour jacket and a Hermes scarf around her neck. Beside her sat a small girl in a private school uniform that Knight recognised.

'All right,' she sighed irritably, 'you'd better get in.'

The girl glared balefully at him as he climbed in, narrowly avoiding the violin case on the back seat.

'What *is* he then Mummy?' she asked.

'Just someone we're giving a lift to, not for long.'

'Is he a tramp?'

'That's not a nice word; just be quiet now.'

Knight was beyond defending himself. He wanted them to know that he was of their tribe, a respectable bourgeois with whom they could happily rub shoulders, but the facts didn't fit anymore. He sat in silence, conscious that his trousers were transferring some of their content to the

43

leather upholstery. It would probably leave a smell, confirming the child's assessment of him.

At the pub, he thanked the woman profusely, strongly sensing her relief as he climbed out. Before he could close the door, he heard the girl ask, 'So if he's not a tramp or a flasher, what is he?'

The pub was set back from the road, which was why he had missed it. Consumed by self-disgust, Knight stumbled inside. The landlord was no more pleased to see him than his rescuer had been. He glared inhospitably at the yeti-like creature who had put paid to his hope of closing early and who needed to ask the price before buying a drink.

Knight took a seat by the fire, even though it wasn't lit. The relief at being out of the snow scarcely raised his spirits. His mood worsened further when he heard the faint ring of a phone that he realised was his. It had been stuffed into the outer pocket of his coat and silenced by the howling wind. His heart sank as he listened to Merv's message saying he was on his way to find him. Ungratefully, he texted back his position and resigned himself to a disagreeable encounter.

Casting round for someone other than himself to blame, he alighted before long on Clementine Lever. He rued the day he met her, castigated her for persuading him to see her again and condemned her for getting under his skin so that he felt obliged to pay some bizarre tribute in the middle of a snowstorm. The one small silver lining was that any guilt he felt was now expunged. He was done with her.

Clinging to this shred of comfort, he sat back and took in his surroundings. It was a plain pub, with scratched wooden furniture and a carpet that hadn't been replaced in twenty years. A menu was chalked on the board: shepherd's pie, sausage and mash, gammon, simple fare with no pretence to gastropub sophistication. He found the homeliness of the place soothing, and wondered how much longer it would survive.

Around the walls were black-and-white photographs of old Sussex. From where he sat he could make out haystacks, steam trains and what might have been a royal visit. Craning his neck to look at the wall behind him he saw pictures of Eastbourne. There was Beachy Head taken from the sea, pensioners in deckchairs with knotted handkerchiefs on their heads, and directly above him a Punch and Judy show. It was taking place in the entrance to the pier, almost opposite his flat. Enchanted, he tried to work out what had changed and what remained since the picture was taken.

To the right of the puppet show was a newspaper kiosk. Standing up to look more closely, Knight recognised the Eastbourne Argus. Then he saw the headline on the hoarding and an odd shiver ran down his spine.

The headline read, 'Body Under Railway Bridge'.

Chapter Eight

Bullock's head was throbbing. He'd never met a woman who could drink him under the table; maybe they had different genes in Slovakia or Lithuania or wherever it was Katya came from. He wouldn't have minded if they'd actually done the business, but towards the middle of the second bottle of Chivas, he had collapsed on his sofa. When he awoke she was gone, along with the bottle. The last thing he needed when he finally arrived at work was to find Knight waiting for him.

'So, it's the same bridge, what of it?'

They were in a bare interview room. Bullock had been bent on a fry-up to settle his stomach. Wafts of bacon from the canteen tormented him as he made do with an insipid cup of coffee.

'It's not just the bridge. The fact is, you have no evidence that she was alive before she got there.'

'And you've no evidence that she wasn't.'

They'd been round this point twice already. Knight regretted having even mentioned the photograph. It gave Bullock the opportunity to insist that he was obsessing about a minor coincidence, while the real grounds for doubt lay elsewhere.

'What was the cause of death then? Was she electrocuted?'

'They're still trying to work it out. It's not easy when the body's in bits, believe it or not.'

'But the temperature was minus six that night – it doesn't take a genius to work out she could have died several hours earlier and been dumped there.'

Bullock felt a fresh wave of nausea and decided that if he was going to be sick he would try to do it over Knight. No one would be able to prove it was deliberate. The thought buoyed him enough to continue the struggle.

'Yes, *could* have. But there's no proof that she was alive earlier and no evidence of foul play. You say she told you that someone stole something from her – what if they did? Are you saying they suddenly turned up out of nowhere and did her in? Where's your evidence?'

Knight felt weary. There seemed no end to the sheer sloth of the man, the complete lack of curiosity that a crime may have been committed.

'That's what you're paid to look for! And if you don't, I'll raise it with the coroner!'

Bullock urged his stomach to punish Knight, but it remained stubbornly inert. The coroner, he was well aware, held him in low regard. If he chose to see things Knight's way it would be another black mark.

'All right,' he lied, 'I'll look into it. What was the name of the bloke you found?' He still couldn't quite believe that Knight had gone to the trouble of researching an unrelated suicide from over forty years ago. It was obviously a sign of senility.

'His name was Giles Askew. He went to Eastbourne College and he owned the farm to the north of the railway line on which he died in 1967. His wife's name was Irene, it's all in here.'

Knight passed him an envelope. Bullock stared at it with abhorrence. This was more than senility, this was some kind of obsessive disorder, possibly the precursor to Alzheimer's or a stroke. The thought cheered him briefly.

'And what exactly do you suggest I should be looking for here?' He tried not to make it sound sarcastic.

'That,' said Knight, with an air of superiority he found infuriating, 'I shall leave to you to decide.'

Outside a great melt was underway. The hedge tops and roofs still bore a thick crust of white, but elsewhere a dirty grey prevailed as the snow turned to slush. Avoiding the temptation of a café, Knight walked back to his car, relieved that the chore was done.

At first, he had tried to brush aside the coincidence, but it clung to him stubbornly. Even though his research revealed not the slightest link between the two deaths, his doubts had spiralled. It was as if Clementine Lever was clutching his sleeve, pleading with him not to let her go. But as Merv had pointed out, he was in no position to conduct any further investigation himself, with which he grudgingly agreed.

It had been awkward in the pub, not least as Merv showed not the slightest interest in the photo. Fortunately, the challenge of pulling the Skoda from the hedge had united them sufficiently to avoid recriminations. Later, they had gorged on pizza and chicken nuggets, made palatable by a smoke. Thus mellowed, Knight had also agreed to dump the whole thing in Bullock's lap. He had no faith in the man, but Merv was right, he could not take this on. He mourned for Bev, the young PC who had been his eyes and ears inside the local police. Her fiancé had taken a job in London and she had transferred to the Met to be with him.

Returning to the freezing flat, Knight engaged once more with the business of survival. There was still well over a week before his accountant returned from holiday. The leafleting agency had no work but there were supermarkets to be researched, job vacancies to be scanned and stews to be made. Most promising of all, Merv was planning another lobster expedition. Knight had not been invited on board on this occasion, which was a relief, but would keep watch at Sovereign Harbour when Merv returned. It seemed there was plenty to do.

But after two days, a degree of ennui set in. Between the tasks he set himself were long, empty hours in which his sole practical objectives were to keep warm and avoid spending money. He read a book about climate change that left him deeply depressed. He watched news reports about refugees and terrorist attacks that had the same effect. Every time he noted the absence of a woman in his life, his mind was drawn to the sprawling mound of flesh on the mouldy sofa. When these torments relented, the fear of being forced from his flat stepped in to take their place.

It was thus not surprising that he found himself returning to the death of Clementine Lever. Set against his doubts and fears, it served as a kind of light relief, much as a sudoku or a crossword puzzle might have done. Having challenged Bullock to look for evidence a crime had been committed, it piqued him that he didn't know how he would go about investigating it himself. The coincidence of two deaths in the same spot was almost certainly just that, yet he supposed it would do no harm to know a little more about Giles Askew. He found it comforting to trawl through the alumni site of Eastbourne College, the lives and deeds of its members conjuring up a world of fraternity and achievement not unlike that of his own school.

There was no mention of Giles Askew, but as this was not an investigation it didn't bother him, at least for a while. But then it did, so he dug deeper and found a testimonial to an ancient teacher who was himself an alumnus and would have been a contemporary of Askew. The discovery pleased him; he had not lost his touch. Not that he was going to do anything about it.

But if he were, where else would he look? Bullock's examination of Clementine's home would have been cursory, its purpose to confirm that the death was a suicide. He recalled the freezing studio, the pictures of decay, the snake-like plait grazing on his thigh. Shifting his mind's eye to her sitting room, he recalled the paintings on the wall. They had resolved by now into a blur of intertwining limbs and torsos, but there had been an odd one out, the Chinese picture of the old man painting a thicket of trees. She had reacted badly when she found him looking at it, though then again she seemed to react badly to life in general. There was not even the beginning of a trail here, nothing the most dedicated police officer would investigate, let alone a waste of space like Bullock.

He had not looked at the contents of the shelves and could not remember if he had seen a cupboard. Nor had he been upstairs. He speculated morbidly on the appearance of her bedroom. Did she have a single bed or a double? What was the state of the bathroom? He pictured a montage of squeezed-out toothpaste tubes and plug holes blocked with hair. Repelled, he turned his mind to business.

*

Merv steered *Adrenaline Rush* through the outer basin, watching the quaysides for any sign of the fishermen. Knight was waiting at the mooring, from where he had just given the all-clear. The *King of Sussex* was on the beach, exactly where it had been when he set out.

Knight appeared none the worse for his mishap in the snow. This was to be welcomed, but it didn't change the fact that he had pushed himself dangerously close to the limit. As for the obsessive interest in the photo, Merv put it down to a combination of shock and exhaustion. He was relieved Bullock had agreed to look into Knight's doubts about the case, however insincere the promise.

As the drawbridge rose, he spotted Knight waiting on a bench in the far corner of the basin, from where he had a view across the boats to the car park. What he didn't notice was the waiter in the glass-fronted restaurant behind him. He had been watching *Adrenaline Rush* since she passed through the lock, and now he was on his phone.

Knight caught the rope and tied up while Merv brought the catch ashore. The Sunseeker was absent today, which was a pity. Another quick sale would have saved them the drive around the restaurants.

'How many did you get?'

Merv lifted the cloth from the tray, revealing half-a-dozen lobsters.

'I reckon there's sixty or seventy quid's worth, and twenty of that's for you.'

'Don't be ridiculous, it's far too much.'

Merv had expected that he would need to cajole Knight into taking the money, but he wanted to get on the road while their luck was still holding.

'All right, we'll talk about it later. You sure the car park's clear?'

'Quite sure.'

Merv drove the van while Knight followed in the Skoda. The risks had fallen to almost zero now; if they had not been seen at Sovereign Harbour there was no reason to suppose they would be seen in town, unless they were extraordinarily unlucky. Yet for reasons of his own, Knight couldn't quite relax. He rehearsed again what he was going to say to Merv, trying to anticipate the reaction. They were on a short stretch of dual carriageway heading west. As they came out of a roundabout, a red Corsa flashed by at speed in the opposite direction.

Merv likewise had a delicate task to perform before the day could be deemed a success. He had chosen a location-finding app that would sit unnoticed on Knight's phone. The breach of trust left him as uncomfortable as ever, but he had sworn to himself that he would never relive the stress of the night in the blizzard.

The opportunity did not present itself until they reached the Lotus Garden, their last port of call. Mrs Chang drove a hard bargain, but Merv fancied her and might have done something about it but for the glowering omnipresence of the much older Mr Chang, with whom she owned the restaurant. Having waited in his car on their previous stops, Knight came in to relieve himself, leaving his coat on a chair by the bar. While Mrs Chang weighed the last two lobsters in the kitchen Merv delved into the pockets, finding first the car keys and then, to his joy, the phone. He had already watched Knight enter the passcode, and now began to download the app. All he needed was for Knight not to notice the loss for ten minutes, whereupon he would slip it back or drop it in the Skoda.

So it might have proved had Knight not taken a wrong turn on his way back from the men's room. Finding himself in an area used for private parties, he came face-to-face with a Chinese painting. Given his whereabouts this would not have been surprising, had not it been the same as the one he had seen at Hillside Grange. It too was a print, hanging between a faded photograph of the Great Wall and a bug-eyed dragon chasing a pearl.

To Merv's disappointment, it was Mr Chang who emerged from the kitchen. He had seen Merv more than once looking at his wife in a way he understood well and didn't like. Without speaking, he opened the till and removed fifteen pounds which he held out for Merv to take. Merv wasn't minded to argue; in five more minutes the app would be downloaded and he needed his wits about him to return the phone. Knight was approaching the bar.

'Excuse me.'

To Merv's surprise, Knight was addressing himself to Mr Chang. Mr Chang was surprised too, unaware until now that the old man was on the premises. If he was a customer, he didn't look like one who had much money.

'What?' he grunted, with a marked lack of hospitality.

'There's a picture in the back room of a man painting some trees. Do you know anything about it?'

'He's with me,' Merv added.

The fact Knight was now associated with Merv in Mr Chang's mind did nothing to advance his cause.

'I don't know about no painting.'

Just then Mrs Chang reappeared from the kitchen. Knight repeated the question; she smiled approvingly.

'That one famous Chinese painting, very popular. Many people have in their house.'

'Do you happen to know what it's called?'

She said something unintelligible in Mandarin. 'It means old person not so strong, have to take it easy,' she explained, glancing meaningfully at her husband.

Knight had not mentioned the picture to Merv, as it didn't seem relevant. Merv assumed he was having one of his spontaneous bouts of enthusiasm, which didn't bother him until he heard him ask Mrs Chang's permission to take a photograph of it. As Knight delved into his coat, he frowned. He patted his jacket and checked his trouser pockets. His face fell.

Thinking the phone might have fallen out while he was in the washroom, Knight hurried back. Merv was consumed by guilt. Mrs Chang observed that old men often forgot things, while her husband sat silently with his arms folded. Taking Knight's keys, Merv announced that he was going to look in the car.

The Skoda was parked near the corner. In case Knight came out, he made a show of opening the door and looking on the floor, then retraced his steps to the restaurant. A red Corsa was parked further up the narrow street. It was like the one he had seen speeding towards the roundabout. It didn't occur to him to give it a second thought.

Knight had already returned from the washroom and, with Mrs Chang's help, was scouring the floor around the bar. Merv waved the phone triumphantly. Suspecting nothing, Knight apologised and thanked Merv profusely before going back to take the photo. As they departed, Mrs Chang smiled sweetly from behind her husband's back. Merv could not be sure, but he thought she was giving him the eye.

Losing the phone had triggered the usual gamut of doubts in Knight's mind about the state of his memory, perhaps justifiably so in that he had forgotten the task he had set himself. Merv's mind was already set on an evening at the dog track, but he did not forget the promise he had made earlier. Before they went their separate ways he produced a twenty-pound note.

'Now look, I know you said you wouldn't take this but it's worth every penny to me to have you on point. I can't do it without you, so please take it.'

Not before time, Knight's memory kicked in.

'Ah, I was meaning to say – instead of paying me, I was going to ask if you could do me a small favour.'

Merv would have given him anything at this moment.

'Yeah, of course, whatever you want, mate, just say the word.'

'Well you see…' Knight ventured hesitantly.

A splinter of doubt pierced Merv's bonhomie.

'I've decided I'm going to take another look at Clementine Lever's house. And I was rather hoping you'd come along too.'

Chapter Nine

Deprived of its shroud of snow, Hillside Grange looked even bleaker than the last time Knight had seen it. A festering rash of moss occupied swathes of the roof, and there were gaping holes where tiles had not been replaced. Nor had the view improved. The white hillside that could have passed for a beginners' ski slope was now a vast expanse of mud.

'How could she live in a dump like that?'

'I think she just got used to it. I think she ignored what was happening around her until she stopped noticing.'

'Or until she decided she'd had enough of it?'

'It's possible, if you believe she lay down on a live rail. There are plenty of easier ways to do it.'

Merv didn't want a debate.

'There certainly are. I'll be up the top then; call me if you need anything.'

Merv returned to the Skoda and moved it further down the road so as not to advertise their presence. His official role was to be the lookout, a reciprocation for Knight's attendance at Sovereign Harbour, but the real job as he saw it was to humour him. That, he hoped, would be the end of the matter.

Hillside Grange had lost none of its power to make Knight feel ill-at-ease, yet it was satisfying to boost the lock on the front door in less than twenty seconds. Beyond the front door was a poky hallway cluttered with rubbish bags that had not made it to the bin. To one side was a narrow staircase with a cupboard beneath it. Not knowing what he was looking for, he fell back on the most basic of formulae, the absence of the normal and the presence of the abnormal. Even this was little use in a setting so thoroughly abnormal. He regretted that her car was not there; presumably it was still in the police compound.

The shelves in the sitting-room contained art books and magazines. Smudges in the dust told him that one or two had been removed and glanced at lately. Several of the pictures were crooked, suggesting a hasty search to see if anything lay behind them. The Chinese picture was still there, beside the chimney breast. The male nude puzzled him again; it was surely worth Merv leaving his post for a few minutes to take a look.

Merv wasn't sorry to get the call. Apart from a BT van, nothing had passed by since he had taken up his position. The withdrawal of a sentry was not strictly good practice, but he was bored and Knight had sanctioned it.

Nevertheless, he felt queasy on entering. The interior of the cottage was every bit as bad as he had expected, and, in the case of the paintings, considerably worse. Knight's obsession had to be nipped in the bud.

'What was she then, some kind of perv?'

He was looking at a picture of the beach beside Eastbourne Pier; the pebbles in the foreground appeared to be withered scrotums.

'I don't know, fortunately, I didn't get to find out. Take a look at this one and tell me if you recognise him.'

Merv inspected the nude with the staring eyes and shook his head.

'Nothing at all. Sorry.'

Knight was not surprised, but felt a tinge of disappointment.

'Alright. Just thought I'd check.'

After taking a last look around the room, he returned to the front door. Merv assumed they were leaving, but now Knight disappeared up the staircase. Steeling himself against further horrors, he followed.

The bathroom was not quite as Knight had imagined it. True, the toilet bowl was cracked at the base, from where a stain spread into the surrounding linoleum, but the ancient tub was clean. It stood on four unpolished brass feet, with no curtain or shower. Nor was there a mirror over the small sink, and, as far as he could see, any evidence of cosmetics, just a worn tablet of thankfully hair-free soap on the side of the bath. There was nothing faintly resembling a clue.

The bedroom displayed the same Spartan severity, except the walls were crammed with more of her paintings. The bed was a single, with a thin duvet that had been pulled aside, revealing a greying undersheet. On one side of the bed was a chest of drawers, on the other a wardrobe.

'Want me to take a look at anything?'

Merv wasn't keen to go through a dead woman's personal effects, but it would speed things up.

'Thanks, take the cupboard and I'll do the chest.'

Knight opened the top drawer, revealing a jumble of laddered tights and shapeless knickers. Never had lingerie seemed so dismal. The remaining two drawers continued in the same vein, with faded leggings and moth-eaten jumpers. There was, however, a small photo-album tucked under a pile of socks. He flicked through an unremarkable sequence of birthday parties and family gatherings which roughly confirmed the little he had found out about her. A suburban upbringing with a librarian mother and a father who was an art teacher; then grammar school, St Martins and a few years of minor celebrity. Marked out by her receding chin, Clementine was unmistakable. There was a smaller girl in some of the family scenes, possibly a sister.

'These any good to you?' asked Merv.

He had been dutifully sifting through a random collection of frocks and blouses that would have disgraced a charity shop, but stacked against the back of the cupboard at the bottom were half a dozen paintings, which he laid out on the bed. They were Chinese, or at any rate oriental, and unlike the prints Knight had seen downstairs and in the Lotus Garden, they were originals. The elderly gentleman was not among them.

Merv was lukewarm in the matter of art. He could see the point of nudes, at least female ones like the redhead in the giant clam, but these were nipple-free to the point of tedium. Knight too found little that interested him. The assorted mountains, rivers and scholars were charming enough in their ways, but none of them matched the grace and serenity of the old man at his easel.

'I wonder why she didn't hang them up.' Merv tried to sound interested.

'You saw downstairs. She only put up her own work.'

'So, what's with these ones then?'

Knight shrugged. There were any number of reasons why a handful of unremarkable paintings could have come into her possession, and with a vivid imagination one might construct fanciful theories linking them to her death. The most likely explanation was that they were no more than what they seemed, unwanted clutter stashed away out of sight and out of mind; he had an ample horde of his own.

'I'll have a last look in the studio and then we'll go.'

'Sure, why not?' Merv agreed cheerfully.

They went back outside and walked through the mud to the studio. Here the door had parted from its lock some time ago, and the police had done nothing to secure it. Inside, there had been some attempt to assess the contents. One or two of the boxes had been shifted around and the screen now stood by the wall. Taped to a shelf unit were some sketches of boats he hadn't noticed before. Merv helped Knight pick through the jumble. Thus it was that he found Knight's picture, which was still on its easel. Merv's spirits rose at last. That the picture was hideous added to its attraction. It was a mad major classic, a trophy to brighten the day.

Merv's body convulsed with suppressed laughter until he could hold it back no more, so much so that they didn't hear the engine. Knight couldn't begrudge him the amusement, he was merely glad Bullock hadn't recognised him. He was tempted to take the picture; one day he too might laugh at it. For the present, it was an apt conclusion to a quest that had led nowhere.

A car door slammed. This time they both heard it.

There was only one way out of the studio, with a strong chance of a face-to-face meeting with whoever had arrived. Their minds as one, they retreated behind the screen. It was as well that they did; no sooner had they taken cover than the door opened.

There was a narrow gash in the screen just above Knight's eyes. Glad of his stick, he raised himself onto tiptoes and peered through, expecting to see a uniform.

It was a woman, and she didn't look like the police. She had her back to them as she went through some drawings on a table. She was wearing a fur bomber jacket topped and tailed by a bob of blonde hair and a pair of body-hugging jeans. As she turned, an impish face revealed itself. It had a small, slightly upturned nose and a delicately pointed chin. A rich, honey-coloured suntan made it hard to tell her age; mid-forties, perhaps. She was carrying a canvas shopping bag.

Knight shifted over silently and motioned to Merv to take a look. She was nearer now, methodically rifling through a cupboard. Merv's eyes were drawn unerringly to the graceful contours of her thighs and calves. He turned to Knight and mouthed a silent phwoar of approval.

She glanced briefly in the direction of the screen but paid it no further attention. Moving to the other side of the studio, she inspected the boat sketches, her body language indicating that she was losing interest. As she made her way back to the door, she came upon the easel. To Knight's slight chagrin, her face wrinkled with distaste. Then she was gone.

Without speaking, they fell into a practised routine. Using the tables and boxes as cover in case she came back, they stole silently to the door. A brand-new Fiesta with a Hertz sticker on the windscreen was parked at the bottom of the track, but she wasn't in it. The kitchen door was open; if she hadn't picked the lock she must have a set of keys. As they crept closer, they could hear her speaking.

'Come on Ray, for old time's sake, I'm as good as I ever was and I need some cash.'

It was a Home Counties voice, faintly husky with a touch of the thespian.

'Thank you, treasure, you won't be disappointed. And definitely yes to a little drink afterwards. See you tonight at nine.'

Now there were footsteps, going away from them across the tiled floor. Merv risked a glance around the kitchen door. She was in the sitting room, scanning the walls. In the far corner, something appeared to catch her eye and she moved out of sight. Seconds later, they heard her footsteps and braced themselves for discovery, but she passed into the hall and went up the stairs.

She had left her phone on the kitchen table. Signalling to Merv to go ahead, Knight brought up the last number. It was a Brighton landline.

Waiting at the foot of the staircase, they heard her searching the bedroom. Something bumped and rattled, wood on wood. There was a cry of delight, or possibly annoyance, and then she was standing on the top stair, shocked to see them.

'Who are you?' she demanded angrily, though with an unmistakable note of fear.

'I was going to ask you the same question. What are you doing with those pictures?' The frames of the Chinese paintings poked out of the shopping bag.

'If you're police, let me see your warrant cards.'

'Actually, I'm a private investigator.'

The last time he had said those words he had been delivering leaflets; this was far preferable. He produced a card and held it up. Merv was looking at him expectantly.

'And this is my associate.'

'So I see.'

She came down the stairs, fixing them each in turn with an engaging smile.

'And are you investigators going to let me past?' she enquired, as if their cooperation would represent a rare and exquisite treat. Standing less than a pace away she took the card and glanced at it. She had dark brown eyes and a mouth that seemed to default to an amused smirk. A scent of lilies and oranges wafted through the air.

'You still haven't answered my question about the pictures.'

He meant to say it with some authority, but it came out like a wry observation one might make to a girl at a party.

'Sorry,' she cooed.

She tried to move past Merv but he shifted to block her way.

'Oh, come on boys, is this really necessary?'

'Sorry love, you heard what the man said.'

Merv thought he had sounded polite, apologetic even, and so was taken by surprise when she drove her knee hard into his groin. He staggered backwards, opening up space for her to pass. Knight was quick enough to grab her arm but she broke his grip as if it were a child's, throwing him off balance. He tottered and fell, clipping his temple on the bannister. With the agility of a gazelle, she fled into the kitchen, snatching her phone as she headed for the door.

It was all the start she needed. By the time Knight was outside, she was reversing fast up the drive, the number plate a blur. Merv hobbled out behind him, bent double.

'Who the hell was that?' he raged, as if it was Knight's fault.

Knight wanted to know too. Maybe Ray from Brighton would tell him.

Chapter Ten

Bullock was on his third Jaegerbomb. The first had been a sharpener in anticipation of seeing Katya again, the second followed the disappointment of learning from one of the other dancers that she no longer worked at the club. The third didn't need a reason.

He wasn't minded to be philosophical. By his standards, he had invested heavily in Katya, going to some trouble to arrange for her violent boyfriend to be found in possession of a healthy lump of crack and then giving him a beating for resisting arrest. But all he had to show for his trouble were a couple of private dances and a lost half bottle of Chivas.

The girl he was watching didn't seem to have had her heart in it, at least not compared to Katya.

She finished her act and disappeared among the tables around the raised stage. Bullock was three rows back, having set his heart on a cosy tête-à-tête before going upstairs. He thought about leaving but the next girl was being announced, a special guest from the sun-kissed beaches of the Canary Islands. Her name was Lolly. Lolly from Lanazarote.

Methodically scanning her parts, he noted the pertness of her breasts, which to his surprise appeared to be real. It was only when he finally came to her face that he saw she was in her forties. The familiar strains of 'Je t'aime' struck up and she began to dance.

She caressed the pole suggestively, then clasped it to her and spun around with her legs stretched out. Next, she leaned back until she was almost horizontal, stretching her free arm towards the audience in a gesture of regal salutation. In the blink of an eye, she had raised her legs over her head and wrapped them around the pole. As Jane Birkin moaned and gasped, she arched her back and flung her arms wide in a pose of rapturous submission. In another barely discernible flurry of limbs, she held her body away from the pole in a frozen star jump, her face alight with triumph. Bullock was mesmerised, so much so it was only now he realised he knew her.

Aided and abetted by the spliff they had smoked on the way over, Knight watched from a table on the opposite side of the room. It had taken curiously little effort to persuade Merv to come with him once the Brighton number had been identified as that of a night club, The South Pole. The ten pounds at the door was a monstrous extravagance and Knight had attracted some odd looks in the queue, but now under cover of darkness he was invisible, an anonymous unit of the intoxicated male herd encircling the stage.

Lolly was on the floor now, lying on her side with one leg hoisted at a right angle. With a wink to a stag and his cohorts in the front row, she slithered to the pole and entwined her body around it, her spine undulating in response to Birkin's gasps with a vigour that would have made her proud. Knight's initial unease about joining a feast for hungry eyes was long gone, along with any attempt to quell the rumbling diehards as they broke their long silence. He was spellbound by her, a heavenly vision adorning the pole like a nymph on a Lalique vase. What astonished him even more was her strength. He had been able to lift his own weight until well into middle age, and as an officer cadet had propelled himself through brutal assault courses with relative ease. She was in another league entirely; the power in her arms and abdomen was inconceivable given her slender limbs and frame.

Merv was having an epiphany of another sort. He had discovered it was possible to fancy a woman who had kneed him in the groin, a notion that ran counter to his deepest beliefs. She finished her act by mounting to the very top and flying her body like a flag, then in one fluid movement she spiralled down and knelt at the side of the stage in front of the stag party. There was a roar of approval as the spotlight faded on her.

'What do you want to do?' Merv asked, noting that she had already moved to the stag's lap, presumably in the hope of adding to the twenty he had already placed in her g-string. Knight slowly gathered his thoughts.

'We'll just keep an eye on her for now. You don't mind staying a bit longer do you?'

Merv acquiesced graciously.

Bullock wasn't happy to see her sitting on the stag's lap, even less so when she led him away for a private dance. Having recognised her, he somehow felt a prior claim on her attention. He also appeared to have finished the third Jaegerbomb. Watching the next dance with one eye, he waited for her to reappear.

Several tables along from Knight and Merv was a wide sweep of stairs leading to a lounge and the dance cubicles. Knight decided to intercept her in the lounge where fewer people would see them. He fairly glided up the shallow steps, savouring the spring of the thick carpet. At the top was a dimly lit bar set amidst a small warren of discreetly spaced tables and chairs, empty save for a scattering of unlikely couples huddled over bottles of champagne. She wasn't among them. There was a cash machine in an alcove beside the candlelit corridor that led to the cubicles. As if contemplating a withdrawal, they sauntered over to it.

The dance was evidently a short one, for in less than a minute she appeared down the corridor. On her arm was the inebriated stag in the last stages of his undoing; before the night was out he would be retrieving his trousers from the sea. As they approached the cash machine, Knight stepped in front of them.

'Hello Lolly,' he said civilly, trying not to let his gaze wander away from her eyes. Before she could object, Merv clasped the unprotesting stag cheerily around his shoulder and guided him away on the pretext of returning him to his mates.

She was livid.

'How dare you?' she hissed.

'I'm so sorry for the intrusion,' he began. 'I wouldn't normally dream of interrupting a lady at her place of work.'

If anything she looked angrier; there was no point in holding back.

'It's just that you assaulted my associate earlier today and I was wondering if we could talk about that for a moment, to save involving the police.'

The mention of the police stopped her in her tracks.

'Look, they were my pictures,' she said more reasonably. 'They came from my father and she should never have had them, okay? That's what this is about, right?'

Knight was thrown.

'I'd rather we started with who you are,' he countered, trying to maintain the air of calm authority.

She looked at him incredulously.

'Are you serious? I'm Clementine's sister! I'm here to clear up all the mess she left behind and I don't need a load of grief about a few stupid pictures.'

It was Knight's turn to be incredulous. He recalled the other young girl in the photograph. Not before time, he remembered she was in mourning.

'I'm very sorry for your loss,' he said sincerely. 'I didn't mean to cause you any distress.'

'Why are you interested in her?' She made it sound as if a normal person wouldn't be.

'Because I don't think she committed suicide.'

She looked at him curiously.

'That's not what the police say.'

Merv rejoined them, visibly on edge.

'We've got company,' he announced quietly.

Bullock had reached the top of the stairs and was lumbering towards them. Lolly seemed even more dismayed than she had been on seeing Knight.

'Evening all,' he greeted them sardonically, and then turning to Lolly, 'I didn't realise you knew these gentlemen.'

'I don't. They were just leaving.'

Bullock was glad to hear it. He had almost despaired on spotting Knight making his way to the lounge with his lowlife sidekick in tow. Now that he was here, he couldn't resist the urge to draw blood.

'Excellent. An elderly gentleman could get a heart attack in a place like this. I take it Mr Knight has told you he did a bit of nude modelling for your late sister?'

A sharp intake of breath told Knight she had recognised him from the picture.

'Oh my god!' She stifled a giggle. Whatever authority Knight had established was turning to dust.

'And I expect he's been telling you about his little theory that someone murdered her.'

Knight wasn't sure himself how much he still believed in his theory, but to be humiliated in front of her by Bullock was unconscionable. He cast around desperately for a way of striking back.

'A theory which you yourself have undertaken to investigate, Detective Constable. Perhaps you'd like to tell me what progress you've made with the Askew family.'

The words rang pompous and hollow in Knight's ears, though Lolly did at least look seriously at him for a second. Bullock dragged his eyes away from her breasts and glared at him witheringly.

'Have you completely lost it?' he demanded rather too loudly. 'Do you really think I've got time to look at every load of old bollocks that people like you drag in because they haven't got enough to do?' Before Knight could reply, a pair of bouncers arrived, giants in dark suits.

'These gentlemen bothering you, Lolly?'

Bullock produced his warrant card. 'That okay for you, boys? I'm guessing you don't want any trouble tonight, is that correct?' The suits took a step back.

'You can take these two out, the lady and I are having a drink.'

Knight felt a reckless urge to roll the dice but Merv was gesturing desperately for them to leave. A small, sane voice found its way through the fog of testosterone and told him it wasn't worth it.

'You haven't heard the last of this, Bullock.' He sounded pompous again, pompous and impotent.

Merv was, if anything, more deflated than Knight. He had wanted to meet Lolly, at the very least assert the fact of his existence to her, but Bullock's presence had set off his visceral aversion to contact with the police. As they were led away, he took one last look at her, amazed not only by her beauty but by the composure that allowed her to dress in nothing but a g-string as if it were the most natural thing in the world.

She was mouthing something to him. It looked like 'I'm sorry'.

Then she blew him a kiss.

Chapter Eleven

It took Knight until the following afternoon to accept there was nothing he could do to make Bullock suffer. He would, of course, make life uncomfortable for him at the inquest, but that was weeks away. The only other course of action was to lodge a complaint about his behaviour, but who would back him up? Revenge, he remembered at length, was a dish best eaten cold.

The Sunseeker was back. From his vantage point on the bench by Merv's mooring, Knight could see the top of her superstructure over the wall between the two basins. It was at once a thing of beauty and a bitter reproach to the depth of his failure.

It was not the only thing of beauty that troubled him. Lolly was a film that played on a loop in his head, but she was also the salt in the wound. Whenever he thought of her, he thought of Bullock too. Struggling to erase the pair of them from his mind, he went to check the car park again.

This time he had accepted Merv's offer of a small payment to ride shotgun. It seemed superfluous, but he had little else to do before his delayed trip to London. From the car park he skirted the outer basin to the lock, picking up Merv's text on the way. By the time he arrived, the inner gates were opening and *Adrenaline Rush* was about to enter.

The return route to the mooring took Knight past the restaurant. Recalling better times, he looked up at the leisured classes dawdling over lunch at half past three. A waiter was looking in his direction, talking on the phone. Was he actually looking at him? He concluded it was paranoia. They had smoked the last of the weed as a consolation after The South Pole; it might be no bad thing to go without for a while.

Merv was all smiles.

There were a dozen lobsters in the tray, some of them over a foot long.

'My God, they're magnificent. What on earth are you baiting them with?'

'The frozen burgers you gave me. I left them out of the fridge and they went off. Stank like hell but our friends can't get enough of them.'

Knight felt pleased to have contributed to the record catch, although it seemed wrong for a decaying burger to receive a free pass to the dinner table via such glorious creatures. Grateful that the day had taken a turn for the better, he tied up the boat and they departed in convoy again on the delivery round.

Merv was on a high. The triumph had blotted out the less pleasant aspects of the previous day, leaving him with an image of Lolly flying round the pole with her legs akimbo. As for the kiss she had blown him, at first he had assumed she was mocking him. But as he pictured her again in the g-string, many times, it seemed more likely that the kiss was genuine, and the apology that preceded it too.

Following behind as Merv delivered the lobsters, Knight marvelled yet again at the strength of that sublimely formed body, the finely toned arm that had thrown him off so easily. He was also keeping a paranoid eye on a blue Golf that had appeared once or twice.

Its occupant Brian O'Driscoll, sixty-four-year-old alcoholic and master of the *King of Sussex*, counted himself a good teacher to his sons. True, they were barely literate, but you didn't need to read and write on a fishing boat. What you needed to understand was that nobody could be allowed to cross the O'Driscolls and get away with it, unless they were demonstrably more powerful than the O'Driscolls. He was proud of how they had applied themselves. It had, of course, been his idea to pay a few quid to Kenny at the restaurant to look out for the boat, and he had also picked The Lotus Garden as the point of interception. The narrow alleyway had no CCTV and was deserted in the afternoons. It also helped that they went there at the end of the run when they would be flush with cash. As they approached the station, he called his boys.

Merv's day meanwhile had yet another blessing to offer, for Mr Chang was not present. As Mrs Chang put her purchases in the tank he gave his eyes free rein, doubly pleased that Knight was in the back looking at the picture again. Perhaps it was the afterglow of the night before, perhaps it was just the absence of Mr Chang, but he felt emboldened.

'Have you ever been fishing?' he asked, slightly surprised by the way the words suddenly came out. She looked up from the tank.

'My father have fishing boat. I go lots of times, help him.' She smiled auspiciously. 'You good fisherman, catch good fish.'

Merv needed no further encouragement.

'Sounds like you're pretty handy then; you can come and help me if you like.'

It was said with a laugh, more a knock on the door than a serious invitation.

'Very busy here, too much work.' She laughed too.

'Tell you what then, come down and see the boat one day – that won't take long.'

She looked at him with some interest.

'You got big boat?'

'It's a fair size,' he lied, 'but I'll probably get a bigger one soon. Does the business though, as you can see.' He gestured to the lobsters in the tank. One of them had landed on its back, a pincer held aloft as it struggled to right itself. From where Merv stood it looked like it was giving him the finger.

'Maybe.' Her head was cocked slightly to one side, as if she was assessing his motives, or perhaps her own.

'We see about it.'

When Knight returned from the back room, he had the fleeting impression that he was intruding, but his mind was still taken with the quiet calm of the picture. He would have bought a print for himself if he had any money.

Merv said goodbye to Mrs Chang with a charm Knight had never witnessed. They stepped out into the dark alleyway, engrossed in their separate thoughts and oblivious to the drizzle that had set in. Had they been fully alert it would have made no difference. The two men in balaclavas were waiting as they turned the corner. One winded Merv with a rustic blow to the stomach, while the other simply pushed Knight off his feet as if he were a skittle. When he looked up, his attacker was holding Merv in a half nelson while the bigger one steadily hammered his face and abdomen with his fists.

'Dad says hi,' he stated in a gloomy monotone.

Merv crumpled to the ground as they fled down the empty alleyway with his wallet. Knight was still struggling to his feet, with an ominous pain in his hip. He staggered over to where Merv was lying, curled into a foetal position with blood streaming from his nose.

'Get me up,' he moaned. Setting his stick aside, Knight bent awkwardly and held out his arms for Merv to take. He came up slowly, with grunts of pain as his chest was stretched.

'Can you make it back to the restaurant?'

'No!' he rasped, trying to catch his breath. 'Not the restaurant.'

'Okay, I'm calling an ambulance then.'

'No hospital,' Merv mumbled. 'I'm fine.'

'You're anything but. We're going to A & E to have you x-rayed.'

'I said no hospital!' Merv was vehement.

'At least let me drive you home. We can come back for the van later.'

'No, just get me in it!'

It was futile to argue. Knight decided to examine the damage himself and make a judgement later. He helped him into the van and followed it back to Merv's flat over the newsagents.

The nose, it seemed, was not broken. It was harder to tell with the ribs, but there was no inflammation to indicate a fracture. The internal organs were another matter. Merv's stomach was a morass of angry dark blotches. If his pulse weakened or his skin turned cold and clammy, it would mean he was bleeding internally. With deep misgivings, Knight agreed they would wait to see what happened.

Conversation was monosyllabic, confined to Merv's essential needs. Having helped him into bed, Knight attended to his own wounds, thankfully no more than a raw graze across the palm of his hand from where he broke his fall. The pain in his hip had abated.

He spent the night on the sofa. Once or twice he looked in on Merv. By the next morning, there were still no symptoms, so after making tea and toast he bowed to the patient's wish to be left alone.

At the flat, he went out onto the terrace. With the wind beating his face, he fought hard against a sour, sickly panic as he contemplated his future. He did not want to leave this place, with its vast sky and horizon, the rumble of rolling water. But it was going to happen, he could feel it coming.

At a loss as to what to do with himself, he went inside to make some coffee. The fridge was near empty; he would have to raid another supermarket soon. Slumped at the kitchen table over a cup of powdered instant and a stale doughnut, he could feel himself giving way to despair.

Eventually, the muffled ringing of the phone reached his ears. Fearful that Merv had taken a turn for the worse, he scrambled to the hall and retrieved it from his coat pocket. But it was not Merv.

'Mr Knight?' asked a familiar Home Counties voice. 'Is that you?'

An odd shiver ran down his spine; it was surprisingly pleasant.

'Yes,' he said waveringly. 'What can I do for you?'

'I think you and I got off on the wrong foot. How do you feel about starting again?'

Chapter Twelve

'So, you modelled for my sister?'

They were sitting in a quiet corner of the bar at her hotel, as far as possible from the coach party that had arrived.

'I did, yes, once. I'm not sure what she made of me.' He thought it best not to add what he had thought of her.

Lolly was dressed more formally than at their last meeting. For this evening's performance she had chosen a dark jersey dress with a plunging zip at the front, accompanied by charcoal leggings. The visit to the club had conferred x-ray vision upon Knight; the off switch was proving elusive.

'But you're a private investigator too?'

He didn't like the way she stressed the 'too'.

'I'd been out of action for a while and business was slow. It didn't seem a bad way of making a bit of money at the time.'

'And did she pay you well?'

'Not very.'

She smiled knowingly. 'Never one to put her hand in her pocket if she could help it was our Clem, poor thing.'

The barman brought their vodkas on a tray. Evidently, Lolly wasn't expected to carry drinks to her table in the normal way. A table of trippers looked on disapprovingly; it wasn't how things were done in Barnsley.

'Put it on my room, Paco.'

'Si señora!'

Paco eyed her with ill-disguised lust and disappeared in a flash of white teeth.

'Anyway, she's gone now. To absent friends.'

They clinked glasses.

'My real name's Laura by the way, but everyone calls me Lolly. Cheers.'

'I suppose I should explain why I had those paintings,' she continued. 'They belonged to my dad but I never bothered to take them with me when I left home. That was years ago, long before she moved into her awful cottage. And when I found the will it turned out she'd left everything to some art charity. So I thought I'd better retrieve them.'

'I see,' he said, as if it made perfect sense, though it didn't entirely. The x-rays weren't helping.

'I don't mean to pry, but was there any reason she didn't leave anything to you?'

She shrugged. 'There wasn't anything worth leaving. The cottage was on a short lease and she had a few hundred pounds in the bank.'

'What about her paintings?'

'Worth nothing. I don't think she sold more than two or three in her entire life.' She shook her head sadly. 'She just went on doing them and forgot to look after herself.'

'Were you close?'

'I thought you said you weren't going to pry.'

The corners of her mouth told him she was teasing.

'We were stepsisters – my dad married her mum when we were both small. My dad was a widower and hers ran off with someone. After we grew up we led separate lives, me abroad mostly and her trying to make it as an artist. She never married or had any children.'

Distracted though he was, Knight noted a discrepancy.

'You said your parents married when you were both small – but surely Clementine was much older than you?'

'That's what everyone thought. But there were only four years between us. Clem was sixty-five.'

Knight was dumbfounded. It didn't surprise him that Clementine looked considerably older than her years, but the news that Lolly was sixty-one threw him into confusion.

'But that means you're…' he stopped short of blurting it out, which seemed to add to her amusement.

'Well, yes I am. I've looked after myself, as I expect you noticed.' The brown eyes bore into him. 'And how old are you, if it isn't rude to ask?'

When Knight confessed he was seventy-three, it was her turn to express astonishment.

'Seventy-three?! That's amazing, I had you down for just over sixty, honestly.'

They clinked glasses again. Knight was giddy with pleasure, ravenous for more knowledge, but she was there first.

'Why don't you think my sister committed suicide?'

Knight explained the bitter anger Clementine had expressed about being the victim of a theft that had left her in penury. This was apparently news to Lolly. She asked if her sister had named the thief, and was mildly disappointed to learn that she hadn't. She listened intently as he described the attempt to extract technical instruction from him, and the doubt surrounding the time of death.

There was also the question of the electric rail. His instinct had been to steer away, but she plainly thirsted for all the knowledge he had.

'What do *you* think?' he asked as gently as he could. 'Could she have done that to herself?'

She exhaled with a shudder.

'No.'

'I'm sorry, but I had to ask. The problem we have is that your friend Bullock won't even consider it.'

She gave him a sharp look.

'He's no friend of mine. If someone did kill my sister, he'd be the last person I'd trust to find them. I think we need another drink.'

She turned to the bar where Paco was staring in her direction. Eyebrows were raised again as he padded to her side, further evidence if any were needed of southern decadence.

'So who were the… Askews was it?'

'Giles Askew was a local farmer who was found dead in the same spot in 1967. It's probably just a coincidence but it's the sort of thing a half-decent policeman would at least look into.'

'Giles Askew, you say?' She had become thoughtful.

'Yes. He had a wife called Irene. Why?'

She frowned, then shook her head. 'No, it's nothing.' They lapsed into silence.

'So you live in Lanzarote?' It felt trite, a cocktail party enquiry, but he didn't want the conversation to be over yet.

'For my sins, yes.' She said it with a wry laugh. 'I train dancers and I dance myself. As you saw.'

He could feel his face flushing. 'What I saw was quite extraordinary. How on earth does anyone ever become that good?'

She did not appear averse to boyish enthusiasm, even if unintended.

'Lots of hours, every day. It's what keeps me going I suppose.' She added, wistfully it seemed to him, 'Not many men ask that.'

Before he could ask more, she leaned forward and stared, not at his eyes but at his chest and arms.

'May I?'

Without warning, she reached out and squeezed the upper part of his arm between her forefinger and thumb.

'I thought so, you've got good arms. You could probably do it too, in fact, I'm sure you could.'

Knight wasn't sure he'd heard her right.

'Do what?'

'Get on a pole. Not the upside-down stuff, just the basic moves. I'm seldom wrong.'

If she hadn't said it so matter-of-factly, he would have assumed she was making fun of him. As it was, he felt a quiet thrill that she should take such a view, however unrealistic.

'Well, I'll take that as a compliment, thank you very much. But...' he didn't wish to sound unduly defeatist. 'I suppose we'll never know.'

She raised her eyebrows in a look that extended a mischievous invitation to play.

'Not necessarily. I have a practice pole in my room.'

Knight didn't recall saying yes. In something of a daze, he went with her across the lobby. At the lift, a Barnsley lady had lost an earring. Out of habit he helped search the floor and found it, much to the lady's joy, and Knight's too when he caught an approving glance from Lolly. The old lady beamed sweetly at her as they all entered the lift.

'You've got a lovely dad you have, you lucky girl.'

The bubble was pricked for the moment but as they rode up in silence, it re-inflated without difficulty. The diehard faction had been quick to note that he was not old enough to be her father and also that she was older than Fran, even though she looked ten years younger. Meanwhile, her eyes were daring him to laugh. They walked down a dimly lit corridor past doors behind which humdrum trippers had been replaced in his mind by frenzied lovers in mind-boggling positions.

In her room, the double bed had been pushed to one side, making room for a pole attached to the floor by means of a solid metal base and to the ceiling by a suction cup. Taking the pole in one hand, she took a few steps and wrapped her legs around it, rotated once then just as casually stepped off again.

'It goes with me everywhere,' she announced fondly. 'And yes, I probably am completely mad.'

She produced a small bottle containing a white liquid and made him rub it on his hands.

'Liquid chalk,' she explained. 'It'll stop your hands slipping off the pole.'

An alarm bell was ringing, belatedly, in Knight's head.

'Are you absolutely sure this is a good idea?' He regretted it immediately, when he saw her face fall.

'Well *I* think you can do it. But only if you want to.'

With the foreboding he had sometimes felt when walking out to bat, he approached the pole and grasped it as she had done. The chalk had dried in seconds, removing any trace of sweat from his hands.

'You take a few steps to gain momentum,' she explained, 'then grab it with both hands like I did and pull yourself onto it. It'll be fine, you'll see.'

He took small, uncertain steps then, as she nodded encouragingly he strode out, clasping the pole in an iron grip.

'Now!' she urged.

Throwing caution to the wind, he heaved himself on, flinging his legs around it in an embrace that might have broken a man's neck. To his amazement, the strength in his arms was equal to the task, certainly for a few seconds. As he flew on the spinning pole, a reckless urge overtook him. He released one hand and held out his arm in a theatrical flourish as she had done in the club, though with considerably less grace.

The combination of weight and centrifugal force undid him. He lost his grip and would have crashed to the floor had she not caught and steadied him, with remarkable ease it seemed. Their faces were inches away, the scent of lilies and oranges all about him.

'That was even better than I thought.' She was gazing at him in what he could only take to be admiration.

He did not confess to feeling dizzy, but allowed her to steer him to the bed where he sat regaining his breath while the room spun on. When he caught sight of himself in a mirror, his face was a dark crimson, though she did not comment on it. His heart was pounding.

'Well, thank you,' he said at length, 'that was quite an experience.' It was far more than that; he had shown his mettle and not been found wanting.

'You can do anything at all if you want it enough,' she said, as she fetched more vodka from the minibar. 'But I expect you know that.'

She kicked her shoes off and sat next to him on the bed.

'Cheers. To Clementine.'

At the mention of her sister, a more serious atmosphere descended, which he did not particularly welcome.

'To Clementine, a remarkable woman.' He hoped it sounded sincere.

She moved up the bed and propped herself against the headboard with a sigh.

'We'll never know what happened to her, will we?'

Knight confessed that they might not. He might have added he was in no position to do anything about it, yet the words eluded him.

'I just wish I could get the name Askew out of my head. I know I'm clinging to straws, but it won't go away. It's stupid of me, I know.'

'It's not stupid at all. Sometimes…' he saw that her eyes were moist. 'Sometimes the memory serves things up for reasons we don't understand, but it turns out to be right.'

She smiled ruefully. 'Not with my memory. It gets worse every year.'

'So, what is it about the Askews?' Knight persisted, for she didn't seem minded to say any more.

Reluctantly, she continued. 'I just have this idea it's a name she might have mentioned once. Only for some reason it's mixed up with an auction house, or something to do with Chinese art. But maybe the name wasn't Askew at all. I really don't know, it's infuriating.'

'Could your Chinese paintings have anything to do with it?'

'I wondered about that too, I'm not sure.'

She shook her head mournfully and stared into space, evidently straining to dredge some long-buried fragment from her memory.

'It's no good,' she said, wiping her eye. Then she turned to him with a vulnerability of which he would not have thought her capable, and took his hand in hers.

'If someone killed my sister,' she said with a tremor in her voice, 'I want to know who it was. I want justice.'

Chapter Thirteen

Merv brooded for two days. Knight called several times, but he didn't want anyone to see him with a face that marked him as a victim. Knight also seemed somehow distracted. He sounded as concerned as ever about the injuries, but only made passing reference to the attack itself, as if he had somehow lost interest in it.

This was not the only reason he had decided not to involve him in his plan. While he knew that Knight could suggest valuable improvements, he was convinced he would also seek to veto it.

With or without his improvements, the project owed much to Knight's influence. Merv had learned stealth and cunning at his side, so that it was not long before he knew where Brian O'Driscoll lived and where he drank. Even more promising, he appeared to hold a strong preference for doing business in cash.

*

Knight had by no means forgotten the encounter. It had simply dropped down his list of priorities, where it jostled with the tasks of keeping body and soul together and the imminent meeting with his accountant. He was in no doubt that something had to be done about the owner of the *King of Sussex*; it was purely a matter of when.

There was one other small task he had set himself before his trip to London. Although he still recognised there was little he could do to satisfy Lolly's expressed wish for justice, he did return to the alumni website and the article about the retired classics teacher.

Oliver Grice had been educated at the school and returned immediately after university to spend his entire working life there. Now he lived in a 1960s terrace of sheltered accommodation near the retail park. What the area lacked in charm, it made up for in convenience. Further along the street was a mobility scooter shop next to an undertakers, and the hospital was a three-minute ambulance ride. The warden let him in and showed him to a modest apartment on the ground floor.

'Come!'

The weedy cry rang out in response to Knight's rap at the door. Grice was waiting for him in the middle of the sitting room, where he stood with the support of a frame. He was wearing a striped blazer and an old boys' tie.

'Mr Lyle, how very good to meet you,' he piped.

Godfrey Lyle was a new creation, an amateur historian concerned with the changing patterns of agriculture in East and West Sussex. Cautiously, the ancient master raised a hand from the frame and held it out for Knight to shake. He was a delicate man, no more than five feet four, who had evidently shrunk since the blazer was acquired. His hand was not much larger than a child's but produced a tight and lingering squeeze, as if hungry for contact.

'It's very kind of you to see me.'

Knight extracted his hand, by no means at ease with the inquisitive, nonagenarian face smiling up at him. There was something about the way he bared his dentures and rested them on his lower lip that was vaguely rodent-like, not to mention the small dark eyes inspecting him with such intensity.

'The pleasure is entirely mine, I assure you. It's not every day I receive a visit from an illustrious historian.'

'Nothing illustrious about me, I'm afraid, I'm no more than a humble hobbyist.'

Plainly not averse to an early offer of deference, Grice motioned Knight to a Victorian settee beside a mahogany table bearing tea and biscuits, then shuffled back to his chaise longue. The antique furniture sat oddly in the small room with its low ceiling and metal windows. Knight wondered if they were family pieces, relics of a more decorous life than the one presently lived. In a practised routine, Grice lowered himself onto the chaise longue and pulled his legs up with his hands.

'Would you mind?' he asked, indicating the tea.

Knight obliged, then bent to pick up a book that had fallen beside the chaise longue. It was the *Satyricon* by Petronius, in the original Latin.

'How very kind. I'll have it here please.' Grice indicated a space by his knee. 'An excellent work, are you familiar with it?'

Knight and his fellow fifth formers had made a point of researching the perversions of the Emperor Tiberius, but Petronius was no more than a name to him.

'I'm afraid not. I did see the film, though, Fellini I think it was. Quite colourful I seem to recall.'

Grice laughed quietly, or rather made a sound like a stammer failing to become a word, his body quivering just enough to send a drop of tea into the saucer.

"The film was nothing," he said at length. "It certainly had nothing like this – *Profert Oenothea scorteum fascinum, quod ut oleo et minute pipere atque urtiquae trito circumdedit semine.*"

He fixed Knight with an expectant gleam that briefly conjured up memories of unwholesome teachers. When no translation was forthcoming, he provided one.

"Oenothea held up a leather dildo which she oiled and covered with small peppers and crushed nettle seeds."

He did the stammering laugh again, baring his fangs. Averting his gaze, Knight found himself looking at a floor vase sporting a chain of satyrs and goats in coitum. Protruding from the top of the vase was a bamboo cane, thin and bending, which could only have been used for one purpose. He wanted to leave but he had only just begun.

'I believe you knew Giles Askew' he said when Grice subsided. 'He's quite an important figure for my book but I haven't been able to find out much about him.'

Grice's mood suddenly changed.

'Askew? Why would anyone want to write about him?' he said with distaste.

'It's really the family farm,' Knight ad-libbed. 'It's an interesting example of the transition to modern farming technology, which would have been well underway in his time there.'

'Well, I don't know anything about that. What do you expect me to tell you?'

'Anything you can. Background material, family, friends, enemies too if he had them.'

'And will you be candid in what you write?'

'Oh yes. The more colour the better.'

His mood seemed to improve slightly.

'Very well. He was a complete shit.'

He let the words hang, with some pleasure it seemed.

'And you can quote me on that.'

Knight nodded enthusiastically and wrote in his notebook.

'I'd be very happy to. What more can you tell me?'

Grice pointed at the notebook as if instructing Knight to take dictation.

'Giles Askew was a bully and a sadist. He was in the sixth form when I was a new boy, and he made our lives a misery.'

'In what way?'

'Beatings, ritual humiliation and what can only be considered as physical torture. He was an animal.'

He had got himself into something of a state. Knight gave him a moment to calm down.

'And you experienced this personally?'

'Of course I did,' he snapped. 'I was his fag for a year. I take it you know what that means?'

Knight confirmed that he did. He too had spent his first year at boarding school as the personal servant to a group of senior boys, although the experience had not scarred him as much as it appeared to have done Grice.

'And did you know him as an adult?'

'Regrettably yes. I had the misfortune to teach his son.'

This came as something of a revelation. Knight's research had found no mention of a son.

'What was the boy's name?' he asked, a little too eagerly.

'Rupert. He was a shit too, but with a father like that it was hardly surprising.'

Knight scribbled furiously. 'Absolutely fascinating. When was he at the school?'

Grice thought for a moment. 'In the 1960s I suppose. But what does this have to do with farming?'

Knight did a quick calculation. Rupert Askew would be somewhere in his fifties or sixties if he were still alive.

'Well, as I said, it's all a question of getting some colourful background. He was a difficult child, you say?'

'He was a brute who would have been expelled if I'd had anything to do with it. I was, however, able to discipline him on many occasions.'

The memory evidently amused him, for the dentures reappeared. He sniggered contentedly, though without recourse to his vocal cords, so that he sounded like an excited pug. A dribble of saliva appeared in the corner of his mouth. The cane caught Knight's eye again and he recoiled at the thought of it being used to visit the sins of the father upon the son.

'And were you aware that he was found dead on a railway track outside Eastbourne?'

The snuffling subsided.

'Naturally. Good riddance, I thought.'

'So what happened to Rupert after his father died? Did he stay at the school?'

'His mother made sure of that. Worked herself to the bone to keep the farm going and pay the fees. Though I can't say I liked her much either, she spoiled the boy. Nothing she wouldn't do for him. I heard later that she sold the farm to pay his debts, more fool her.'

'And do you have any idea where he is? He might be an interesting person for me to talk to.'

'No idea at all, thank god. In prison with any luck.'

There was one more question which he'd left till last in case it aroused suspicion.

'This may not be something you'd wish to comment on so I'll quite understand if you'd rather not talk about it.'

Grice sat up, his curiosity piqued. Knight remained silent for a moment.

'Well yes, go on then.'

'To your knowledge, was there ever any doubt as to whether Giles Askew committed suicide?'

Far from finding the question distasteful, Grice evidently took a malign interest in his tormentor's demise.

'I saw him at a parents' meeting. It was the week before he died, that's why I remember. She was there too. It was the usual thing. She wouldn't hear anything bad about the boy, and he wouldn't hear any good. For which, of course, he blamed the school. And he stank of drink, as he always did.'

'Did he seem depressed?'

He waved his hand as if to bat away the interruption.

'He made his usual threats to send Rupert somewhere else, and was, of course, extremely rude to me. But I heard him talking to the rugby coach later on. That was the last time I saw him alive.

He paused, searching for the thread and finding it again.

'They were arranging to have a drink after half term. But a week later he was dead. It did strike me as odd at the time, but I didn't honestly care if he'd killed himself or not.'

He leaned forward with a childish eagerness.

'Do you think somebody bumped him off?'

Knight wasn't sure what he thought. People could keep up a façade for years. But Askew sounded like the kind of man who revelled in dishing out pain, and in his experience that could keep people going for a long time.

'I don't know, but from the way you describe him he doesn't sound the type.'

'Well, let's hope he wasn't!' Grice piped fervently. 'Let's hope the bastard got what he deserved!'

The ancient classicist sank back, exhausted by the effort.

Knight put his notebook away.

'You're not going are you?'

'I think I've taken up enough of your time already. As I said, it's extraordinarily kind of you.'

Whether Grice should be pitied as a victim or condemned as a pervert no longer interested Knight; all that mattered was not to be in his presence a moment longer. It seemed his host had other ideas.

'No no, you must stay. There's so much more to talk about, you haven't told me anything of your school days yet.'

'I'd absolutely love to, but I'm afraid I have another appointment. Goodbye, Mr Grice.'

Knight held out his hand but it wasn't taken. Grice pitched forward, clutching his stomach and gasping for breath.

'My medication,' he wheezed. 'Up there, quickly.'

There was a small bottle of capsules on a shelf above the chaise longue. While Knight fumbled with the lid the gasping grew worse.

'Where's your alarm? I'll get the warden.'

'It's not working,' Grice moaned.

Knight splashed cold tea into one of the cups and thrust it at Grice, with a capsule at the ready.

'No, I don't take them like that!'

He looked again at the label on the bottle and saw what he hadn't noticed before. The capsules were suppositories. His patient meanwhile was struggling to undo his trousers.

'Quickly!' he pleaded plaintively. 'If you don't do it within thirty seconds I could die.'

Knight's instinctive response was to help. But, as he tugged at the trousers, it soon became apparent that Grice wasn't wearing underpants. Whether it was that, or the way the small dark eyes were drilling again, the fortitude bred by decades of military discipline abandoned him.

'I'm going for help!'

'No, please!' Grice begged.

Aghast at his cowardice, Knight raced to the warden's office. He tried telling himself that Grice would die soon anyway, and that a sudden death was better than a protracted one, but none of it would wash. All he knew was that he was not going to insert a suppository into Oliver Grice.

'You have to come!' he barked, as he burst into the office. 'Mr Grice is having an attack of something.'

The warden looked at him in alarm for a moment, then frowned.

'It's not the suppositories is it?'

'Yes, what of it?'

He closed his eyes and groaned.

'I'm very sorry,' he sighed. 'He usually goes for younger men so I didn't think he'd try it on with you.'

Seeing Knight's expression, he added, 'I'll have to have another word with him. Sounds like he's getting desperate.'

*

Knight retreated to a pub and shelled out recklessly on a large vodka, though it did little to expunge the memory. The targets of his anger alternated between Grice for his stomach-turning subterfuge and himself for going there in the first place. Lolly hadn't asked him for help and he hadn't offered, so why had he embarked on this preposterous goose chase?

He went back to the flat and sat in the cold. By way of proving once and for all that it was indeed a goose chase, he spent the rest of the morning on the phone. Lolly had mentioned an auction house, so now he called every single one he could find. Needless to say, none of them had heard of Rupert Askew. At first it was satisfying, but then he began feeling twinges of disappointment. Eventually a profound tedium set in and he felt a peace of sorts approaching.

It was then that the well-bred voice of a receptionist at Pernil Goode in London's Bond Street informed him Rupert Askew no longer worked there.

Chapter Fourteen

In a café off Bond Street, Knight nursed an overpriced cappuccino amongst a chattering band of art dealers and wealthy shoppers. He didn't want them to know he had a sandwich in his pocket he had made himself because he couldn't afford to buy one, or that he had four pounds to his name until his state pension arrived.

Far from waving a magic wand, Reuben Gerwitz had chided him for letting his affairs slip so far before seeking help. Given Knight's age, no amount of financial sleight-of-hand could change what he had spent months trying to deny: the flat would have to be sold.

That evening, at his son's house, his depression had deepened. There was talk of redundancies at his son's work, but also dissatisfaction with his grandson's state school, raising the ruinous spectre of private education. This was where grandparents were meant to ride to the rescue with trust funds blazing, though short of selling up and disappearing beneath the waves, there was nothing he could do. He did not mention his own troubles.

And yet.

Perhaps it was a delayed effect from the session of indoor rugby that morning before his grandson departed for school, or perhaps it was the minor triumph of having unearthed a lead of sorts, but as the minutes ticked away until the appointment at Pernil Goode he felt his burdens lighten. It helped too that Lolly had been unstinting in her praise when he told her what he had discovered. Try as he might to banish the image of her on the pole, he was snared by the knowledge that they were practically of the same generation. He was failing to banish this thought too when he left the café with a spring in his step and set out on the short walk to the auctioneers.

The junior Chinese specialist studied the figures on her screen, the sick feeling welling up in her stomach. The auction would close to new items in less than a week, and on the present showing the department would make little over half its target. There had already been a memo preparing them for job losses if revenue continued to disappoint; as the most recent arrival, she would be the automatic choice.

However, a slim chance had emerged that she might live to fight another day, so she was pleased when reception called to say that her visitor had arrived. She climbed the stairs from her cramped basement office, praying that he wouldn't be another fraudster. As part of her daily routine, she saw any number of cheats and chancers who insisted that the uninspiring twentieth-century copy they had bought in a junk shop the previous week was an imperial masterpiece which had been in the family for generations. But that was the job; she was paid to spot fakes.

On the phone, at least, Aubrey Beauchamp had sounded genuine. When she saw him waiting at reception in his crumpled linen suit he looked genuine too. She breathed a provisional sigh of relief.

Knight thought she looked tired. In her late thirties perhaps, groomed to perfection in a brittle sort of way. She didn't wear a wedding ring, not that this told you much. It had taken all his powers of gentlemanly persuasion to obtain a meeting rather than send her scans of photographs. Moved by his pitiable fear of technology, she had agreed to see him.

The niceties completed, he opened the briefcase and took out an A4 envelope.

'I hope these are good enough,' he began apologetically. 'I've never got round to having them done by a professional.'

He laid the pictures out in front of her, letting his hand tremble a little.

'Ideally I'd have tried to keep the collection in the family, but my children aren't interested and it's getting to the point where I can't afford the insurance anymore.'

86

He wished it were true. On a rough calculation, the pieces he had found online were worth over a million pounds.

She started to say how sorry she was but, as she picked up the first photo, she froze, and the tiredness seemed to leave her.

'May I ask when you bought this vase, Mr Beauchamp? It's quite an unusual piece.'

Which indeed it was. A little under three hundred years earlier it had been the personal property of the Emperor Qianlong. Knight took the picture from her and gazed at it fondly.

'Ah yes, probably my favourite. My father bought it when I was a child. He's the one who started the collection, I just followed in his footsteps really.'

It was not an unfamiliar story. She went slowly through the other pictures, the Tang incense burner, the Ming wine cup, the exquisitely carved jades, and saw the promise of redemption.

'And you have provenances?'

'Oh yes, all filed away. That's one thing I am quite good at.'

For a moment, her poker face gave way and she smiled. Knight felt a fleeting sensation that his moral compass might be a few degrees adrift, but it was too late to reset it.

'I'd need to see them, of course, but I'm extremely confident we can get you some excellent prices. Perhaps I could come and visit you in Eastbourne?'

It was time to up the stakes.

'There is one other matter. I'm afraid I was only reminded of it this morning when I looked through my father's papers.'

She nodded assent, eager to please.

'I'd like Rupert Askew to be involved. He handled nearly all of my father's purchases and did very well for him. Is he in today by any chance?'

A faint warning bell rang in her mind but it was no more than a murmur, the equivalent of a hairline crack on an otherwise perfect piece.

'I'm afraid he isn't,' she apologised. 'He hasn't worked here for some time.'

'Oh.'

Knight frowned and sank back in his chair.

'That's a pity. I'd rather hoped to rope him in on this. Can you get him on board as a consultant or something?'

'I honestly don't know where he is,' she apologised, 'but I can assure you we have all the people we need to do an excellent job for you.'

'Oh,' he said again, this time with a hint of petulance. 'Well, I'm sure you can, but I think I'd like to have him all the same if you don't mind, I'd find it reassuring. Surely someone here must know where he is?'

He put one of the photos back in the envelope.

'Mr Beauchamp.' She lowered her voice. 'I'm not really supposed to tell you this, but I feel you ought to know. Rupert Askew left under something of a cloud.'

'Really? Oh dear.' He made it look as if this had come as something of a blow. 'What did he do?'

'I'm afraid I'm really not at liberty to say.'

'I think I need a bit more than that to be honest. This is an important decision for me, I need a few facts.' He harrumphed and put another photo in the envelope.

'No, please.' She leaned in conspiratorially. 'You absolutely did not hear this from me, but Rupert Askew was accused of a very serious theft. He is *not* someone you should trust with selling your collection.'

There was no need to feign surprise. Floundering for a second, he fell back on a peevish incredulity.

'Well who did he steal from? Was there any proof?'

'I really can't say. Perhaps… if I had a word with my head of department. May I take these?'

'By all means.' He gave her the envelope and adopted a more conciliatory tone. 'I don't mean to be difficult, but I really would like to get the facts straight before I make up my mind. He can't be that difficult to track down, surely?'

As she went to find her superior, the hairline crack expanded marginally, enough at least to entertain the possibility that Aubrey Beauchamp might fall into the category of things that were too good to be true. She took out the photos for another look.

Knight waited for twenty minutes, wondering why they were taking so long. For want of anything better to do, he visited the men's room, a sumptuous affair with marble basins and thick cotton towels. The world of Aubrey Beauchamp was cosseting to body and soul; he could get used to this.

Eventually, the receptionist was instructed to take him to a glass-fronted meeting room on the first floor. Here he waited again, noting that the security guard from downstairs had shifted position to a seat in the corridor outside. It was only when he saw the set of the two women's faces that he realised all was not well.

The head of department was cast from the same mould as her junior colleague, but two decades older.

'I understand you'd like to contact Rupert Askew,' she began, with a formal charm that was not unpleasant. 'Would you mind telling me why that is?'

'As I explained to your colleague, I'd like to hear his side of the story. I take it you have no objection to that?'

The charm evaporated.

'Shall I tell you what I think, Mr Beauchamp? I think you're working for Clementine Lever. And that being the case, you'll be aware that we have an injunction prohibiting her or her representatives from entering the building.'

Knight made a show of bewildered outrage but his mind was not on it. Another fruit had dropped into his lap, a massive one he could barely digest. He continued to bluster, threatening to complain to the chairman, but cut no ice.

'Perhaps you could tell me about this piece.' She was holding up the picture of the Qianlong vase.

'I've already explained,' Knight spluttered indignantly. 'It was part of my father's collection.'

'You're quite sure about that?'

The two women looked meaningfully at each other.

'Would you excuse us for a moment?'

They stood up abruptly and left the room. He watched as they engaged in a tense conversation a few feet away on the other side of the glass. As a commercial spook he had learned to lip read, but it was darker out in the corridor and he struggled to pick out words. With no detectable urgency he slid open the camouflaged lens cover on his stick and touched the tiny pressure pad on the handle to activate the camera.

The dumb show lasted less than a minute, after which the older woman took out her phone and made a call. When they returned he wished he had quit while he was ahead.

'I'm not entirely sure why you came here, Mr Beauchamp, and I don't think that's your real name. What I do know is that the Qianlong you say you inherited from your father was sold by us in New York six months ago. I expect when we research the other pieces we'll find they don't belong to you either.'

Knight heard the clatter of stumps and bails. To his eye, the vases and jades on the internet had seemed much alike, a medley of mountains, pearls and dragons. He had grossly underestimated the observational powers of the women standing before him.

'All right, you got me.' He put his hands up in mock surrender. 'I'm a private investigator. And I'm not working for Clementine. She's dead. I'm working for her sister.'

If anything they viewed him with greater distaste than before.

'I don't care whom you are working for. You've attempted to deceive us and I'm following company policy. The police are on their way.'

'But that's ridiculous!' he objected angrily. 'All I want is to find Rupert Askew!'

Ignoring him, they swept out of the room again. Before she closed the door, the junior specialist fixed him with a withering glare.

'Can I just say, Mr Beauchamp, you're a lousy fake.'

He made straight for the door but the guard was there before him. The lock clicked. He hammered on the glass, demanding to be let out, but the guard went back to his seat and refused to look at him.

It would not be the end of the world if he had to talk to the police, but he had always taken it as a point of honour not to allow himself to be held against his will. He remembered something he had seen in the washroom downstairs and rapped on the glass again.

'I need the loo!'

The guard shook his head. When Knight repeated the request he looked away. The police would arrive in minutes, seconds even. He had to get to the men's room.

On a table in the corner was a large bronze pot with a mouth about a foot wide. According to the display card, it was a Japanese Meiji planter. With some difficulty, he lifted it down then undid his trousers. With one hand on his stick and another on the table, he began to lower himself. The guard relented instantly.

'I've got diarrhoea,' Knight cried, as he entered the room. 'Get me to a loo quick!'

Clutching his trousers, he allowed himself to be taken to a washroom further down the corridor. The guard followed him in.

'You're not going to stand there are you?' he bellowed at parade ground strength. 'Have some bloody respect, for god's sake!'

Reluctantly, the guard retreated to the corridor. Praising the gods that the cubicles were empty, Knight pushed open all the doors save for the one furthest from the entrance. He pulled it shut from the outside, jamming it with a few sheets of toilet paper. On the ceiling was a smoke detector. He lit another sheet and held it aloft on the end of his stick.

The alarm went off throughout the building.

To his credit, the guard was only tempted for a split second to run and save his skin. He burst in, smelling the smoke in the air but more intent on the closed cubicle at the end of the room. To his shame, he failed to see Knight standing beside the door behind him.

Knight hurried to the stairs. The people streaming out of offices and galleries paid him little attention, but already he could hear the guard yelling at him to stop.

At the head of the staircase was a porcelain Buddha. He took it from its plinth and turned to face his pursuer.

'Catch,' he shouted above the wail of the alarm.

It was a gentle lob, much as his eight-year-old self might have passed a rugby ball from the back of the scrum. It was also a ridiculous thing to do, he thought afterwards. If the statuette had smashed, he would have been lucky to end up in a hostel, let alone a bungalow. For the catcher's part, the likelihood that he was holding an object worth several times his salary froze him to the spot. By the time he had restored the Buddha to its plinth, Knight was halfway down the stairs, followed by a throng of bodies heading for the front door. Among them, as he looked back, were his two interrogators. Together with the security guard they were trying to push their way past colleagues and clients, who found their behaviour objectionable and let them know it.

Catching his breath, he stumbled out into Bond Street past a pair of policemen standing aside for the crowd to exit.

'Are you all right, sir?' asked one of them kindly.

'I'm fine, thank you,' he gasped. 'I just wish they'd told us about the fire drill.'

Slipping in front of a gaggle of Chinese tourists, he turned at the first corner and kept going.

Chapter Fifteen

At Brown's Hotel on Albemarle Street, there was a lounge where he had met clients during his years at Commercial Intelligence, charging eyewatering sums to an expense account. In his current circumstances, the prices seemed all the more stupendous, though the quality of service had not diminished; the request to delay his order until his associates arrived was accepted without question.

The video had transferred automatically to his phone. By adjusting the light level and zooming into the women's mouths, he was able to start transcribing the scrap of conversation he had managed to record. It was hard going. Some words emerged easily – 'police', 'mention', 'circumstances' – but even at full zoom it was a question of listing the options and trying them out until they made sense, a verbal Rubik's Cube. After an hour, he was confident enough of what he had.

'Supposing he tells the police what he told us?' the junior specialist asked.

'Then they can deal with it. I don't want him back here under any circumstances. I've had strict instructions.'

Here she seemed to grow thoughtful for a moment.

'Unless…'

'Unless what?'

'He didn't mention Abigail Samuels did he?'

'Who?'

'Doesn't matter. Before your time.'

That was when she took out her phone to call the police.

The waiter was eyeing him dubiously. Knight looked at his watch again and tutted, aware that the pretence was wearing thin. It was time to make a decision.

He now knew that, at some time in the past, Clementine had been looking for Rupert Askew. The injunction suggested she may have taken her pursuit to extremes, perhaps creating a disturbance at Pernil Goode. It didn't prove that he'd killed her, but it made him in all likelihood the thief she blamed for her poverty. And now there was Abigail Samuels. A search revealed the usual array of marketeers, therapists and American academics, but one stood out from the rest. She was the owner of an investment consultancy that bore her name, less than a mile away on the other side of Mayfair. Her leisure interests included an art collection.

For five minutes, Aubrey Beauchamp became a high net worth individual seeking a last-minute appointment before flying home to Lichtenstein, but her secretary informed him that the diary was full.

He was practically on her doorstep; the lure was/irresistible. Taking leave of the waiter, who expressed his condolences impeccably, he set off.

Mayfair had once been a playground of sorts for him, a warren of clubs and dens of overpriced vice through which he had slipped like a shadow, a patient observer and cutter of deals. Even then it had seemed a closed world to him; a network of handsome yet anonymous terraces punctuated by lavish displays of wealth.

That much hadn't changed. In Berkeley Square a Bentley Continental, a snip at a hundred and eighty thousand, leered at him from a showroom. The poker-faced buildings hadn't changed either. He passed hedge funds and private banks, their names marked on small brass plaques or inscribed discreetly next to the entry buttons, or not mentioned at all.

He turned into South Audley Street. Despite the rain that had set in, he felt buoyed to be closing in on a target. Like its neighbours, the building was a brownstone house on five floors, of which Samuels Global Resources occupied the top two. The website showed an immaculately presented woman in her sixties, with a deep tan and curly black hair. She would be hard to miss when she came out, which was why he hoped to find a café from which he could observe the entrance.

Cafés, however, were in short supply at this end of South Audley Street. The rain was coming down harder, casting the first shadows of doubt over his decision. In five minutes, he could be at Marble Arch Station and on his way to Victoria. It was then that Lolly called.

She hadn't heard of Abigail Samuels, but practically purred with appreciation when she learned what he'd unearthed.

'And you're outside her place now?'

Knight confirmed that he was, unleashing a further torrent of congratulation and encouragement. The conversation was shorter than he would have liked; it was hard to hear everything she said against the noise of the traffic.

Raising the collar of his army coat and pulling the bobble hat over his forehead, he proceeded down the street. His fortitude was swiftly rewarded. On the other side of the road, a house was covered in scaffolding. The workmen had left for the day, defeated by the rain. It had a colonnaded porch that nestled beneath its own roof, fit for the Georgian aristocrat who had first lived there. Knight squeezed through a gap in the traffic and climbed the stairs.

There were some sacks of cement and a large tub of something grey. Collapsing gratefully onto the tub, he rested for a full minute, his arms wrapped tight around his chest. From here he had an unrestricted view down the street to the entrance of Abigail Samuels' building. It seemed he had committed himself, so he dug in.

Shifting the sandbags was backbreaking work. By and by he had, if not a daybed, a padded perch to make the experience bearable. The problem was the cold. His coat was soaked through but there could be no question of taking it off. He was also starving. Long overdue second thoughts were starting to emerge when a fur-clad lady approached beneath an umbrella.

'You poor man,' she said kindly, pressing a pound into his glove. She was on her way before he could explain the misunderstanding.

But then he wondered if he needed to. As the afternoon drew on, more passers-by took pity on the huddled figure. He quickly came to terms with any sense of shame, telling himself that he was not actively soliciting contributions and therefore not a beggar. As proof of this, he refrained from placing his bobble hat on the bottom step where it might earn him more, although later he relented on the grounds of operational efficiency. It became a game, guessing who would be the next to make an offering, the businessman, the off-duty nurse, the priest from Mount Street.

It was towards four o'clock when the student found him. He wore a hat like Knight's, over a shock of ginger hair.

'You all right friend? You homeless?'

'No, as it happens.' Knight's teeth were chattering. 'Just stopped to shelter from the rain, but thank you.'

There was nothing to be done about the exhaustion in his voice, which the visitor took as plain evidence that he was in denial. It was also quite clearly the voice of a bourgeois, which only went to show how far the crisis had spread.

'Listen friend, the reason you're homeless is that the bankers and the Tories have ripped you off just like everyone else. We have to stand together, you know what I'm saying?'

Knight didn't necessarily disagree, and took the flyer the young man offered. He would happily have chatted to pass the time but, at this moment, a chauffeur-driven Jaguar drew up outside Abigail Samuels' building. Seconds later, she appeared at the front door.

Watching the old man struggle to his feet and scuttle down the steps, the student imagined he had somehow scared him away; perhaps he was not yet ready to confront the pressing need for revolution. But then his behaviour grew stranger. Racing down the opposite pavement, he was waving agitatedly at the symbol of capitalist oppression that was drawing away from the kerb. Next he was getting into a taxi.

The Jaguar was three cars ahead. Knight told the driver he had missed his friends and to follow it wherever it went. He had no idea how much money was in his pocket, perhaps enough for a few minutes in the cab while he tried to conjure up another move. In the event they scarcely covered a quarter of a mile before joining a queue of traffic outside the Grosvenor House Hotel in Park Lane. Along the driveway in front of the main entrance, a line of police was holding back a crowd of chanting protesters. Knight shovelled a fistful of coins through the partition and hurried after the Jaguar, only to see the chauffeur open the door and escort his employer into the building.

Knight fell in behind a procession of Burberry coats. A policewoman was waving them on to the door, keeping an eye out for any demonstrators who might be tempted to join their ranks. She gave Knight an odd look. He didn't seem to belong where he was, but nor did he fit the bill of disaffected youth. On the mistaken assumption that he was harmless, she let him pass.

In the lobby, the cause of dissent was revealed. The hotel was playing host to a property investment seminar whose proudly declared aim was to shift yet more of London's housing stock into the hands of private landlords. Abigail Samuels was listed as a keynote speaker, but first there was to be a champagne reception in the ballroom. The only problem was, he hadn't been invited.

At the ballroom entrance, guests were being checked in against a list. Not all of them had their invitations, which didn't appear to be a problem. Knight backtracked to the cloakroom, where he waited for a suitable subject to approach the long queue. When an elderly, bewhiskered investor appeared, he made his move.

'Dennis!' he exclaimed joyfully. 'I wondered if you'd be here.'

'I beg your pardon?' The accent wasn't English.

'Dennis Kampner – didn't we meet at the Brussels thing?'

The man shook his head, regarding the wet stranger with a degree of distaste.

'My name is Hector Rodriguez,' he replied stiffly. 'I believe you have made a mistake.'

'Oh!' Knight covered himself in confusion. 'I'm so terribly sorry, I was convinced it was you, I mean him. I'm afraid my memory's playing tricks on me.'

With further apologies, he bade the man farewell and returned to the ballroom. The cloakroom queue was worth a good five minutes, not quite time to complete his mission but enough to keep a toehold in the game.

Praying that his new namesake was not a star of the property world, he presented himself at the reception desk and affected a Spanish accent. It was not a good one, but the attendant was from Latvia and gave him the badge without question. Entering the throng, he spotted his quarry deep in conversation with some Arabs. Nearer to hand was a long table laden with food and drink. It would cost precious time, but he couldn't pass up a chance to eat. With one eye on the reception desk, he shovelled vol-au-vents, salmon blinis and cocktail sausages into his mouth as discreetly as he could. He was thus ill-prepared for the interruption.

'Put on a good spread, don't they? Mind you, it's the least they can do considering what they charge us.'

The young man had a shiny suit and a weasely face with a broken nose, ideal for intimidating tenants. Knight casually scratched his own nose, allowing his hand to cover a furiously chewing jaw.

'Indeed,' he managed at length, 'it's not cheap is it?'

Knight moved down the table towards the mini-kebabs. Annoyingly, his new companion followed.

'So, what kind of portfolio do you run then? Residential, office, industrial?'

'Actually I'm a newbie, just thinking of testing the water.'

Failing to notice that the man was inspecting his badge, he bit into a kebab and turned away, hoping this would signal the end of the conversation.

'So where you from then?'

'Eastbourne,' he mumbled.

'Eastbourne? Thought you'd be from somewhere hotter with a name like that.'

Knight thought he heard the bails coming off again, but the calories had begun to kick in.

'My father was Argentinian,' he confided, 'but, as it happens, I've never been there.'

The weasel seemed disappointed.

'Still,' he persisted, 'there's nice pickings to be had in Eastbourne, don't know why you're bothering with London.'

Despite everything, Knight's curiosity was piqued. The real Hector Rodriguez had yet to appear at the reception desk.

'Why is that then?' he asked, swallowing hard and moving on to the chicken satay.

'Very simple. You've loads of old people – no disrespect – who can't afford to hang onto their properties, and if you can get to them with a cash offer before they go to an estate agent, you're quids in. Leafleting's good, cost you next to nothing.'

Knight felt a strong urge to plunge the man's head into the exotic fruit gateau, but then thought of a way of putting him to good use.

'You don't know Abigail Samuels do you? I've heard she's a good person to talk to.'

'Abigail? Everyone knows Abigail. Want me to introduce you?'

Only partially forgiving him, Knight followed to where the famed adviser was taking leave of the Arabs. She looked even better than the picture on her website; tall with a full figure sheathed in a silk cotton skirt suit. A princess in Gucci.

'Abigail! There's someone I'd like you to meet.'

She didn't bat an eyelid at the crumpled apparition; the wealthy came in all shapes and sizes.

'How do you do Mr…' She squinted at his badge. 'Rodriguez?' She frowned sharply. 'You're not Hector Rodriguez, he's over there.'

At the reception desk, the genuine article was arguing with the attendant. Abandoning the social niceties, Knight turned to his now redundant companion and issued a command.

'Would you leave us please, this is something of an emergency.'

Without a further glance at him, he took the startled woman lightly by the elbow and ushered her a few steps away.

'Who are you?' she objected angrily; even investment bankers didn't treat her like this. Hector Rodriguez and the attendant were approaching across the crowded room.

'I'm a private investigator. I don't usually do things this way but I need you to tell me everything you know about Rupert Askew, now.'

At the sound of the name, her face turned to thunder.

'Are you trying to blackmail me?' she hissed.

She didn't find out. There was a roar from the entrance as an advance party of about twenty protesters burst in, followed by half-a-dozen police. Rodriguez and the attendant froze in horror as the new arrivals set about upturning the tables and pouring champagne onto the floor to chants of 'hands off homes' and 'bloodsuckers out'. To emphasise the message, if a little too obviously, some of them began to spray the assembled company with red paint. A policeman wrestled one to the ground, but now more protesters poured in, followed by more police, until the ballroom was a sea of flailing bodies and spilt food.

Abigail Samuels had retreated to the edge of the room. Knight followed, keeping a watchful eye on the sprayers. As rucks went it wasn't especially vicious, certainly not up to the standard of drunken squaddies in an Aldershot pub on a Saturday night. He took quiet pleasure in seeing the weasel with a stripe of paint down the front of his suit.

'Don't worry,' he reassured her. 'This won't last long.'

Nor would it have, but for the smoke grenades. The police had been gaining the upper hand, but now the room began to fill with an acrid fog that stung the eyes and throat. Knight noted with a sneaking respect that the protesters had donned gas masks, which turned the engagement back in their favour. Before the smoke reached him, he took a deep breath.

Mrs Samuels remained rooted to the spot, her body convulsed by an uncontrollable fit of coughing. Knight pulled her to the floor where the smoke was less dense and gave her his bobble hat to hold over her mouth. His eyes on fire, he guided her on all fours to the door where he had seen waiters entering from the kitchen. On reaching it, he allowed himself a gulp of noxious air before hauling himself to his feet, pulling her by the wrist to indicate she should do the same. But the door refused to open. Through the din he heard a babble of fearful voices on the other side.

'Open the bloody door!' he bellowed. He barged it with his shoulder, but only enough to panic the kitchen staff into calling for reinforcements. As he tried again, a spray can loomed up through the smoke, followed by a gas mask on a mane of ginger hair.

The unexpected sight of the bourgeois pauper among foul capitalist scum threw the insurrectionist. Unsure which target to prioritise, the traitor or his consort, he hesitated for a fatal split second. Holding up his coat as a screen, Knight charged. There was a muffled objection as he made contact, but then a sudden impact that sent him staggering backwards. Lowering the coat, he saw the student in the arms of a burly policeman, with another at his side.

Knight pointed to the kitchen door. 'There's more of them in there,' he rasped. 'They're blocking the way.'

The second policeman charged at the door. This time it flew open, scattering the terrified Filipinos and Bangladeshis clustered behind it. Taking his protégé by the arm, Knight pulled her along in the policeman's wake. Searching in vain for a culprit to demolish, he paid the elderly couple no further attention. Nor did anyone else challenge them as they fled through the kitchen and found their way to a service lift.

Chapter Sixteen

'I met him five years after my husband died. I went on a dating site and my date didn't turn up. But he did.'

She sipped her whisky, a twenty-year-old single malt. They were sitting in her apartment overlooking Hyde Park. She'd been grateful for being spared the paint, but still refused to talk until he told her that Rupert Askew had killed someone, which was only a slight exaggeration of what he believed. They had shared a cab, for which she had paid.

'He'd also been stood up, or that's what he said. I think that was how he operated, finding women like me online and then showing up as someone else so that the agency couldn't trace him. He used a false name, of course.'

They were facing each other across a glass coffee table the size of a bed. On the shelves and walls were Chinese pots and paintings, softly bathed in light from invisible sources. Elsewhere, a grand piano was covered in silver-framed photographs. She had her legs tucked up on a white sofa that looked like a minimalist sculpture, identical to the one she had allocated to him.

'I was flattered. He was young and good-looking, I was lonely, and for a while it was good. We had a lot of fun and spent a lot of money, mine mostly. Not that I minded. What made him so interesting was that he knew about Chinese art, although he was vague about where he worked. One day, he offered to value my jade collection, and I agreed. A month or so later he disappeared and that was the end of it, or so I thought.'

She took another sip of whisky; Knight was on water. In the cab he had come close to being sick but had managed to disguise it.

'Did you ever speak to him again?'

'No. I called the number he'd given me but it was dead. I just assumed he'd lost interest and didn't have the guts to say so. I was damned if I was going to run after him. And then two years later, I happened to see one of the jades in a catalogue at Pernil Goode. It fetched fifty thousand.'

'You mean you didn't know it was missing?'

'I was careless, I admit it. I bought the collection on impulse, not something I advise my clients to do. Then I lost interest and put them in a cupboard. Didn't even bother to get them insured.'

Knight was seized by a righteous anger of which the ginger radical would have approved. He wanted to tell her that fifty thousand was his entire debt, until he saw it would be shameful.

'But you had no idea that this one piece was worth so much?'

'No idea at all. I only paid twenty thousand for the whole lot. But that happens sometimes, a piece flies and you don't really know why. You might say I had a stroke of good luck followed by a bad one.'

'So what did you do?'

'I kicked up a stink at Pernil Goode, of course. I even found out his name from the dealer he'd used to place the piece. But I didn't have any paperwork, or even photos. Needless to say, he had a detailed provenance, all forged of course, but there was nothing I could do about it. So, in the end, I let it go and moved on.'

'You didn't think of going to a newspaper?'

'And be on the front page of the *Sun* as the millionaire widow who fell for her toyboy? I don't think so.'

She was still wary of him. There was a ruthless intelligence at work which intrigued her, along with a sense of danger to which she'd once been more partial than she was now. His physical state was another matter. He needed restoration, a lot of it, and that took time. She drained her glass, tentatively imagining him in a decent suit.

'Do you have any idea where he is?' Knight asked.

'None at all. And I don't have a photo of him. For some reason, he wasn't keen to have one taken.'

The whisky had gone to her head, which didn't stop her having another one.

'Did he know about your art collection before you met him?'

'Oh yes, it was in my profile. The main attraction, I'm sure.'

She took a deep swig. There was one thing she hadn't told him, for somehow it mattered what he thought of her. But she had a reckless streak and the whisky knew where to find it.

'There's something else.' The words were slightly slurred.

Sensing her discomfort, Knight thought she had lent him money or involved him in her business.

'He was into... kinky stuff.' Another mouthful. 'He took me to a couple of clubs where... well, it doesn't matter. I went along with it because he told me I should open up to new experiences. And not long before he disappeared I... I let him beat me with a cane.'

The confession hung between them like some strange mutant fruit that had unexpectedly appeared on an otherwise normal tree. Misshapen and malodorous, it repelled him at first, though in its very perversity it showed her in a new light: naive perhaps, and fearful of abandonment, but also an experimenter prepared to throw off the chains of prudery. She had guts. He didn't ask if she'd enjoyed it.

'I'm sorry you ran into him,' he replied at length. 'It seems to me you were just unlucky.' It could also have been much worse, he thought.

She excused herself and walked a little unsteadily to the kitchen for water, motioning Knight to stay seated when he offered to fetch it for her. Only employees and waiters did that anymore. The sense of release was physical, breathing a lightness into her limbs. She was grateful that he didn't seem shocked.

Gulping the water from a bottle, she found herself reconsidering the restoration project. But then she was reminded of a more current venture, the personal trainer who seemed to worship the ground she walked on and had no interest in canes. One thing at a time, she told herself.

'You must let me buy you a new coat, yours is ruined.'

Knight was attached to his coat and declined politely. Most of the paint would come out; what remained would be a battle scar. She didn't offer to pay for dry cleaning, for which on balance he was glad, but she did instruct her chauffeur to drive him back to Eastbourne.

Sunk in the leather upholstery, he half dozed, half daydreamed, assembling what he knew about the life of Rupert Askew. It was a gratifying haul that he would take pleasure in laying before Lolly. At the outer reaches of south London, the mid-evening traffic began to thin. Before falling into a fitful sleep, in which he possessed dazzling wealth and the perfect body of his youth, he reflected that it had been a most satisfactory day.

But it wasn't over.

Chapter Seventeen

Merv's eyes were locked on the entrance to the Fishermen's Club. Twenty yards away, obscured by other cars, was O'Driscoll's Golf. The red Corsa, he had by now established, belonged to one of the sons. If ever O'Driscoll decided he'd had enough to drink, it was here in the car park that he would be relieved of his money bag. He'd been in the bar since seven, now it was nearly ten.

It wasn't technically a mugging, of which Merv would have disapproved. This was a serious matter of restoring property to its rightful owner, no less justified than removing weapons from dodgy houses in Belfast. Short, sharp and as brutal as necessary, but not nearly as dangerous.

He had also assumed it would be much easier. More than once, a passer-by had come close to seeing the infrared binoculars. Nor did it help that the batteries were running low and he had no spares. He was wondering whether Knight would have prevented the oversight when the club door opened.

It was probably a man, but with the light from the doorway behind him the only thing that matched was the build.

There was a thump on the roof of the van. Terrified, Merv dropped the binoculars.

Finding nothing of interest, the seagull was gone again in an instant. The target meanwhile disappeared among the cars. If it was O'Driscoll, he would be driving away in seconds. Merv sprinted in the direction of the Golf, pulling the balaclava over his head. But the Golf was unattended. Elsewhere, an engine started up and a pair of headlights made for the exit.

Merv exhaled slowly. Checking first that he was alone, he went once more through the sequence of events that would shortly unfold. O'Driscoll would go to the driver's door, which faced away from the clubhouse entrance. Merv would step out from behind the adjacent SUV and give him one in the mouth followed by a knee in the guts. This would continue until the contents of the bag were made available. There wasn't the luxury of someone to hold him in position, but the knuckleduster would compensate for that.

He tried out the position behind the SUV again. The height made it perfect; O'Driscoll would be visible from at least four cars away, maybe more, which meant the restricted peripheral vision caused by the balaclava wasn't a problem. Raising himself by the door to peer through the side window, he failed to see the mirror and hit it with his shoulder.

The alarm hit him like a shockwave. He sprinted for the van, only to see a man and a dog approaching from the road; the man was looking straight at him. His mind a blank, he turned and fled in the direction of the clubhouse. Behind it was a workshop, beyond which lay the beach where the fishing boats were laid up, the *King of Sussex* among them. He looked back. The alarm was still sounding, but there was no sign of the dog walker or anyone else.

He asked himself what Knight would do. The advice, possibly unwise, was to stick it out. There was a stack of lobster pots at the side of the workshop, offering a better view of the clubhouse entrance. Safely installed, he recovered his composure enough to convince himself the mission remained on track. The door opened.

It was not O'Driscoll. The owner of the SUV inspected his vehicle briefly, switched off the alarm and returned inside. Resigned to waiting until the bar closed at eleven, Merv resumed his vigil.

The first hint of trouble was a distant siren. He told himself it meant nothing, certainly no reason to panic, until the blue flashing light swept into the car park. The police car circled once, teasing him with the possibility that it would lose interest and drive out again. But on completing the circuit, it ignored the exit and continued round to the clubhouse entrance, not twenty yards from where he stood. Two officers stepped out.

While one of them went inside, the other shone a torch, the beam playing for a moment on the stack of lobster pots. The fragment of Merv's brain still capable of rational thought told him there wasn't enough light to penetrate the pots and expose him, but it was drowned out by a primordial shriek demanding instant flight. As soon as the beam passed on, he ran blindly to the beach.

Perhaps the policeman saw him, or perhaps he was merely being diligent, but from behind a hull Merv saw the torch beam raking the pebbles. Amidst the jumble of boats and equipment, was some kind of metal shed with a piece of fishing net hanging through the open door. He darted to it and climbed in behind the bundled net. Unable to find the handle, he clasped the side of the door and pulled it shut as far as it would go.

From outside, he could hear the crunch of boot on pebble.

'See anything?' an unnervingly deep voice shouted.

'No.' The second voice was much closer.

The door opened and the torch played over the net.

'Probably shat himself and legged it.'

Merv was close to validating the first part of the officer's theory. Meanwhile, his colleague had arrived.

'Jesus, why don't they just put up a sign and say help yourself?'

One of them kicked the trailing net back inside and slammed the door shut.

Merv waited for a full ten minutes until there was silence except for the muffled splash and hiss of the waves. Squeezing out from behind the net he searched for the door handle. Probing the area where it should be, his fingers found something sharp. Throwing caution to the wind, he switched on the phone torch. The bare stump of the shaft was thick with rust and there was a jagged break where the rest of it had sheared off, taking the handle with it. He scoured the floor and the folds of net; there was no handle.

He made a painful attempt to turn the shaft with his fingers. When that didn't work, he began a frantic search for a tool. Behind an oil drum he found a net cutter. With his heart in his mouth, he tightened the blades around the stump and turned. The stump broke off.

Some time elapsed until he could engage with the fact that somebody would have to come and let him out. Jabril owed him a favour for the speeding points, as did Alice from the allotment for the seeds he'd given her; he even considered Mrs Chang. Somebody, anybody, would do, as long as it wasn't Knight.

*

Refreshed by his sleep in the Jaguar, Knight waited for the lift to come. Lolly had yet to respond to his message suggesting that they meet the next day. On an impulse, he had asked her to the flat for lunch, an invitation which with hindsight he was questioning. He would never have invited a client to the flat, but she was not a client. Was she a friend? As he pondered this and the meagre contents of his fridge, his phone rang.

It was something of a disappointment to see that the caller was Merv. He felt a pang of guilt too, conscious that he had neglected him over the past few days. Nothing, however, could have prepared him for the news that he was trapped in a shed on the beach by the Fishermen's Club. As the lift doors opened invitingly before him, he turned and went back out to his car.

Further details followed as he sped along the seafront. He wasn't morally offended by what Merv had proposed to do, but he was shocked by the enormity of the risk. It was poor judgement but also a reproach; this was his battle too and he hadn't been present.

The door opened without difficulty.

'Thank you,' Merv mumbled. 'I'm really sorry.' Radiating humiliation, he could not look Knight in the eye.

'Not your fault, you were unlucky.' The words rang hollow.

'No, I was an idiot. It's all right, you can say it.'

There was a surliness that discouraged further questioning, but it couldn't be left yet.

'Why didn't you tell me?'

'Because I didn't want to put you in danger. Can we leave it please?'

They'd reached the Skoda, which he'd left by the van.

'I'm thankful for that, but I still wish you'd told me. We'll come up with something. I don't know what, but we will.'

As he spoke, the club door opened and the man himself appeared. They both dropped down beside Knight's car.

'I'm going to do him,' Merv whispered fiercely. 'Don't try and stop me.'

Merv chanced another look, which was as well. Behind O'Driscoll, a woman had come out for a cigarette. Knight could see there was something odd about the way the man was walking, slow and ultra-cautious, as if he were a stroke victim taking his first steps. O'Driscoll was drunk. If it were not for the presence of the smoker, he would be ripe for the taking.

But perhaps the smoker didn't matter.

'Merv, get the van and block the entry lane.'

Merv was bewildered.

'You what?'

'Just do it – now!'

Succumbing again to the spell of Knight's authority, Merv did as he was bid. O'Driscoll didn't notice him, nor did he react when Knight got into the Skoda and drove off.

The only way in and out of the car park was through two parallel lanes. Knight took the exit lane and parked just outside it. The van arrived next and blocked the inbound lane. O'Driscoll was still fumbling with his keys.

Eventually the Golf approached, moving rather too quickly for Knight's liking. As it entered the exit lane he reversed the Skoda across its path. There was a squeal of brakes and a bang that shook him.

Knight stepped out. O'Driscoll was gaping at him through the windscreen, a picture of rage mingled with disbelief. He heaved himself out, venting his fury without restraint. Only then did he recognise Knight.

'What the fuck…?'

Knight noted with pride that his timing had been perfect: it was the Golf that had run into him, not he into the Golf. The damage itself was barely noticeable among the other scuffs and dents.

'That was careless,' he said calmly. 'You've done a lot of damage to my car.'

For a second he thought the drunk was about to launch himself at him, but the van door opened and Merv stepped down. O'Driscoll's rage gave way to fear.

'What do you want?' The confident voice of the bully had degenerated to a submissive croak.

'I think a thousand should do it. It's going to need a new panel and a respray.'

He gaped at Knight with his mouth open. The penny had yet to drop.

'But you… it was your fault, you did it deliberately!'

'Did I? I'd say your judgement was impaired because you're over the limit. By quite a lot as it happens. If we can't agree I'll have to ask the police to join us.'

Knight took out his phone and pressed a few random keys while O'Driscoll frantically juggled the chances of flight and the reaction of his wife if he was banned again.

'I'd like to report a collision with a drunk driver,' Knight was saying. O'Driscoll crumbled.

'All right! But I've only got five hundred, you can look if you don't believe me.'

He held out the bag for them to see. Merv took everything, ignoring the promises of violent retribution that Knight was recording with his stick. It was a perfect moment, tarnished only by his failure to pull off such a coup by himself.

Knight was jubilant. To the victor the spoils. Yet for him too there was one small blemish on an otherwise matchless outcome, a niggling spoilsport of a thought that came up out of nowhere and took him by surprise. He wished Lolly had seen it.

Chapter Eighteen

Gripping the pole with her thighs, Lolly hung like a bat from the roof of a cave. She found comfort in seeing the world upside down; it had become a ritual of everyday life. Tensing her abdomen, she raised herself until her face was level with her toes, counted to three and dropped back slowly. The burn was intoxicating. Repeating the manoeuvre, she fell as she always did into a meditation in which she sorted and resorted her concerns until they formed a landscape she could make sense of.

Chief among them was Bullock. Since the night at the club, he had sought her out several times, not only there but at the hotel. He had offered himself as a worthy ally in a dangerous world, although it was obvious that, for the moment, the only danger she faced was from him. Bullock was small fry compared to the Russian gangsters who owned La Manzana del Paradiso, but he could not be ignored.

She showered and set about her face. The price of Clarins in England had come as a shock, but then Lanzarote was one great duty-free shop; she reproached herself for not bringing more.

Knight on the other hand was a gift, quite possibly from the gods. He might even be that rare thing, a man you could rely on. There was certainly no question in her mind as to who was more likely to track down her sister's killer. But gifts from the gods, she knew from long experience, had to be treated with caution.

After the hydrating cream came the toning oil. She applied it generously, taking care to smother the wrinkles she had recently discovered just below her neck. Although barely visible to the untrained eye, they were a blemish that could not be tolerated. There were standards to be maintained, for as long as she could afford it.

She rifled through the crammed wardrobe, well worth the excess baggage fee. Far from finding the invitation to lunch inappropriate, she relished the prospect and was bent on looking her best.

*

Knight squeezed the vacuum cleaner back into the cluttered cupboard and forced the door shut. It was the first time in weeks that he had given the flat a proper clean, and now he had he felt mildly elated.

The soup was ready. In a nod to economy, he had used a bedraggled cauliflower from his most recent foray, cutting off the unwholesome parts before liquidising it in chicken bone stock. For everything else, including the chorizo, cream and herbs for the soup, he had proudly paid. The Chablis was an undeniable extravagance, as was the gravadlax, but fully deserved in the light of his triumph over O'Driscoll. The lobster was an afterthought. It had lain forgotten in the bottom of the freezer since their second expedition; when he saw it, he felt compelled to extend the menu.

Inevitably, his thoughts were drawn to the last time he had prepared a meal in comparable circumstances. Cooking for Fran had been something else altogether, a purposeful display of plumage that might lead to greater things. This was absolutely not the case with Lolly, he reminded himself, because absolutely nothing was going to happen between them. He had even resigned himself to the prospect that this could be their last meeting. Drunk on the thrill of his exploits in London, he had sobered up to the memory of his meeting with Reuben Gerwitz. From here on, he had resolved, all his energy would be focused laser-like on financial reconstruction. There could be no question of even contemplating a pro-bono investigation, let alone one for which he possessed no resources.

As he polished the wineglasses for a third time, the doorbell rang.

'What an amazing place!' she exclaimed.

Today, it was a cashmere trenchcoat, over a silk blouse and black leather trousers. He tried not to stare as she admired the airy sitting room, the Chesterfield, the paintings, the table set for two.

'And what's out there?' By way of reply, he opened the door to the terrace.

The wind had dropped and a pale winter sun shone in a clear sky, dispensing an imaginary warmth into the air. Lazy and unruffled, the sea was a lake of summery blue pencilled with a few thin streaks of white.

'Oh my god, the view, it's just like home.'

'You live by the sea?'

'Three blocks back from the beach. If you crane your neck on the balcony you can see the ocean. Not like here, it's out of this world.'

She was right, he could not give it up.

'What are those?'

Her eye had fallen on two bed-shaped objects covered in tarpaulins. He unhooked one of the covers and pulled it back, revealing a business class airline seat.

'My pride and joy. I got them from a client a few years back. Try it out if you like.'

She sat down and played with the controls, bringing up the seatback then adjusting the footrest until she had spread herself like a Roman senator at a banquet.

'This is absolutely mad. I love it.'

He pictured Fran in the identical pose and remembered where that had led. He repeated the mantra, nothing was going to happen.

'Let's go inside and have some lunch.'

Focusing his mind on facts and probabilities put him on firmer ground, even as she enthused over the soup. The discovery that Rupert Askew was connected to Clementine provided enough of a prompt for her to recall a few more details, albeit hazily. She thought he might have been a boyfriend for a short while, though she couldn't recall meeting him. It disturbed her to hear that Clementine may have been looking for him, still more that he had an appetite for sadism.

'Where do you think he is? Could he be around here somewhere?'

'If he's the person who killed her, he might not be far away. The problem is we don't know anything about her movements in the run-up to her death.'

'I might be able to help you with that.'

Lolly opened her handbag, a Prada according to the logo. She was no Abigail Samuels, but didn't seem to lack the trappings.

'They brought the car back and I went through it. I hope that's okay.'

Any sense of affront that she had encroached on his territory was forgotten as he read the receipts. The first was for a car service a few days before her death. Between then and when her body was found, there was a difference of sixty-four miles. Unless she had used public transport, she had not strayed far. But it was nothing compared to the second. The day after the modelling session, she had bought a bag of aquarium gravel from a pet shop. Knight felt a tingle down his spine; there could be no doubt now about Clementine's intentions.

'She must have seen him somewhere,' Lolly was saying, 'because otherwise how would she know where to go to use what you told her? You can't do surveillance without knowing where to look.'

They were eating the lobster. She deftly cracked a claw and hooked out the meat, clearly no stranger to the process.

'So what next?'

And there it was.

His embrace of realism included an intent to be scrupulously honest with her. The truth was the police were infinitely better equipped to find Rupert Askew, and there were now grounds for investigation that even Bullock could not ignore.

'If it was me, I'd go to the Askews' farm,' he began, 'but your best chance of finding him is to go to the police. There's enough circumstantial evidence now to oblige them to investigate. If I was in your position, that is what I would do.'

A weight lifted from his shoulders. He was not entirely happy for it to go but his conscience felt clean; he was sticking to the path.

Lolly crumpled.

'I won't go to the police,' she said quietly, staring into her lap. 'It's not just Bullock, I know I could go to someone else but…' she sighed despairingly. 'I have no faith in them, I just don't.'

'But I'll help you. I'll go to the top, to the Commissioner if I have to. They would have to act.'

'No.'

She seemed resigned, defeated even. It was the first time he had seen her like this.

'I just don't have it in me, it's as simple as that.' She paused, pursing her lips as if tasting something bitter. 'And I don't have any money to pay you to do it. I'm sorry.'

The mention of money threw Knight off balance. It cast him in a mercenary light, the last thing he wished.

'It isn't about money,' he protested. 'It's just that I'm limited in what I can do for you.'

She smiled. It was a small, wistful offering that nevertheless felt like the sun coming out from behind a cloud.

'You've done enough already. And look what I've done to you in return.'

She gestured to the bruise on his temple from where he had fallen on their first encounter. Then she frowned and peered at it more closely.

'Can I take a look at that?'

He had not been aware that the bruise looked particularly bad; before he could reply she began to explore the side of his head with her fingertips.

'You haven't had any headaches or blurred vision?'

He thought back to the dizzy spell at the supermarket, but that was before the fall. There had been another in the taxi with Abigail, though he didn't recall a headache or trouble with his eyes.

Her fingers moved to the side of his neck.

'Oh my god, you're completely locked up.'

With mounting concern, she widened the investigation to his back, squeezing on either side of his spine.

'I can't leave you like this; let me work on it for you. Please.'

Bewildered by the turn of events, Knight allowed himself to be led to the sofa. He sat as instructed with his back to her while she perched on the armrest, kneading his shoulders. He didn't detect any particular easing of his muscles, but the fact of being touched by her was as exhilarating as the sensation itself.

'You have the most extraordinary back,' she murmured. 'It's like a bodybuilder's.'

Knight was thrown again. As a young man he had been justifiably proud of his physique. Even now, it compared well with others of his age, but only because the bar was set so low.

'Well, I did do a bit of weightlifting when I was in the army,' he confessed modestly. 'A very long time ago.'

'Ah. I did wonder. Which bit?'

'Intelligence mostly. And a few years in the SAS.'

'The SAS? So you're a trained killer?' He couldn't see her face, but he could hear she was teasing.

'Fully trained and at your service.'

They laughed together; another first. In the space of a few minutes her mood had performed an about-turn. Where would it go next?

'So, tell me Mr SAS, what exactly would you do if you went to the farm and the marina?'

He nearly missed it. She was close enough for him to feel her breath on the back of his neck, putting him in danger of sensory overload. It was like playing a fast bowler in a heavy mist, except it was she who was playing him.

'Why, are you thinking of becoming an investigator like your sister?' He didn't disguise the hurt.

There was another peal of laughter.

'I don't think so, I'm not nearly brave enough. To be honest, I think I'll probably fly home tomorrow.'

'Tomorrow?!' It popped out like a mismanaged champagne cork.

'Yes, tomorrow. I'll never know what happened to her, but I'll live with it.'

Knight ran into a sudden turbulence.

He heard himself saying, 'There's nothing to stop me going up to the farm'. She was working her thumb in tiny circles around the nape of his neck, while her hand caressed his scalp. 'Honestly, it'll take no time at all.'

'No, I can't allow it.'

'Really, it's nothing, I promise you!'

She came and sat beside him. Her eyes were full of wonder, as if they had discovered something profound.

'You really mean that, don't you?'

'Yes, of course.'

She reached out and put her hand on his cheek.

'I think you're an extraordinary man, and I believe if anyone can find him it's going to be you.' She took an audible breath, as if steeling herself for a fateful decision.

'All right, I'll stay for a few more days. Thank you.'

She leaned forward and kissed him on the cheek.

Knight was in a daze as he served the coffee. Soon after that she had to leave. At the door, she kissed him again and begged him to be careful.

On autopilot, he drifted around the flat and tidied up, somehow remembering to turn the heating off. When he cleared the plates he noted how cleanly she had picked her half of the lobster. As he scraped its remains into the bin, the severed head slipped away and fell onto the floor. He picked it up and held it for a moment. The blackened eye sockets stared at him balefully, as if conveying an accusation or possibly a warning. He found it somehow offensive and threw it unceremoniously into the bin.

Walking back to her hotel, Lolly felt a familiar glow of satisfaction. She had perhaps overdone things with the bodybuilder reference; it was always hard at the outset to judge how much encouragement they needed. She sensed she had done enough, but there was certainly nothing about him that disinclined her to do more if required.

Chapter Nineteen

The cold light of day did little to persuade Knight that he had acted irrationally. It was right to help a bereaved woman in her quest for the truth, despite the unruly stirrings she provoked. He did not intend to discuss his findings with Merv, whose take on such matters was invariably one-dimensional. As to the stirrings, they were a cross he was prepared to bear.

He had thus come to an arrangement with himself. The question of the flat would be postponed for a further two days while he found out what more he could about Rupert Askew. He was well aware that he was holding the flimsiest of threads, but he liked the familiar feel of it between his fingers, the wait for the faintest tug.

The farm began to the north of the railway and spread out over a hundred acres or so of West Sussex. When he came to the bridge he slowed down, picturing the rails beneath it with the snow falling outside. Today it was unremarkable, as was the road along which he had trudged to the pub. A little further on, he took a narrow lane to the north.

Todhurst Manor Farm lay on a plain that rose to a wooded hill at its far extremity. Over centuries the soil had dutifully churned out bread and meat for the surrounding populace while lining the pockets of its owners, including the Askew family and now a Qatari investor. From the lane he turned down a track past frost-tinted fields to a cluster of grey buildings. It was an efficient, charmless place, a metal barn flanked by a newish grain hopper and a prefabricated bungalow. Knight arranged his notes and eased himself back into the character of Godfrey Lyle, amateur historian.

To the farm manager, the visit was a welcome distraction. He lived alone in the bungalow, his wife having had her fill of country life and upped sticks. He happily shared what knowledge he had, but it wasn't much more than what Knight already knew. The farm had been sold by Irene Askew to the sheikh's property company some twenty years ago. Since then it had been run by a succession of managers, of whom he was the most recent. He didn't know what had happened to Mrs Askew or her son, nor was he aware of their importance in the history of local farming. Knight was beginning to fear that the journey had been wasted when he revealed the gem he had been saving.

'I do have someone here who can tell you a lot more though. Old Bert used to work for the family. In fact, he should be here now. I told him to come and join us.'

He tried calling, but either Bert wasn't answering or the signal had failed again. They walked down the side of the metal barn. The first section was filled with towers of hay bales, the next with vehicles and then a lambing pen. It was all on an industrial scale that banished any idyllic vision of duckponds or blazing log fires in an ancient house. That was what was missing, Knight realised, a farmhouse. The prefabricated bungalow was too new for the Askews to have lived there, so where was it?

'Bert's been here ever since they sold up,' the manager was explaining. 'The company sort of inherited him and then found it couldn't do without him. I know I couldn't.'

Beyond the barn was a low, featureless building with a corrugated iron roof. It had the air of a punishment barracks, compounded by a sickly sweet smell that grew stronger as they approached. Inside were a dozen or so pig pens, their occupants arranged in ascending order of size. It reminded Knight of school, the first formers gambolling chaotically about their enclosure while the seniors truffled for stray food pellets and occasionally snapped at each other. At the far end was a door on which hung a rusty piece of metal, inscribed with the name of the occupant on the other side, one Boris.

'That's where he'll be,' the manager announced. 'You're not squeamish are you?'

Knight assured him that he wasn't. The door opened into a private enclosure about ten feet square, carpeted with filthy straw.

'Bert, did you not get my call?'

Bert turned from what he was doing. He was a mountain of a man, well into his sixties, with eyes set much too far behind his forehead for

119

Knight's comfort. He put down the plastic jug he was holding and took a battered phone from his overalls. Meanwhile his other hand continued with its task.

He was kneeling amidst the straw next to a pig several times the size of the largest ones in the pens. It was a male, as evidenced by what remained clamped in Bert's other hand while he inspected the cracked screen of his phone.

'Sorry Mr Gordon, didn't hear it go off.'

'This is Mr Lyle, the gentleman I told you about.'

To Knight's relief, he didn't offer to shake hands.

'Very pleased to meet you, sir. I hope you don't mind if I carry on. Boris doesn't like it if he is interrupted.'

'Boris is the father of all the pigs you saw next door,' the manager informed Knight proudly. 'He doesn't get on the sows much anymore though; it's so much more efficient to do it this way.'

Boris didn't seem to mind. His head and the front half of his torso lay flat on what looked like a small vaulting horse, but which Knight recognised from his grandparents' farm as a dummy sow. His eyes were closed and he lay perfectly still, apparently untroubled by the notion that this might be second best.

'I understand that you worked for the Askews,' Knight ventured, averting his eyes from Bert's ministrations.

Bert beamed warmly, if somewhat inanely, at the author.

'A very fine family,' he replied reverently, 'one of the best. If you worked for the Askews in them days you was counted lucky.'

He spoke slowly, with a rare trace of what had once been the local accent, stretching the vowels and missing out the t's.

'And the son, Rupert, you must have known him when he was a boy. What do you remember about him?'

Bert's eyes lit up.

'Oh, young master Rupert. Lovely boy he was, always ready with a smile and a wave. I can see him now, riding over the fields on his pony, bless his little heart.'

It didn't sound like the Rupert that Knight had heard about.

'What about Giles Askew? What was he like?'

'Oh, he was a fine man too. Every Christmas he saw to it that we had a pudding and a bottle of whisky. And the puddings was all made in the farm kitchen, better than anything you ever had from a shop. And what they'd do, they'd put a couple of half crowns in the pudding so you had a bit of extra money to spend on Boxing Day. And then…'

'That's very interesting, Bert,' Knight broke in. 'It must have been a terrible shock when he took his life.'

The pig man shook his head mournfully.

'It was a hard time, but they kept themselves to themselves mostly. I just came in and did my job you see, that's what we all did. Now my foreman, old Sid, he could have told you a lot more but he's dead now, went a good ten years ago. What happened was the doctors…'

He went off on another ramble, all the while attending to Boris and collecting the offerings in the jug. Knight became desperate for a change of air and scenery. Bert was a dead end.

'They must have been very grateful to have you. I don't suppose you know what happened to Rupert or his mother after the farm was sold?'

'No sir. I never saw them again.'

'Where exactly did they live? I'd imagined them in a big house but there's only the bungalow now and it looks quite recent.'

Bert frowned.

'Oh no, they didn't live here, not a family like them, they was up at the manor. Very fine house that, and I've heard it said…'

'It's on the northern boundary on the other side of the hill,' the manager interrupted, sensing Knight's frustration.

'But you don't live in it?'

'I wish,' he said ruefully. 'The company sold it a couple of years ago along with a bit of the forestry land. What's the name of the old lady who lives there, Bert, the one you do odd jobs for?'

'That'd be Mrs Fisher, sir.'

'And who lived in it before her?' Knight enquired of the manager again, despairing of getting any sense from Bert.

'No one. The company wanted the managers to be down here so they left it empty. There was talk of the Sheikh using it but I don't think it was big enough for him. I expect that's why they sold it in the end.'

The conversation was brought to an abrupt halt by an ear-splitting eruption from next door. It seemed a fight had broken out in the fifth form, a serious one given the alacrity with which Bert abandoned his task and raced away to restore order. Alarmed by the vehemence of the squealing, the manager followed him.

'Sorry about this,' he apologised, 'Bert might need some help.'

Knight had no desire to witness the spectacle. What he had seen already was depressing enough, added to which was a suspicion that, on some counts, Boris could be said to have enjoyed a more successful sex life than his own.

Boris himself had opened one eye. Added to the curtailment of his pleasure, the shrill cacophony from his offspring confirmed that something was wrong. In his mind, the wrongness was strongly associated with the stranger standing before him. He clambered off his indifferent paramour.

At first, it struck Knight as entirely normal that the pig might wish to stretch its limbs after its long sojourn on the dummy. Even as it approached, he assumed it wanted merely to say hello, as a dog might. A vicious bite on his calf suggested otherwise. He backed off, attempting to prod the animal away with his stick. Yet the more he prodded the more infuriated the pig became. Intent on wrapping its jaws around Knight's thigh, it charged vigorously.

A hundred kilos of unfettered id sprang upon Knight, snapping at his face and neck. He rolled himself into a ball, his shouts for help drowned out by the squealing multitude on the other side of the door. If he had stopped to think, he might have realised that the safest course of action would be to play dead, but his instinct was to inflict pain, to counter savagery with savagery. Lashing out blindly, his hand caught hold of something gristly. Not knowing or caring what it was, he pulled it with all his might.

The technique worked, though not as Knight had intended. Rather than run away squealing, Boris rolled off Knight and lay on the straw beside him. Hoping to drive the beast further away, he repeated the ploy. Boris closed his eyes.

Only now understanding the true nature of his deliverance, Knight hastily relinquished his hold. Grabbing his stick, he crawled hurriedly away towards the door. It was evidently not an outcome that Boris found acceptable. One eye opened again.

Bert and the manager were removing the ringleaders when Knight crashed through the door with the prize boar in pursuit. With a surprising turn of speed, Bert sprang from the pen and launched himself on top of Boris like a forward going into a ruck in front of the goalposts. He was plainly no stranger to the process. As Knight fled the building with the mortified farm manager behind him, the last thing he saw was Boris hanging upside down in Bert's massive arms, wriggling violently but ineffectually on his way back to the bedroom.

*

Ten minutes later, Knight sat in a layby, regretting his refusal of the offer of a clean coat. Fending off questions and apologies, he had leapt into his car and driven like the wind until a glance at the speedometer warned him to get a grip. Now that he had, he felt little better. Failure he could take, if grudgingly, but for it to be accompanied by an abasement even worse than the experience with Grice left him on the brink of despair.

There was only one way to recover a small scrap of recompense for his efforts, and that was to see inside the house where Rupert Askew had spent his childhood. Mrs Fisher would know nothing, but something might have been left behind, some random fragment of the Askews' life that would let him move another step closer. Clinging to the fast-disintegrating thread, he started the engine.

After a mile, the lane began to climb, the fields giving way to oak and birch. At the crest, the woodland continued downhill to a patch of open meadow and spread out again beneath it. The farmhouse stood behind the meadow in the lee of the hill.

Knight stopped and looked through the bare trees. It was a seventeenth-century manor house with tall skinny chimneys and dark columns of leaded glass, something he might see in *Country Life* while waiting at the dentist.

An ungated driveway led through the meadow to a landscaped garden that surrounded the house. The lawn at the front was dominated by a huge oak tree. Counting the first-floor windows, he reckoned there must be at least six bedrooms. As a manor house it was modest by the standards of its time, but it struck him as an odd choice of place to live alone.

He rang the bell and waited. At the end of the driveway was a barn that possibly served as a garage, but the doors were closed. Peering through the windows on either side of the front door, he saw an elegantly furnished sitting room and a kitchen with a long oak table and a modern Aga. When there was no response, he took a walk around the house. At the back he could see a large billiard room and a pantry that backed onto the kitchen. There was also a padlocked trapdoor which must have been used for taking deliveries down to a cellar. Behind him, a kitchen garden ran down the hillside to where the woods began again. It was the setting for a perfect childhood, an opportunity that had been grossly squandered. Resolving to come back another day, he returned to the car.

At the last moment, out of habit, he turned quickly and scanned the windows. On the first floor, a woman's face moved back sharply behind the curtain.

A degree of belligerence overcame him. He was not in the habit of imposing on elderly ladies, but he had promised himself the small consolation prize of seeing inside the house and was not going to be denied.

A little after the third ring, the door opened a few inches. Behind the chain he could make out a heavily wrinkled face between a neat perm and a tweed suit. Far from objecting to his presence, she stared through the narrow gap in a mildly curious way without saying a word.

Knight apologised profusely for the intrusion and briefly explained his interest in the Askews.

'I'm Godfrey Lyle by the way, sorry, should have said.' He smiled charmingly. 'How do you do?'

Still, she said nothing.

'You are Mrs Fisher, is that right?'

Her eyes flickered in recognition of something. He had a better idea of the face now, a pointed chin and a thin nose that gave her a faintly avian appearance.

'Yes,' she said, with a smile which exposed dark yellow teeth and gums worse than his. He repeated his request for a few minutes of her time and a chance to see something of the house.

'Who are you?' There was a meekness about the way she spoke, as if she were a child asking an adult to explain something. With a sinking heart; he repeated his name.

'What have you come about?'

Knight recoiled. He was not at his best in the presence of dementia, a fate he dreaded as much as Merv dreaded the police.

'Mrs Fisher,' he said slowly, as if to the child he had heard. 'I wanted to see your house because I'm writing a book.'

She frowned, as if struggling to make any sense at all of what he had said. It seemed all the more incredible that she should be alone in this place.

'Mrs Fisher, is there someone who comes and looks after you, a carer perhaps?'

There was another flicker of recognition. She raised a bony forefinger and pointed at him.

'You're not the carer. You smell.'

There may well have been a way to gain her confidence and enter the house, but he wasn't even tempted. It barely bothered him to feel the thread snap. There were only two things he wanted now: to forget this day had happened, and to have a bath.

Chapter Twenty

Merv scrubbed the deck of *Adrenaline Rush*, shifting the grime that had built up during his stewardship. A conveyor belt of squalls from the Atlantic had kept him off the sea for several days, making him glad of the money he had shared with Knight. He had seen nothing of O'Driscoll and didn't expect to, now that a video disc of his threats had been left on the windscreen of the *King of Sussex*. For this too he had Knight to thank.

The only shadow over an otherwise satisfactory state of affairs was a sixth sense that Knight was up to something. It wasn't anything he had said, but rather what he hadn't, an evasiveness that crept in when asked how he had spent his day or what he planned for the next. But short of asking him outright what he was playing at, there was little he could do about it. Seeking solace in a fry-up, he drove into town.

The place he had in mind was a greasy spoon a couple of streets back from the beach. As he approached, he recalled that Knight had pointed out Lolly's hotel on the way back from the Fishermen's Club. It was not far beyond the turning to the café. On a whim, he ignored the turning and drove on.

Outside the hotel, the traffic had come to a standstill. For once he didn't object; it gave him time to stare up at the bedroom windows, idly speculating which one of them might be hers. If he'd been on a job for Knight it would have taken him two seconds to invent a reason for an unannounced visit. But his mind was a blank, stalled as it was in the memory of the blown kiss. He was woken from his reverie by the sight of a woman waving at him energetically from the pavement in front of the hotel entrance. It was her. Judging by the Marks and Spencer bag in her other hand, she was returning from a shopping trip.

Merv was paralysed by indecision. The traffic was moving again; he could wave back and drive on by, or he could... what? As he dithered, drawing slowly away, she solved the dilemma by pointing into the hotel and beckoning him to follow her.

He left the van in a side street and hurried back, resisting the urge to run. On entering the hotel lobby, he felt self-conscious in his grubby overalls. The odd looks were instantly forgotten when he spotted her in the bar, her smile guiding him in like a tractor beam.

The smile faded when he was close enough for her to see the bruises on his face.

'Oh my god,' she exclaimed, 'what happened to you?'

'Not a lot.' He tried to make it sound breezy. 'Little difference of opinion with someone. No big deal.'

'Not with Tom?' she asked anxiously.

It might have seemed an odd question had he not been fixated on the low-cut leopard print camisole that appeared when she took off her jacket.

'No course not, no big deal. All sorted.' She seemed relieved to hear it.

'Would you like something?'

He asked for coffee. She caught the waiter's eye in a second, faster than he ever did, though he was not to know that the eye in question had been glued to her since she checked in.

'I owe you an apology,' she confessed, once Paco had departed, casting a disapproving look at Merv as he went. 'I panicked, and I know now I didn't need to.' There was an earnestness that made it impossible not to forgive her.

'One of those things,' he shrugged.

'And are you okay? No problems or anything? You know.'

He was taken aback by the frankness of the question. The parts to which she had referred responded appreciatively, adding to his confusion.

'No, I'm fine,' he replied, awkwardly.

She put her hand to her mouth, as if she had committed a faux pas.

'Oh dear, I've embarrassed you, haven't I? I'm sorry, I'm like that with bodies, you get a bit blasé when you spend half your life stark naked.'

Paco caught the last sentence as he delivered the coffee and raised an eyebrow. She ignored him.

'So, you're Tom's right-hand man. That must be exciting.'

Merv confirmed that it was. She listened with rapt attention as he recounted various incidents that showed him in a favourable light. It was a unique experience to sit with a woman as beautiful as this and be the sole focus of her attention. Even his ex, a looker in her day, had never taken a comparable interest. 'How amazing,' she murmured once or twice, and then when he had finished, 'I'm so glad he has you at his side. I can't tell you how grateful I am for that.'

The doubt he had been nursing took form at last.

'He's, er, not working for you at the moment though, is he?'

She looked wrong-footed.

'I… well, I assumed you knew. He's been looking into a couple of things for me, yes. Did he not say anything to you about it?'

'No, nothing.'

'Or about me?'

He shook his head, unable to disguise the shock, or rather the disappointment. She backtracked quickly, downgrading the scale of Knight's activities, but Merv was not to be thrown off so easily.

'So what exactly has he done for you?' He knew Knight wouldn't have approved of the question, but that was Knight's problem. Lolly outlined the steps he had taken in searching for Rupert Askew, still attempting to downplay their importance. Merv listened with mounting disquiet.

'Well, he hasn't said anything to me about it.' A petulance had crept into his voice. 'But I've told him I'm busy, so he's probably holding off until he knows I've got more time.'

She nodded sagely.

'I think you're absolutely right. I mean, you're his enforcer aren't you, so he only calls you in when things become serious, isn't that how it is?'

Merv had never thought of himself as Knight's enforcer; he warmed to the idea.

'Yeah, that's about it. I don't mind a bit of rough stuff now and then.'

She smiled knowingly. 'That's what I thought the first time I saw you. I can read bodies you see, and when I looked at you I could see the strength immediately. You weren't ever a bodybuilder were you?'

Merv was tempted to embellish his CV still further, until he saw that the truth was more flattering.

'No, I guess it's just the way I am.'

'Lucky you.' The imp came out to play, flashing a conspiratorial smile that might have meant more. Merv's mood improved considerably.

'So, how did you get into dancing then?'

'Oh that. Very long story, very boring. But you'd be good at it, I can tell.'

'What me?' He was relaxed enough to laugh now.

'Yes, you.' She laughed with him. 'Don't look so surprised.' It seemed she had suddenly been visited by some kind of inspiration, for her eyes widened and her mouth dropped slightly open.

'Now, there's a thought,' she mused. Merv waited for enlightenment.

'You see, I'm still trying to think of a way of making up for the very bad thing I did to you, and maybe that's it.'

'That's what?'

'Just a minute.'

She reached across the table and squeezed his biceps firmly.

'Oh, yes!' It was said with the pride of someone discovering a fact that proves them right. She put her hand on his and squeezed it more softly than she had his arm.

'You know, I think you really might like it if I gave you a lesson.'

*

On the other side of town, Bullock clung to the handrail of the running machine, head bowed in contemplation of his pounding feet. Occasionally obscuring the view, his stomach hung like a sack, bouncing with each stride. It was a bigger sack, he noted, than when he had last been to the gym a year ago.

He wasn't quite sure what had prompted the spontaneous visit; most likely frustration with his work. The drowned girl remained unidentified, despite the hours he had spent liaising with do-gooders at homeless hostels and missing persons charities.

Another possible explanation for his presence in the gym was the belief that he was on a promise, if the encounter in the hotel bar was anything to go by. Lolly had made several excuses when he asked her to meet him there, so instead he had waited for her one evening when he knew she was in. She had made more excuses but agreed to one quick drink, during which he progressed as far as getting a hand on her thigh.

Katya had slapped him for less, but Lolly had merely rolled her eyes and called him naughty, before shifting his hand to his lap and somehow flitting away before he could object. That, to Bullock, was a promise, and with it she entered the legion of women who in his eyes were destined to have sex with him.

He stumbled off the treadmill to the chest press. It too seemed harder than before, even after he reduced the weight. The seat felt smaller, the resistance more stubborn as he thrust the handles away and hauled them back into his chest. In an unusual act of deferred gratification, he decided to give it another ten minutes before going for a beer.

*

Merv's arms were aching, but his hands were locked in place by the chalk. On her command, he stretched his legs out in front of him.

'Remember to breathe,' she called. 'And smile.'

He fixed his face in a rictus grin and sucked through his teeth.

'That is so beautiful! Now lift and wrap your legs round the pole.'

The muscles in his thighs and abdomen locked tight again as he raised his legs a further forty-five degrees. On the previous attempts she had helped at this point, now he had to do it alone. With a cry that could have come from a delivery ward he forced his legs ever upwards, like the hand of a clock creeping towards twelve. His body convulsed as he made one last heroic effort, and his toe touched the pole.

The sheer relief of getting there undid him. His legs flopped and his hands came away, but already she had arms wrapped around him so that he did not fall.

'You are amazing,' she whispered. 'I've never seen a man do it so easily the first time.'

Merv forgot his failure to complete the task. He was conscious of her body pressed hard against his, only now slowly decoupling as she took a step back and admired him. He could smell something flowery.

'Why don't you take a shower and I'll check you haven't hurt your back?'

He was pretty sure that was what she had said.

'Yeah, why not?' he heard himself reply, and floated in a trance to the bathroom.

The assault of hot water brought him back to his senses enough to take stock of what was happening, or rather what might happen next. Whatever it was, the answer was yes. His last brush with romance had been a one-night stand with the burger lady from the dog track, who had out-drunk him comprehensively only to take the shine off things by being sick in the early hours. Here he was in a dream from which he never wished to wake. He dried himself with a towel several times the size of any that he possessed and prepared for the next instalment.

There was, however, the question of what to wear. He hadn't bothered with jeans under the overalls, and his boxers, while clean, were fraying around the elastic. The towel, he realised, represented the best of both worlds. It was a sop to modesty if modesty was required, and easier to discard than the boxers if not. Holding his stomach in, he wrapped the towel around it and sallied forth.

'Anything hurting?' she enquired, as she led him to the bed.

In truth, nothing hurt. He'd felt a sharp pull on his back and shoulders when they briefly took the weight of his tumbling legs, but the combined effect of the shower and his anticipation of what lay in store relegated the pain to a dim memory.

'A bit stiff in a couple of places,' he answered cheerfully, though regretting the choice of words. 'But it's all good. What do you want me to do?'

She told him to lie on his front with his legs apart, so that she could kneel between them.

'I'm just going to check you haven't damaged any tissue. I doubt it, though, your body's in incredible shape.'

Lightly placing her fingers on his shoulder blades she rotated her thumbs in the flesh below, softly to begin with, then pushing into the knotted muscle, kneading and stretching, a cocktail of pain and pleasure hitherto unknown to him.

'Sorry, was that too hard?'

'No,' he lied, 'hard as you like.'

The way ahead unfolded in his mind. When she finished with his back she would ask him to turn over. She would smear the oil on his chest, rubbing it in firmly at first, then applying a lighter touch as she worked down to his stomach and finally the towel, which she would surely remove. Already his vision was gaining in credibility; the pressure had eased off and her fingertips were tracing a figure of eight that shifted up and down, criss-crossing his spine and once or twice brushing against the towel barrier. He willed her to dismantle it, but instead she murmured into his ear.

'You know, I meant it when I said I was glad Tom has you by his side.' She said it as if the thought had just entered her head. 'It means a lot to me to know you'll be there when he needs you.'

It wasn't quite the direction he'd imagined the conversation would take, but he wasn't about to disagree.

'Course, I'll be there. As long as the old bugger asks me.'

'Oh he will. And then…' Her fingers reached the towel again, nudging it half an inch lower. 'And then I'll be in your debt. I won't forget that.'

Her voice came closer. He inhaled the flowery essence, as much of it as he could take down.

'What I'm saying is, Merv, I need you. Do you understand that?'

'Yeah,' he mumbled hoarsely. The figure of eight was nearing the towel again.

There was a knock at the door.

She removed her hands as if they'd strayed into a flame. 'Shit,' she muttered. 'Who is it?'

'Delivery,' boomed a voice that sounded unpleasantly familiar.

Bullock knew she was in because one of the cleaners was keeping him informed on pain of having her visa renewal blocked. It didn't strike him as impolite to turn up uninvited; it merely ensured she wouldn't have to worry about looking easy by agreeing to a date. He found that many women felt inhibited in this way. Besides, in a rare concession to gallantry, he had stopped at a petrol station and bought flowers. It took a moment to sink in, after he'd said 'surprise' and proffered the wilting bouquet, that she wasn't especially pleased to see him.

'Detective Constable!' she exclaimed, with a note of panic. 'This really isn't a good time.'

'Course it is,' he reassured her. Out of habit he took a step into the room but she was too quick and closed the door on his foot, quite painfully.

'Don't be like that,' he cajoled. 'Here.' He pushed the flowers through the narrow gap.

'No! I said, it's not a good time!'

Something wasn't right. He was always prepared for a bit of token resistance, but she had lost her composure in a way that didn't make sense, until a disturbing possibility occurred to him.

'You got someone in there?' It was his work voice.

Merv had so far lain silent. His first reaction on realising who the visitor was had been to hide, but it was swiftly overtaken by the appeal she had made to him less than a minute earlier. It was a clarion call, surely, to grow a pair. He sprang from the bed and went to her side just as Bullock forced the door open. He gaped at Merv in disbelief then rounded on Lolly.

'What is he doing here?'

Merv was seized by the zeal of the righteous.

'What does it look like?' he roared.

Never far beneath the surface, the rhino in Bullock broke free. He charged blindly at Merv with some vague notion of expelling him from his territory.

Merv hit peak testosterone. As Bullock lunged, he swung his head as he had done in many a bar fight and nutted him on the bridge of his nose. Lolly screamed.

Bullock screamed too and staggered away with his face in his hands. 'You're under arrest,' he managed to whimper, though showing no inclination to come back for more. As he stumbled through the caution, Lolly went to him and prised his fingers apart.

'Steve, are you all right? Oh my god!' Bullock's nose was bleeding copiously.

'He's under arrest,' the servant of the people insisted. Lolly motioned urgently at Merv to leave and took Bullock's hand in hers.

'No darling, you can't do that,' she cooed. 'It was you who started it and that's what I'll have to say if anyone asks me. Now come.'

She led him to the bathroom, protesting but not resisting. At the door, she turned back to Merv.

'Another time,' she mouthed, before disappearing inside.

Merv's valour had drained fast since the moment of impact. He was aware of having crossed a dangerous line; also that the towel had fallen off some time ago. Much that it pained him to abandon the field to Bullock, he dressed swiftly and left. Another time, she had said. Amen to that.

Lolly wiped away the blood and staunched the flow with an earbud, tutting and cooing all the while. He wasn't the first savage beast she had soothed, and wouldn't be the last.

'There was nothing to be upset about,' she chided him gently. 'I was giving him a lesson, that's all.'

'You what?'

'I was teaching him on the pole, it's part of what I do, silly.' The rage seemed to be subsiding.

'You give lessons?'

'Yes, why not? Now stay still.'

She anointed his nose with the cheapest cream she had. There was a tightrope to be walked here; if she tried to get rid of him too quickly he would become angry again, but if she lingered too long he would rediscover his purpose. Already his hands were starting to wander. Reluctantly, she recognised that a sacrifice would have to be made.

'You can have a lesson too if you want. But not right now, and only if you're good.'

Five minutes later he was gone, though not without an ungainly tussle at the door which required her to unclamp his hands from her bottom while somehow feigning a fit of giggles.

She flung herself down on the bed, exhausted. Bullock was becoming a serious distraction. It didn't bear thinking what could happen if she complained and he retaliated by running a check on her; he had to be kept sweet. But Merv, at least, was onside now, of that she felt confident. Anything or anyone who tilted the odds in Knight's favour had to be seized upon without hesitation. It was, after all, a question of justice.

Chapter Twenty-One

In other circumstances, Knight would have welcomed Merv's new interest in Clementine's death. It had surprised him to hear Merv concede that he may have been wrong in his approach to it, and how he had begun to share Knight's unease about leaving the matter with Bullock.

If there had been anything useful for Merv to do, he might have accepted the offer to help him take another look. As it was, he preferred to keep his disappointment to himself, and with it the quandary he faced. He did not wish to reveal to Lolly that he had hit a brick wall. If he called her, he would be obliged to tell her, which meant there would be no further reason for her to stay. But if he didn't, he feared she might leave anyway, quite possibly without telling him. Trapped in a no man's land of indecision, he found himself on Google Earth again.

From the road the house was barely visible. The aerial view showed the garden and meadow in high summer, a tranquil idyll for the rich tucked away from prying eyes. He moved over the house, the distorted chimneys looming up like malformed limbs. At the back was the kitchen garden he had seen, beyond it the woods where Rupert had once played, or hidden from his violent father.

The shot had been taken in early summer. The trees were in full leaf but spaced far enough apart to reveal an occasional patch of the woodland floor. When it dissolved into a blur of pixels he scrolled on, peering into the hidden depths of the wood as if some primordial Beast of Sussex might be hidden there, fully aware that he was procrastinating.

It was the beast's eye he spotted first, or rather a smudge like a leopard's spot, caught in a ray of light that had briefly penetrated the lower reaches. What struck him was how the colours were at odds with their surroundings. The centre of the eye was black, and around it were streaks of brown and purple mixed in with green. To Knight it looked oddly autumnal.

He saved a screenshot and enlarged it. The result was a formless array of dark tones, strikingly inappropriate to the season. At a certain resolution he could see the colours being repeated. It was a pattern he dimly remembered, but his memory stubbornly refused to say from where.

He made a hasty deal: if half an hour's contemplation took him no further he would admit defeat and go to the estate agent. Half an hour became three quarters, and then an hour. At one stage he dozed off for a few minutes, awaking none the wiser. At last, he sprang from the sofa, unnerved that the day was slipping through his fingers.

*

The estate agent's office was deserted save for an elderly woman deep in conversation with a man in a dull grey suit. Irritated that there was no one else to see him, Knight sat down and waited.

From what he could hear, the woman's husband had died and she was going to live in Doncaster with her daughter, a prospect she viewed with some trepidation. The adviser oozed sympathy. She was doing the right thing, and fortunate to be doing it in the current market rather than in a year when the market would definitely drop. Listening to the hogwash, Knight was reminded of the obnoxious investor at the property seminar. When the word 'bungalow' was mentioned, it was all he could do not to get up and leave.

The woman sat facing away from him. From her voice it was hard to guess her age, but what convinced him she must be truly ancient was the hairnet. He had not noticed it before, the finely woven strands all but matching the dark hair beneath. Shapeless and drab, it drew him in, adding to his disquiet much as Clementine Lever's plait had done. He pictured himself taking her place somewhere in the dreary extremities of the town while she descended to the next level, the last if she was lucky. But there was something else about it. In the way it clung to her head, it provided the jog to his memory that told him what he had seen beneath the trees next to Rupert Askew's old home. It was a camouflage net.

Forty minutes later, he found the dirt track which led from the lane into the woods, a few hundred yards below the house. The estate agent had practically pleaded with him to stay, easily detecting the insincerity of his promise to return later. Feeling no remorse whatever at having abandoned his mission, he skirted alongside the track to avoid leaving footprints. Soon he came to a padlocked gate and a fence with a sign prohibiting trespassers. He didn't fancy a climb, but his pick slid into the cheap padlock virtually unchallenged. He felt a familiar satisfaction as the tumblers moved aside and the shackle sprang open.

It was only mid-afternoon, but under the flat grey clouds that threatened further snow an eerie twilight prevailed. Little had been done to manage the woodland. Between the oaks and chestnuts, large patches of bramble and holly had been allowed to flourish, denying him a clear view through the trees. He didn't see the second fence until he was nearly upon it. It stood about ten feet high, with a slanted crown of barbed wire and a gate wide enough for a vehicle to pass through. Beyond it, covered in camouflage netting, was a low building. He was about to take a closer look when he noticed the camera on top of a fence post, pointed at the track.

Shrinking back into the trees, he inspected it through his binoculars. It was a make he recognised, a low-cost model that didn't offer a motion detector. But it usually came with a sixty-degree lens; it might well have caught him. He recognised the lock on the gate too. It was an altogether more serious proposition than the one he had just picked; well beyond his capabilities.

Keeping under cover, he followed the line of the fence in a rough circle around the building. The netting covered the roof and the top half. It was a timber structure, oak planking he thought, with solid shutters over the windows. On one side was a door under the eaves. It was much more than a shed; it was some kind of cabin or summerhouse. A cannabis farm even.

There were three more cameras. If he was right about the lenses, they covered all of the perimeter save for a gap opposite the back of the cabin. Someone had skimped or miscalculated; he put his money on a cowboy consultant. Yet the intention was serious: whoever owned this place had gone to extreme lengths to shut out the world. If there was an innocent explanation, which in his mind would include a cannabis farm, it was inside the summerhouse and he wanted to see it for himself.

He moved behind a sprawling holly tree where he thought the gap was. Peering through the leaves, he saw a sensor wire embedded in the fence. Remembering Merv's offer of assistance, he took out his phone but put it away again. For reasons he couldn't identify, he wanted to keep this for himself a little longer.

If he couldn't get through the fence, he could at least see what happened when the alarm was activated. Not far from where he stood was a fallen tree that had been left to rot. Without much difficulty, he prised away a branch as thick as his arm. It was about the length of a javelin. The last time he had held one, more than half a century ago, he had achieved a creditable second place. Trying to recall the optimal stance, he took up a position a few yards behind the holly. The problem wasn't so much the weight or even the height of the tree, it was the sodden earth that denied him a run-up. He swayed backward and forward, arching his back until it hurt, and let fly. The tip of the missile disappeared into the topmost branches, leading him to assume he had failed, but a moment later he heard a clatter as it hit the fence. He braced himself for the blare of a siren, but there was none.

Retracing his steps, he fell back to the first gate. He had left his car further up the lane and wanted to be as close to it as he could, but with a view of the track. He reasoned that, if anyone came, they would arrive by road, the only other building in the vicinity being Mrs Fisher's house. She was an unlikely cannabis farmer, unless that was what had done for her memory. A few yards off the track beyond the fence was a thicket of brambles, dense enough even in its leafless state to render him invisible. He tore into it, ripping aside the spiky tendrils with the hook of his stick until there was a gap big enough to shuffle into, feet first on his backside. Through the loose network of tendrils in front of him, he could see the gate less than twenty yards away.

Normally, he would have assessed the potential drawbacks of his strategy. The fence could be faulty, or whoever owned the alarm might decide an animal was responsible. More to the point, if he had miscalculated the camera angles, they would almost certainly have a picture of his face. None of it mattered. A mild mania had overtaken him since his departure from the estate agent, triggering a compulsion to break free and damn the consequences.

A vehicle was approaching. The engine note changed as it slowed down. He willed it to turn onto the track, but it picked up speed again and accelerated out of the bend.

After half an hour, his spirits remained mostly undimmed. He decided that if no one came in the next ten minutes he would return and break in at night. If somebody did appear, he would follow them. Either way, he would make it his business to find out what was in a camouflaged summerhouse less than half a mile from Rupert Askew's old home.

More cars passed. Ten minutes turned to twenty before the mania eased off enough for him to consider a tactical withdrawal; for example to the relative comfort of his car. However, he had pushed himself into such a tight cavity that the brambles were now firmly ensnared in his coat and refusing to release him. With barely any elbow room, he hacked with his stick at the stalks he could reach, frantically trying to enlarge the space around him. He began to feel a sense of déjà vu, with Grice and the pig mocking him as he blundered afresh into a new fiasco. After several minutes of exhausting effort, he had carved out enough extra volume to accommodate a small dog. As he paused to draw breath, he heard a car approaching.

It changed gears and slowed down as the others had done; then came a muted splash as its tyres hit the wet track.

Chapter Twenty-Two

Knight peered through the creepers. Somehow in his thrashings he had obscured the view, for now all he could see was the side of a silver car and a dark coat next to the gate. A male voice broke the silence, speaking in what sounded like Arabic.

Abandoning his attempts to shift the bramble, he flicked the switch beneath the metal crook and hoisted his stick cautiously. A touch on the screen of his phone brought up a flickering image of an Audi. Knight turned the periscope slowly until he could see the owner's back. He was about six foot two, well-built, with shiny black hair that hung over the collar of his coat. The gate swung open and he turned back to the car, looking straight into the lens. It was a well-fed, sensual face in its late twenties or early thirties. The car moved off down the track.

Throwing caution to the wind, Knight tore savagely at his spiky prison, flailing and stamping until he had ripped himself free of the last tendrils. Pulling the broken stalks from his coat, he hurried back to his car. The Audi had come the same way as he had, so the driver would not have seen the Skoda around the bend further up the hill. The bet had to be that he would go back the way he had come. Knight drove down far enough to have a view of where the track joined the road. After a few minutes, the Audi reappeared. As he expected, it headed back towards town. Accelerating loudly, the young man barely glanced in Knight's direction. He waited until the car was out of sight and followed.

Knight raced through the narrow bends in the gathering dusk. Where the lane straightened out, he spotted the Audi a quarter-of-a-mile ahead behind a horsebox. Even if the driver was a pro, he would find it hard to tell if the headlights behind him were from the car that had been parked on the hill. He hung back all the same, allowing one vehicle to overtake him then staying on its tail.

In the busier streets at the edge of the town, it was easier to stay hidden, but as they entered the warren of terraces behind the shopping mall a builder's van blocked his way. He squeezed past, only just catching the Audi's tail-lights as it disappeared into a driveway beside a parade of shops.

Knight drove past and pulled into a space opposite the parade. Half of it was given up to a DIY emporium. Occupying the rest were a Polish supermarket, a kebab shop and a tanning lounge, each of them separated by doors that led to the flats above. He crossed the road and walked slowly to the driveway. It led to a delivery yard, where the Audi was in a slot reserved for the kebab shop.

He walked back along the parade again. There had been a solitary server and a small queue of customers in the kebab shop when he went past a few moments ago, no face that he recognised among them. Now there was an extra body behind the counter. At first the white jacket threw him, but there the young man was, slicing into a tower of dripping meat. Knight retreated to the Skoda, wondering if he'd missed a stray look. There was no reaction, the slicing and serving continued unabated. Keeping an eye on the shop window, he played back the recording.

A secondment to Oman had left him with a smattering of Arabic, not enough to make any sense of what he heard save for one word. Khal. It always came together with Malik, which he knew to be a name. Uncle Malik.

The queue replenished itself enough to keep the servers busy. How was it that a kebab chef was responsible for the security of a jealously protected site in the rural heartland of East Sussex? At a stretch, he could be moonlighting for a security company, though he hadn't arrived in a van or worn a uniform. And how had he received the alarm? He didn't look like he owned the property, so presumably he worked for whoever did. Uncle Malik perhaps.

Now he had his phone to his ear. He was jabbing agitatedly with his free hand, evidently unhappy about something. A moment later, he came out from the counter and made his way to the street. Rather than go to the driveway, he opened the front door next to the shop and disappeared inside. A few moments later a light went on in the first-floor window.

Knight wanted to see inside the flat. The problem was, he didn't know who else lived there, if anyone, and it would take time to find out. But then the light went off again and the young man returned to the street, having changed back into the coat he was wearing earlier. He went to the driveway and after a moment the Audi reappeared.

Knight followed, confident that he hadn't been spotted. For the moment he was content to let events unfold, revelling in the confirmation that his powers remained intact. If it was a blind alley, if it was pure self-indulgence, he didn't care; he had earned a moment of respite and would squeeze every last drop from it.

The target headed east. Reaching the dual carriageway, he darted impatiently from lane to lane, once leaving Knight to guess the way at a roundabout. They seemed to be approaching the northern entrance to Sovereign Harbour.

He felt an odd mixture of confusion and excitement as the Audi turned in, possibly leading him to some bizarre link between the kebab chef and the captain of the *King of Sussex*. The reality proved more mundane; the car took the turning to the retail sheds that graced the fringe of the complex. Knight hung back at the slip road, waiting for cover. When he reached the row of outlets the young man was getting out and making for a sports store. He parked a few rows away and followed him inside.

Crossing the threshold, he was transported into a dense jungle of display stacks, heaving with football shirts and lurid track tops. Taking a baseball cap as he went, he prowled down the narrow aisles between the towers of sweat-shopped merchandise, assailed by the unrelenting thud of drum and bass. Apart from a security man at the front door, the place was all but empty.

He spotted him looking at a display of wetsuits. Bowing his head and pulling the peak of the cap over his face, he inched closer and pretended to inspect some swimming trunks. There was something sullen, he thought, about the young man's body language as he rooted through the hangers and cast his selections into the trolley, almost as if he didn't want to be there. Of more immediate interest, he had taken his coat off and draped it over the trolley's handles.

Knight moved up to the beach towels. The trolley was parked with its handle facing him, a mere two yards away, and the man had his back to him. Taking a selection of towels, he broke cover and dropped them beside the trolley. As he bent to pick them up, the young man glanced round and saw a bent, elderly figure in a filthy coat and a ridiculous cap. He didn't see Knight's hand, under cover of a towel, snaking into the pocket of his coat. Nor would he have been unduly concerned, because that pocket was empty.

Knight fell back to the body boards. He could not repeat the trick; the best he could hope for was to get a shot of a credit card at the checkout, where the reluctant shopper was now heading. He tracked him down a parallel aisle, but then there was a pause at a display of golf clubs. He watched him take down a driver and test the weight.

The display was on a mammoth four-sided stand. Knight shifted cautiously to the side opposite the clubs. The trolley with its beckoning cargo was parked half across the aisle, but the young man didn't have his back to it now. Somehow, he needed to be shifted.

A trio of skinheads had arrived, not by the look of it with any serious buying intent. They were standing by a wall of trainers, arguing loudly about which ones looked gay. Between them and the golf display was a low-rise cluster of shoeboxes, affording a direct line of sight to the golfer as he tested the clubs. Knight saw a move. The potential consequences didn't bear thinking about, but he wasn't thinking; in a matter of seconds the target or the shoe critics would move on.

He took a golf ball from the shelf. There were still no staff to be seen; the cameras he would have to risk. With his second ambitious throw of the day, he hurled the ball at the skinheads and ducked out of sight behind the display.

There was an angry shriek from the largest of the trio, a cadaverous six-footer in last season's Chelsea shirt. It seemed the ball had struck him behind the ear, for which he blamed the one person present who happened to be holding a golf club. The heated denial only added to his anger, fuelling a tirade of insults. While the confrontation raged, Knight scurried down the aisle. The young man had his back to him now, the skinheads' powers of attention were at full stretch. Nobody noticed as he slipped his hand into the other pocket and found not only keys but a wallet.

In the Skoda he rifled through the cards. The man's name was Bahir al-Masri, the address appeared to be the kebab shop. Tucked away in a corner there was also a small badge that might once have been on a uniform. It featured an eagle and some Arabic text which meant nothing to him. As he photographed his haul the skinheads came out and disappeared among the cars, paying no attention to him. Next he turned his attention to the keys, which he photographed against a page of his road atlas to fix their size. A moment later Bahir came out, a look of thunder on his face. While he scoured the ground around the Audi, Knight photographed the last two keys, ready to drive away fast if he was seen. His guess was that Bahir would go back inside the store, but now the skinheads reappeared and gathered around him.

The abandon with which Knight had pursued his quest evaporated as he confronted its unintended consequences. It had seemed safe to assume that no great violence would be committed inside the store, but outside was a different matter. Horrified at what they might do, he decided he had no choice but to intervene.

In the event, his services were not required. When the skinheads closed in on their prey, they were met by a battery of blows and kicks that left them winded and bleeding, one of them clutching his rib cage as he writhed on the ground. It was a polished, clinical display, black belt at least, and mercilessly executed.

His attackers having fled, Bahir went back into the store. With a new respect, and not a little apprehension about any future dealings, Knight drove past the Audi and dropped the wallet and keys beside it.

Chapter Twenty-Three

Merv thought Knight looked shattered. His eyes were struggling to focus and the bags were worse than usual, even for one thirty in the morning. He also had two bandaged fingers.

'You should have said, we could have done them on the vice in the shed.'

'Too late for that now,' Knight grunted.

He had grossly underestimated, or forgotten, how long it took to make keys. His concentration fading, he cut another notch around the pattern he had glued to the top of a tin can. He had checked and rechecked the pattern against the scale of the map; one tiny blemish could render his efforts worthless. Beside him on the desk in his study were three completed Yale keys and one that looked like a miniature axe. This, he guessed, was for the gate or the summerhouse.

'Want me to put some tape over those ends so you don't cut yourself again?'

He accepted gratefully, still surprised at how readily Merv had agreed to help. His apologies for not being able to pay had been brushed aside, nor had there been any mention that the chances of finding Rupert Askew were vanishingly small. If anything, Merv's curiosity was even greater than his own. He was intrigued by the badge, which neither of them could identify, and it was at his suggestion that Knight had posted the image on a collectors' site. Of far greater interest was the ownership of the land. According to the Land Registry, the property and the area around it were held in a Jersey trust, concealing the identity of the owners. In Knight's experience it usually indicated questionable behaviour of some sort, if not outright criminality.

Willing his hand to stay steady, he made one more incision and held the final key up to its counterpart on the laptop screen. It was the double-bladed axe design, similar to the one he had just completed.

'What do you think?'

Merv studied the real key and its screen image, painstakingly adjusted and measured to make it exactly life-sized. He had only seen Knight do this once before; a hurried attempt on a delinquent husband's love nest that had not succeeded. Here the workmanship was of a different order.

'I'd say that's pretty good. You've pushed the boat out for her, haven't you?'

It struck Knight as an odd choice of words.

'How do you mean exactly, pushed the boat out?'

'You know, gone to a lot of trouble. Don't blame you mate, she's a lovely lady.'

As Merv feared, Knight bristled.

'What's that got to do with it? I made a promise and I'm keeping it.'

Sure you are, Merv thought.

'How is she anyway?'

'I don't know. I haven't seen her for a while.'

This was technically true. He had finally called Lolly, trying to sound positive about what he had unearthed. She too was intrigued by the camouflaged building in the middle of the woods though, unlike Merv, she wasn't slow to point out that its proximity to the manor house didn't mean much, given the passage of time. He thought he caught a trace of disappointment in her voice, but she did not say anything more about leaving.

It was gone two in the morning when they reached the kebab shop. The lights were off throughout the building. To Knight's relief, the silver Audi was parked at the back, suggesting its owner was safely asleep. While Merv kept watch, he fixed a tracker under the rear bumper then removed the valve cap from one of the tyres. With a delicacy he might have applied to the dismantling of an IED, he inserted a core-removal tool and turned it with a pair of pliers. With an ear to the valve, he listened for the first hiss of escaping air, ready to abort if he overdid it and set off the car alarm. At last it came, a barely audible whisper that told him the tyre was on its way down. He replaced the cap and Merv helped him back to his feet.

Twenty minutes later, they left the Skoda down a track near the bend where Knight had stopped before. While Knight dealt with the padlock Merv fixed a camera to the bramble, pointing back towards the road. They passed through the gate and the woods swallowed them up.

In the pitch darkness, Knight felt his weariness lift. Action beckoned and he was well-prepared; beside him, Merv remained ebullient.

'What if we do find a dope farm in there?' he whispered. 'We can't just go away empty-handed, can we?'

'I think it would be our public duty to take away as much as we can,' Knight whispered back. 'The vulnerable youth of the nation deserve no less.'

Merv laughed, though he was less relaxed than he seemed. It was a low-risk job, not much more than a midnight stroll in the woods, but in the light of what he'd done to Bullock's face, he was more concerned than ever to avoid the attentions of the police. Which he would, as long as Knight stuck to the plan.

The inner fence loomed up out of the darkness. While Knight donned his balaclava, Merv checked the feed from the gate camera to his phone. They had agreed Knight would go in alone, leaving him to watch outside should someone come from a direction other than the road. As plans went, it was excessively cautious, which suited him down to the ground.

Knight was ready. Merv straightened the head torch for him and switched it on.

'Twenty minutes tops, or I'm coming in to drag you out.'

'That won't be necessary. I'll let you know if there's anything worth seeing.'

Leaving Merv in the cover of the trees, Knight approached the gate. He felt uncomfortable walking into the gaze of the cameras; it always went against the grain, no matter what precautions he had taken.

The first of the two axe shapes fitted snugly in the lock but wouldn't turn. Shifting it forward and backward didn't help. Nor did increasing the pressure, which risked bending the tin. It had to be the second key. He pushed it into the lock but it only went in half an inch and was reluctant to come out. Cursing his workmanship, he wrenched it free and tried again with the first one, vexed by the looming prospect of cutting the fence. As if punishing the key for his own failure, he applied full pressure and the lock opened.

His heart beat a little faster when he saw that the door was fitted with the same model. The second key slid in smoothly and began to turn, only to come to a halt three quarters of the way round. He made several more attempts, backing off each time as he sensed the metal starting to buckle. Somewhere in the cutting was an imperfection, an invisible slip of the hand or eye which blocked his way as surely as a slab of concrete. He was wondering what the chances were of finding a fallen tree trunk to serve as a battering ram when he remembered that he had pulled this key roughly from the gate.

Holding it up to the torch, he peered at both sides of the bit, but it was hard to focus through the narrow eye-slits. Conscious of the seconds ticking by, he removed the head torch and peeled off the balaclava. Rotating the key, he could see no obvious signs of damage, no nicks or scratches, until he looked down the shaft as if he was seeing it from inside the lock. It might have been a trick of the light, but the more he looked the more it seemed that the edge of one of the axe heads was not entirely straight. He removed a glove and ran the two sides between his thumb and forefinger. On one side the metal passed smoothly across his skin; on the other he sensed the faintest scratch.

'How's it going?' Merv's voice crackled in the earpiece.

'Not now,' he replied tersely.

The pliers were still in his pocket. Holding the key against the door he pressed the tip of the pincers into the corner of the axe head while levering the shaft towards him. The freezing air was starting to numb his fingers, making it hard to judge if there was any difference. The view down the shaft suggested otherwise, although now there was the suggestion of a kink in the opposite direction. Reconciling himself to defeat, he tried again. With a meaty click, the lock surrendered and the door swung open.

Huddled beneath a tree, Merv re-read the texts he had received from Lolly. The experience of seeing himself described as an exceptional man of rare integrity was entirely new. There was also a voicemail; the one occasion on which she had phoned him back only for him to miss the call. It was crystal clear from her tone that she meant every admiring word; the one thing Merv knew about sincerity was that you couldn't fake it.

However, he was beset by the first stirrings of a guilty conscience. It couldn't be plainer Knight was sliding into obsession, for which he had ample form. But by offering to help, he now saw, he was hastening the downfall. What it all came down to, after the duty and honour stuff, was that Knight thought he was going to get his leg over. But it obviously wasn't going to happen, just like it didn't with the last one. Knight hadn't admitted as much, but it was as plain as day that she had dumped him because he was too old. This was why he needed protecting from himself. If tonight took them no closer to finding Rupert Askew, which it wouldn't, he would think of another way of looking for him, and then another, until he had completely trashed himself again. Merv was not going to let it happen, and if along the way he got lucky with Lolly, then that was a bonus. In fact, it was more than a bonus; it was fair compensation for his trouble. But he would have to be discreet, very discreet.

Knight, by now, was in a state of some confusion. He had told Merv he was in, but what he was in didn't make sense. There were no booby traps, bodies or sacks full of weed. Instead there were tables, chairs and a pair of settees, and in one corner a counter with shelves of bottles behind it. The banality of the place offended him, its one saving grace the mystery that anyone would go to such lengths to hide it.

'So what you got?' Merv asked, at last.

'I don't know. It seems to be some kind of bar.' Knight couldn't disguise his disappointment. 'I'll get back to you.'

There were three doors along the side of the room. Superfluous though it seemed, he switched on the bodycam and opened the first door. Squeezed in behind it were a curtained shower and toilet, with a small basin between them. Equally cramped, the second room contained a desk with a chair on each side, as if for private business. In the drawers were receipts for items such as wood sealant and insecticide. On the top was a desk calendar which served as a diary, with reminders to buy gas canisters and mousetraps, the humdrum routine of country life. He flicked back several weeks. Some of the dates were marked with a cross, but otherwise there was nothing more controversial than a note to buy shower gel and shampoo. Why would anyone want or need to take a shower here? It didn't feel like a holiday home, and even if it was then why did it have to be kept a secret?

He found the answer in the third room. It was a little larger than the other two, enough for a double bed and a chest of drawers. By now, he was speculating some eccentric hermit came here to commune with nature, and was half-expecting to find thick walking socks and waterproofs. It therefore added to his confusion to find an impressively wide selection of lingerie. Only it was not the type of lingerie with which he was familiar. With the uncomfortable sensation there was something voyeuristic in his actions, he inspected several neatly arranged piles of leather thongs, spike-studded bras and crotchless knickers, in addition to garments whose function he could only guess at. He was glad Merv wasn't there to provide a running commentary.

It became apparent the collection was intended for more than one woman, because the items came in several sizes. At the back of one of the drawers, he made a further discovery, a box full of condoms, lubricants and sex toys. Finally, it dawned on him what went on in this place. Call it a club, call it a brothel, or maybe a location for porn films, people came here to have sex. There was no male attire, which suggested that the women who took part were there solely for the pleasure of the men. He wondered how willingly they did so. The effort that had gone into securing the building added to his misgivings. For the male participants, if not the women, the stakes must be high. Yet it did not seem nearly luxurious enough for the usual suspects such as businessmen and celebrities, let alone for politicians or the senior clergy. Perhaps times were harder than he thought. The only type of person who would fit the bill was Bullock, which made the place feel all the more tawdry.

There was a decision to be made – how badly did he want to know who came here? He had no particular desire to watch them in action, but nor could he bring himself to accept that he was done; the dog and the bone had yet to be parted. His one remaining video transmitter was in his pocket. It was a valuable piece of kit, an IP camera which passed itself off as an innocuous coat hook. It would be easy enough to retrieve; the question was where to put it.

Merv checked his watch; fifteen minutes so far. He had been keeping an eye on the feed from the gate, but even at this distance a pair of headlamps would penetrate the woods the moment a car entered the track. He also had a link to the tracker telling him the Audi hadn't moved. For want of anything else to do, he listened to Lolly's voicemail again.

Even through cheap earphones there was a caressing, winsome quality that took him back to the moment she had whispered in his ear while he was on the bed. As he abandoned himself to the memory, a highly unorthodox thought stole up on him. It was, he had already decided, his duty to protect Knight by discouraging him from further involvement. But this didn't mean that he himself might not volunteer, discreetly of course, to offer his own services. It would be for a limited period, perhaps until Lolly came up with the goods he took to be on offer. He could not be accused of stealing a client for the obvious reason that she wasn't one.

Unaccustomed to strenuous moral debate, Merv found his mind going round in circles, not helped by the sound of Lolly's voice in his ear. As soon as he removed the earphones, he became aware of something treading through the dead leaves.

Craning his neck cautiously around the tree, he expected to see a fox or a deer. But the shape was human. It was walking beside the fence towards the gate, which Knight had left open. He jerked his head back behind the tree as the figure passed yards from where he sat.

Knight was fixing the coat hook to the wall beside the front door when Merv's panicky hiss burst out of his phone.

'Company! Hide ! Now!'

He stumbled into the bathroom and hid behind the curtain just as the light went on in the bar. He made ready with his stick; if he charged out, the element of surprise might see him to the gate. It was as well he didn't. The next thing he heard was a distinctive metallic click, the sound of a safety catch. It was followed by a shout from Merv.

'Oi you! You looking for someone?'

Merv hadn't seen the gun. As far as he could tell when he looked round the tree it was a small man on his own, easily taken out if things got physical. When the barrel swung towards him he flung himself to the ground.

Knight reeled from the blast. It took a moment to realise that the curtain was intact and he was not the target. He heard the snap of a shotgun breaking open and a faint click as a new cartridge went in, then footsteps moving fast towards the fence. He left the shower and peered round the front door in time to glimpse a dark form flitting into the trees. There was no sign of Merv. But what he did see as he scanned the brightly lit room was what he had failed to look for when he first entered: in the opposite corner, where the wall met the ceiling, was a motion detector.

Dismayed by his blunder, he hurried to the gate and listened. Away to his left, he could hear the dead leaves being trampled.

'Merv, are you receiving?'

There was no response. Another shot rang out.

'Merv, come in!'

Knight plunged into the woods to the right of the track, barely able to see his hand held out in front of him. Every now and then a torch beam flickered through the branches over to his left. As long as it was moving so was Merv, unless he was lying shot and the gunman was looking for the body.

Halfway down the track he crossed over. He'd managed to move ahead of the light and intended to lie in wait for the shooter to cross his path. But now the light went out.

He flattened himself against a tree and listened again, trying to judge how many pairs of feet he could hear. He had only seen one person at the summerhouse, but it didn't mean there wasn't another, or more, waiting in the woods. Could he hear something being dragged along, or was his imagination slipping its leash?

He needed something to throw, to fool the gunman into shooting at the spot where it landed. With each shot he would move closer, until there was a chance of rushing him on the reload. That was the theory. Bending to scour the ground for an object, he heard a twig snap behind him.

Even twenty years ago, he might have managed to pivot and launch a kick. As it was, he had scarcely begun to move when an arm locked itself around his neck. He flailed wildly with his stick and jabbed his elbow into the assailant's ribs, but the grip only tightened until he couldn't breathe. A menacing yet familiar voice whispered in his ear.

'Drop the gun or I'll break your neck.'

Even as he said it, Merv inhaled the musty aroma of Knight's coat. They both froze. From somewhere between them and the summerhouse came the rustle of a slow, steady tread, growing fainter.

It felt like a good time to leave.

Chapter Twenty-Four

Knight's chest was tight, his lungs aching as Merv all but dragged him the last hundred yards to the car, acutely aware they were sitting ducks if the shooter's friends arrived.

'It's fine, I can drive,' he wheezed between breaths, but Merv had already taken the keys and was opening the passenger door to bundle him in. He didn't resist; it was Merv's call. He had been shot at twice, the first blast flying over his prone body, the second sending a ricocheting pellet perilously close to his ear as he ran through the woods.

'I'm sorry I got you into this,' Knight managed to say as they took off, too fast for his liking. 'I had no idea anything like that was going to happen.'

'Yeah well, now we know.'

It was said with an edge, but quite what it meant remained unexplored; a car was approaching, its headlights on full beam. Merv cursed and braked hard, pitching Knight into the ageing seatbelt until it locked. By the time he looked round, the tail-lights had disappeared.

'Did you get a look at his face?'

'No. All I saw was the gun. Single barrel, or I wouldn't be here.'

'Do you think he was trying to hit you or warn you off?'

'Dunno, didn't stay to ask.'

Merv clearly wasn't in the mood to talk, but there was one other question he felt compelled to ask.

'How did he manage to get so close before you saw him? I could hear him when he was looking for you in the woods and he must have been a hundred yards away, it doesn't make sense.'

It was meant in the spirit of rational enquiry, but it wasn't taken that way.

'I don't know, all right? Maybe I heard something and thought it was an animal, but when you've been shot at it gets a little bit difficult to remember things, or maybe your memory's perfect all the time!'

Knight was taken aback by the outburst. He had underestimated the effect of the shooting on Merv.

'I'm sorry,' he said, 'didn't mean to push you. There's something else you should know.'

He had expected Merv to be furious about the motion sensor, but he almost seemed relieved.

'Well, there you are,' he muttered, 'everyone screws up sometimes, it happens.'

He gripped the wheel less tightly as they left the lane and the street lamps began again.

'So, what was in there that someone thought it was worth shooting me for?'

As Knight shared his findings, Merv relaxed, demanding a detailed description of the lingerie. He was less interested in the identity of the gunman, whether it was a panicking amateur or a hardened criminal. Either way, he took the view it was none of their business.

'And was there anything else, you know, to connect it all to this Rupert bloke?'

'Well no, there wasn't. There might be some other lines I could follow, I'm not sure yet.'

'Well, you've had a good run with it, she can't complain.'

This jarred, but not as much as what came next.

'So when are we going to tell her?'

'I'm not sure,' he replied guardedly. 'I'm quite happy to see her alone, though. I wouldn't want to waste any more of your time over this.'

Merv cackled. 'You're joking, mate, course I want to be there. Unless you're desperate to be on your tod with her.'

'I am most certainly not!' Knight felt himself bristling, but told himself he was being ridiculous. After everything that had happened, how could he possibly refuse?

'I'd be more than happy for you to come.' He hoped it sounded sincere. 'I'll talk to her in the morning and let you know when.'

Too right you will, Merv thought.

*

Lolly was in bed browsing through back issues of the *Antiques Trade Gazette* when the call came. She didn't like the sound of Knight's terse account, but there hadn't been much that she'd liked lately. Avoiding Bullock, making her own fruitless enquiries, contending with an outcrop of crow's feet that stubbornly defied her potions – life was full of bitter pills, and here by the look of it was another.

Not that she blamed Knight; she had seen for herself that the task was all but impossible. But she had allowed herself to believe in him. Dazzled by his early successes, she had convinced herself the day was approaching when she would have Askew in her sights and do what she had to do. She would, of course, hear them out this evening as requested, because it was only polite. There was one small consolation; if she left the next day she would not have to give Bullock his lesson. Abandoning the world of antiques, she logged onto easyJet.

Knight, too, was bowing to the inevitable. Top of his list was to return to the estate agent, though it kept dropping to second as he cleaned the kitchen, cleared the mouldy food from the fridge and reacquainted himself with the washing machine. The slow, boring chores gave him comfort. He even cleaned out the car and brought his mud-caked wellingtons up to be scrubbed.

While he worked, he replayed the events of the previous evening. The question that baffled him was where the shooter had come from. The nearest building was Mrs Fisher's house, though someone could have left a car further down the lane and walked from there through the woods. As to the shooter's identity, it was possible that Bahir had managed to find another car. If he hadn't on the other hand, who was it? Uncle Malik? But this way madness lay. Merv was right, it was none of their business.

By late afternoon, a semblance of order had been restored, though he had still not called the estate agent. Urgently seeking nourishment, he retrieved a quiche and a Swiss roll from the back of the freezer and microwaved them in turn, devouring most of the quiche in the time it took to defrost the cake. It was only his intention to eat a slice or two, but soon most of that was gone as well.

Replete if somewhat bilious, he took his phone to the sofa with the firm undertaking to make the call after a ten-minute nap. Yet his mind refused to relax and his steadily bloating stomach reproached him. At last, disgusted by his cowardice, he brought up the number and stared at it grimly, his thumb poised. But in a last-minute stay of execution, the phone rang.

At first, he thought he had triggered the ringtone by mistake, but there on the screen it said caller unknown, plain as day, and the ringing continued.

'Is that Mr Knight?' an anxious voice asked. It was male, faintly accented, and could have been from anywhere.

'Yes, how can I help you?' he replied, trying not to sound surprised.

'I am praying that you can, Mr Knight. It's my daughter, she has been with bad people and now they are saying she is the one who gets the drugs for them. The police have charged her for being a dealer and I don't know what to do anymore.'

'I'm very sorry to hear that.' He was all business now, alert to opportunity but also deceit. Many conversations began like this; what followed was seldom straightforward.

'Who am I talking to please?'

'My name is Singh. I found your website and read how you saved the woman who is in prison for killing the old ladies. Please, I need to see you today. I will pay whatever you say.'

Desperate promises of money were likewise to be taken with a pinch of salt, but nor could they be ignored. Even if the man was only telling half the truth, there was the chance of a down payment.

'I'd be glad to help if I can, Mr Singh.' He didn't wish to sound too keen, but it wouldn't do to appear unduly diffident. 'Are you quite sure it has to be today? I am a little tied up at the moment.'

'Please, it must be today. I am going away on business tomorrow; if we leave it until I come back I'm afraid it will be too late. Mr Knight, I am begging you.'

He built an instant and possibly unfair picture in his mind; the panicking absentee parent confronted with a crisis but unwilling to do any more than throw money at it. But who was he to judge, if some of it came in his direction? It was just after five; they were due to meet Lolly at seven.

'I can see you for an hour if you meet me in the bar of the Grand Hotel at five thirty. There's a consultation fee of a hundred pounds and it's fifty an hour after that.'

Knight wished he'd asked for more. The distraught father declared his undying gratitude and swore to be on time. Daring to hope that a new chapter was opening just as a wretched one closed, he shaved and looked for something clean to wear.

*

The Grand Hotel was Knight's default meeting place for new clients. Half a mile from his front door, it conferred an air of patrician gravitas that it suited him to cultivate, but also offered opportunities to see and not be seen. He arrived early and took a seat in the sun lounge from where he could watch the entrance. Hidden by the *Daily Telegraph*, he was indistinguishable from his fellow occupants.

Mr Singh had described himself as short and dark, in a blue suit. Five thirty came and went, but no such person appeared. Concerned he had missed him, Knight walked slowly down the colonnaded lobby and surveyed the bar. Irritation and disappointment welled up in equal measure. He continued his walk, inspecting the leaden landscapes and portraits lining the walls, then doubled back past the bar again. Disappointment gave way to suspicion. If the man in the blue suit was a fiction, it could only be because someone wanted a chance to observe him.

Once the idea had lodged in his mind, it became irresistible. Pretending to send a text, he scanned the lobby and the lounge beyond for candidates. There was a sprinkling of business people huddled over contracts and spreadsheets, a tea party involving several wheelchairs, a tense nanny escorting a bawling child to the bathroom; nobody was taking the slightest interest in him. Unless it was the figure he caught in the corner of his eye, dipping back into the corridor where the nanny had gone.

He wavered between flight and pursuit. There was every chance he had imagined it, that the client was simply late or had changed his mind.

It happened. But then why hadn't he called? The corridor was empty, the gents likewise save for an octogenarian in an MCC tie, sipping champagne as he stood at the urinal. Back in the corridor, a passing waiter listened politely to his enquiry about a mislaid brother-in-law; he had seen no one.

In an attempt to calm his nerves, he paid a king's ransom for a large vodka and took it back to the sun lounge. It didn't help, so he had another. The fact he had failed to spot anyone only added to his unease – if they could avoid detection, it meant they were good, very good. He recalled how he had taken off the balaclava before entering the summerhouse and neglected to put it back on again. Perhaps he had missed a camera in the same way he had missed the motion detector, or perhaps he had been wrong in believing that the camera on the gate lacked infrared. But then how had they managed to identify him and track him down? Was it the business card he had given to Clementine Lever, or was it O'Driscoll? A fresh wave of paranoia swept in; O'Driscoll had money, enough to pay for a professional if he wanted one.

Rather than go straight to his car, he walked along Grand Parade in the bitterly cold rain that was sweeping in from the sea. After fifty yards, he turned abruptly and walked back, assessing the handful of passers-by. Save for a teenager in a hoodie, their faces were obscured by umbrellas. He returned to the driveway of the Grand Hotel and waited; none of them turned round. Nor was there any sign of a silver Audi or O'Driscoll's Golf.

The Skoda was in the side street next to the hotel. As he climbed in, he thought he glimpsed someone turning away under the streetlamp at the corner. Through the rain-spattered windscreen, it was hard to judge if the figure had been watching him, let alone if it was a man or a woman. He was seeing ghosts; he had to get a grip.

Lolly's hotel was at the other end of the seafront, half a mile beyond the pier. Rather than drive straight there, he headed the other way into the smart residential streets behind the cliffs. The mirror was empty for a few seconds, then a single headlamp appeared. He took the next turning and stopped, waiting for the headlamp to follow. A moment later a pizza delivery bike sped by.

In the next street, the pizza man was outside a house, opening the box on the back of the bike. Knight drove past slowly, trying to catch a look at his face, but he had his helmet on. He continued towards the station, checking his mirror every few seconds. It didn't help that the rear wiper had not worked in months. The station clock caught his eye. It was five to seven. The prospect of being late maddened him. He accelerated past the station and, as he did, a pizza bike reappeared briefly at the roundabout behind him.

It was not necessary to run the red light, but a cocktail of exhaustion, anger and fear drove the pedal to the floor. What he had not noticed was the police car in the service road beside the station.

*

Merv was about to knock when he heard Lolly's voice. At first, he thought Knight had arrived early, which annoyed him, but then he realised she was on the phone. 'That's terrible,' he heard her say. 'What are they going to do to you?' She sounded sympathetic, though not without a tinge of irritation. He would have been happy to listen longer, but two guests were making their way down the corridor.

She kept the phone to her ear as she answered the door.

'Yes, but he's just arrived.' She barely looked at Merv. 'Surely he can tell me all about it?' There was no mistaking the irritation now. 'I understand that, but there's nothing to stop you and me meeting another day. Here, I'll pass you over.'

'Merv?' Knight sounded more than flustered; he was on the edge of losing it. A confusing tale emerged of a mystery client, a pizza bike and a breathalyser, the upshot of which was that he had been detained for further testing. A part of Merv felt he ought to go at once to the police station, though he saw quickly that it would change nothing. Besides, Lolly had already signalled her preference to go ahead with him alone. Knight, thankfully, was reaching the same conclusion. 'Look,' he said, with undisguisable reluctance, 'I think you'll have to do this and report back to me. Do you think you can manage on your own?'

Merv prickled but let it go.

Lolly, meanwhile, had occupied one of two chairs at the small table by the window and indicated he should take the other. It felt oddly formal.

'I'm so sorry about Tom,' she said. 'I wouldn't have taken him for a... I mean it's such bad luck. I hope he doesn't lose his licence.'

'He sounded pretty sure he wouldn't, let's hope he's right.' The chair was uncomfortable. Merv eyed the bed longingly. 'Like you say, it was bad luck. Shame he can't be here.'

'Well, at least you are. So tell me, what happened last night?'

It struck him that she had wasted little time in getting down to business. He had expected more small talk, certainly some expression of concern for his welfare in the aftermath of the shooting. Perhaps it would come when he reached that part of the story, which he now related in detail.

She listened intently, never shifting her eyes from his. When he got to the exotic underwear, she allowed herself a small smile, when he described the gunshots she expressed authentic concern, though not quite as much as he would have liked. Yet he did not feel resentful; her voice, the wafts of scent and the steady inquisition of her eyes saw to that, as did the cropped halter top exposing a few inches of her impossibly flat midriff.

'So, the gunman, where do you think he came from? Isn't it a bit odd that he managed to get so close before you heard him?'

Merv shuffled uncomfortably in the hard seat. 'I've wondered that too. Maybe I did hear him and thought it was an animal or something. I honestly don't know.'

She didn't look convinced.

'So, apart from the fact this place is near where the Askew family lived, there was nothing Tom could find to link it to them?'

'No. He reckons it was only built a couple of years ago, so they were long gone.'

Lolly was silent for a moment.

'Tom said there might be some other avenues he could explore. Any idea what they are?'

Merv had been expecting the question. Despite his belief that he was acting in Knight's best interests, notions of betrayal and disloyalty had continued to dog him. Now, as another waft of orange blossom came his way, he understood right was on his side. It was time to throw his hat in the ring.

'The reality is, there isn't any more he can do. If Rupert Askew is in Eastbourne, Tom's run out of ways of finding him.'

She didn't seem surprised.

'I suppose that's it then,' she said with regret. 'Thank you for being honest with me, Merv. I really appreciate it and I'm incredibly grateful for everything you've tried to do. But there's no use flogging a dead horse, is there?'

There was a finality about the way she said it he hadn't reckoned on. It was all the more unwelcome in that she was raising herself from the chair.

'No, hang on!'

She paused, suspended in motion over the seat.

'I didn't say it was necessarily over. There still are things that can be done, it's just Tom's reached the end of the road and he can't do them. But I might be able to.'

With a questioning look, she sat down again.

'What things?'

Merv had given this bit some thought. Even so, it was fairly vague.

'I've got quite a few contacts round here.' He dropped his voice. 'Some of them prefer to stay under the radar, if you know what I mean. But there's not much goes on they don't know about, and when they don't, they know someone who does. So, I'd be happy to make a few enquiries for you.'

For once, she looked unsure of herself.

'That's very kind, Merv.' She hesitated, scrutinising him with what he took to be fascination. 'So, these are people who, how can I put it, move in circles Tom wouldn't necessarily have access to?'

'Got it in one. He knows a lot of people, obviously, but these are like, you know, a bit special, fingers in lots of pies, and they only talk to people they know they can trust.'

This, at least, was accurate. There was Kemal who did the knock-off Armani gear, Marek who imported the counterfeit fags from Poland, not to mention Jabril who currently had a nice line in out-of-date chicken nuggets, or goujons as he had learned to call them. They were tight-lipped to a man, even with Merv, which was precisely why it wasn't dishonest to claim they could help; he had no idea what they didn't know.

She still appeared less than enthusiastic.

'Well, let's say they had… valuable information. Wouldn't they expect to be paid?'

'No, course not! These are my mates we're talking about; they wouldn't want money for giving me a hand, any more than I'd want it

161

from them. And I wouldn't want any from you, that's what mates are for, right?'

'Well,' she said, possibly brightening a touch. 'Thank you, Merv, I'm very touched. But how long do you think it would take to get an idea?'

'A few days. You're not leaving just yet are you?'

Lolly didn't like making snap decisions. She preferred to ease the truth out of people, coaxing and encouraging them, only applying pressure when necessary, finely calibrated to avoid antagonising them. She took pride in her skills and delighted in their use, much as a fisherman might take pleasure in landing a salmon. The problem with Merv was one of value. He was safely in the net and had been for some time, but how much he was worth to her she didn't know. And there would be a catch; there always was.

'I hadn't quite decided. I've already stayed longer than I'd planned, but I could always come back if you found something.' She let that one hang and gauged his reaction. The mouth turned down and the forehead wrinkled. He wasn't buying it.

'But I'm sure I could stay another day or so,' she went on, before he could say anything. 'Enough for you to make a few enquiries.'

As she expected, he cheered up immediately.

'Well, that's great, sorted then. I'll put out a few feelers and see what I come up with. But I'd rather you didn't say anything to Tom if that's all right, don't want any hard feelings. I do my best to look out for him, but he doesn't always like it.'

'No, of course, I quite understand. And thank you, Merv, this is incredibly generous.'

'Yeah well, like I say, it's all about helping your mates, isn't it?'

There was an uncomfortable silence. The catch was on its way, telegraphing its arrival through the nervous expression on his face; the way he swallowed once or twice as he plucked up courage. She was minded to let him stew, to savour his awkwardness as he staked his claim. But she reminded herself that he wasn't a bad man, just a normal one. For better or worse, she had made her bet; she should do what she could to see it through.

'Was there something else, Merv?'

'Well, it's funny you should mention that.' His relief was palpable. 'I think I did something to my shoulder when I took a dive to dodge that shotgun. You think you could take a look at it?'

*

Knight was not surprised when the second test proved negative, given that the first was borderline.

The suspicion that he was being picked on for his age was borne out by a lecture from a humourless sergeant on the reaction times of elderly drivers, further stoking his wrath. It therefore seemed wise to pay heed to the small voice counselling self-preservation and an early night, but as he approached the seafront the thought of his cold, empty flat depressed him. When he reached the building, he drove on.

Outside Lolly's hotel, the same small voice counselled him again. He was tired to the point of delirium and haunted by a pursuer who might be real or imaginary. But now that he was here he craved the consolation prize of seeing her; to go away without it became unthinkable.

There was, of course, no guarantee she would still be there. He tried Merv but he wasn't answering. It was approaching nine, he would have left some time ago, presumably with other fish to fry. Should he call Lolly? When they had spoken earlier she had sounded put out, as well she might be. Instinct, or perhaps fear, told him that if he called her now he might be smartly dismissed. This too became unthinkable. It would be poor manners to arrive unannounced, but he had reached a point where manners were a luxury. He would go to her room. If she was in, she was in. If she wasn't, so be it.

He had to walk up three floors because the lift was out of order. This gave the small voice a further opportunity, so that when he eventually reached her door he had changed his mind again several times. He thought he could hear her, or perhaps it was the television. It would be shameful to eavesdrop. Throwing caution to the wind, he knocked.

'Who is it?'

She sounded on edge, exasperated even. He looked down the corridor; the stairs were too far for him to stage a retreat.

'It's me, Tom.' There was an uncomfortably long silence. He heard something click, and then her footsteps.

Despite the tension he had detected, she was perfectly composed when she opened the door.

'I didn't think you were coming tonight,' she said coolly. 'What happened, are you all right?'

It wasn't the greatest of welcomes, but he hadn't been dismissed.

'I've been better. I was just passing by and I should have rung but my phone was out of battery.' He had the uncomfortable sensation that she could see right through him. 'If you're not busy I thought maybe I could add to what Merv has told you.'

'Yes, of course.' She ushered him in. 'Merv is still here,' she added casually, 'he's just in the loo.'

The bathroom door opened and Merv came out. It may have been his fragile state of mind, but Knight formed the immediate impression he was less pleased to see him than Lolly was.

'Bloody hell, mate, are you all right?'

Knight was not all right. He had taken the stairs too quickly and his heart was still pounding. Added to which, Merv's presence had thrown him. What had he been doing here for nearly two hours? He felt the tightness gripping his chest again and had to grab at the side of the table. Lolly was there in an instant, helping him into a chair.

'Oh my god, do you want me to call a doctor?'

'No!' he growled. The whole situation had become unnervingly surreal, the tightness, Merv's presence, the flashes of double vision. Not to mention the ruffled bedspread and Merv's trainers on the floor. Lolly brought him a glass of water.

'Tom, you don't look well.'

'I'm absolutely fine.' It was an effort to keep his voice level. 'I just need a couple of moments.' He downed the water, spilling some of it on his chin.

'I think I'd better take you home, mate,' Merv said, through gritted teeth.

'I said, I'm fine.'

'Mate, you're not fine.' The irritation was unmistakable now. 'Let's get you back to the flat and into bed.'

The combined frustrations of the evening fused into a toxic ball of resentment and rage. Control of events may have slipped through his fingers some time ago, but he was not going to be nannied by Merv.

'Will you stop acting like a bloody nursemaid!' Knight shouted. 'If I say I'm okay, I'm okay, and that's a bloody end to it!'

'What is your problem?!' Merv shouted back, shocking them both into silence.

'I think you'd both better go,' said Lolly.

Knight waited until they reached the stairs before letting rip again.

'For once and for all, will you get it into your head that I do not wish to be treated like a child! There is absolutely nothing the matter with me.'

'You're not well!' Merv bellowed.

'And you're not a bloody doctor!'

Merv finally lost patience. The time had come to let Knight have the truth, with both barrels.

'No, I'm not a doctor, but I can see when you're losing it. And right now, trust me, you have lost it! Forget about her, it's not going to happen. She's not interested and she's bad news for you! And now we're going home!'

Suddenly it all fell into place. The disturbed bedspread, the trainers, the reason why Merv had stayed so long.

'I don't believe it,' he sputtered. 'You're after her yourself!'

Merv's face said it all. Knight erupted.

'She's my client, how dare you think you have the right to try it on with her!'

With which he departed downstairs. The shock of discovery had left Merv mute, despite the anger unleashed by Knight's ferocious attack. To cap it all, he turned at the landing and bellowed again.

'Go on then! If it's a bit of rough she wants you're obviously the man!'

Knight drove home, no longer bothering to check the mirrors. Sitting at the kitchen table, as if in a trance, he surveyed the horrifying rubble of a day that had started with a modicum of promise. He felt no regret for what he had said to Merv. It was a gross enough impertinence for him to impugn his motives in the way he had done, but to pursue Lolly was unforgivable. It was a betrayal eclipsed only by the loathsome question as to whether she had been minded to reciprocate.

There was nothing on television he wanted to watch, nothing in the fridge he found remotely tempting. At least, the flat was no longer an eyesore, although by the sink his muddy boots were still awaiting attention.

As an officer cadet he had found it soothing to polish his boots after a day that went badly, and in the weeks after Roz died he had found solace hunched over an old sheet of newspaper while he shined his shoes, even if they were clean. He did not quite find solace now, but the red mist did turn a lighter hue as the mud was rinsed away. If anything had happened between them, it could not have been much. Lolly had not seemed dishevelled or out of breath when she opened the door, nor for that matter had Merv when he appeared.

Somehow, perhaps, he would put all this aside, along with the points on his licence, the fine he couldn't afford and the likelihood he had stirred up a hornets' nest of enemies he didn't need. He turned a boot over under the running water and scrubbed the tread. Some small stones fell out into the sink. At first, he thought nothing of it, but as the water washed away he stared in disbelief.

Scattered around the drain were half-a-dozen pieces of brightly coloured gravel.

Chapter Twenty-Five

Knight held the gravel in his cupped hand and ran the tip of his finger over the fragments as if they were gemstones. His head swam with where he'd been, and with regret that he hadn't cleaned the boots sooner.

Repairing to the sofa, he cast his mind back. The days folded into each other, randomly exchanging events as if to torment him. He had worn the boots the previous night, starting at the kebab shop and ending at his apartment. Before that was the night he had found the summerhouse. And before that? He remembered being glad of them at the farm, which also meant he must have been wearing them at Mrs Fisher's house. The permutations bred like rabbits with each new scene, defying any attempt to impose order.

He switched on the reading lamp and inspected them again. They gleamed seductively, issuing an invitation tinged with malevolence. It was not too late to make the short journey to the kitchen and deposit them in the bin; there would be little shame in it. Rather than that, he texted Lolly.

At eight sharp, she was on his doorstep. It had been her idea to meet at this hour, the flight being at midday. Even without having seen the stones, she had felt a rush like cocaine when Knight described them. There was a fine line between the courage to hope and the folly of wishful thinking, between gritty persistence and flogging a dead horse, a line she trod frequently. At this moment she could not say which side of it she was on.

The horse in question did not look good. Knight had risen at the last possible moment and cut himself shaving even as she rang the bell downstairs. Inevitably, she was as radiant as ever. Jolted from his torpor more surely than by a double espresso, he led her to the sitting room.

She turned the pieces of coloured gravel over in her palm as he had done, with an intensity that told him he had been right to call her.

'Where do you think they came from?'

He noted with satisfaction how she hung on his every word as he reeled off the places, though frowning as the scale of the challenge became apparent.

'It's perfectly possible, of course, that they're not from Clementine at all,' Knight concluded. 'But I thought you should know.'

'Thank you, Tom.' The warmth that was absent the previous evening had returned. 'Which do you think is the most likely?'

'I really don't know. But it's harder to see why she'd feel threatened in a public place like a kebab shop, so maybe not there.'

'Unless it was round the back where he parks his car. What about the farm?'

Knight shrugged. 'It's possible she was taken there, though I didn't get the impression the man in charge was a murderer.'

'Unless he didn't know about it. What about the other one, the pig man?'

'I thought he was a bit of a simpleton, I wouldn't bet on him either.'

'So, that leaves the woods, the summerhouse and the old lady's place. I'd put my money on the summerhouse.'

He was struck by how efficiently she sorted and assessed the facts. There was a sharp, analytical mind at work that he hadn't had the chance to appreciate before.

'What about the camera?'

'If anything moves it switches on and sends me an alert. There's been nothing so far, but I've checked and it's working.'

She pounced on it. 'What about the man with the gun, did it get him?'

'He didn't come in far enough to trigger it.'

'Pity.'

He almost felt as if he should apologise, but he understood why she was interrogating him; he would be the same if somebody killed one of his own. He also realised he hadn't given much thought to what came next.

'The truth is,' he said, 'you'll never know for certain unless you go back and search everywhere, and even then you're looking for a needle in a haystack.'

She nodded thoughtfully. 'It would take time. Time and a lot of luck.'

'A lot of luck.'

'And there's no point going to the police,' she added. 'They're not going to get excited about a few stones.'

An unspoken question hung between them. Now that it did, the prospect of scouring East Sussex for pieces of gravel seemed unattractive. It must have shown in his face, for she put her hand on his arm and changed the subject.

'Why don't we look at the video? You never know, there might be something.'

He had wondered whether to show her the footage. He did not consider himself a prude, but nor did he warm to the thought of inspecting exotic lingerie with her. Or rather, there was a part of him that did warm to it, which he would rather she didn't know about.

She watched like a hawk, asking him to stop and replay sections so she could identify the types of liquor behind the bar or the brand of shampoo in the bathroom. In the office shots, she wanted to go back over the dates on the desk calendar.

'What do you think those are? The party nights?'

Knight played the images frame-by-frame. The marked dates recurred every few weeks.

'It's as good a guess as any. He pointed at the screen. 'There's another one next Thursday.'

'Maybe we should go.'

He felt his face tingle, even though he knew she was joking. Meanwhile, she was pointing out another date.

'Isn't that the day before Clem was found?'

It was, but what of it? Not that he could criticise her for clutching at straws.

When it came to the lingerie, she wrinkled her nose in distaste.

'Who designs this stuff?' she muttered, as much to herself as to him. 'I mean, look at that!'

He freeze-framed on a pair of black rubber cups, each with a hole in its centre. They were studded with teat-like protuberances which gave them the appearance of giant viruses; only the attached straps enabled him to identify them as a brassiere.

'What is it about our breasts that people want to make them look so ghastly?' she complained bitterly. 'You do realise you're meant to stick your nipples through the holes so they look like the odd ones out? Among all the worm things?'

Knight hadn't thought of it that way. Now that he did, the idea repelled him.

'I have to say, I don't see how that's erotic,' he confessed readily, keen for her to know that they agreed.

'Well exactly! How can anything be better than a naked body?'

They watched the rest in silence. He wanted to express his approval of naked bodies, but in a way that wouldn't show he was thinking of hers. To his regret the moment passed, though he would have been pleased to know she was calculating the cost of changing the flight.

'I'm sorry about Merv,' she said.

Knight was thrown deeper into confusion.

'Well, I'm sorry too, I'm afraid I didn't behave very well.'

She shook her head. 'It wasn't your fault, he was out of order. I don't think he should have spoken to you the way he did.'

It was music to his ears; he wanted to hear more.

'Merv is an excellent man but he does have a tendency to fuss.' Emboldened, he added, 'I hope he hasn't been bothering you.'

It sounded intrusive, indelicate even. Far from taking offence, she smiled wryly and laughed.

'If I didn't know you better, I'd say you were jealous.'

He felt his face glow again. 'But listen,' she went on, 'Merv is just a big kid, really. I'd hate to think I'm the cause of you two falling out.'

'Of course you're not,' he tried to reassure her. 'It's just… I'm afraid I found his behaviour unacceptable.' How pompous it sounded. 'What I mean is, he pushed me too far and I didn't like it.'

'I know, he had no right to. But I don't think he meant badly, and you have such a good partnership. It would be a tragedy to lose it.'

She shook her head sadly.

'Besides, it's my fault as much as his.'

Having lain dormant, Knight's suspicions elbowed their way to the fore.

'Why do you say that?'

'Because he's made up his mind I'm interested in him. Hand on heart, I've done nothing to encourage him, but it happens all the time with

170

men I meet, and to be honest it's a pain. They decide they fancy me and then they get obsessed.'

She took his hands in hers.

'I'm so glad you're not like that.'

Knight was stupefied. It must have shown, because she apparently felt the need to explain herself in more detail.

'I like it that you're not all over me like a rash. Men have no idea how boring it makes them. But you understand that, and I've no idea if you fancy me or not, but if you do, you haven't rubbed my nose in it.'

He tried to say something witty about aspiring to be more than a rash, but she hadn't finished.

'And the irony is, it's one of the things that makes you so attractive. They broke the mould when they made you, Tom.'

As he stared into the headlamps, she leaned forward and kissed him on the lips. It was not a searching kiss, there was no ingress or entwining, yet it reached every corner of his body, setting off a dance of pheromones performed with no less grace than when he was eighteen. Undone by hope, he sent his hand in search of her face only for her to shift away abruptly.

'I'm sorry,' she whispered. 'I couldn't help myself, I had no right.'

'There's nothing to be sorry for,' he managed to say. 'I think you had every right.'

She let out a little gasp of relief, or perhaps even joy.

'That's good to hear,' she murmured, then straightaway the smile faded. 'I should go now.'

Knight protested, but she was on her feet, getting her bag.

'Please don't make this any harder for me,' she begged. 'I don't want us to do something we'll both regret later.'

She was at the door almost before he was on his feet.

'You will call me, won't you?' she asked anxiously, and then she was gone.

Going down in the lift, she passed through a complicated melee of emotions. One of them, unusually, was guilt. There was something magnificent about Knight, but also a vulnerability that, for once, caused her to question her actions. Then again, her mother had never tired of telling her that you couldn't make an omelette without breaking eggs, and on the whole her mother's advice had been sound.

Chapter Twenty-Six

For twenty-four hours, Knight was borne on wings. Had anyone ever told him a day would come when he would volunteer to scour East Sussex for pieces of gravel, he would have given them short shrift. Now he had volunteered, it felt neither as irrational nor as onerous as he might have imagined.

Naturally, he regretted the rupture with Merv. It was understandable he might develop a schoolboy infatuation for one such as Lolly, and as a reasonable man Knight was prepared to overlook it. He also took satisfaction in having proved him so profoundly wrong. 'She's not interested, mate,' the words echoed contemptibly in his mind, their sting expunged. They delighted the diehards, who had returned to the fray insisting his capitulation to celibacy be questioned.

It was only now, as he left the woods, he sensed his mood changing. As a mature student he had taken ecstasy once or twice; the comedown was not unlike what he experienced now, an onset of greyness which made him twitchy.

He had begun at the rear of the kebab shop, cautioning himself to expect nothing and not overly disappointed when this proved to be the case. It was likewise no great blow to find nothing at the farm, where he claimed to have dropped a cufflink on his previous visit – though not, he insisted, anywhere near Boris. From Bert, he had at least been able to confirm no one else lived at the old farmhouse, and that the widowed Mrs Fisher had a helper who came in several times a week.

Like Lolly, he had his money on the summerhouse. The track itself had yielded nothing. Short of scraping off the surface and sieving it, there was little hope of identifying anything in the mud. The real blow was that the lock had been changed. He had partly foreseen it, but a faith of sorts had kept him going, a mischievous inspiration now exposed for what it was. He had left the old farmhouse till last, not wishing to disturb Mrs Fisher unless he had to.

It was impossible for him not to see his mother in her, the glacial slide from vitality and wit to trance-like stupefaction. From what he had observed, she was in the second half of the descent, still aware of who and where she was, but with a memory that went back a few seconds at the most. It would get much worse than this. Basic routines would fade until she was no longer able to make a cup of tea. Speech would follow then, bit by bit, her motor skills unless she was lucky enough to be carried off by something else first.

With fear had come guilt, a bully of equal magnitude. The visit would confuse and upset her. He told himself that whatever pain he inflicted, it would not be for long and she would forget about it almost immediately. The harm done would equate to what, the uncertainty of waiting for a bus that was late, the frustration of searching for a lost phone? But how could you know? A part of him hoped she wouldn't be in.

Rather than go straight to the door, he stopped and walked slowly with his eyes glued to the gaps between the paving stones. Here and there, a stunted blade of grass or a small weed poked up out of the cracks, but no gravel.

He had intended to ring the bell as soon as he reached the door but decided instead to continue searching the outside of the house before embroiling himself in tales of lost cufflinks. After examining the ground by the entrance, he progressed unhurriedly round the side of the house to the rear. The sitting room was empty, as was the billiard room. At the trapdoor he inspected the padlock. There was a dim picture of it in his mind from before, lying at a certain angle that didn't appear to have changed.

As he approached the kitchen, the light came on. If he suddenly appeared at the window she would be terrified; worse still, she may even still have the wit to call the police. Pressing himself against the wall he peered around the window frame.

She had her back to him, standing at the kitchen table opening a box of teabags. She could still make a cup of tea; it was a mercy of sorts. The kitchen itself was sumptuous. The Aga glistened, the units and the table were solid oak. She had money, another mercy. Summoning his courage, he broke cover and rapped on the glass.

Rather than spin around, she turned slowly and fixed him with the blank stare he had witnessed before.

'Mrs Fisher,' he called, 'there's no need for alarm.'

Either she couldn't hear him through the double glazing or she took his entreaty at face value. She remained where she was and continued to look at him without any hint of recognition or curiosity.

'Mrs Fisher, might I come in for a moment?'

When she did not reply he went to the kitchen door and knocked, again without eliciting a response. He returned to the window and saw she had not moved. It was a good enough excuse to call it a day; he could finish his walk around the house and be gone, with minimal damage inflicted. Showing her the picture of Clementine was a waste of time, a pedantic piece of box-ticking. Perhaps it was the same box-ticking which guided his hand to the doorknob as he passed by. Disobligingly, the door was unlocked. It was not with the regimental motto ringing in his ears that he opened it, but a sickness in his stomach.

'Mrs Fisher, you probably don't remember me, but I came to see you about my book.'

It was said with the kindliness of a vicar who had popped in on an ailing parishioner. Her eyes showed a glimmer of interest. She raised a hesitant finger and pointed at him.

'Are you the plumber?'

Knight took a deep breath.

'No, Mrs Fisher, I'm not the plumber. I'm a visitor and my name is…' His memory failed him. She looked at him in an almost friendly way, as if welcoming him to the club.

'Lyle,' he remembered at last. 'Godfrey Lyle. Look, why don't we sit down?'

She obeyed without hesitation. It disturbed him all the more to have total power over her; so too would any opportunistic thief who decided to take an interest in the house. But then he imagined her in an old age home, gazing into space from a row of armchairs, and the risk seemed worth it.

'Mrs Fisher, I'd like to show you a picture.'

There was no point in pursuing his cover story. He unfolded the picture of Clementine and laid it before her. It had been taken several years ago at a gallery in Eastbourne. The face was less haggard, but the plait was unmistakable. He searched for a glimmer of recognition, a widening of the eyes or the arching of an eyebrow. There was arguably some small tremor of reaction, but he knew he could be willing it to be there.

'This woman is Clementine Lever,' he said calmly. 'Have you ever seen her?'

Mrs Fisher frowned.

'Is that Mummy?' she asked, then with the beginnings of a smile. 'Is she coming to see me?'

'No, she's not coming.' He slowed his speech to a crawl. 'But she may have been to the house in the woods. Do you know about the little house in the woods?'

This time the flicker of recognition was unambiguous, enough to kindle in him a small spark of anticipation.

'Is she Goldilocks?'

He counted to three.

'No there's a summerhouse in the woods behind your garden. Do you know the woods I mean?' He was starting to interrogate her.

'I don't go in the woods,' she answered, as if it were a confidence. 'I don't like bears.'

He decided to make one more attempt and then extricate himself as tactfully as possible. 'Do you know Rupert Askew? He used to live in this house.'

'Rupert was a bear,' she replied, with more certainty than she had displayed until now. 'Rupert was a good bear.'

'Yes, he was a good bear. But this is a different Rupert. He used to live here, in this house.'

As he had feared would happen, she grew anxious.

'Here? Is he here now?'

'No, he lived here before you.'

Her eyes fell back to the picture.

'Is she his friend?'

'She used to be, but they're not friends anymore.'

'Why not?'

She was starting to fixate. Next would come an eternity of meandering questions to which no answers would satisfy her.

'He stole something from her. Look…'

'What did he steal?'

Knight rose.

'I don't know. It's been very nice seeing you again, Mrs Fisher. I hope I wasn't interrupting you.'

He was about to leave the way he came when the front door slammed. 'Afternoon, Mrs Fisher,' a female voice cried out, accompanied by the wiping of feet on the doormat. From the front window he saw a small Toyota of a certain age, its arrival muted by the double glazing. Before he had time to compose himself, a middle-aged woman in a cleaner's tabard bustled in from the hallway.

'Oh, hello,' she hailed him cheerily, 'I wondered whose the car was,' and then to Mrs Fisher, 'Sorry, didn't realise you had company. I'll start in the sitting room shall I?'

Mrs Fisher remained silent.

'Actually, I was just going,' Knight announced blithely. 'I'm afraid I've taken up quite enough of Mrs Fisher's time already.' But the new arrival seemed more concerned with her employer.

'Mrs Fisher, are you all right?'

'Want to lie down,' she said quietly. 'Can you take me upstairs?'

Clearly worried, the woman helped her out of the chair. If she was having some kind of attack, Knight knew he had triggered it. It would add to his shame if he abandoned the carer to deal with the situation on her own.

'What is it?' she was asking anxiously. 'Shall I call a doctor?'

The old lady shook her head. 'Bed,' she mumbled. She flinched when Knight took her arm.

Together they guided her from the kitchen into a hallway which ran past the sitting room to a staircase at the rear.

'Who did you say you were?' the carer asked, in a tone that suggested the onset of suspicion. She was also looking with disapproval at the trail of dirt his boots had left on the plush cream carpet. Knight hurriedly explained his status as local historian and seeker of cufflinks, which was readily believed.

'I don't suppose you ever knew the Askews when they lived here?' he added, as they reached the foot of the stairs, but she confessed to being a newcomer. Their charge meanwhile removed her arm from Knight's clasp

176

and seized the banister. She mounted the stairs steadily with the carer beside her, from which he inferred that his services could be dispensed with. The carer appeared to agree.

'I think we can manage now, Mr Lyle,' she called over her shoulder. 'Would you mind letting yourself out?'

Only too happy to oblige, Knight retreated down the hallway past further evidence of Mrs Fisher's wealth: a gilt mirror, a mahogany console table replete with Georgian candlesticks and a silver bowl full of orchids. Ordinarily, he might have lingered for a moment, but he craved passionately to be gone. It was only as he was about to slam the door that something he had glimpsed fought its way to the front of his mind. He grabbed the door before it shut and returned to the table.

There was no sound from upstairs. He bent over the silver bowl to inspect the inscription closely. Six Chinese characters, each about half an inch high, were engraved across the front. Yet the bowl itself was clearly not Chinese.

The first character he was sure he had seen before. It was as if someone had struggled to write a lower-case t, placing the bar in several positions before giving up and crossing it out. The second one he remembered because it looked like a television aerial. Somewhere on his phone he had the picture of the elderly artist. He could hear voices from upstairs now, an offer to bring a cup of tea. His fingers stabbed at the screen, bringing up texts and weather forecasts until at last he had it. He zoomed in on the characters and compared. They were identical.

Chapter Twenty-Seven

The clouds had cleared, sending the temperature plunging below zero. The padlock was solid but cheap. Knight lifted the trapdoor slowly, alert to the slightest hint of a creak. In the woods behind him, a fox barked, heedless of the cold in his quest for a mate.

Feeling ahead with his stick, he eased his way down the stone stairs and switched the head torch on. There was no sign of an alarm; evidently, Mrs Fisher or whoever was responsible for her affairs didn't share the same obsession with privacy as the owners of the summerhouse. The walls were lined with densely packed wine racks.

The first bottle he took out was a 1996 Pomerol. In the days of money, he had been given one by a client, and only after drinking it had discovered it was worth over a thousand pounds. There were at least two cases of it. He pulled out several more bottles from different racks; Montrachet, Musigny, Krug, the names flashed before him. He could not begin to calculate the value. Had she once been a collector, or was this the work of a deceased husband? He had spent the afternoon in the nearby villages making discreet enquiries about family and friends, but apart from a florist who recalled delivering a display some months ago, no one knew anything about her. According to Bert, she had moved in on her own and started showing signs of dementia shortly after.

On the other side of the cellar, was a second set of steps. If he had the geography right, the door at the top would open into the passage between the staircase and the billiard room. It was open. Switching off the torch, he prepared to cross another line.

It took a moment for his eyes to accustom themselves to the darkness. Feeling his way through the hall to the console table he carefully lifted the silver bowl and took it into the sitting room, closing the door behind him before he turned on the torch again. There was no question of the bowl being anything other than English, or at least European, probably eighteenth century. He had speculated endlessly about the significance of the inscription. Mrs Chang had said it had something to do with taking life easy in old age, which he assumed made it the title of the picture. But perhaps it wasn't the title, perhaps it was a proverb or a saying that could appear anywhere, from teapots to bumper stickers. He had said nothing to Lolly yet, not wishing to present her with another random coincidence.

He set the bowl aside and turned his attention to the room. A pair of wing armchairs faced the stone fireplace. Elsewhere, a chaise longue stood beneath a window and, at the far end, a glass-fronted display cabinet housed more silverware. There was nothing here that was not among the best of its kind, yet even allowing for the cold beam of the torch something was lacking; it felt more like a collection than a home.

Opposite the fireplace was a bureau which yielded bills and bank statements. He leafed through them, quickly establishing that she enjoyed a spectacular income from an investment bond. There was no indication who managed the money for her.

He replaced the bowl and returned to the rear of the house, stopping at the foot of the staircase. Reassured by the silence, he went on to the billiard room. It was an oddly masculine place, the oak floorboards uncarpeted, the panelled walls bare save for a wild boar's head over the fireplace. In the centre was a full-size table, its sprawling green baize glowing eerily under the torch beam. The tips of the cues were scarcely marked, the chalk had been used once or twice. Whoever played here was not a regular, and he doubted it was Mrs Fisher. A drinks cabinet offered single malts and vintage cognac, as well as an opened box of cigars abandoned carelessly among the bottles.

He steeled himself to go upstairs. Having seen the effect of his presence on her earlier, he dreaded what might happen if she came upon him at three in the morning. The staircase was thickly carpeted and appeared to have been recently restored, allowing him to ascend without a murmur from the boards. At the top, he faced a corridor stretching the length of the house, with doors on either side.

The first was a bathroom. As with everything else, no expense had been spared. A polished copper tub vied for attention with a cavernous walk-in shower. The top half of the vanity unit brimmed with potions and perfumes, many of them unopened. Was that because she forgot she had bought them, or did someone lavish gifts on her, more than she could use? The absurd thought crossed his mind that Mrs Fisher had a lover. She was in the next room. A strip of moonlight around the curtains helped him make out the shape of her hair against the pillow. Straining his ears, he heard the steady whisper of her breath.

He didn't notice the other dark shape further down the bed until it raised itself and shot towards him. Before he could pull the door shut the cat was rubbing its flank around his legs and making a noise like distant machine-gun fire. When he tried to toe it back into the bedroom, it wailed loudly and hissed before slipping contemptuously through his feet into the corridor. He waited for Mrs Fisher to turn and open her eyes at him, but she slept on.

Knight closed the door and crept away. To his annoyance, the cat insisted on joining him, having forgotten or forgiven the affront. There were three more rooms. Save for carpets and curtains, the first two were bare; plainly no throng of children and grandchildren flocked here for Christmas and birthdays. The third partly challenged this view. There was not only a bed but, on the windowsill he could make out the shape of a teddy bear. Switching on the torch, he saw a wardrobe and a set of shelves full of model aeroplanes.

At one end of the wardrobe were a Barbour and a tweed suit. He worked his way along the rail, building up an image of wholesome country life. But then the garments grew smaller. Cricket whites and rugby shirts gave way to a youthful tuxedo and a prep-school uniform. At the far end hung a christening gown. He found it bizarre, but also unspeakably sad; perhaps this was some kind of shrine to a loved one no longer present.

At one end of the mantelpiece was a photo album, propped between two undistinguished vases which might have been made at school. Resting his stick against the fire surround, he took the album down and leafed through the first few pages. In every photograph there were only two subjects, a young woman he soon recognised as Mrs Fisher and a baby who became a toddler and a young boy. Knight's skin prickled. As the boy became a man, he knew he had seen him before, and when he posed with his mother against the backdrop of a Sunseeker in a palm-fringed marina, he remembered where.

He never knew whether it was the cat's paw or its tail he trod on. As he reeled from the discovery, a sudden unsteadiness in his legs led him to shift his balance. It let out a hideous shriek and raced to the door, where it yowled and scrabbled frantically. Knight thrust the album back onto the mantelpiece, only to compound his clumsiness by striking a glancing blow to the larger of the two vases. It toppled off and shattered on the hearth.

For a moment he was paralysed, aware only that the cat was still scrabbling noisily to get out. Switching off the torch, he went to the door and was about to open it when he heard her footsteps in the corridor outside. He shrank into the wall.

The door opened and the cat shot out. He heard a grunt of annoyance. To his intense relief the door began to close, but then she hesitated. In a voice that managed to be both hopeful and melancholy, she addressed the darkness.

'Is that you, Rupert darling?' she asked.

Chapter Twenty-Eight

Merv dismounted from the van and went round to let Mrs Chang out. She seemed to expect it, sitting stock-still until he opened the door.

It had done wonders for his spirits when she accepted the invitation to catch some free samples. It was perfectly above board – she was a valued customer, which he had pointed out more than once. It also boded well that Mr Chang was attending to their other restaurant in Worthing.

Her eyes lit up at the spectacle before them.

'Very beautiful boats,' she intoned reverentially. 'Lot of money.'

Here was the one false note in an otherwise faultless overture. *Adrenaline Rush* fell some way short of the vessel he had described, not least in the matter of creature comforts. He suspected Mrs Chang valued them highly. For this reason, a quick, trouble-free start was essential; the sooner they were out to sea, the sooner the thrill of the chase would work its magic on her.

'Is it that one?'

She pointed playfully at an elegant cabin cruiser, leaving no doubt she would be delighted if it were.

He dismissed it with the authority of a connoisseur. It was too slow, the handling was poor, in short it had no class. 'You see mine's more of a sports car,' he explained. 'You know like one of those vintage ones, a proper classic.'

She frowned. 'Vintage? Like wine?'

He was wondering whether to claim that boats made in certain years were more highly prized than others when his heart missed a beat. *Adrenaline Rush* had disappeared.

The two sailing yachts which had been moored on either side of her for weeks were still there. Normally, the roof of the wheelhouse was just visible between them, but now it wasn't. As they drew closer, Merv breathed again, if only briefly. *Adrenaline Rush* was indeed present, but sitting so low that the water had nearly reached the level of the deck.

'This one?'

Mrs Chang seemed aggrieved to learn it was.

'This one sinking,' she stated, more in disapproval than sympathy. 'This is not good boat like you say.'

Creditably, Merv maintained a veneer of calm.

'You wait here. I'll sort it out.'

Mrs Chang had no intention of going any nearer than she already was. Merv scrambled down onto the foredeck, regretting his ignorance of boats. Could they just spring leaks, like vans when they rusted or roofs when tiles fell off? He suspected not. The broken door to the wheelhouse confirmed as much. It swung open on its hinges, the dented metal and scratched paintwork showing where the crowbar had been. A sharp stink made his eyes water. It seemed to be coming from the hole in the floor of the wheelhouse someone had drilled, the hole through which they had poured acid down into the aluminium hull.

The bilge pump was dead. So were the lights and the engine, because the O'Driscolls had drained the battery. He went to the aft deck and pulled up the inspection hatch while Mrs Chang watched sceptically from the pier. His reflection stared back at him from the water in the hull.

'We no go for lobsters today,' she pronounced, unhelpfully he felt.

*

Waiting for the marina manager to appear, Knight was still drunk with pride. It was true luck had played its part, but it was a luck born of persistence and nerve, not to mention ingenuity, skill and fine judgement. Certainly, Lolly thought so; her veneration sat like a medal on his chest.

When the manager came out of his office, he was not especially surprised by his visitor's rumpled suit and unfashionable overcoat. Yacht owners were an unpredictable bunch, especially the titled ones.

'Sir Crispin,' he greeted him cordially. 'Sorry to keep you waiting.' He didn't mention a boat had been sunk, which would have reflected poorly on the marina's security standards.

'Not at all, it's I who should apologise for dropping in out of the blue. I won't hold you up for a second longer than I need to.'

This seemed to please his host, as did the reasons for the flying visit: an unintended detour that had taken him past the marina en route to the airfield, coupled with a desire to spend more time in the old country now that he was bored with St Raphael and its exorbitant mooring fees. The manager was able to assure his guest there was no shortage of berths at highly competitive rates.

'Well, that's excellent,' Knight enthused. 'By the way, you come highly recommended by an old friend of mine, Fisher. I take it you know him?'

'Richard Fisher?'

'That's the one, we used to play polo together.'

Suitably impressed, the manager confirmed Richard Fisher was a highly valued client whose boat was the pride of the marina.

'Mine's not quite in that league,' Knight admitted, 'just a humble Benetti. Where's the silly bugger gone by the way? I was rather hoping to cadge a drink.'

'He's off to St Malo again,' replied the manager, unable to see what could possibly be humble about a Benetti. 'One of his regular jaunts. I think he likes the wine.'

Knight gave a hearty laugh.

'Never says no to a drop of Bolly, our Richard, nothing but the best for him. That Sunseeker of his really is quite something.'

'Actually...' the manager stood up and went to a chest of map drawers. 'I've got a picture of *Mamma Mia* somewhere here. Well, not just of her, but she's in it. I keep meaning to get it framed, but you know how it is.'

He produced an A2 sheet with a charcoal drawing of the inner harbour. *Mamma Mia* was clearly visible in the foreground at her mooring berth, with a tangle of masts and sails behind her. A chill went down Knight's spine as he recognised the style and remembered the sketches of boats he had seen in Clementine's studio.

'It was done by a poor woman who committed suicide on the railway not long ago,' he confided. 'It was on the news, quite a story.'

'Not bad at all.' He tried not to sound too interested. The date next to the signature was two days before their encounter with the mugger.

'Sorry to hear about the woman. How did you get hold of it if I may ask?'

'She'd been here a few times over the past month, sketching the boats. I took a liking to that one and she sold it to me. From what she said, she was quite an important artist.'

Knight's pride took a dent for having missed the link; this was surely where the trail had started for her, a chance sighting of Askew on deck or on the quayside even as she was drawing.

'Well, you may have found yourself something very valuable, congratulations. When's he coming back, by the way?'

Pleased to be praised by a knight of the realm, the manager made a quick calculation.

'He's usually away for three days, so I wouldn't be surprised if he was back tomorrow.'

Knight thanked him for his time and promised to be in touch about the repatriation of his yacht. He had left the most delicate enquiry until last, waiting until they were nearly at the door.

'You know what?' he announced, as if touched by a stroke of genius, 'I might just change my plans and hang on for a bit to see him. Is he still living up at his country mansion?'

The manager looked blank.

'You know,' Knight prompted, 'up by Todhurst Manor farm. He has his mother there, she's not well, unfortunately.'

'I didn't know that,' the manager confessed, 'he's never mentioned it.'

'Ah well, he does buy property like it's going out of fashion. So where is he then? Knowing him, it'll be a few millions' worth on the seafront.'

Now it was the manager's turn to show off a nugget of information.

'Not the seafront.' He pointed across the inner harbour. 'He's over there. The penthouse on the left.'

*

Juggling fact and speculation, Knight hurried to the building. Since being cast out of Pernil Goode, Rupert Askew had somehow become rich enough to get his hands on over ten million pounds' worth of boat, and in all likelihood the farmhouse plus the land in the Jersey trust too. Yet, whatever he'd stolen from Clementine couldn't possibly have been enough to pay for it all. Perhaps there were other victims, or perhaps he'd become involved in some kind of crime which had nothing to do with her. In which case, why had he killed her, if indeed he had? Could she have witnessed some outrageous perversion at the summerhouse and threatened to expose him? It was hard to imagine what degree of depravity would drive someone to murder in order to cover it up.

He reached his destination only to find the way barred by an electronic security gate. Thwarted, he made his way to the café where Lolly was waiting. As he crossed the bridge over the inner basin, he could not help but glance over to where *Adrenaline Rush* should be. She was hanging from a crane, her prow and wheelhouse out of the water with the stern submerged.

His first instinct was to help. He could see Merv standing beside a pair of men in overalls but, when he raised his arm and waved, he turned his back. Unsure if Merv had seen him, Knight walked on. It was not a betrayal, he told himself. Whatever had happened, there would be nothing he could do about it.

Knight was the last person Merv wanted to see. His ruin complete, he watched the water pouring from the six-inch hole directly under the wheelhouse where the acid had pooled. His anger for the moment was directed at Charlie Fleece for not renewing the insurance. The crane alone was going to cost half of his available cash, never mind what it would take to fix the hole. Mrs Chang had gone home in a taxi; he'd been required to pay for that too. For all he craved an ally at this moment, there was no way he could let Knight witness the scale of the disaster for which he partly blamed himself. Hidden between the two much larger boats, *Adrenaline Rush* was, he now realised, invisible to the security cameras.

He was relieved when Knight moved on. It allowed him to turn his mind to more important matters, the first of which was what he was going to do to O'Driscoll.

*

'I think you're right.'

Lolly took a sip of cappuccino, leaving a slim line of frothed milk on her lip.

'She saw him here when she was sketching. She wanted to keep tabs on him, so she fooled you into telling her how to do it. But then she saw something she wasn't meant to, and he killed her.'

Unhurriedly, she wiped away the milk with the tip of her tongue.

'It could also have been Bahir,' he reminded her. 'Or it could have been his uncle Malik. But it's all circumstantial.'

There was an edginess about her. She had insisted on coming when he mentioned his plan to visit the marina office. A few moments ago, when he had pulled another rabbit from the hat in the form of Rupert's address, there had been another outburst of adulation, but it gave way quickly to the adept marshalling of facts and guesswork he had witnessed before. There had been no mention of the kiss.

'If it is all circumstantial, does that mean the only way to get him is with a confession?'

Uneasy about the implications of the question, Knight agreed it was. 'Is that feasible?'

It didn't feel like a request, more an assessment of his capabilities. Many decades had passed since he had done anything remotely like that; it was not a prospect he relished.

'It's not impossible. But a forced confession wouldn't stand up in court. You'd have to trick it out of him, or one of the others.' He had done that too, but with backup. And money. 'It wouldn't be easy,' he concluded lamely.

'I know it wouldn't. Which means for now all we have is the penthouse. Do you think you can get us in? Please?'

She reached across the table and took his hand. Whether it was the perfectly curated texture of her skin, or its temperature, or some bio-magnetic quirk which chose this moment to rear its head, it was hard to say. But the necessary charge was duly imparted, providing a compelling resumé of everything that had been said in the kiss.

Half an hour later, they were at the security gate, Knight bearing a gift bag. To the casual observer, it would have contained wine or perhaps something stronger, not a bottle of supermarket water wrapped in tissue paper. They waited until a neighbour returned from lunch and let them in, not doubting they were the uncle and aunt of an absent resident who wished to deposit a gift outside his door. After noting that the old man looked exhausted and possibly out of his depth with such a glamorous wife, the gentleman gave them no further thought.

For the chosen few, the preferred entrance to the penthouse was via a lift which opened inside the apartment itself. For anyone else there was a tradesman's entrance at the top of a flight of stairs from the floor below. Both were operated by electronic key cards.

Having bid farewell to the neighbour, they rode to the penultimate floor and walked up the stairs. Knight could see at a glance that nothing he possessed would take them past the electronic lock, while the door itself looked impregnable. To his mind, it was a task that called for delegation.

Lolly thought the idea was completely mad, yet she marvelled at the transformation which ensued as he made the call. He morphed, effortlessly it seemed, into a querulous old fool, fearful and obdurate, implacable in his refusal to take no for an answer. Was he a madman or a magician? She had inspired many men to reach beyond their natural limits and knew the signs when they were reaching too far. Men were like car engines, they overheated if you ran them too hard. She reflected too, as they waited, that she bore the full responsibility for this. But she owed it to herself, if not to Clementine, to get through the next forty-eight hours or however long it took. All she could hope for Knight was he would come to no harm.

The fireman was polite enough at first; the chance to ogle high-end real estate was a respite from the training tower in the cold. But soon he found the old man intensely irritating. He seemed to wear his fearfulness as a badge of honour, refusing all attempts at reassurance.

'And did you smell smoke as well, madam?'

Lolly assured him that she had. It was more a burning smell she thought, perhaps an electrical one. Something similar had happened to her grandmother, not enough smoke to trigger the detectors until it was too late. To the fireman it made no sense at all, but she, at least, appeared relatively sane. Like the neighbour before him, he wondered what she saw in the old fool; it could only be money. His colleague waited at the foot of the stairs, watching the trio clustered around the door. He had formed much the same impression.

The first fireman produced the set of key cards he had brought from the fire station. He would have preferred to use the lift, the idea of arriving inside the apartment appealed to him. Unfortunately, there were rules about escape routes, even when the chances of a fire were vanishingly small.

Knight caught Lolly's eye as the door opened. He noted the way her mouth dropped open a fraction as if she had witnessed a miracle, and how she was looking at him with something approaching reverence.

'Will you wait here please, sir?' The first fireman went on ahead, followed by his colleague. He subjected Lolly to a stare of unstinting approval on his way past, which he was sure she returned.

On the other side of the door, was a spacious foyer where the lift entered the apartment. Beyond it were two passages branching left and right, leading to the living areas. When the firemen were out of sight, Knight followed with Lolly behind him. They were in the kitchen, admiring the appliances.

'Have you found it?' he enquired anxiously.

'Sir, you can't come in here.'

'I beg your pardon?'

They both glared at him, their patience wearing thin. It didn't matter, a few more seconds was all he needed.

'Go and wait at the door please; I won't ask you again.'

'I'm perfectly entitled to be here,' Knight objected. 'This is my nephew's property and I have every right to represent his interests!'

Dropping all pretence at civility, one of the firemen took Knight firmly by the arm.

'Out! Now.'

'How dare you!' Knight shook himself free and backed out of the kitchen. 'If this is what you get for taking the trouble to report an emergency, it's the last time I'm doing it!'

The fireman sighed. 'We're very grateful sir. Now, will you please… just… leave.'

Knight harrumphed and did as he was bid. 'Darling,' he called petulantly, 'we have to go, we're not wanted here.' On his way through the foyer he complained loudly to her about the lack of respect for responsible citizens who didn't shirk their duty, and made a point of slamming the door loudly.

After stretching their appraisal of the penthouse and its contents for as long as they dared, the firemen departed too. Passing the built-in cupboard opposite the lift, one of them detected an aroma of oranges. He took it to be an air freshener, and made a note to buy one for his wife as a birthday present.

Chapter Twenty-Nine

Knight waited two floors down until they came out. They were laughing, a harsh, locker room cackle about something they couldn't wait to tell the others, though he couldn't hear what it was. Through a window opposite the lift shaft, he could see the fire engine below. When it departed, he returned to the top of the stairs, replaying in his mind's eye the look on Lolly's face.

She was in a state of excitement as she opened the door, though it wasn't about his stroke of genius in letting them in.

'I've found his office,' she announced, leading him down the passage to a large room at the far end of the penthouse. She was already wearing the latex gloves they had picked up when they bought the water. At a window overlooking the harbour was a Bauhaus desk, the top drawer of which was open.

Knight's face clouded. 'You haven't moved anything, have you?'

'Of course not! Look, this was in it.'

The diary was bound in crocodile skin, with scrawled entries that were mostly names of women and restaurants.

'That's good, well done,' he said grudgingly. It was, too. She had made a point of finding an office first, as he would have done. He photographed the pages on the bodycam.

'No, here.' She pointed to the space for the following day. It was empty, but the date itself was discreetly underlined just as it had been in the summerhouse. Going back, there were several more.

'They're the same ones, I'm sure I remember them. Something is happening tomorrow in that cabin; it has to be.'

Knight was adrift for a moment, thrown by the significance of the find but more by the way Lolly was rifling through the remaining drawers with the assurance of a pro.

'We have to be quick,' he said, in an attempt to assert himself. 'Look for phones, laptops, and anything of Clementine's he might have kept as a trophy.'

'And photos,' she added, without looking up. 'We should split up. You start in the room opposite and we'll work our way to the other end.'

Knight hesitated, wasting valuable seconds. She might miss something, but they'd achieve twice as much if they did as she said. Already she had finished the desk and was turning her attention to the bookshelves.

'Well, go on then!' She seemed surprised that he was still there.

'Don't forget to check the floors for gravel,' he told her as he left, even though he knew she would.

The room opposite was the master suite. It boasted a titanic four-poster bed and a bathroom clad in black granite. He found it oppressive; beneath the luxury was an unspoken aggression, a declaration of power.

There was time for no more than a frantic skim of the surface. If the fire service had contacted Askew, he would send someone immediately, possibly Bahir or the gunman from the woods. There was a wrap of cocaine in the cabinet and another in the pocket of an Armani suit, but nothing to link him to Clementine.

Lolly was already in the main reception room, sixty feet of trophy furniture and silk carpets bounded by floor-to-ceiling glass. He watched as she looked behind the pictures and filleted a cocktail cabinet.

'I'll do the sofas,' he informed her.

'Already done them, there's nothing.'

He took himself to the kitchen, where he delved into the backs of cupboards and pulled out the drawers to look beneath them. The fridge was given over largely to champagne; he scrabbled in the compartments, hoping in vain to find Rohypnol or Ketamine.

His frustration mounted. It wasn't just the lack of time, it was the way Lolly's single-mindedness seemed to relegate him to the sidelines. He told himself he was being ridiculous. She was closing in on the man she believed had killed her sister – how did he expect her to behave? And how would she react, he now wondered, if justice eluded her?

On his side of the passage, there remained a guest bedroom and a gym that looked as if it was never used. From her side, he heard her leave the sitting room and move on. He found nothing. There was no safe, no weapon, no computer. There had been a printer and a router in the office; presumably he had taken the computer with him. They had already stayed too long.

'Lolly!' he shouted. 'It's time to go.'

She heard him but didn't answer. Instead she took out her phone and started to photograph the room she had just walked into. It was no worse than the handful of others of its type she had seen, but still made her feel slightly ill. Potentially, it was also gold dust.

'Lolly!'

Knight strode in purposefully, only to stop in his tracks as he saw what the firemen had been laughing about. He had never actually visited an S and M dungeon, but this was what he took it to be, even though it was in a penthouse rather than the bowels of the earth. The walls were lined with glass cabinets displaying whips, canes, probes and items of clothing he didn't recognise; from the ceiling hung a leather harness sporting stainless steel shackles. In the centre, was a circle of screens painted with nymphs and satyrs engaging in improbable acts of congress reminiscent of Grice's floor vase, though with a greater emphasis on pain than pleasure.

Incongruously, Lolly was snapping everything with the zeal of a Japanese tourist.

'See what's behind the screens,' she instructed him. 'And look for pictures, he may have taken pictures.'

Knight felt his grip slipping. He couldn't understand why she was photographing everything when he was getting it on the bodycam.

'We leave in exactly one minute.' It was an order.

One of the screens in the circle was mounted on wheels so that it could serve as a door. When he pushed it open, he was assailed by multiple versions of himself, reflected from the mirrors on the backs of the panels. In the middle of the circle was a low plinth covered in crimson velvet. On top of it lay a double coffin. This, in itself, was shocking enough; what truly awed him was the carving. Reclining on the coffin lid, knees raised and legs akimbo, was a carving of a naked woman sculpted from the same piece of wood. Only she wasn't quite a woman. The gaping mouth, the bulging eyes and above all the cartoon breasts were explicitly in the style of a blow-up doll.

A dozen or so Lollys arrived. Without hesitating she raised the phone; a dozen or so flashes dazzled him.

'I'm going to see if I can open it,' he announced tersely.

With deep foreboding, he moved from corner to corner, feeling beneath the rim of the coffin's lid. Every few feet there were air holes in the side, which gave him some comfort; if there had been a body inside for any time it would surely smell by now. Halfway round he found a gold-plated disc embodied in the wood, with a smaller disc at its centre.

'You may want to look away,' he warned, but she was busy lining up a shot.

Despite the air holes, he felt a keen sense of dread as he pushed the button. With a hydraulic hiss, the lid ascended, not sideways as it might have done in a vampire movie, but vertically on four wooden posts. The lid was now a canopy. What lay beneath it were not human remains, but a bed.

'For god's sake!' she muttered.

It was not a bed for those in search of a good night's rest. It was a pit, or rather a playpen, in shiny black PVC with soft padding that reached to the top of the coffin's sides. A small shelf had been built across one of the corners, beside which was a button like the one on the outside. Laid out neatly on the shelf, as if on a surgeon's tray, were clamps, forceps and an ominously large dildo. There was also something small that looked vaguely like a corkscrew.

'I hope he rots in hell,' she spat as she stepped in to get closer.

Knight's desire to leave suddenly boiled over.

'Lolly, you really don't need to do that! Can we please get out of here.'

Still she paid no attention. Recalling their first encounter, he didn't fancy his chances of dragging her away. It would have made no difference even if he had succeeded. As he threatened unconvincingly to leave without her, they both heard a distinctive ping that announced the arrival of the lift.

Knight stole to the open panel. He could hear a rancorous male voice, heavily accented. As it drew closer, he picked out the name Richard more than once. His mind grappled ineffectually with the options, all of them bad, until he heard a faint hiss behind him. The canopy was descending, and Lolly was beckoning frantically for him to join her. He could think of a host of reasons why it was lunacy, but at that moment he didn't have a better idea. He scurried to the coffin and half dived, half fell through the shrinking gap, whisking his stick away an instant before the lid clicked shut.

They lay motionless, scarcely breathing. The voice receded as the visitor moved away down the passage. Knight turned onto his side and tried to raise his body, only to bump his head on the lid.

'What are you doing?' she whispered accusingly.

'Trying to get to the button. When the lid opens we run for the door.'

The problem was their heads were at the wrong end of the bed, whose size was in any case designed for close contact rather than people in bulky street clothes, in her case a copious chinchilla coat. She had to flatten herself against the side while he performed a kind of slow-motion dive around her head, dragging himself on his elbows like some slow primeval creature that had failed to evolve competent limbs. He could scarcely bend his back and had no more than an inch of headroom, which meant that his skull was pressed hard against her hips. Any sense of the exotic was wasted on him, the more so when his back mutinied and he found himself stuck with his head wedged between her thighs.

'Let me try,' she whispered.

He was starting to sweat. Her kneecaps dug into his scalp as she squirmed past, face down. The button was not even close. Only then did it occur to him how else he might reach it.

'The stick, can you get it to me?'

'I'm lying on it. You'll have to reach.'

He stretched his arm and found her shoulder. As he burrowed into the chinchilla it became evident that he would either have to circumnavigate her breast or pass his hand directly beneath it. He twisted his shoulder painfully, adjusting the angle to avoid contact.

'You're going the wrong way,' she hissed.

She was able to arch her back fractionally. His fifteen-year-old hand would have been no less agitated, but before this could become a moment of apotheosis, or even cheap farce, his fingers found the tip of the stick. He worked it steadily until it emerged from beneath her shoulder, allowing him to reach with his other hand and withdraw it.

His first attempt on the button was stymied by the instruments on the shelf. He stabbed blindly, at last detecting the metal plate; the button would be a few inches to the right. Like a snooker player poised over the final black, he drew back the stick but then stopped dead. The voice had returned. It was somewhere in the passage by the sitting room, then it was at the dungeon door.

'Listen to me. I will not tell you again to calm down.' He spoke with an icy calm, struggling to hold back his anger. 'We don't know it was him. All they said was an old man with a young woman.'

He came in.

'I told you, there's no one here. I'm in your little playroom now. You think I like to look at this stuff?'

They heard the screen on wheels being pushed aside, followed by a snort of disgust.

'You are a sick man, you know that? You're lucky Bahir is on the boat with you and it's me who's seeing this and not him!'

He felt Lolly stiffen. She had managed to straighten her body so that they were spooning, squeezed together as if glued. Contorting his neck, he squinted through one of the air holes. Knight's bet was that the dark, middle-aged man with a gun in his hand was Malik. Oddly, there was a smear of white paint on the trousers of his expensive suit.

'I already told you,' he snapped, 'I have dealt with it. After today he is not a problem anymore, he's gone. Which part of that do you not understand?' He spat a curse in Arabic. 'Okay, where do I find it?'

He was moving round the coffin toward the button. It might have been sensible at this point to surrender, perhaps concocting some unlikely story and then making a dash for the door at the first opportunity. Lolly's presence put paid to the thought. As Knight saw it, the best chance would be to ram him with the stick as soon as the lid began to open, going for the gun and then the throat. His hand lodged against something sharp; the corkscrew object had fallen from the shelf. It could do the job for him if he stayed alive long enough to get in close.

But the lid didn't open. As Knight braced himself for the onslaught, the man lost the battle with his temper.

'You do not blame me for this!' he exploded. 'This is your fault, your problem, and me who has to fix it. You do this one more time and I find someone else, you understand that?' He fairly shouted the last sentence, with which he was gone.

They took the stairs, Lolly flying ahead despite his entreaties to stay close. He caught her up at the last landing, checking the lobby.

'He's gone,' she said, her voice unsteady. 'Please, I need a drink.'

*

The hotel bar was filling up. He had suggested his flat, only to recall there was nothing to offer her. She wouldn't wait while they found a shop. In the car she had been terse and withdrawn but, by the third vodka, she had regained some of her composure. By the fourth, she was the coolheaded strategist again.

'We're still not quite there, are we?'

The presumption that the next step ought to be ready and waiting up his sleeve was not lost on him.

'No, we're not,' he replied guardedly. 'We have evidence that he's a pervert, but it's not against the law.'

'More's the pity. And it doesn't put him with my sister either. What we need is a full forensic search at all his properties, which isn't going to happen.'

He could have done with a coat of varnish on the truth. What he had just pulled off was nothing short of sensational, even if he had failed to unearth a smoking gun.

'Not without going to the police. I can try, but I still don't see them buying it.'

'Then all we have left is the camera in the summerhouse, is that right? Unless you can get a confession from one of them.'

Knight had told her this was a last resort; now its time had all but arrived. The unvarnished truth in this instance was that, without Merv to help him, the odds were impossible.

'It would take time. And a lot of planning.' With little chance of success, he was going to add.

'Just in theory, how would you go about it?'

Knight bristled. Less than an hour ago their bodies had been squeezed together in an intimacy that surely merited at least a passing reference, but it was as if the event had never happened.

'First, I have to get one of them on his own, preferably Askew. It couldn't be under duress because anything he said wouldn't count in court. And then…'

What then? Beating a confession out of him wouldn't count either, even if he was prepared to do it. 'I'd have to fool him somehow; make him believe we have more evidence than we do,' he concluded weakly.

He could see that Lolly was likewise unconvinced.

'It's a very long shot, isn't it?'

She didn't seem disappointed. It was just an option which had been crossed off the list.

'So, all we can do is hope that something happens in the summerhouse tomorrow and the camera catches it. There's nothing else, is there?'

He remembered one other small scrap and threw it in, conscious of scraping the bottom of the barrel.

'I sent the Chinese inscription to a professional translator. I'm not holding my breath but I'd like to know what it really means.'

For a moment, it was as if he had startled her. She seemed to catch her breath, but then said, somewhat flatly, 'I can't see how that will help. Let's just hope the camera works tomorrow.'

He was on the verge of pointing out that the camera had never failed before, when an uncomfortable thought occurred, one that might explain her state of mind.

'Lolly,' he asked gently, 'have you thought what happens if we can't prove anything?'

She shrugged. 'I suppose I'll have to cross that bridge when we come to it.'

'Are you quite sure about that?'

She looked unsure of herself. Something of the old vulnerability resurfaced, as if a bubble had been pricked.

'What do you mean?'

'You know as well as I do that nothing that happens tomorrow is likely to prove who killed your sister. So are you sure you aren't thinking of taking the law into your own hands?'

She was silent for a moment, her eyes engaging with his in a way they hadn't for a while.

'Supposing I was. Would you help me?'

Knight felt the ground sway beneath his feet. A torrent of emotions played havoc in his mind, chief among them a profound sense of foolishness that he had allowed himself to be deceived.

'No!' he protested sharply. 'That would make you no better than him, and how do you know you wouldn't end up dead yourself?'

He was half expecting tears, but, in the literal twinkling of an eye, she turned everything upside down again.

'Of course, I won't, you silly thing.' The mischievous elfin smile was there again. 'But I'm allowed to fantasise about it, aren't I? Wouldn't you?'

Knight was no less confused than he had been a moment ago.

'I suppose I might. But you haven't answered me – what will you do if we can't get any proof?'

The elf grew serious.

'I'll ask if I can lean on your shoulder and let you guide me for a bit longer,' she said softly. 'That's if you're willing. You see…' she swallowed. 'No other man's ever stood by me like you have. I've never known this.'

Sincere though she sounded, there was something odd about her choice of words, as if there were a whiff of pulp romance about them. But the tears were real enough, and now she had smudged her mascara. He reached into his pocket for a tissue and came up against something sharp.

Lolly looked aghast at the object in his hand.

'Where did you get that?' she asked. 'Don't hold it up for everyone to see.' Paco gave them an odd look as he passed by.

'It was in the coffin. I was going to use it on him if I had to.'

She frowned. 'I beg your pardon?'

'With the spiral bit. I think it's some kind of corkscrew.'

With pronounced distaste, she picked it up and examined it discreetly. About four inches long, green with white flecks, it consisted mostly of a bulbous ovoid about the size of a pheasant egg. One end was gently rounded, the spiral protruded from the other.

'It's jade,' she explained. 'Carved from one piece, Chinese probably. But it's not a corkscrew.' She pointed to the spiral. 'This is meant to be the tail of a pig, the rest is its body. Can you see the face?'

Knight looked more closely. Faintly abraded on the rounded end were indeed the snout, eyes, and ears of a pig.

'So what is it then?'

'You really don't know?'

Something about the way she said it made him wish he had left the thing in his pocket.

'It's a butt plug. You know what that is, don't you?'

He did. He felt a revulsion, not so much at the purpose of the object as from the recollection of the peanuts he had taken at the bar with his unwashed hand. More than that, he felt stupid for not recognising it. She would think him naive and unworldly, though there was no telling what she would have thought if he had known what it was. Most of all, he felt cheated out of a moment. She had been opening up to him again, he had been about to wipe away a tear, only to be plunged into the depths of grossness.

Lolly, too, seemed knocked off her stride. Which she was, though not because of a lewd artefact. To have any chance of keeping the truth at bay, she needed to keep him close now.

'There's something else I need to ask,' she said, then with a faint tremble in her voice, 'please don't think you have to say yes, you've done so much as it is.'

Grateful to be back on familiar ground, Knight would gladly have agreed to anything, however rash the promise.

'I'll do whatever I can,' he replied, 'as long as it doesn't put you in danger.'

She took a deep breath.

'I don't want to be alone here tonight. Can I stay with you?'

Chapter Thirty

The sole occupant of the freezer was a packet of chicken nuggets. Elsewhere were the remnants of an onion bhaji and a bag of salad turning to slime. Had he been eating alone, he might have ignored the salad and settled for the rest in the microwave, but he persevered and found a potato in the cupboard beside an ancient can of peas and a stock cube.

Having cooked the nuggets, he chopped them up with the bhaji and the salad, after washing away the slime. Yearning for pancetta, he diced the potato into cubes. Accompanied by the peas, the assembled ingredients joined forces in the stock to produce a creditable minestrone, which he left to simmer.

The status of the meal was open to question. The degree of care lavished on unpromising material suggested high hopes for the evening ahead, which the diehards were keen to promote. Their opponents reminded him Lolly was unpredictable, that hope must be treated with caution, but most of all he also found himself imagining how Merv would have construed his efforts.

Merv's presence in his thoughts was persistent. He tried to swat him away but he kept popping up at odd moments, with a message as beguiling as it was crass. You're on a promise, mate, he could hear him saying it. He tried his best to dismiss the notion of a ripe fruit about to drop into his hands, reminding himself that she was vulnerable, alone, frightened by the ordeal in the penthouse; small wonder she should look to him for refuge. Did he mean to exploit that? But she had said, 'I want to stay with you tonight,' – not 'can you put me up?' or 'do you have a spare room?'

The muddle followed him into the office, where he had set up the camp bed for himself. Was that sending the right message? Should there even be a message? He felt paralysed by indecision, made worse by the fatigue which had begun to steal over him.

The sofa beckoned. She had said she would come at eight and it was now a little after seven thirty. He had no intention of falling asleep, though it would have been a release from the dizzying prospect that a drought was about to end. Strive as he might to filter it out, Merv's voice provided a steady drumbeat to his thoughts.

*

Descending in the lift, Lolly ran through her options. If Bullock was in the bar, she would go back to the first floor and take the service stairs to the alleyway behind the hotel. If he wasn't, she would check the street from the main entrance. The tricky part would be the walk to her car, where he might appear at any moment. He had tried to corner her several times, turning every excursion into a cat-and-mouse game. Somebody was spying on her, but she had no idea who it might be. She hoped it wasn't Paco. The closest call had been when he turned up drunk at her door in the early hours of the morning. She had pulled the duvet over her head and waited, her heart pounding, until the night manager coaxed him away.

He was not in the bar or waiting outside. Head into the wind, she strode out, ready to turn tail the second he appeared. Seeing the way clear, she crossed the road and upped her pace. Unusually for her, she was unsure of her ground. The plan was simple enough, the getaway as sound as any she had contrived, yet she could not deny that her chances of success would be higher with Knight at her side. She had even felt a strong urge to put her cards on the table and tell him the truth.

But that would have meant breaking the golden rule. All the bad things that had happened to her were the result of putting her trust in a man, and by learning not to do so she had taken back control of her life. The very fact that she had considered relinquishing it suggested her judgement was clouded. This made it harder to focus on the other question that exercised her: should she strike immediately or bide her time?

She heard the car before she saw it, the familiar Neanderthal growl of the twin exhaust followed by angry hooting as the black BMW shot across the oncoming traffic and stopped on a double yellow line a few yards ahead. She turned and walked back immediately, not daring to let him see her run. She had no chance. Her flesh crept as an arm with a strong whiff of B.O. descended on her shoulder.

'Steve! How amazing; what are you doing here?'

He squeezed hard enough for it to be a warning and pulled her into a doorway.

'Are you sure you're pleased?' There was a malevolent delight in his voice. 'I could have sworn you were avoiding me.'

'No, you silly, of course not! I forgot something at my hotel, that's all.' The tedium of it was getting to her, the sheer energy it took to dazzle and charm.

'Going somewhere nice?' He was looking at her overnight luggage, a Valentino leather tote.

'No, just a bit of shopping. Can't bear throwing away all those bags they give you.'

He smirked. She smirked back and ran a consoling fingertip along his jawbone.

'I haven't been avoiding you, I promise. And I haven't forgotten your lesson either. I've just been run off my feet.'

'Fair enough. How about now then?'

She made a face sorrowful enough to announce a bereavement.

'Oh Steve, I can't. I'm on at the club tonight.' Then, as if struck by inspiration, she added, 'What about the end of the week? I'll have calmed down by then and we can enjoy ourselves without having to rush.'

'No. Has to be today.' With the satisfaction of a poker player revealing his fourth ace, he produced a document and held it out for her to read. She didn't need to, the Interpol heading told her everything there was to know.

'Oh that!' She managed a giggle. 'No one cares about that, it's just a stupid misunderstanding.'

'The Dutch police seem to care about it. They think you had a little something going on with one of their top fraudsters, which is why they wanted to talk to you. Only you left in a bit of a hurry.'

'But I'm not wanted here,' she cajoled. 'I'm not on any list or they would have stopped me at the airport.'

He grinned wolfishly. 'Your friend's on the list. Interpol didn't rate you as it happens, but the Dutch still have a warrant out for your arrest. Which means that really I should take you in.'

She cursed him for digging so deeply. He was not unlike Hendrik, equally pickled in testosterone, though Hendrik had a body to die for and a lot of money. Not that she'd seen as much of it as she deserved.

'So shall we stop messing about? What do you think?'

Seeing the ugly glint in his eyes, she wanted to squirt them with the pepper spray in her pocket. Instead, she bit her tongue. The plan would be in tatters if he followed through on his threat.

'Steve, this is so unnecessary, you don't have to force me to see you. I thought you knew that.'

She couldn't repeat the fingertip on his face. It was either take his hand or adjust his tie. Opting for the latter, she played her last card.

'Look, I really do have to go to the club tonight. Why don't you come tomorrow morning? Wouldn't that be a nice way for us to start the day?'

He shook his head.

'No. More than happy to start at the club, though. Get in the car, I'll take you there.'

*

Knight was swimming with Lolly in the sea. He could see their house in the hills above the beach. Now she was in the garden, halfway up a slender palm tree. She was spinning around it slowly, an outstretched hand beckoning him to join her. Wrapping his arms around the trunk, he pushed himself up with his feet, only for her to retreat higher and vanish. And now something was buzzing, an electric saw it seemed, for the tree was toppling.

He awoke with a start, the electric saw revealing itself as his phone vibrating on the coffee table. When he saw the time, he thought she had been and gone, but the text told otherwise. 'Unavoidably detained, so sorry. Will try to come later. Love you, Lolly xxx'

His call went straight to voicemail. Not trusting himself to sound composed, he didn't leave a message. He considered going to her hotel, only to see how foolish he would look if there was an innocent explanation. It seemed he had little choice other than to take the text at face value.

The short sleep – it was now eight thirty – had done nothing to refresh him. In an attempt to fight off the fatigue, he forced himself to revisit his list of outstanding tasks. Finding and signing the letter to appoint the estate agent should have taken seconds, but it was an age before he could bring himself to write his signature. When the dirty washing only amounted to half a load, he fell into an exhausting debate as to whether he should run the machine now or wait until there was more. In the same vein, he felt bound to turn the heating off but couldn't face the thought of being cold again. The suspicion that he had caught a bug was confirmed when a mild nausea began to take hold. The injustice of it infuriated him; that on this, of all nights, he should fall prey to some niggling virus.

Digging deep, he found a kernel of defiance, small but imbued with the grim determination of a kidney stone. Whatever it took, he would stay awake.

*

Bullock, by contrast, was enjoying his best evening since the flight of Katya. There had been private dances with champagne paid for by Lolly, and many banknotes thrust into her g-string, or rather one that he had used repeatedly and was now back in his pocket. She had refused to remove the g-string. 'Not in here,' she'd pleaded, with the obvious concession that it would happen somewhere else.

Now he lay on the bed in her room, watching her ride the pole. He had wanted to go to his flat but she insisted on keeping her promise of a lesson, hinting mysteriously at a special surprise awaiting him at the end of it. There seemed no reason not to indulge her, besides which it would be easier to order room service for breakfast than have to explain where everything was in his kitchen. Honed over many years, his judgement was that she wouldn't dare to lodge a complaint against him. Nevertheless, he had made a point of bringing an additional insurance policy, and so was glad she was in the bathroom when the champagne arrived.

'Ready,' he called to Lolly when the man had gone. He poured two glasses then quickly tipped the powdered Rohypnol into one of them.

'Happy days,' he toasted her.

'Happy days, darling.'

He took back her glass and replaced it on the tray. He didn't want her passing out just yet.

'I think it's time for that special surprise you told me about.'

Her lips twitched wickedly.

'So do I. But first, you have to show me what you're capable of. Over here.'

She put a chair next to the pole then, from a small pot, took a dab of something white which she made him rub on his hands.

'To help you grip,' she explained. She stood on the chair and smeared some near the top of the pole. 'You put your hands up here. I'll help you with the rest.'

It wasn't clear to Bullock how this might open the gates of paradise, but he went along with it. He took her place on the chair and placed his hands where she had instructed.

'Now bring your legs up.'

This much was just about possible. He lifted his feet from the floor, bending his knees so his legs were tucked in beneath him.

'No, straight out in front of you.'

This was different. His back and thighs ached immediately but, before he could abandon the position, she stepped back onto the chair and took hold of his feet.

'That's amazing,' she purred. 'And now, we're taking these all the way to the top.'

Bullock was appalled.

'You are joking, right? Let me down.'

'What?' She sounded shocked. 'Steve, you can't be serious. Even Mervyn managed it, and he's half the man you are.'

With renewed purpose, Bullock strained every sinew. Without her support it would have been impossible, even with it his stomach muscles threatened to implode at any moment. Yet, as his feet approached their destination, he felt the wind in his sails. It was a shame he was facing away from her. He estimated his head must be at about the level of the g-string; he pictured the shimmering sequins and much else. What he could not see was that she was supporting him with one hand now, while the other removed a small tube of Vaseline from behind the very sequins that danced in his mind's eye. She squeezed some of it onto the pole directly below his hands.

'Amazing,' she breathed as his toes reached the top. 'Now, wrap your legs around the pole.'

For an instant, he gloried in his triumph, though with the removal of her support he felt his hands slip fractionally down the pole. Then he felt no grip at all, only an excruciating explosion of pain in his shoulder as it hit the floor with his full weight behind it.

*

Knight rode out another wave of nausea. At first, he had thought it was flu, but now he suspected food poisoning. He cast his mind back over what he had eaten in the last twenty-four hours, which turned out to be a tub of potato salad. It was two days over its date, or so he had thought. He made his way unsteadily to the bathroom and put a finger down his throat, retching unpleasantly but producing no more than a trickle of bile.

On the return journey, he paused at the bedroom door. The weariness which had begun earlier was now an exhaustion that left him limp and barely capable of thought. He didn't want Lolly to see him like this, so what exactly was the point of the battle to stay awake? He was taking off his shoes when he heard the buzzing sound again and felt the phone vibrating in his pocket. It would be her, saying she was on her way at last. Fate had found another way to mock him.

But it wasn't Lolly at all. It was the camera alert.

*

Lolly was in an A & E cubicle at Eastbourne General Hospital, and by no means rid of her burden yet. A display of distraught compassion, operatic in its intensity, had not been sufficient to convince Bullock the fall was a shockingly unfortunate accident. Under threat of arrest, she had thus been obliged to accompany him in the ambulance. As she expected, having done it to herself more than once, the triage nurse had provisionally diagnosed a fractured collarbone. He was propped up on a trolley bed with his eyes closed. Every now and then he opened them to check she was still there.

'Painkillers,' he mumbled. 'Find my painkillers.'

It was pathetic, the nurse had already given him more than enough. Chafing to be gone, she went through the jacket she had hung on the back of a chair. In one pocket she found a brass knuckleduster, a particularly brutish model adorned with spikes. Disgusted but not surprised, she put it back. In the next, was a pack of paracetamol and a loose strip of capsules she assumed was part of it. When she recognised the Rohypnol logo, her opinion of Bullock hit a new low.

Twenty minutes later, he was staring into space. She felt no compunction. This was what he had intended for her, his guarantee that he could use her body like a toy and leave her remembering nothing. So it would be for him; she only regretted there wasn't more she could do to make him pay. What worried her was that the amount she'd given him would only see her through the next few hours, and she needed him out of the way for longer.

She glanced through the curtain. The nurse who had seen them was hunched over a computer screen at the central desk; elsewhere an orderly was trying to placate an aggressive drunk; no one was anywhere near their cubicle. Reaching into her handbag, she sought out the object that wasn't a corkscrew and inserted it as far as it would go into the part of Bullock's anatomy where the sun didn't shine.

*

Knight watched again as Malik carried a crate of liquor to the bar and unpacked the bottles. He set out glasses on the tables, then came back to the entrance for a pair of Marks and Spencer bags containing towels, which he took to the bathroom. And that was it. After a quick look round, he switched off the light and left. A few moments later, darkness and the absence of motion brought the recording to an end.

He had played it many times, more to distract himself than to spot a detail he may have missed. It seemed clear to him what was happening: the alcohol was for the guests who would be arriving in the next few hours. It was less obvious what form the party would take, given that there was only one bed; perhaps they drew lots. Not that he cared. His eyes insisted on shutting, so to stay awake he had to prise them open every minute or so. Having abandoned the food poisoning theory, he had forced down the minestrone in the hope it would give him strength. But the nausea had returned with a vengeance, accompanied by a blinding headache.

To avoid dozing off, he had stationed himself at the kitchen table rather than the sofa. Now that the minestrone was poised to make its comeback, he had to move. For the first time in weeks, he had to lean heavily on his stick to get to his feet. A slow-motion race to the bathroom ensued, which he lost badly. Well short of the toilet bowl he was sick, most of it discharging onto his trousers.

He tipped the seat shut and sat down. There had been a report in the paper that winter flu had claimed two old ladies at a rest home. Out of pride and complacency, he hadn't bothered with the free vaccination offered to the elderly, an act of hubris he now regretted. Fearful that he might at any moment topple to the floor, he set about peeling off the trousers.

His vision was blurring. He fixed his eyes on the floor in front of him, trying to keep it in focus. At first, he thought he might be hallucinating; by the airing cupboard there was a white mark he was sure he hadn't seen before. When he looked away and back; it was still there.

Something told him it was important to know more. Clutching the sink and then the towel rail, he tottered to the door and opened it. Inside, the cupboard was spattered with white paint. A half-full tin from when he had glossed the woodwork had been knocked over. It had been replaced where he had left it on the shelf, but perhaps not exactly. He tried to picture it the last time he had looked in the cupboard, but his mind was closing down fast, serving up a shifting mosaic of sick, white paint, a white stain, trousers, Malik... he looked beyond the shelf to the boiler behind it. There were scratches around the screws on the flange where the flue entered the wall. He slid open the small inspection hatch to look at the flame inside the boiler. It was burning bright yellow.

As he backed out, his legs gave way. He crawled to the passage, knowing that it wouldn't be enough because the carbon monoxide would have filled the flat by now. Clinging to memories of assault courses and overnight marches, he inched towards the sitting room, assailed by siren voices imploring him to curl up and lay his ravaged body to rest.

Chapter Thirty-One

He was being peppered with icy pellets, and a crackling barrage that could have been gunfire rang in his ears. One eye opened and was greeted by a swarm of dancing white dots.

The hail had come in the early hours, an outlier of snowstorms on the other side of the Channel. He was lying on the terrace. Or rather his head and shoulders were, his legs trailed behind him in the sitting room. He was numb with cold.

A warning bell sounded dimly as he dragged himself inside. It all came back to him; he was in no man's land between the gas and the freezing hail, and the only way out was to turn off the boiler.

Facing the elements on his hands and knees, he took in deep breaths of the freezing air until his lungs ached. Despite the open door, the concentration in the flat would still be high, lethally so if he wasn't quick enough. A brutal forced march ensued. He came close to collapsing again when he reached the boiler switch. Shouting and singing to stay awake, he dragged himself around the flat opening the windows, sucking in lungfuls of air at each one.

Returning to no man's land wrapped in his coat and a duvet, he pulled a chair next to the open terrace door and collapsed into it, attempting to identify the pertinent facts. He had taken in enough carbon monoxide to make him pass out, which meant the levels in his blood would take hours to subside. It would leave him vulnerable to further attack until he replenished enough oxygen to make his brain and body halfway serviceable. As to the long-term effects, he didn't want to know.

He sat for half an hour braving the cold, steadily absorbing the clean air. When he felt strong enough, he made a foray into the kitchen to turn the kettle on, then shuffled back to the chair. He repeated the manoeuvre when the kettle boiled, and sat warming his hands on a mug of tea.

There was no question in his mind that Malik was responsible, and that he had known where to find him since the night of the pizza bike. When the tea had done its work he made another foray, this time into the bathroom. As he expected, when he unscrewed the flange and moved it aside there was a ball of rags packed tightly into the flue. Nor did it surprise him that the CO monitor was dead and its battery missing.

The stench of his discarded trousers meanwhile was inducing a fresh bout of nausea. His stick had fallen beside the toilet bowl. Prodding the tip through the belt, he delivered the stinking garment to the washing machine. This time he ran it.

Any number of neighbours could have let Malik into the building, just as he had duped the man at Sovereign Harbour. It was a hazard he accepted, but the front door was meant to be safe. He was wrong. With the aid of an old-fashioned magnifying glass, he found shiny scratches in the lock. The realisation that it had been picked shocked him almost as much as the poisoning. The lock was not cheap, he had chosen it on the basis that it lay well beyond his own abilities. It incensed him that a superior talent could brush him aside so easily.

He had to warn Lolly. Malik hadn't mentioned her by name, but it didn't mean he couldn't find her if he wanted to. His phone, however, had gone missing. It wasn't on his desk or behind a sofa cushion or in any of the other places he usually mislaid it. He thought back. It had definitely been in his trouser pocket when he returned from Lolly's hotel. Foreboding turned to panic when he realised where the trousers were.

Even when it was switched off, the machine would not allow him to open the door in mid-cycle. A sodden trouser leg taunted him from behind the glass, reminding him nothing on the phone was backed up and hadn't been for months. A spurt of wrath put a screwdriver in his hand. Kneeling awkwardly, he forced the tip into the door seal and leaned in hard, only for the screwdriver to spring loose and nick him painfully on the wrist. Cursing the machine for its stupidity, he sat on the floor and waited for it to complete the programme.

The phone was dead. His fingers were still too numb to prise the back off, so he left it in the kitchen and went to the office. There was still one burner phone in the drawer, but now a new obstacle stood in his way;

Lolly's number was in the device he had drowned. With the patience of Job, if lacking his piety, he waited for the computer to boot so he could look up the hotel's number. There was a mail from the collectors' site; it could wait.

The receptionist asked for his name and left him on hold. Expecting to be told there was no answer, he was almost startled to hear her voice.

'Tom, I'm so sorry about last night,' she said, before he had a chance to speak. 'I'll explain everything when I see you.'

He was more than curious to know, but it would have to wait.

'Lolly, you have to listen to me and do exactly what I say. You can't come here.'

Her voice went cold. 'Why, what's happened?'

Underplaying how close a call it had been, he gave her a terse summary of events.

'Do you think they know where I am?'

'It's possible. You have to stay in your room with the door locked, do you understand that?'

'For how long?' She didn't sound pleased.

'For as long as it takes. Don't open for anyone until you're absolutely sure who they are. I'll come later. I don't know when.'

'Have you told the police?' she asked, anxiously.

'Not yet.'

She went quiet for a moment.

'What are you going to do?'

'I don't know. I'm still working on it.'

He thought he heard her exhale sharply.

'Okay, I'll stay.' She paused. 'Why didn't you call me on my mobile?'

It was another question Knight didn't want to hear.

'I meant to. I must have hit the wrong button.'

'Oh.' She didn't sound convinced. 'What about the camera? Did you find anything?'

On firmer ground, he told her about Malik's visit to the summerhouse. She was hungry for detail and keen to speculate about what might follow. He might have found her interest odd had he not been anxious to avoid the subject of the phone.

'And nothing's come through since then?'

'No. Stay in your room,' he urged her again.

'I will. And Tom…' Her voice changed key. 'Be careful.' If only for a moment, he felt a grain of comfort.

He went back to the bathroom with a new battery and brought the CO monitor to life. The gas was all but gone. The priority now was the phone. He made more tea and warmed his hands on the cup until he could feel his fingers again. When at last he prised the back off he saw that the inside was almost full of water. Having removed the battery and all the cards, he dabbed the interior with an ear bud until most of it was gone. In the depths of his wardrobe was a fan he sometimes used in the summer. He set it up on the kitchen table with the phone propped against the bread bin, and left it to run.

Passing his office en route to the bedroom, he saw he had left the computer on. He was about to shut it down when he remembered the mail from the collectors' site. It was a chatty, if long winded, missive from somebody who had time on their hands, but it came with an unwelcome sting in its tail. The badge, it seemed, was once the property of the Military Intelligence Directorate of the Syrian Arab Republic.

The little Knight knew of Syrian military intelligence was that they were to be avoided, even in Eastbourne. Yet far from weakening his resolve, the revelation only served to stoke the outrage he already felt. A dangerous cocktail of anger, patriotism and bloody-mindedness coursed through him.

As to their involvement with Askew, he doubted it was government business. There had been a few grams of cocaine at the penthouse – the most likely explanation was that they were bringing it in on Askew's yacht and distributing it from the summerhouse. This would explain the fence and the cameras; presumably the sex parties were a way of keeping the clients sweet.

Knight put himself in Malik's shoes. If he found out he was still alive, surely he would attempt to strike again? The more he thought about it, the more it struck him that Malik should be offered the opportunity. Drawn into the open, he could take his turn at being the prey; then he would be made to talk. For this, of course, he would need to be in one piece. It called for a form of entrapment that would be overwhelming but non-lethal. As Knight's anger turned from fire to ice, a plan was not long in coming.

The challenge was the place. He needed somewhere remote enough for there to be no witnesses, yet easily accessible for him to make his preparations. There were farm buildings he could think of, and quiet corners of the retail estate, but they were either too big or ran the risk of a passing security patrol. It had to be a small, cramped space where nobody ever went. He cast his mind back through sheds, barns, boats and tunnels, and came at last to Hillside Grange. Clementine's cottage couldn't be seen from the road.

Equally encouraging, the rooms were small enough to concentrate the blast.

Chapter Thirty-Two

He took the stairs down to the service entrance at the rear of the building and looked out past the bins to the small car park. Given what he intended, he had taken steps not to be recognised. A low-brimmed hat, thick spectacles and a beard would be enough as long as he kept an eye on the ubiquitous CCTV cameras.

He had left the Skoda on the seafront the previous evening. If Malik was watching the building, that was where he would be too. Unless he wasn't alone. Edging to the end of the bins, he checked the road outside. Without his phone, there was no way of telling if Bahir's Audi was on the move. Malik's car was as yet an unknown quantity, though unlikely to be any of the modest saloons and hatchbacks lining the pavements of the quiet side street. After watching for a minute he set off, checking behind him every few paces.

In the event, the shopping trip proved uneventful. His mood improving, he went to Iceland and bought a party pack of frozen ribs on special offer. At the corner of the street that led to the rear of his building, he paused and scanned ahead. Unless the elderly lady looking down on him from her window had been hired to spy on him, he was safe as far as the service entrance. At his front door, he peered into the lock at the minuscule smear of paint he had left; it was unscratched. In the bathroom, the monitor reading was normal.

The assembly was straightforward. He needed to minimise shrapnel, which could be lethal, so the storage jars he had chosen were made from soft plastic rather than glass. The two large ones had wide mouths with screw caps, and stood a little over a foot high. Donning a pair of latex gloves, he wiped everything for prints and half-filled them with the baking powder. Having replaced the caps, he filled the smaller jars with vinegar, again taking care to screw the caps back on tightly. The rest would have to wait until the cottage.

The phone was still dead, even when he tried another battery. That left the Browning. He retrieved it from the cupboard on the landing outside his flat and set about cleaning it. Only when he was satisfied it was in perfect order did he contemplate the ribs. They were meant to be eked out over the next few days, but he cooked the whole pack. Heedless of the consequences for his digestion, he ate them all as he rehearsed the operation once more. At around nine, he packed everything in a holdall and went out through the service door again, this time with the Browning in his pocket.

It was harder now to see if anyone was waiting in a car, harder still when he went up to the corner and surveyed the seafront. With his heart in his mouth he plunged into the road and hastened to the Skoda.

He drove slowly around the block until he convinced himself that nobody was following, then headed out of town. It hadn't crossed his mind yet that what he was intending might indicate a diagnosable mental condition of some kind; now that it did he found he didn't care. The dogs of war had been let slip, and he was cheering them on their way.

At Hillside Grange, he climbed the stairs to the bedroom and began setting up the first of the two stun grenades. He had made several promising ones at school, and a much larger version on a drunken night at Sandhurst which had nearly cost him his commission. While they were child's play to put together, the effect was dramatic. The mixture of vinegar and baking powder in the confines of the jar would unleash an eruption of carbon dioxide followed in seconds by an ear-splitting bang as the jar exploded. The blast and the noise would render anyone within a few feet briefly senseless, or worse if he had overdone the quantities. The symmetry was not lost on him; a counterstrike of gas against gas, with the difference a single atom.

He placed one of the large jars on the bed and tied a length of black string around its neck before removing the lid. With extreme caution he opened one of the smaller jars and lowered it until it rested on the baking powder, acutely aware if it spilt the reaction would start immediately. Having screwed the cap back onto the large jar, he led the string to the door and passed it through the keyhole before tying it to the handle. The door opened outwards; when it did the jar would topple.

He repeated the process in the bathroom. Here the door opened inwards, which required a complicated routing of the string around the sink. Now it was the turn of the bait, the radio he had bought in a junk shop. Playing softly behind a waste bin on the landing, it would attract attention as soon as the front door was opened. The batteries would last three days, but he meant the trap to be sprung long before that.

Returning to the ground floor, he cleared himself a space in the cupboard under the stairs and rehearsed the move from the front door. He would need to be at least twenty seconds ahead of his pursuers.

Finally, he called the harbourmaster's office. The manager had left for the evening, but a helpful woman was charmed by Sir Crispin Devereux into revealing that *Mamma Mia* had berthed in the early hours. That would mean Bahir was back too. Running on a seemingly limitless flow of adrenaline, he drove to the kebab shop. When Bahir saw him he would call Malik, of that much he was convinced. After that it was down to luck as to whether Malik would come, and how quickly. He would give it an hour and keep returning until they bit. Either way, one or both of them would be offered the chance to follow him to Hillside Grange.

But Bahir wasn't there, or at least he wasn't behind the counter. The Audi was parked at the back, so presumably he was upstairs in the flat. Returning to the front of the building, Knight joined the sparse queue inside the shop. It was around ten, the lull before the post-pub storm. The smell of the meat caught him off guard, rekindling a ravenous hunger that had evidently not been sated by the ribs. He ordered a kebab and a large portion of chips.

'Is Bahir upstairs?' he asked the young woman in the headscarf as she took the money.

'You know Bahir?' She sounded surprised, as well she might. Something about his eyes struck her as faintly manic; that and the fact he hadn't shaved in two days.

'Everyone knows Bahir, we're very good friends as it happens. Is he up in the flat?'

She shook her head. 'He's been away, not come back yet.'

'Ah. Do you know if he's with his uncle Malik?'

'Who?'

He didn't get the impression she was holding out on him.

Knight indicated the other servers. 'Do any of them know?'

Several short exchanges took place in Arabic and Turkish; heads were shaken. But they all took a good look at him; there was no way Bahir could fail to find out he'd been there.

'Well, if you see him, tell him Tom Knight was here. I'll be back tomorrow morning.'

He circled his building twice before leaving the Skoda at the rear and taking the service entrance again. The lock remained unscratched. He had already eaten most of the chips in the car; now he fell upon the kebab.

But what started as a celebratory feast soon lost its allure. The successful opening moves of a counter-attack had, as ever, brought on a high. Now, as he munched at the fatty meat in the cold stillness of the flat, the first flickers of doubt stirred. How could he be sure that Malik or Bahir would actually follow him? And if they did, could he be certain they wouldn't have time to get back down the stairs before the explosion? He had taken care not to make the grenades too powerful, but what if he had made them too weak?

There had been no response from Merv. Tempting though it was to call again, it was obvious that he didn't want to talk. The greater temptation was to call Lolly. Having convinced himself it was better for her not to know about the trap, he fretted that she would find a reason to go to the cottage without telling him.

Postponing the decision, he made another attempt to resuscitate the phone. His mood brightened somewhat when he saw that the fan had done its work. Grateful his blunder could go unnoticed, he watched the familiar logos come to life.

It was, therefore, with mixed feelings that he realised the camera had been triggered again in the early hours of the morning; he would have to confess after all. He wasn't in the mood for naked flesh, but he played the video. Perhaps he would recognise one of the guests, not that he could see how this would help him now.

The image was gratifyingly sharp, the sound only slightly muffled. He was left in no doubt as to what was taking place, only it wasn't a drugs deal or an orgy. It was an auction.

Chapter Thirty-Three

Grim-faced, Lolly sat on her bed watching the video. Knight was on the chair by the pole, vaguely dissatisfied that he had somehow ended up sitting here and not beside her. She was wearing a short satin dressing gown over a silk camisole and culottes which came down to her calves. He averted his eyes. Given what was on the screen, the male gaze would not go down well.

In the foreground she could see the backs of half-a-dozen men. They were sitting at the tables facing the bar, from behind which Rupert led the proceedings. Next to the bar, a smiling Malik urged on the bidders. Beside him stood a girl, Somali possibly, little more than a teenager. What she was wearing had come from the chest of drawers in the tiny bedroom. His hand was clasped around her upper arm as if he had caught her in some act of delinquency. Lolly enlarged the girl's face. She looked terrified.

'My guess is he picks them up on the French coast,' Knight said gravely. 'A yacht that size will have a motor launch – I think he uses it to get them on board and then drop them somewhere near here when he's done the crossing. Afterwards, he sails back into Sovereign Harbour as if he's been on a pleasure cruise.'

Knight recalled the parade of girls. They were East African and Arab, about twenty in all, some even younger than the Somali. Each sale was punctuated by lewd exchanges between Malik and the buyers, with occasional contributions from Rupert that seemed to fall flat. He wondered what type of hell the girls had exchanged for this one, and how they might be free now if he had seen the video in time.

When it finished she closed her eyes, as if reeling from what she had seen. Which indeed she was, though not entirely from horror as Knight supposed. The video changed everything.

'The bastard,' Lolly seethed. She turned to Knight. 'We need to get this onto my phone too – there's no other record, is there?'

'Don't worry, I've backed it up.'

'All the same, best to be sure. Won't take a moment.'

Already, she was tapping and swiping the screen again, setting up a hotspot from which to transfer the file.

'You're a genius, Tom,' she added, in case he needed reassurance. 'I think you've nailed him.'

'I'm pretty sure there's enough to send him to prison,' Knight said, with due modesty. 'He won't be given as much as he would if we proved he killed Clementine, but he'll go away for a long time.' He paused. 'The question is, can you live with that?'

She could, but not with what came next.

'Because I think I should go to the police, tonight. I'll go right to the top, they can't ignore this. And if they do, I'll post the video online.'

Having been a few steps from delivering the final blow, Lolly found herself walking a tightrope. He was right, of course, the sooner the search for the girls began the better. She couldn't be seen to disagree with that, nor did she wish them to take their chances for an hour longer than was necessary. But it all came back to omelettes and eggs. Regrettably, the police would have to wait.

'You're absolutely right,' she said, 'but it's time you stopped blaming yourself. If it wasn't for you, they wouldn't stand any chance at all.'

'I suppose not,' he said, quietly.

She could see he was far from forgiving himself. It was a novelty to encounter such strength of principle in a man. She found it admirable, attractive in its way, but deeply impractical. It crossed her mind again to tell him everything, but she had her principles too.

'I'm worried about you. Come and sit here with me.' She patted the side of the bed.

Knight had been intending to leave and go to the police station. After that, he did not know. The video had brought things to an end in a way he could not have anticipated; the victory felt somehow hollow. A few minutes would make no difference.

She made him sit with his back to her, and ran her fingers up and down on either side of his spine.

'You're completely locked up. I'm not surprised after everything you've been through.'

'I've felt better,' he confessed.

'And you'll feel better again. I'm going to make sure of it.'

She plunged her thumbs into his shoulders.

'Your back's like a piece of wood. You must be in a lot of pain.'

He was in some pain, now that he thought of it. It wasn't what he would call a lot, but the sympathy was welcome. And the touch, even through his shirt. The mere fact of it was already encouraging a more positive view of the world.

'It's because you're worried about the girls, isn't it? What might be happening to them.'

He hadn't been thinking about them at that particular moment, but now he did the weight of responsibility returned.

'I'm sure you're right.' Just a little longer, he told himself; there was no need to forego these few morsels of indulgence.

She stopped massaging and wrapped her arms around his chest, resting her head on his shoulder.

'I'm worried about them too. It makes me wonder…' She hesitated.

'Wonder what?' Knight turned his head so that their cheeks touched. She rubbed against him affectionately with a little murmur of pleasure, and whispered in his ear.

'I'm not saying you should do this, but there may be a quicker way of finding them than going to the police.'

*

In the pitch dark, Merv picked his way across the pebbles, his footsteps silenced by the wind.

No one had seen him when he left the van outside the Fishermen's Club and made for the beach, carrying a thirty-litre jerry can and a crowbar. He heaved the jerry can over the side of the *King of Sussex* and clambered onto the deck. The boat sat at the top of a steep shingle bank, its stern facing the sea. The wooden rollers beneath it stretched as far as the water's edge.

He jemmied the door of the wheelhouse and let himself in. The first fire would start here. At the stern, was an access hatch above the engine, which was where the rest of the petrol would go.

There had been some missed calls from Knight but he had not listened to the messages, determined nothing should distract him until the job was done. That said, the boat's controls held a certain fascination. Merv did not consider himself a thief, but it interested him to know how things could be stolen. What he saw here struck him as only a little more difficult than an old car, of which he had borrowed a fair number before they started filling them with computers.

Not that he had in mind a joyride in the Channel, but the idea of the *King of Sussex* ablaze on the sea like a Viking funeral appealed to him. Hotwiring the ignition would be child's play, and the tide was coming in. He climbed back down onto the beach and went to the prow.

The lights of the Fishermen's Club were out, there were no late-night dog walkers. Satisfied he was alone, he inspected the cable to which the boat was tethered. It led to the motorised winch which hauled her up the beach from the sea. All he had to do was pull away the hook and heave; the rollers and the incoming tide would do the rest.

It was certainly worth a try; if nothing else, it removed the risk to the neighbouring boats. His conscience agreeably clear, he went to fetch the second jerry can.

*

Knight was not so much questioning his judgement as failing to make any kind of judgement at all. Little by little, as the glow of wellbeing spread down his spine, he saw she might be right. The quickest way to find the girls could well be to spring the trap, which he had finally felt obliged to tell her about, and extract information from whoever he caught. There were, of course, some serious pitfalls, not least the risk of prosecution. On the other hand, she was absolutely right that the traffickers would give the police nothing, at least at first, and certainly not the names of the buyers. If he was lucky, he could provide the crucial shortcut.

'Just think about it,' she was saying. 'But don't rush into it. Let it wait and take your time.'

He didn't feel like rushing anywhere. There was another reason why the idea appealed to him. Although Rupert and Bahir would not be hard to find, he knew nothing of Malik's whereabouts. The idea of him walking free stuck in Knight's throat. If there was any chance it would be Malik who opened one of the doors, he didn't want to miss it.

'I'll think about it,' he said, groggily.

'Good. But first we have to make you better.' She sounded relieved. 'No rushing. We'll do this together, we're a good team.'

She was still sitting behind him, her legs stretched out alongside his own. Her arms were wrapped round his chest. Knight's mind went into overload. He searched for a way to steady the boat for long enough to regain the power of rational thought. To the fury of the diehards, he alighted on a mantra and repeated it to himself: nothing was going to happen.

She planted a light kiss on his neck.

The diehards poured through the gap. It was an invitation, surely, or at the very least an overture to which he was bound to respond. The question was how. He needed to be facing her, but this would require a degree of deftness on his part. If he drew his legs up, he could roll onto his knees and swivel round, though it would risk crushing her thigh if he performed the manoeuvre clumsily. Mindful of her advice not to rush things, he played the move through in his mind while seconds ticked away.

His phone pinged.

It was lying on the bed beside Lolly. Knight's instinct was to throw it at the wall, but already she had picked it up.

'Sir has mail,' she said drolly. 'Would sir like me to put this on mute for him?'

'Yes, why not.' He tried to make it sound casual, but the bubble was burst, the moment lost.

He wavered between a second attempt and a return to the mantra, but now the mail had registered its presence in his mind, it wouldn't go away. It rankled that he couldn't banish it, and the more it rankled the clearer it became he should stick with the mantra.

'I'm sorry,' Knight sighed. 'Just let me take a quick look.'

'You need to rest,' she purred. 'Slow down, let it go.' But already he had taken the phone.

'It's the translation of the Chinese inscriptions on the pictures and the bowl.' He didn't know why he was telling her this; it was scarcely relevant in the circumstances. 'It means *The Blessings of Old Age*. Does that ring any bells?'

'No. What are you doing?'

What was he doing? He had begun the search out of habit, keying in the words without thinking. Too late, he realised it was a crass breach of bedroom etiquette. Yet it seemed no offence was taken, or swiftly forgiven if it was. In one fluid movement, she wrapped her legs around him and pivoted about his torso as if he were an outsized pole. It was by no means effortless – he heard a little gasp of exertion – but she landed softly between his knees, facing him.

'You don't see it, do you?' she cooed. 'Your mind keeps running away with itself and so you never have peace. It's time to change.'

She was undoing his shirt. Knight was stupefied by the suddenness of it, as if he had fallen through a wormhole into a world constructed from the most improbable concoctions of his imagination.

'I...'

'Sshhh.'

Lolly silenced him with a lingering kiss, her fingers working nimbly down the buttons. He entered something akin to an out-of-body experience, looking down on them both as she removed the rest of his clothes, and then her own.

'I want you,' she whispered. 'I've wanted you since I saw you.'

Deaf to any hint of cliché, Knight returned from the ceiling to a body bombarded by sensation as the dance of pheromones struck up once more, only now it was a riot. Something was breaking free in her, he was sure of it, anointing him as her chosen one in a rush of fingers, tongues and skin. And eyes. All the while she fixed him with a stare of beseeching, almost frantic intensity, sometimes breaking into a smile, sometimes overtaken by rapture, as she brought about a rejuvenation that was nothing short of miraculous.

At first, they made love slowly. Buffeted between rhapsody, gratitude and disbelief, Knight gave himself up to the scene he had craved since he first set eyes on her. He felt a fierce yet tender devotion, and with it the intoxication of a fabulous victory. He had defied his enemies, defied murder, and he had defied his age.

But if it was indeed the eighteen-year-old Knight who had somehow slipped through the decades to reclaim his kingdom, a change came over him as they made love faster. Very soon he ceased to be the version of himself in the hayloft on the neighbour's farm or on the back seat of his ancient Austin. Instead, he became the disheartened youth gasping for breath on his first assault course, his lungs bursting as the sergeant screamed obscenities at him. At first, he ignored the tightening in his chest, ploughing on as it were, defying the odds even as the tightness became a wracking, stabbing pain which engulfed him.

Croaking and wheezing frantically for breath which would not come, his vision faded and the world went black.

*

Merv unscrewed the cap from the jerry can. He was confident now that the launch would work. First, he would soak the places he had identified, with any surplus to be poured over the lobster cages. Then he would detach the cable, if necessary heaving from the prow to help the *King of Sussex* down the rollers. The slope was steep and the tide was coming in; he didn't anticipate a problem. Finally, he would light the rags and throw them onto the deck.

He took a last look around the wheelhouse. Part of him was saddened at the boat's impending demise. She was older than *Adrenaline Rush*, blunt and weathered in a way that appealed to him. In another world, she would have been his. Hardening his heart, he was about to tip the petrol out when his phone rang.

For a moment, he had the absurd idea Knight had found out what he was doing and was trying to stop him. But it wasn't Knight, it was Lolly. She was distraught.

'Merv, please, I need your help! It's Tom, he's had a heart attack.'

Chapter Thirty-Four

The cold gel from the electrodes sent a shiver through Knight's chest.

'You been overdoing it a bit then?' the nurse asked, not unsympathetically. She reminded him of one of the girls in the video, only she was from Sheffield.

The pain in his chest had eased, though not by much, and his breathing had stabilised enough for him to speak if he kept it short. He watched the needle trace a jagged graph along the paper.

'What's it showing?'

'Not a lot; it doesn't always tell you everything you want to know. Look on the bright side though, at least you're not a smoker.'

Technically, what he had told them was true; he hadn't smoked a cigarette in months. What he hadn't mentioned were the decades before that, or the weed.

'Are you quite sure you can't see anything?'

'It's really for the doctor to say. Just try not to worry; whatever happens you're in the right place.'

Knight could have sworn he detected a flicker of amusement. There was no disguising the fact he had been naked when the paramedics arrived. He had come round just as they were whisking him out of the hotel past startled guests. 'Poor old bugger,' a sorrowful lady had sympathised, 'that's just how my George went.' The ambulance ride was a blur of faces and monitors, but mostly the crushing pain in his chest.

He tried to read the nurse's expression as she watched the graph. She didn't display anxiety, but she would have been trained not to. Besides, this was routine for her; she would not be unnerved at the prospect of seeing another old man die.

'Your friend seems very nice. Have you been together a long time?'

'Not that long, no.'

He wondered what was going through her mind. Did she think he and Lolly had met up for some unlikely bout of casual sex, possibly paid for, which had gone wrong? Or did she think they were a couple? He asked himself the same question, reflecting morbidly that their coupledom could be short-lived. And what, for that matter, did Lolly think?

The nurse tore the paper from the ECG machine and gave him a knowing look.

'I'll tell your friend she can come back in. You mind you behave yourselves.'

She left the cubicle and, a moment later, Lolly took her place. She seemed overwhelmed, panicked even, which he took to mean she too feared for his life.

'What did she say?'

'Nothing really. We have to wait for the doctor.'

'I'm so sorry, Tom.'

He heard a tremble in her voice, made more poignant by the soft ping of the monitor in the background. Her fear fed his own, but it was also a solace. As she bent and kissed his forehead, he was taken by the notion of her bidding him farewell on his deathbed; if only for a moment, he was at ease with it.

'I'm so, so sorry. But I have to go now.'

Knight thought he may have misheard her, but she was edging away out of the cubicle.

'I'll be back as soon as I can. And there's someone here to see you.'

As if by some cruel conjuring trick, she was replaced by Merv.

'Hello, mate,' he said awkwardly.

Half a dozen questions fought it out in Knight's mind until a victor emerged.

'Where did Lolly go?' he asked. Merv seemed taken aback.

'Dunno mate, she didn't say. I'm here now.'

He said it with a pointedness that suggested his presence demanded greater acknowledgement. 'She called me,' he added, as if Knight needed it spelt out for him.

'Sorry Merv, I'm not myself. I'm glad you're here, thank you.'

A silence hung over them. There was a chair at the foot of the bed. Merv moved it next to Knight and sat down, inspecting him with palpable unease.

'So how bad is it?'

'I don't know, they won't say. I've still got pain in my chest, not as bad as it was but bad enough.'

'Jesus.'

It wasn't the first time he'd thought Knight was about to expire, but the setting and the props made it far too real.

'Listen, Tom…'

Knight knew what was coming, and he didn't want to hear it.

'No, please. It was my fault. I said some dreadful things I wish I hadn't. I'm so very sorry.'

'I said some bad things too. I was an idiot.'

Knight managed the trace of a smile.

'I'd say that makes two of us.'

Merv felt a sharp stab of self-reproach as he took the outstretched hand. Knight's haggard face, with its wayward stubble, the tightness of his grip and unwillingness to let go, created a semblance of farewell for which he blamed himself. This was what came of taking his eye off the old fool, worse still for letting a woman of all things come between them.

'So how did it happen?'

Knight felt this was not the moment to test the fledgling peace which had broken out.

'I went to see her about something I'd found out to do with her sister. I should have waited for the lift, but I was late and I ran up the stairs. That's when it came on.'

Merv's face grew sombre as he pictured the scene.

'And what, someone found you passed out on the stairs?'

'Not exactly. I made it as far as her room, and she called for help.'

White lie though it was, Knight was sickened by the deception.

'There's a lot more to tell,' he said, by way of changing the subject. 'Askew and his friends are trafficking women into the country. He brings them in on his boat and drops them somewhere near the coast.'

As Knight told the story, Merv found the events progressively surreal, peaking with the description of the stun grenades at the cottage. Even to Knight, it sounded preposterous when said out loud. A logic of sorts still ran through the events but, in Lolly's absence, it somehow felt thin. Nevertheless, the conclusion remained crystal clear.

'The problem is this – if they know about Lolly and where to find her, they'll go after her too. And I wouldn't put it past her to go after them on her own.'

Knight sank back onto his pillow, overcome by a deep sense of failure.

Merv was at a loss for words. It was less than a week since their falling out; in that time Knight had dug himself in the shit to a record-breaking depth.

They were interrupted by the arrival of a junior doctor, who seemed slightly thrown by Merv's presence.

'You are Mr Knight's… friend, is that right?' Merv confirmed he was. She turned to Knight, again with an air of mild surprise.

'And how are you feeling?'

'About the same. The pain is still there, just not as bad.'

'I see.' She wrote something down. It struck him as ominous, though he couldn't read her any better than the nurse.

'So what did the ECG show?'

She weighed her words carefully.

'I'm not quite sure yet. We need the results of your blood tests and then I'd like the consultant to see everything. The best thing for now is to move you to an observation ward.'

'But you must know something!' he protested. 'Surely you can tell if I've had a heart attack, or if I'm about to have another one?'

She smiled understandingly.

'I do appreciate how worried you must be. All we can say for now is it's not unknown for… for more elderly patients to suffer cardiac arrest after vigorous sexual intercourse, which is why we need to proceed cautiously. On that point, I'm afraid I have to ask you both whether you were using protection.'

Merv uttered a profanity and fixed her with a glare of limitless abhorrence.

No stranger to the incivility of the British public at times of stress, the doctor pursed her lips and consulted the notes again.

'It says here quite clearly…'

'No!' Knight interjected in a hoarse bark. 'That was the friend who brought me in. This is another friend.'

He closed his eyes, willing a second attack to claim him.

'Oh.' She glanced at Merv indifferently. 'My apologies.' Closing the folder with a snap, she informed them an orderly would arrive soon, and left them to a long silence. Knight kept his eyes closed, trying to focus on his heart rate. Merv stared at the blue curtain. When nothing was forthcoming from Knight, he took it upon himself to break the ice.

'So you shagged her then?'

It was a desecration all the more painful for being entirely predictable, but one Knight had no choice but to bear.

'Yes, I did.' A part of him wanted to add, 'Do you have a problem with that?' but he didn't let it.

Merv frowned, as if he were grappling with a tricky piece of algebra. 'You shagged her and it gave you a heart attack. I'm just getting the facts straight here.'

'Yes. So it would seem.'

Knight wondered if Merv expected him to apologise for this as well. But why should he? He had done nothing wrong, other than make himself the target of violent criminals and abuse his body until it fell apart. He fell again to thinking about what was in the ECG that the doctor wouldn't tell him.

Merv too lapsed into morbidity. He imagined a funeral, with Knight's family he had never met. Lolly would not be there, of that much he was sure. Thinking of her alerted him to a possible upside, at least from Knight's point of view; if this was indeed to be the end, it wasn't such a bad way to go.

*

Bullock shuffled cautiously down the corridor with the aid of the walking frame he had taken from the old man in the bed opposite. He wasn't supposed to be on his feet, but the craving for a cigarette had left him unable to sleep.

The procedure itself had been quick once they finally got round to him. A sedative had seen to it that he remembered only a few random details, notably a speculum on the surgeon's table that he recognised from his porn collection. Subsequently, a pump of some kind had been inserted into his nether regions, inflating them dramatically while the surgeon sought out his prey. There had been a suppressed snort of laughter from someone when the offending item was removed. He was still sore and had yet to risk exercising his bowels. That apart, the thing which chiefly occupied his attention was what he intended to do to Lolly.

He couldn't afford to arrest her. A court appearance would lay bare the details of their relationship, leading to a tabloid feeding frenzy and his sacking. The solution he had in mind was the very least she deserved, yet the risks left him hovering on the brink. Even though the man he had earmarked for the task was as good as they came, he would lose much more than his job if it went wrong.

Wavering between thirst for revenge and habitual cowardice, he noticed a bed emerging from the lift further down the corridor. Bizarrely, the orderly pushing it was accompanied by Mervyn Watson. Bullock stopped and peered at the man in the bed. It was Knight.

Forgetting the cigarette, he followed them at a safe distance to the ward where he himself had spent some of the previous day. He watched through the swing doors while the bed was wheeled into one of the rooms. The duty sister meanwhile had taken receipt of Knight's notes and begun to leaf through them. After a minute, she was called away, leaving the nursing station empty. Unchallenged, Bullock went to the counter where she had left them. Learning of Knight's recent medical history, he found the tipping point which made up his mind.

*

Merv awoke with a start when the tea trolley collided with a drip stand. It surprised him he'd managed to fall asleep in the upright armchair, and that a thoughtful nurse had draped a blanket over him. Knight was still sleeping.

They had not spoken again about Lolly. He tried not to think about them together, but the sheer weirdness of it continued to engross him. Lying there with his eyes closed, Knight could just as easily be a corpse; only the subtle movement of the blanket as he breathed indicated otherwise. He would not have looked much better a few hours ago, and yet she had chosen him. Or rather she had snared him. As a child, he'd watched a documentary in which a praying mantis ate her partner after having sex with him, and the image had imprinted itself on his memory.

Now it returned, just as the consultant entered with an entourage of student doctors. A moment of truth was approaching.

For Knight, it was something of a crash landing into the new day. About half-a-dozen young men and women were gathered around his bed, led by a short, bald man who was asking him how he felt. After this, there was no further invitation to join the conversation. Knight became a repository of symptoms on which the consultant's acolytes were required to speculate, the consultant himself basking in their esteem as he put them down with polished irony. Strokes were discussed, pulmonary clots, and a discussion about his blood which he didn't understand. His family history was raised, causing some of the audience to nod solemnly, although one of them sniggered when her neighbour whispered something in her ear; they obviously knew the circumstances in which he had been found. Eventually, he could bear it no more.

'Excuse me,' he interrupted testily, 'when you've finished playing your games do you think you could just say what is actually the matter with me?'

This was addressed to the consultant, who was not used to being spoken to like a private who had mislaid his boots. He shot Knight a glare of pure malevolence, which resolved quickly into a sarcastic smile.

'Certainly, Mr Knight. As far as we can see, you have a gastro-oesophageal reflux condition, most likely brought on by poor diet and binge eating.' With all the condescension he could muster, he added, 'You're probably more familiar with the terms heartburn and indigestion. There will be a prescription for you; please try not to leave without it. Have a pleasant day.'

He swept away with his entourage, some of whom were openly laughing. Knight felt a crushing weight of humiliation, followed by a joy almost as intense as what he had experienced with Lolly. With it came the stirrings of renewed faith in his invincibility. He had broken free from the jaws of death, or rather they hadn't even come close, and now life was welcoming him back with open arms. Anything was possible.

Merv had witnessed the exchange from the back of the gathering.

'Heartburn? You had heartburn?' he said slowly. Realising that he may have sounded less than euphoric he went on, 'That's brilliant, mate,' but this too lacked a certain exuberance and could have sounded sarcastic.

He didn't know what he felt, whether he should shout for joy or wring Knight's neck.

Knight didn't notice. His mind was rebooting, gleefully reinstalling the capricious network of hopes, convictions and cravings which had pertained until a few hours ago. He got out of bed.

'What are you doing?'

'I need to call Lolly. If she thinks I'm stuck here, she might try to do something on her own.'

Merv was aghast. It seemed Knight was seriously contemplating going through with his bomb plot.

'Are you thinking of doing what I think you're thinking of doing?' he asked, as calmly as he could.

Knight didn't hear the question. He had been about to look in his coat for the phone when he remembered the Browning. A sobering shiver ran down his spine as it dawned on him he had entered the hospital with a loaded gun. Had it been found he would be under arrest now, with a policeman in the ward ready to take him in.

But when he patted the hidden pocket inside the lining, he made a discovery that was no less disturbing. The Browning wasn't there.

Chapter Thirty-Five

Bullock adjusted his position on the inflatable ring he had acquired upon discharging himself. A sympathetic nurse had given it to him, impressed by his determination to deal with a crisis in a major investigation.

Despite the discomfort, he was able to take satisfaction from the speed with which he had expedited matters, considerably faster than if he had been doing his day job. Beside him in the car was one of his trusted regulars, a part-time football hooligan and full-time thief with an unyielding drink problem. From another of his protégés, a fence who had shopped the thief twice without him knowing it, Bullock had secured the promise of a crate of whisky. For a few minutes' low-risk work, it was an offer the thief had accepted without hesitation.

Outside, the promised snow had arrived. It was still at the picturesque stage, falling like tickertape over the street beside Lolly's hotel. Her car was some fifty yards away, facing towards them.

Still fearful for her visa, the cleaner had taken little persuasion to continue assisting him. It seemed she was reliable, because now Lolly appeared at the corner.

'Remember,' Bullock instructed his helper, 'teeth and nose, break everything you can. Soon as anyone pays attention, you run.'

Lolly opened the tailgate and heaved the heavy suitcase in. As ever when a project approached its crisis point, she was hyper-alert. It was the expensive ski mask that caught her eye, somehow incongruous beneath the hood of an army surplus anorak. As the first blow fell, she shied away and took it on her shoulder. The brute force of it sent her staggering a few paces into the empty street, far enough for her to rebalance and turn. As if performing an impromptu can-can, she delivered two sharp kicks between the legs of the advancing stranger, causing him to double up in pain while she took out the pepper spray and squirted it in his face. As his hands shot from his groin to his eyes, she kicked again, inducing a further howl of agony and a swift retreat.

Her throat dry, she slammed the tailgate shut and threw herself into the car. She might have panicked, had she not been consumed by a murderous anger. When the attacker covered his face with his hands, she had instantly recognised Bullock's knuckleduster.

*

The wait at the hospital dispensary was interminable. Sandwiched between Merv and a thin woman with a hacking cough, Knight had yet to come to terms with the news Lolly had checked out of her hotel.

'Think about it, if she's any sense she'll be on her way to the airport. She's probably there already.'

'That's not possible, she would have told me.'

Merv bit his tongue. He had a single objective, to get Knight home and into bed. The fact that she had done a runner didn't surprise him in the least. The fact it surprised Knight told him there was a long road ahead before he finally let go.

'Even if she was leaving, why would she take the gun and not tell me? And why did she take it in the first place?'

'Because she found it in your coat when she was getting your stuff together and didn't want you to get nicked. She probably hid it in her room somewhere.'

'Then why hasn't she said anything? Can't you see? It was her idea to stick with the cottage plan rather than go to the police. That's a much better reason for going off the radar.'

Merv despaired. She'd obviously dumped him, so why couldn't Knight just move on like a normal bloke?

'So, what you're saying is,' he replied patiently, trying hard not to sound disparaging, 'that right now, she's parked up outside the kebab shop waiting for Bahir to clock her and call his uncle?'

He wished he'd kept his mouth shut.

'My god,' Knight muttered. Next, he had his phone in his hand and was tapping agitatedly on the screen.

'Mate, come on, you know she's not going to answer.'

'I'm not calling her. I want to see where Bahir is.'

Knight waited fretfully for the link to the tracker to open. When it did, he wasn't any the wiser. The car was to the north of the town, approaching the country lane that led to Todhurst Manor.

'Well, he's not going to the cottage, is he?' Merv pointed out hopefully. 'So, if she did go to his shop he obviously doesn't know about it.'

'Unless she's in the car with him.'

Adding to Merv's disquiet, Knight was fumbling in his wallet now.

'I'm sorry, Merv, I know you don't approve and I'm not asking you to get involved.'

'Now what are you playing at?'

For some reason, he had taken out his bus pass and was rising to his feet.

'I'm going back to get my car and then I'm going up there. Please don't try to stop me.'

Momentarily incapacitated by his friend's further descent into lunacy, Merv watched him go. Then, with the fatalism of a soldier returning to the trenches after a spell of leave, he got up and followed.

*

From the end of the driveway, they could see the silver Audi beside the front door of Todhurst Manor. There were two sets of tyre tracks and the snow was settling fast; the second car had left not long ago.

'I can't see a thing through all this.'

Merv passed the binoculars to Knight. He peered through the snow, trying to detect any sign of movement at the windows. All he could say for certain was that the lights weren't on.

'Can we at least go to the door?'

The deal they had made was that they would look for any obvious sign that Lolly was at the house, in the absence of which they would return to the flat.

'And what if someone opens it and points a shooter at us?'

Knight debated with himself; it wasn't at all far-fetched.

'We drive down, turn the van round and keep the engine running.'

'And then?'

'We see what happens.'

Unhappily, Merv drove up to the house and did a three-point turn, readying the van for a quick getaway. There was no hint of any reaction from inside. The remnants of breakfast were on the table in the empty kitchen, a silver coffee pot and a toast rack with a couple of slices left in it.

Knight opened the door and reached down with his stick to steady himself.

'Excuse me, we didn't say anything about getting out.'

'I won't be a minute.'

He slithered awkwardly to the ground, his feet instantly wet as the snow covered his shoes. Faced with the unwelcome choice of letting him go alone or forfeiting the quick getaway, Merv switched off the engine and followed him to the back door.

The first suggestion that all was not well were some drops of blood on the doorstep. The door was open. There was more blood dotted across the kitchen floor, a trail that led past the table towards the front passage. Knight listened. All was quiet save for the tick of the clock on the wall.

Signalling to Merv to stay close, he moved to the passage door and listened again. If there was anyone waiting with a gun on the other side, they were as good as trapped; even if they made it back outside they would still be sitting ducks. He opened the door a crack, with Merv ready to shoulder it shut. The passage was empty.

There were stains on the pale carpet. As Knight looked into the sitting room, Merv beckoned him back urgently to the passage. The front door, he now saw, was studded with shotgun pellets. In dumb show, Merv pointed towards the rear of the house from where the gun must have been fired.

There were more stains at the entrance to the cellar. The door was ajar. Holding the end of his phone between his finger and thumb, Knight shone the torch through the gap, waiting for it to be blasted from his hand. Throwing caution to the wind, he looked down the empty steps.

'Armed police,' he shouted. 'Come out with your hands up and you won't get hurt.'

There was a light switch just inside the door. He flicked it on, illuminating the rows of bottles. When he was halfway down, he could

237

see a rack in the far corner hanging open on its hinges. Beside it a man in a dark suit lay on his back. It was Malik.

The wound in his chest had soaked his shirt and emptied onto the stone floor, as if he had fallen into a pool of blood. His eyes stared lifelessly, yet with a dread that told of an excruciating final moment. In the wall behind the open wine rack was a safe, its contents no longer present.

'Jesus Christ, you don't think she...' Merv cut himself short, aware that the same question must be passing through Knight's mind. If it was, he didn't show it.

'Look at the blood,' he said, evenly. 'There's none between here and the top of the stairs.'

'So?'

'He was shot from about where you're standing now. The body wasn't moved, or there'd be a trail across the floor.'

Merv could see the logic of Knight's thinking, though a more compelling logic was to leave immediately. Knight seemed to agree. Without a further glance at Malik, he made his way back to the steps.

'Good thinking, mate, time we weren't here.'

'Not quite.' Knight picked some shot from the wall. 'I think the blood in the passage and the kitchen belong to someone else. Whoever it was took a hit in the cellar and maybe another one as he ran out. He knew he wasn't going to make it to the front door, so he sidestepped into the kitchen.'

Or she.

'It means the trail goes the other way – he went out through the kitchen.'

At the back door, they found what the sight of the blood on the kitchen floor had caused them to miss. Sheltered under the eaves of the house, the ground was barely touched by the snow. But a few feet away, where it lay thick, was the ghost of a footprint, followed by more. In between were faint dashes of red. Fast disappearing, the trail led down towards the woods.

They were approaching the tree line when Merv stepped on something hard and called for Knight to stop. He felt his stomach churn when he saw the phone in Merv's hand. It was the same make as Lolly's; she could have dropped it while trying to call for help. Bracing himself for the worst, he followed the vanishing footprints to the edge of the wood, where he saw a pair of outstretched legs beneath a tree.

Bahir sat with his back against the trunk, his eyes closed. Knight felt his pulse, it was beating, but his skin was icy cold and beside him the snow was stained red around his upper thigh. Merv rolled him onto his side. At the back of his thigh, the fabric of his trousers was shredded and blood was seeping from the raw flesh.

They dragged him back to the house, or rather Merv did while Knight held the leg aloft to keep the blood in his core. While Merv peeled off the trousers, Knight hunted in the kitchen drawers for clingfilm. Together, they wrapped it tightly around the wound then laid him on his back with his head on a cushion and his legs propped up on a chair.

'How much you reckon he's lost?'

Knight peered at the wound again through the clingfilm. There was no tell-tale spurt, just a steady ooze.

'It doesn't look like the artery's badly ruptured, but we don't know how long he's been bleeding. He needs an ambulance.'

Merv blanched. 'They'll send the law, you do realise that?'

Bahir groaned. It might have been the warmth of the kitchen or the turbulence of his journey there, but he was alive for now.

'Use his phone. Don't say it was a shooting, tell them he had a heart attack.'

Knight filled a glass with water and splashed some of it in Bahir's face. He groaned again and his eyes flickered. On seeing Knight they widened in alarm.

'Please. Don't kill me.' It was barely a murmur.

'That depends.' Not wishing Bahir to know help was coming, Knight signalled to Merv that he should leave the room. He put the glass to Bahir's lips and let him drink.

'Tell me who shot you and who killed Malik.'

Either the shock of his awakening had been too much for him or his mind was fleeing from the pain. His eyes closed again and his head flopped to one side. Knight took it in both hands and rolled his eyelids back.

'Bahir, tell me who it was and I'll call an ambulance.'

He mumbled something.

'Say that again.'

'It was her,' he rasped. Knight felt the back of his neck prickle.

Merv returned and knelt beside them. A discreet nod said that the call had been made.

'Who? Who was it?' When there was no reply he splashed more water in his face and raised his voice almost to a shout. 'Was it Lolly?'

His eyes flickered open again.

'Lolly,' he muttered, and then something that sounded like busted, or bastard.

'Where is she? Where is Lolly?!'

Merv put his ear close to Bahir's mouth as he mumbled again. At a loss, he offered him the glass and waited while he drank.

'He might have said bandstand. Did you say bandstand, mate?'

Bahir nodded.

'Twelve. Twelve at bandstand,' he whispered. 'Malik say no. She shoot him. Shoot me.'

His eyes closed again. This time there was no waking him.

Knight looked at the clock; it was half past eleven. While Merv felt for a pulse, he took Bahir's car keys from his coat.

'Stay with him until you hear the ambulance, then meet me down there.'

The fact that it was unmistakably an order annoyed Merv. He opened his mouth to object but Knight had gone.

*

Knight left the Audi west of the pier and walked the last twenty yards to the stairs leading down to the beach and the bandstand. Hatless against the snow, he cut a sorry figure with his back hunched and his coat pulled over his head. Not that anyone was watching; as far as he could tell, the seafront was deserted.

At the bottom of the steps, he looked into the open space in front of the stage. In the summer it would be filled with chairs for concert goers, now it was empty and the snow lay undisturbed. Keeping to the back wall, he moved on until the bandstand itself came into view. Facing the land with its back to the beach, it was a sprightly Art Deco structure boasting classical columns and a bright blue pointed roof that could have graced a mosque. He peered into the shadows behind the columns, but they too yielded nothing.

Although it was not yet twelve, he began to wonder if he had sent himself on a wild goose chase. Twelve could mean anything: people, a house number, a bus. Or a beach hut? But the beach huts were further along, not by the bandstand. He decided it made more sense to go back to the road; if anyone was coming it would more likely be by car than on foot. Checking that the walkway along the beach remained deserted, he retreated to the Audi and watched.

There was at least a chance that Lolly was alive. He could take some comfort, too, that Malik had not been killed with the Browning, though her implacable drive to hunt down Rupert Askew spoke volumes. So did her unwillingness to involve the police. Was that why she had encouraged him to persevere with the stun grenades, because it would prevent him from calling them? But at that point she hadn't known he was carrying a gun, so it seemed unlikely she was planning an assassination. Or did she know? She could have looked in his coat without him knowing. It was a scattering of fragments which refused to fit together.

Outside, a near-empty bus crept by. He was about to call Merv when he noticed the half-completed search he had begun on the phone before Lolly suddenly alighted on his lap. He played the moment back. At first, she had been mildly disapproving when the alert sounded, yet she had not been offended when he opened the mail and typed in the translation. Far from it, she had begun to undress him.

The entries for *The Blessings of Old Age* were at first humdrum, mostly bible sites and self-help gurus, but then came a link to the *Daily Mail*. The article was five years old. As he read, some of the fragments slid together. They didn't form a picture, if anything they added to his confusion, but the implications dumbfounded him. He was still reeling when Lolly's rental car passed by. She slowed and pulled into a spot just beyond the stairs to the bandstand.

Knight knew he was playing catch-up, though he had, as yet, no idea from how far back. As he got out, a people carrier with darkened windows shot from the road opposite Lolly and skidded to a halt beside her. He could see a hooded man with a briefcase in his hand. What happened next was unclear. The briefcase vanished briefly and a rag appeared. Then the door of Lolly's car was open and she was being dragged out.

Knight could smell the chloroform as he closed in. Askew was hauling her limp body between the two vehicles and didn't grasp the nature of the approaching threat until the metal handle of the stick caught him on the side of his head. The quilted hood absorbed some of the blow, but he dropped Lolly and shrieked. The second blow caught him on the kneecap and sent him scrambling back into the people carrier without even a token resistance.

Holding the stick awkwardly under his arm, Knight dragged Lolly back to the Fiesta. Slight though she was, it was all he could do to heave her dead weight onto the passenger seat. He was trying to force her legs into the footwell when a second man loomed out of the snow. He was the same height as Askew, but twice the breadth.

There wasn't time to take a swing. Knight jabbed at his throat, but the stick was wrenched from his hand and a gargantuan fist drove into his face. As he went down, he smelt chloroform again, far stronger now. Before the rag blotted out his vision he remembered where he had last seen the giant. It was in the pig shed at Todhurst Manor Farm.

*

Merv had no intention of being anywhere near the house when the ambulance arrived. Almost as soon as Knight had gone, he gave Bahir more water and tightened the clingfilm. Then he ran to the van. Halfway down the hill an ambulance sped by, easing his conscience.

At the pier, he got stuck behind a gritting lorry, forcing him to wait while a breakdown truck went by on the other side, followed by a people carrier. He looked at the windscreen but the occupants were hidden behind a curtain of snow. By the time he made it past the gritter he was outside Knight's building. He looked up at the terrace, likewise shrouded by the snow, and hoped irrationally that he was there.

He spotted the Audi and drove past, straining for a glimpse of him. When he saw the Fiesta, he stopped and pulled in beside it. The churned-up snow told him something had happened here, perhaps only minutes earlier. It was something bad. Lying beside the car was Knight's stick.

He tried Knight's phone and wasn't surprised when there was no answer. For the first time in his life, Merv considered calling the police. The last time Knight had gone wandering in the snow, he had survived by the skin of his teeth. Now, he had disappeared again, only with a dead body and a missing gun thrown in. But Merv had sworn never to let it happen again.

He went back to the van and opened the location app. He would have given anything for Knight to be home, even if it meant he was with Lolly, even if he was on his way back to hospital with a real heart attack. The icon on the map offered no such comfort. Knight was at Sovereign Harbour.

Fifteen minutes later, Merv looked down at the serried ranks of boats from the edge of the car park. Knight had told him about the penthouse; it seemed a likely contender but the icon was on the far side of it. Hurrying along the deserted quays, he clutched at the few straws left to him. Perhaps he had just forgotten his stick, perhaps they had taken a taxi here and were closeted in one of the bars while she told him it was over.

When he reached the other side of the basin, the icon had shifted again. It was hovering around the harbourmaster's office and then, bizarrely, it appeared to be on the water. When he reached the lock below the control tower, he understood why. Barely visible through the falling snow, *Mamma Mia* was crossing the outer harbour towards the open sea.

Chapter Thirty-Six

Knight awoke in total darkness. It took him a moment to recognise the motion of a boat at sea. The dull roar he could hear must mean he was close to the engines.

He was wrapped from head to foot in something heavy that bore down uncomfortably against his back and calves. By pushing with his hands, he could make out a hard, lumpy surface. He pushed again and attempted to wriggle his hips. It may have been wishful thinking, or it may have been that he shifted by a fraction of an inch.

Like an insect labouring to break free of its chrysalis, he pushed and squirmed for some twenty minutes until his head emerged, as if from the mouth of a tunnel. It was still pitch black. When at last his arms came free, he found the metal chain that was wrapped around the tarpaulin in which he was encased. Taking the links in his hands he thrust with all his strength until he was out.

His phone was gone, as was his stick. He got to his knees and groped blindly. Beside him was something smooth and rounded with a rope attached, to which he clung as he rose unsteadily to his feet. Gradually, the contours of the object revealed it to be a landing craft, a rigid inflatable by the feel of it. He was in the tender garage at the boat's stern. Somewhere beyond the landing craft would be the hatch which rose up for it to be launched into the sea.

There had to be a way into the engine room. At odds with the pitching motion, he found a wall and inched along it until his fingers touched a handle. On the other side of the door, there was a dim glow from a control panel. A glance at the labels confirmed he was on *Mamma Mia*. In front of him, a narrow corridor opened out into the engine room, where two massive diesel engines filled the cramped space with a deafening roar. There was also a flight of stairs. A large wrench on a tool rack caught his eye; it would do as a weapon. Grateful for the handrail, he climbed the stairs and cautiously opened the door at the top.

Delivered with a blast of snow, the smell of the sea quickened his senses. He was on the main deck, beside the tinted windows of the salon. The lights inside were on, which would hide his presence. Cupping his hands to the glass he risked a look; the salon was empty.

At the glass door, he stopped and looked in again. There was a clear line of sight past the bar to the dining table, after which came a partition with a passage on either side. He went in and rested for a moment in a chair behind the corner of the bar where he couldn't be seen.

The overwrought interior was no more appealing than before, but he knew now where the money had come from to pay for it. Five years ago, a pair of Chinese billionaires had fought each other for *The Blessings of Old Age* in the saleroom at Pernil Goode. A mid-ranking minor classic, the painting had been expected to fetch a few tens of thousands at the most but, in their aversion to losing face, the billionaires had bid each other to twenty million. He had little doubt Askew had stolen the painting from Clementine Lever. What he couldn't believe was that Lolly didn't know about it. He would be sure to ask if they both came out of this alive.

*

Merv's second call of the day to 999 had not gone well. He had used Bahir's phone again and stupidly stated the same false name. It was a fact not lost on the police operator who had just dealt with a fatal shooting in the countryside. She had been more interested in who he was than the story he had to tell, which she didn't seem to believe anyway. Thus he had come to a fateful decision.

The tide was already halfway up the beach when he reached the fishing boats, praying that the snow had kept the O'Driscolls away. The *King of Sussex* was still there. It took less than three minutes to hotwire the ignition. He unhooked the cable then put his shoulder to the hull and heaved with all his might.

*

Knight passed silently through the salon. At the partition, he took the passage on the left, at the end of which were two more flights of stairs. One went up to a closed door which he guessed must open into the wheelhouse. The second led down to where the cabins would be. There, he decided, lay his best chance of finding Lolly.

They were not cabins as he had experienced them on troopships. Wrench at the ready, he entered the first one and was greeted by the brassy sheen of a high-end business hotel. It didn't contain Lolly. Nor did any of the others. He was beginning to fear she was dead and he was alone on the boat with Askew and the pig man when he found the briefcase.

It was lying on a bed in the biggest cabin. Beside it was a holdall full of men's clothes, some of which he recognised from the wardrobe at the manor house. They were stuffed in haphazardly, the sign of a panicky getaway. He opened the briefcase, fully expecting to find the incriminating records of the trafficking operation. In a sense he did. The briefcase was stuffed with cash.

It was a mixture of fifties and twenties, used and new, tied in thick bundles. He couldn't help but stop to make a rough calculation; there couldn't be much less than half a million pounds. He gazed at the banknotes, transfixed. They gazed back at him like a stray dog hopeful of a home. Thus far his objectives had been to find Lolly and stay alive; now a third one slyly volunteered.

As he climbed back to the main deck the boat slowed down. His intention was to hide the briefcase behind the bar before turning his attention to the occupants of the wheelhouse. Bereft of forward motion, the boat pitched unpredictably, reducing him to a snail's pace as he swayed through the salon like a drunk. He was barely within striking distance of the bar when he heard voices.

They were some way behind him, on the far side of the partition. Without thinking, he launched himself through the salon door onto the deck and staggered chaotically back to the stairs. He lost his footing and went down on his backside, realising too late that, if *Mamma Mia* had been stopped by a mechanical fault, they would be going to the engine room.

He rolled away and dragged himself behind one of the engines as they reached the top of the stairs. For a few more seconds, he still had the advantage of surprise. He put down the briefcase and made ready to strike with the wrench. Bert entered first, turning to steady Askew as he stumbled in behind him. The light came on.

'We'll do the small one first,' he shouted over the noise of the engines. Askew didn't reply.

From his hiding place, he saw that there were two ways into the tender garage, one on each side of the hull. As if he were tending a child, Bert helped Askew to the door opposite the one Knight had found.

'Just do your best to keep calm, sir, it won't take long.'

As they disappeared, he broke cover and crept behind them. The dark outline of what looked like Askew was clinging to the launch craft. If he turned even slightly, he would see the empty tarpaulin on the other side. But now there was a loud mechanical whine and a dim shaft of light from outside. The stern was opening, letting in a fresh blast of snow and air. Bert joined Askew by the launch. Between them on the floor was another tarpaulin, wrapped in chains.

'You ready then, sir?'

Askew responded with an unsteady croak, as if he were close to a breakdown.

'I can't do it. You'll have to.'

'Now come on Master Rupert, you know what we agreed, and you know it needs two of us.' It was said more with regret than reproach, not that Askew was listening.

'No, I won't!' His voice shook. 'You've got to do it, I'm ordering you! Just make sure you use this first.'

Knight flattened himself against the bulkhead as Askew burst through the doorway. It was the perfect moment to strike, but the peculiar exchange had thrown him. Without looking back, Askew stumbled across the engine room and vanished up the stairs. Bert knelt down beside the tarpaulin. He had Knight's Browning in his hand and was fumbling with the safety catch.

This time Knight didn't hesitate. The pig man looked up at the shadow lumbering towards him, its features obscured by the light behind.

'I'm sorry, Bert,' Knight whined. It was a poor imitation of Askew, but enough for Bert to hesitate for a split second. The wrench struck the top of his head and the gun fell from his hand.

It wasn't Knight's intention to kill him, but if he had he would shed few tears. He retrieved the Browning and went back for a roll of electrical wire he had seen. Only when he had bound Bert's feet and hands, did he check his pulse. Evidently blessed by a thick skull, Bert was alive.

So was Lolly. She moaned as he dragged her from the tarpaulin and hauled her across the floor. For want of anywhere better, he laid her down behind the engine where he had hidden. Her pulse was steady. Encouraged, he looked for something to rest her head on. There were some folded wetsuits on a shelf. He slipped a pair beneath her head and called her name. She didn't respond.

He went back to Bert and searched his pockets. There was a wad of cash and a passport, along with a rag that still smelt of chloroform. Blood was dripping down his forehead, breaking into a spidery delta over his nose and cheeks as if he had absconded from a low-budget horror film. He groaned and his eyes opened.

'Bastard,' he coughed.

He was lying on his side with his hands tied behind him. His body convulsed as he tried to get to his knees, only to sink back defeated by its own bulk. Knight crouched beside him and showed him the gun.

'Where is this boat going?' he asked evenly.

Bert turned his face and spat. It was a feeble attempt, most of the saliva dribbling under his chin.

'Go fuck yourself,' he mumbled. 'I serve the family, not you.'

Knight pressed the barrel to his knee.

'Very commendable. How do you feel about life in a wheelchair?'

He tried to roll away, again to no avail.

'Let's try that again. Where are we going?'

'He wouldn't tell me. I don't think he even knows himself.'

Knight removed the barrel from Bert's knee and placed it in his ear instead.

'This is how your pigs go, isn't it? Quick bolt into the brain, maybe you'd prefer that?'

'It's true, I swear it!' He was getting the message now. 'He's running, he's scared of what they'll do to him. I've nothing to do with it, I swear.'

Knight saw red.

'Is that so? You were going to shoot us both and dump us in the sea, but you've got nothing to do with it.'

Bert flinched.

'He was supposed to do it! I was only meant to be here if he needed me.'

Knight's finger tightened on the trigger. No one would know if he pulled it all the way.

'Who else is on board?'

'Just Master Rupert and his mother, I swear it's the truth!'

Knight thought about clubbing him back to sleep, but relented and stuffed his mouth with the rag.

Lolly was still out. With no realistic prospect of moving her anywhere else, he felt her pulse again then climbed back to the deck.

There was no guarantee Bert was telling the truth but, if he was, the odds had turned on their head. Askew was a coward who would put up no resistance when ordered at gunpoint to turn the boat around. If he refused, he'd get the same treatment as Bert. As for piloting the boat, it couldn't be that hard to work out the controls. He felt a stab of pity for Mrs Fisher, or rather Irene Askew. Torn from the safety of her home, she could have no idea what was playing out as her son fled from justice.

He made the tortuous journey back to the wheelhouse and listened at the door, wondering if Bert had fooled him. What if there were other conspirators he wasn't aware of, or another prisoner? Only once had he hit a civilian figure on the firing range. The moment insisted on coming back to him as he flung the door open and burst in with a brutish roar.

There were no hostiles, just one civilian in the form of Irene Askew, who sat gaping at him in trepidation from the co-pilot's chair. He lowered the gun quickly.

'Mrs Askew, I promise I won't hurt you. Please tell me where your son is.' He tried to sound reassuring, to little effect. Dwarfed by the oversized chair, she sat motionless with her mouth open, breathing heavily.

'Where is Rupert?' he said slowly. 'I'm his friend and I've come to help him.'

He thought he saw a glimmer of understanding.

'Do you go to school with Rupert?' she asked nervously.

There was no point spending another second with her.

'I'm sorry to bother you, Mrs Askew. Just stay where you are and everything will be fine.'

He closed the door and returned to the bottom of the wheelhouse stairs. Askew must have gone to the lower deck, perhaps to take refuge in his cabin until Bert returned. But in that case he would know the money was gone, so why was there no sound of a frantic search? By way of answer, came the sound of retching followed by a toilet flushing. It was somewhere very near.

Built into the partition between the stairs and the dining table was a bathroom he hadn't noticed. Rupert Askew emerged and turned in the direction of the bar.

Knight felt a predatory rush of blood. He hadn't expected Askew to drop so sweetly into his lap. Daring to hope the end was in sight, he followed him into the salon and steadied himself on the dining table.

'Stop where you are and turn round with your hands up.'

Askew was reaching for a bottle. He spun around like a startled cat, his arms springing to attention when he saw the gun.

'Don't shoot!' It was a high-pitched cry, a bizarre falsetto Knight found somehow grotesque.

He pointed the gun at a chair on the opposite side of the table.

'Over here. One wrong move and I'll take great pleasure in using this.'

Staring as he might at a ghost, Askew approached the table.

'Sit down and put your hands on your head. Take them away and I start shooting.'

He obeyed without hesitation. Knight sat down diagonally opposite, the Browning trained on Askew's chest. Locked into the boat's motion, he wouldn't miss.

'Where's Bert?' Askew stammered.

'Dead,' Knight lied.

Askew shuddered. Knight found it gratifying. He held all the cards now, and his captive knew it. He batted away the thought that one of the cards was a briefcase full of cash.

'I've got money,' Askew pleaded, as if reading his mind. 'Just name your price, anything you like and we'll say this never happened.'

'I don't want your money, I want to know why you killed Clementine Lever.'

At the sound of her name, he recoiled and shook his head agitatedly.

'I swear on my life I didn't touch her. Please, you have to believe me.'

Knight squinted down the barrel.

'No! I'm begging you, please put it down.'

He started retching again, yet kept his hands religiously on his head. Knight put the gun on the chair beside him out of Askew's sight. There was no point pushing him further over the edge than he was.

'All right, who was it then?'

'It was Malik,' he snivelled. 'I tried to stop him but I couldn't.'

'And who killed Malik?'

'Bahir did.'

As if unburdened of a dreadful truth, he moaned and sobbed uncontrollably. Knight felt a macabre satisfaction. He wasn't convinced about Bahir, though the idea was appealing in that it didn't point the finger at Lolly. For a few moments, he watched the sorry performance as he might the aftermath of a car accident. There was something exaggerated, almost theatrical, about it that eventually disgusted him.

'For god's sake, man, pull yourself together,' he barked.

The raw authority of the order had an immediate effect.

'All right,' Knight said more reasonably, 'now tell me who shot Bahir.'

Askew seemed to relax then, to Knight's bewilderment, he replied petulantly, 'You know what? I don't think I want to tell you.' Then he rose to his feet and added, his voice rising again to a squeal, 'You filthy scum!'

Knight reached for the gun but it wasn't there. Nor was the chair. He turned and saw it had been moved out of his reach. Beside it stood Irene Askew, pointing a shotgun at him.

Chapter Thirty-Seven

At first, Knight was in denial, clinging to the notion this was a form of dementia he hadn't seen before.

'Mrs Askew, I think you should put that down,' he requested, in what he hoped was a reasonable tone.

She stared at him almost in disbelief.

'My god, you really are that stupid,' she said, in wonder as much as contempt. She glanced at Rupert. 'Don't just stand there, get the gun.'

The full weight of his folly descended on Knight like a block of stone. There was a demonic quality to the creature standing before him. In the blink of an eye, she had transformed from the object of his pity to a ruthless predator, a shrivelled and deadly crone from the Brothers Grimm.

Rupert meanwhile took the Browning and stood beside her.

'Quite a good actor, my son, when he needs to be. Takes after me – not bad at dementia, am I?'

Rupert said nothing. After his moment of bravado he seemed scarcely less fearful than before.

'Get up.'

Knight rose to his feet. Rational though she sounded, in her eyes he saw a being maddened beyond repair. She would pull the trigger.

'Out on the deck.'

Knight took an unsteady step backwards. Smaller and slighter, she had much less difficulty in keeping her balance, even with the shotgun in her hands. It was a single barrel Purdey. He could try to rush her and hope Rupert wouldn't use the Browning, but at this range she couldn't possibly miss.

'All I can say is, you're an exceptionally intelligent woman, Mrs Askew. Might I ask, was it you who shot Malik and his nephew? Because if it was, you did the world a favour.'

It was an educated guess, but he was still shocked by the reply.

'They deserved it, trying to steal our money. Keep moving.'

'Why outside?'

'Why do you think? Can you see him cleaning the carpet?'

There was a resentment about the way she said it, which Rupert plainly didn't like. If he could keep her talking, there was a chance.

'What about Clementine Lever, did she deserve it?'

This time she seemed less certain of herself.

'She was a slut and she shouldn't have come looking. He wouldn't do it, so I had to.'

'Well, I don't blame you,' Knight sympathised. 'She threatened your business, importing the women.'

It went straight under her skin.

'No!' she protested furiously. 'It was their idea, he'd never have done anything like that on his own.'

'Mummy stop it!' Rupert pleaded.

'You be quiet!' Agitated though she was, the barrel never wavered.

'I should have put a stop to it but he listened to them, not to his mother.'

Knight nodded gravely.

'I'm very sorry to hear that, Mrs Askew. And it was very foolish of you, Rupert, because your mother had to clear up the mess like she's doing now.'

'Shut up!' Rupert yelled.

Knight ignored him and turned back to Irene. It made sense now, the rot that ran through the family and the madness it brought in its wake. He had a strong suspicion, too, how the first body had come to be in the tunnel.

'Because he's never had the guts, has he? Because his father beat them out of him. And that's why you killed him too, didn't you?'

'Yes,' she spat, 'and it's the best thing I ever did. Get out!'

They were approaching the threshold. He might be able to twist his body around the glass and grab at the barrel, but she was less than a yard away.

'Stop. Rupert, open it for him.'

Watching Knight nervously, he pushed the door open and stood to one side, the Browning in his hand.

'Move.'

'No, wait,' Knight pleaded. 'You haven't told me about Clementine's sister; what did she do to you?'

Disgust rippled across the pinched face.

'The little cow tried to blackmail us. With that video I expect you made for her. Going to share the money, were you? Or was she going to run off with it on her own?'

Irene laughed as the composure drained from his face.

'No fool like an old fool, is there, Mr Knight?'

It wasn't just what she had said that had rendered him speechless, it was the surreal incident playing out behind Rupert's head. Seen only by Knight, the ghostly outline of Lolly's face pressed up against the tinted glass. It was there for a second and gone.

He played a last, forlorn card.

'Why don't you make him do it? Give him the chance to be a man.'

'Just shoot him!' Rupert begged.

Knight reached for the glass door frame in the vain hope of pulling himself out of the line of fire. Instead, he lost his balance and fell out onto the deck. When he looked up, they were both standing over him.

'On your knees.' Glad of even a moment's respite, he complied.

'Go on then,' she said to her son, 'show the bastard.'

Unable to look Knight in the eye, Rupert moved behind him while she kept the shotgun trained on his head. Still he shrank from the task.

'This is for Bert,' he said, at last.

There were two loud bangs, and Knight toppled over.

Merv cursed. He had tried to bring the *King of Sussex* alongside *Mamma Mia* to get a closer look as she wallowed in the swell, but now he had rammed her in the bow. The fishing boat ground along the yacht's hull until the aft deck came into view, revealing two bodies and a third person knelt over one of them. He reversed the throttle too late and the *King of Sussex* surged past while he spun the wheel to bring her around.

Knight's head throbbed. It had hit the deck hard, which he only realised when he felt for a wound and found no blood. Irene was crouched over Rupert, letting forth a low, unearthly keening. The Browning had fallen a few feet away. She saw him move but he got there first, shouldering her aside as she lunged for it.

'Enough!' he commanded. 'It's over.'

The shrivelled face looked back at him, its eyes incandescent with hatred. Her hands were smeared with blood.

'No,' she hissed. 'You die too.'

She was on her feet before he could stop her. If she went for the shotgun and tried to reload he would shoot, but she fled to the salon door and disappeared inside. Only now did he turn his attention to Rupert. His eyes were frozen in a glassy stare and his head lay at an unnatural angle to his shoulders. Most of what lay below his face had been blown away, leaving a tangled hollow where his throat and neck had been. It was speckled with the pellets that hadn't made it all the way through.

The *King of Sussex* was making a slow circle fifty yards off the stern. Knight wove his way back to the door, fearful there could be another gun on board. She was not in the salon or waiting behind the bathroom. His own gun didn't feel right. He climbed back up to the wheelhouse and tried the door. It was locked. He stood to one side and hammered with his fist.

'Open up!' The parade ground bellow collapsed into a hoarse splutter. 'If you don't, I'll blow the lock away.'

As he aimed the Browning, he saw it was pitted from where it had taken some of the blast that killed Rupert. The first bullet tore into the wood around the lock but didn't break it, the second never reached the firing chamber. He tried to pull the magazine out but it was stuck fast. When he hammered again the boat began to move. The smoother motion was a welcome relief, but it came at a price. She had said he would die too, and he suddenly understood how. They were accelerating into the world's busiest shipping lane, where she meant them to die together.

He had to return to the engine room. If Lolly was there, they had a chance on the launch. If she wasn't, a cruel choice awaited.

The engine room was empty. Nor could he see the briefcase; wherever Lolly had gone, she had taken it with her. Dreading the moment of decision, he opened the door to the tender garage and saw his prayer answered, though not as he might have hoped. The launch was poised at the end of the platform with water pouring around it, while Lolly knelt in the stern attempting to push it free.

'Hurry!' she shrieked, as if he were late.

Leaving Bert to his fate, Knight charged and dived as he might over a try line, only to fall short as the boat slipped away. His fingers scraped down the hull onto the perimeter rope and his body slid into the icy water.

Merv didn't see them come out. The launch was suddenly there, spinning in the wake of the yacht before it disappeared into the swell. It crested the next peak at a dizzying angle with a lone figure huddled inside and something trailing off the back. In the fading light, if he misjudged the throttle and went past them, he wouldn't see them again.

The freezing sea gripped Knight's body like a vice. He was hyperventilating, desperately trying to keep his head above the surface while the launch plunged and climbed between the waves.

'Lolly! Help me!' he cried feebly.

He didn't think she'd heard him, but a hand poked out tentatively over the side.

When the boat crested the next peak, Merv saw Knight clinging to Lolly, whose legs were wrapped around the aft bench. He cut the throttle and watched with a mounting sense of dread as they disappeared down the much larger wave that followed.

Knight was above the boat as it began its descent. He had managed to haul one shoulder over the hull, gravity would do the rest.

'Pull!' Lolly screamed.

As he tumbled in, he glimpsed the *King of Sussex* rearing up over the next peak, at the top of the wall of water they were about to climb. He lashed out blindly for a handhold, and then what gravity had gifted, it snatched away again.

The Channel swallowed him indifferently. He went in feet first with barely a splash, the light dimming as the sea closed over his head. A dark object sank past him; it looked like a briefcase.

When he came up, the launch had gone, but behind him he could hear an engine. The swell lifted him high enough to see Merv with a boat hook, reaching out to Lolly. He heard his name being shouted before they slipped out of sight.

It was too late anyway. He came up twice more, gasping for breath and pawing at the water as the last of his strength ebbed away. He couldn't feel his legs. When he sank again, he knew it was for the last time.

There was no fast forward replay of his life, no closing montage of his parents, of Roz, his children or his grandson. Nor was there any pain, just the impossible tightness in his chest which would end if he could bring himself to open his mouth. It would be quick; no hospital beds, no care home fees, no shameful slide into dementia. He was ready, if not willing.

And then, he saw the lobster pot.

It was descending past him on a line, like some strange pelagic lift bound for the sea floor. As if he had pressed some invisible button, it stopped. He reached out and wrapped his arms around the line, then his legs, so that, as he slipped down, he found himself straddling the top of the cage. Next, he was being borne aloft. When he broke the surface, he continued rising, swinging violently over the heaving water while the winch motor squealed and Merv lunged with the boat hook.

As if tiring of the game, the sea sent a wave which casually flicked Knight over the railing into a tower of lobster pots that crashed about him as he fell onto the deck.

Before he passed out, he was sure he heard a distant foghorn.

Chapter Thirty-Eight

Merv had been pleasantly surprised to find Knight ironing his clothes. It was one of the skills they had each learned in the first week of basic training, so he didn't find it odd. But it was an act of initiative, taken without being prompted, and as such it marked a turning point.

The fact that Knight was still alive mystified him. When he had thrown the lobster cage into the sea, it had been little more than a frenzied gesture, made without the slightest hope of seeing him again. He thought it was the spot where he'd seen Knight go down, but amidst the rolling waves it could only be a guess. There was something hallucinatory about the experience of seeing his catch break the surface, as if it couldn't possibly be Knight sitting on the cage, even though it couldn't be anyone else. How many lives did the man have, and who had said he could have them?

He knew, too, that Knight was far from rejoicing. He hadn't perked up at the freshly caught lobster, the prize catch of an expedition with Jabril in a borrowed kayak of dubious provenance. More worrying was the flash of paranoia Knight had displayed at the shopping centre. They were coming out of the chemist together when he suddenly convinced himself they were being followed, insisting on a complicated detour to throw the imaginary stalker off their trail. It was possibly the medication; they had come away from hospital with a shopping bag full of it, which he was making Knight take.

Not that Merv was immune to paranoia himself, though he considered his to be of the healthy variety. The O'Driscolls still had no idea how their boat had come to be beached a hundred yards from where it was tied up, but there was no question who would be their prime suspects. When he reached the van, he scanned the street carefully before getting in.

He would come back that evening. In the meantime, there was the hole in *Adrenaline Rush* to pay for. Here, there was a glimmer of hope. Marek had acquired a pallet of Ukrainian Merlot, and Merv knew a man with a printing machine which did vintage wine labels.

*

Knight ran the iron down the sleeve of a rumpled linen shirt he hadn't worn in years. He worked slowly, resting his weight on the board, repeating the stroke with painstaking precision until the creases were overcome.

The first few days had passed in a blur. Merv had taken control of his life, shepherding him through police interviews, hospital visits and the attentions of journalists. He had submitted gratefully, even permitting the hated estate agent to send a prospective buyer. Now, through slow, repetitive, chores such as the ironing, he was in the early stages of getting a grip.

The lobster was not helpful in this respect. It had been consigned to the sink, where it lay perfectly still at the bottom of a bucket of seawater. Occasionally one of the antennae twitched, the only sign it was alive. Knight felt an unwelcome affinity with the creature, not least for its unquestioning pursuit of questionable bait. Their shared familiarity with lobster cages likewise induced memories he needed to push from his mind.

Merv and Lolly had dragged him into the wheelhouse, quarrelling over how he should be carried. While Merv stood stonily at the wheel, she checked his bones for breakages and rubbed his hands tirelessly.

'I'm so sorry,' she kept saying. 'I was going to share it with you, I swear I was.' Merv let out an involuntary bark of laughter, after which she said little more. She found a blanket and covered him with it.

It was dark when Merv beached the fishing boat. The snow was still falling, screening their chaotic exit into the shallows. Knight was too weak to climb down. After another heated exchange, Merv lifted him over the side and Lolly took him on her shoulders. They carried him to the van and laid him out in the back where she knelt over him while they drove, still rubbing his hands and begging forgiveness.

With a stab of annoyance, he saw he had scorched the shirt. He threw it on the floor, frustrated by Lolly's obstinate presence in his thoughts.

Forsaking the ironing, he turned to the vacuum cleaner. The noise of the motor and the crackle of detritus flying through the fan gave him a stronger foothold in the present, not that his list of tasks offered any cheer. On the kitchen table was the contract he had promised to post to the estate agent before the end of the afternoon. The knowledge that the briefcase had been washed up on the beach and handed in made the envelope's presence all the more harrowing. At first, he hadn't mourned the money, scarcely having made its acquaintance before it was snatched away. Now it stung every time he imagined a life that included it.

Money there would, of course, be, but in a form that spelt defeat. The offer had come out of the blue from a newly retired accountant, keen to secure the flat before embarking on a world cruise with his wife. He had accepted the inflated asking price suggested by the estate agent and sent a surveyor within days of Knight accepting it. Merv had urged him to see the quick sale as a stroke of immense luck, yet he couldn't. It filled him with a dread all the worse for knowing the date of his departure.

But Merv was right. He wouldn't starve, he wouldn't be homeless or trafficked as a sex slave, or suffer the torment of seeing a child grow into a monster. Others had not been so lucky.

The unluckiest of all, it seemed to him, was Irene Askew. Her misfortune was to have survived the collision with a cargo ship that happened a few minutes after Knight was plucked from the water. According to an eyewitness, the starboard side of *Mamma Mia* hit the stern of the ferry as it passed. It said something for the boat's construction that she did not sink, despite the crushing blow to her hull. A lifeboat was launched and Irene Askew was removed forcibly from the wheelhouse after her rescuers broke down the door. The last he had heard she was under guard and heavily sedated, facing three charges of murder and one of manslaughter.

Bert could be counted lucky to be alive at all, given no one had found him until *Mamma Mia* was towed back to Sovereign Harbour. His misfortune was ever to have met the family, which he had served all his working life. He had signed up not once but twice, first as a boy and again when Irene Askew returned to the house after her son bought it back. She had paid him well to be her rock and protector – as well she might, for it was Bert who had carried her husband into the tunnel after she killed him. He had nearly succeeded in ending Knight's enquiries when he warned her to expect the visit of the amateur historian, giving her time to prepare herself. Now he faced two charges of attempted murder and one of perverting the course of justice.

Nor would Knight have swapped with Bahir, charged with people trafficking and being an accessory to murder. It was he who had caught Clementine outside the summerhouse and dragged her inside, much to the consternation of the gathered bidders. It turned out that she had indeed dropped a small handful of gravel, which was found by the forensics team following Knight's interview. At Malik's insistence, Bahir and Rupert had taken Clementine to the farmhouse. An angry altercation followed, in which she demanded money in exchange for her silence. Rupert was prepared to pay, but Irene settled the matter with a silver candlestick which broke her skull, witnessed by Bahir.

Bahir's bad luck had begun much earlier when his uncle recruited him into Syrian military intelligence, only for the family to fall out with a more powerful clan. Malik had brought his money and methods to England, finding in Rupert a willing partner for his new venture in the supply of refugees to the sex trade. Bahir had chosen to stay under his wing; his parents were long dead, his sisters married off courtesy of Malik to elderly Lebanese businessmen.

Malik's misfortune, or rather misjudgement, was to have chosen Rupert as a business partner. According to Bahir's confession, Malik had found him in a London casino, rapidly losing the money that remained after he'd spent the greater part of it on the Sunseeker; the house and land by comparison were a fleabite. The lucrative offer was snapped up with enthusiasm and the business began well, the girls delivered by Malik's associates to a remote beach east of St Malo then taken aboard by Bahir in the launch. At the receiving end, Malik waited for the merchandise to be dropped at dead of night between Eastbourne and Hastings.

The first blow to the relationship came when a girl fell out of the launch and drowned. Bahir blamed Rupert for refusing to wait for a squall to pass; Rupert blamed him for not replacing a missing lifejacket. It was nothing compared to the row over Clementine. Rupert had a meltdown, leaving Bahir and Bert to place her body on the rails under the bridge that had served his mother many years earlier.

The last straw was when the blackmail video arrived. Malik had dissolved the partnership on the spot, demanding a massive sum in compensation. When he made the mistake of threatening Rupert, Irene shot him. The only reason she hadn't finished off Bahir was Rupert screaming at her to stop.

And so he came finally to Rupert himself. His bad luck had been his father. In the end his downfall had hinged on one small, random incident, a fleeting glimpse of a Chinese inscription on the silver bowl in the hallway of Todhurst Manor, at the very moment when he was about to abandon the investigation. It was a cynical display of bravado on Rupert's part, an arrogant piece of self-congratulation that had cost him dear. If Knight had not seen it he would still be alive, free to inflict untold suffering on desperate women.

The vacuum cleaner cut out. He hadn't heard any dirt passing through it for some time or noticed that the motor had raised its voice, so it hadn't occurred to him to change the bag. He hunted for a new one, only to find an empty box. Weary of therapy, he made a cup of tea and sat at the kitchen table. Focus on the positives, Merv had told him. At the chemist, he had found a leaflet about depression and taken to quoting from it. Like a patient teacher with a slow child, he had reminded Knight many times what the positives were.

At the top of the list, most of the girls had been found and the police believed they were close to getting the rest. Second, though for Merv it was first equal, Knight had scored. Yet the diehards were muted in their triumph, and not only because of Merv's choice of vocabulary. For now that he had done the deed, the question as to whether he would ever do it again remained as unanswerable as it had been to begin with. The third positive was his stick. Retrieved by Merv, it stood propped against the kitchen table. He picked it up and laid it across his lap as one might a small child or a cat. Not in a position to return his affection, it nevertheless exuded a trustworthiness he currently treasured above any declaration of endearment.

'Why didn't you tell me the truth?' Knight remembered asking Lolly.

'Would you have helped me if I had?'

He still didn't know. She had bewitched him enough to break the law and risk his life for her, but would he have joined her in an act of blackmail? He couldn't rule it out.

'It was my picture, you see, from my father when he died. I told you that. I left them with Clementine for years because they weren't really my thing. I meant to get them one day, but we couldn't stand each other and I never got round to it.'

He must have looked nonplussed, because her mouth turned down and she let slip one of her little sighs.

'Yes, I lied about her too. We hated each other from the moment our parents introduced us, and it never stopped. I wasn't sad when she died. I know that's hideous of me but there it is.'

He felt the weight of his folly again as he remembered her tearful pleas for justice.

'So you always knew about the stolen painting, and what it was worth?'

'Yes. I was furious with her for being so stupid. And then she refused to report it because she knew she couldn't prove anything, and she was terrified of how ridiculous she'd look. She already was ridiculous, though.' The last came with a flash of resentment.

She paused, perhaps to rein herself in, or to find strength for what came next.

'I wasn't surprised when they said it was suicide; the only thing that shocked me was the way she did it. But when you said his name, I knew he had to be involved. And that gave me a chance of getting back a bit of what was mine.'

She looked every bit as downhearted and defeated as when she had been playing him, only now he had no doubt that what he saw was real.

'For my old age, you see? There won't be a lot waiting for me when my looks are gone.'

He heard the fear, felt it blow on the embers. And an aching disappointment. She had come astonishingly close, only to lose on the final roll of the dice.

'What will you do?'

'Just keep trying. What else is there?'

In that moment, he forgave her. He saw, or perhaps chose to see, not a fraud but a lone warrior, a soldier of fortune adrift in a censorious world. There was one more thing he had to know, indelicate though it was to ask.

'Did you make love to me…' he began, but it sounded so buttoned up. 'Did you have sex with me to stop me finding out about the painting, or because you wanted to?'

She smiled wryly. The imp returned fleetingly to her face, as if taking a final bow.

'Would you believe me if I said both?'

When the van stopped, she bent down and kissed him; a long, lingering caress that fanned the embers into a modest glow.

'Thank you for saving my life,' she whispered, as Merv opened the door. And then, in the unsettling way she had, she was gone.

They were at the bandstand, where she had left the rental car. He wanted to go after her, convince her she should stay at the flat until her strength returned, but he was spent. All he could think was that he would give anything to see her again.

She did leave one parting gift, or rather a piece of uncleared ordnance which could have cost him dear. It emerged that, an hour or so before she and Knight were abducted, Bullock received a text expressing her abject apology for abandoning him. It came with an invitation to meet privately at Hillside Grange and set the record straight. He hadn't been badly injured, no more than a bang on the head when the blast from the first device propelled him through the bathroom door, thereby triggering the second. Knight was interviewed under caution but, in the absence of fingerprints or witnesses to his shopping expedition, no charges were brought. Once the storm abated, he forgave her for that too, and saluted her cunning.

He took the empty mug to the sink. From its watery cell on death row the lobster renewed its claim on his attention. He decided he didn't want to eat it, much less plunge it in boiling water. Meanwhile, the envelope lay on the table, a vile, toxic thing he didn't want to touch. It could no longer be postponed or avoided, but he saw now how the blow might be softened.

First, he went onto the terrace, hoping the view of the sea would somehow bolster his resolve. Instead, he found himself comparing it with the view over a DIY centre from the one-bedroom flat the estate agent had shown him. Sensing another bout of panic, he returned indoors and left as quickly as possible.

He attracted a few curious looks as he carried the bucket across the road to the beach. The choice was between dropping the lobster off the end of the pier or letting it take its chances from the water's edge. His judgement was that its legs and antennae might snap if they hit the surface at an unfavourable angle, so he had opted for the beach. Following this, he would go without fail to the postbox.

He advanced towards the sea, wishing he had thought to wear his wellingtons. Primed by a biting onshore wind, the breaking waves sent fizzing sheets of water at breakneck speed over the pebbles.

Lifting the lobster from the bucket induced an energetic twitching of its tail. It would have been easier, he realised, to remove the rubber bands at home with a pair of scissors. He took a glove off and tugged at the first one, his fingers draining quickly of warmth. Provoked, the lobster prodded with its other claw, harmlessly enough, but once the first band was released it realised it had more to offer, snapping spiritedly at Knight as he attempted to remove the second band. His feelings towards the ungrateful creature cooling rapidly, he was too engrossed to hear the crunch of feet on the pebbles until they were almost upon him.

As the band came off, he spun around to see a powerfully built man in a tailored greatcoat, the man Merv had accused him of imagining at the shopping centre. His mind went into overdrive: too smart for the O'Driscolls, too flash for CID, perfectly credible as a hit man sent by a vengeful pimp.

'Are you Tom Knight?' he asked coldly.

The nearest people were more than fifty yards up on the seafront. If he had a silencer, he would be well on his way before anyone noticed a body lying in the shallows.

'Who are you?' Knight demanded. He took a step closer. He still had the lobster in his hand; if the man showed any sign of reaching for a gun, he decided he would throw it at him. His coat was unbuttoned at the top – if the lobster could gain purchase there it might lash out at his throat, creating time for him to take another pace forward and take him with the metal end of the stick. He clutched his new comrade tightly, preparing to send him into battle.

The stranger stared disapprovingly.

'Paul Harris, Mayfair Associates. Can you confirm that you are Thomas Arthur Knight, please?'

He knew the agency. They did high-end financial investigations and charged a fortune. Nevertheless, he watched like a hawk while the man opened his coat and produced a licence.

Knight lowered the lobster.

'All right, let's say it's me. What do you want?'

The investigator all but rolled his eyes, intimating the encounter was beneath his professional dignity, which in truth it was.

'I have a letter for you from Mrs Abigail Samuels.' An envelope and a printed form appeared. 'She didn't have your address,' he added, as if Knight were at fault in some way. 'I need you to sign for it.'

Knight's relief gave way to irritation. The lobster meanwhile had taken to agitating its tail again. He was gripping it by the back of its head with his fingers out of harm's way, but the sensation as it squirmed was deeply disquieting.

'Is that a pet?' the investigator asked, not in a tone he would have employed with a hedge fund director.

'No, it's not. Excuse me.'

Knight turned away and hurriedly assessed the speed and strength of the breaking waves. To get the lobster far enough out for it not to be washed straight back, he would need to advance quickly behind the receding water then retreat even faster before it lashed out again.

With the aid of his stick, he took a Chaplinesque run-up then, with an elegant underarm action, dispatched the lobster as if it were a bowling ball as far into the sea as he could. The retreat was less successful, the next wave catching him effortlessly.

The investigator was horrified.

'You do know how much those cost?' he asked, as Knight signed the form.

'Yes I do,' he replied crisply. 'You're welcome to get him out again if you want.'

The investigator took the form and left without saying a word.

Knight resented the intrusion of Abigail Samuels into the meagre consolation prize he had awarded himself. If he'd been able to take his time, his feet would not be soaking wet. Nor, at this precise moment, did he wish to be reminded of her vast wealth. He supposed it was a message of congratulation; the story had been on the national news twice so it was no great surprise that she knew. As for the expense of sending a private investigator to find him, it would mean no more to her than the cost of a stamp.

'Dear Tom,' the note read, 'I hope this reaches you safely. Well done for getting the bastard; I couldn't believe it when I saw you on television. Please get in contact, it would be lovely to see you. Please also accept this small token of my appreciation. With fond regards, Abigail Samuels.'

Enclosed was a cheque for fifty thousand pounds.

Thanks and Acknowledgements

I am immensely grateful to the many people whose advice and support made this book possible. In particular, I would like to thank Wesley Emmott for his excellent research, and Elainea Emmott for teaching me the finer points of pole dancing. Also my agents Gaia Banks and Lucy Fawcett, Mark Cable, Selene Emrys Jones, Felicity Maidens, Kate Malone, Bob Page, Peter Pring, David Reed, Adam Whittington, Roland Wilmer, Marie Wright and my wife Kate for her unstinting encouragement.

Most of all, much love and thanks to my dear friend, the late Gervase Bradford, whose extraordinary life was the inspiration for Tom Knight.

Also Available

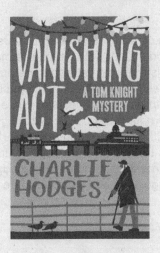

Vanishing Act
(A Tom Knight Mystery 1)

Tom Knight is a private investigator well north of 70. After years of solitude following the death of his wife, he finally returns to the dating scene and meets the enchanting Fran.

Fran is on duty when three elderly ladies in her care at a retirement home are found dead. A syringe with traces of heroin is found in her bag and the police leap to the obvious conclusion. It falls to Tom to prove Fran is innocent and unmask the real killer, going undercover at the care home and relying on everyone's tendency to underestimate the elderly in order to succeed.

Proving that you're just as young as you feel, the Tom Knight mysteries combine delicious comedy with a precision engineered plot.

OUT NOW

About the Author

In a glittering career since leaving university, **Charlie Hodges** has worked as a TEFL teacher, a marketing quack and Father Christmas in a department store. He has also written extensively for television, with credits ranging from *Emmerdale* to *Shaun the Sheep*.

Charlie was born in Durban, South Africa. He lived there until the age of 15 before moving to England where he was educated at Tiffin Boys' School in Kingston upon Thames and Jesus College, Cambridge. He lives in Tunbridge Wells with his wife, two teenage sons and a bad-tempered Jack Russell.

Note from the Publisher

To receive updates on special offers and news of other humorous fiction titles to make you smile – sign up now to the Farrago mailing list at farragobooks.com/sign-up.